THE UNDERLYING HAND

THE UNDERLYING HAND

BOOK ONE OF THE DIVINE CHRONICLES

ROGER KOCH

Copyright © 2021 Roger Koch.

Paperback: 978-1-63767-060-6
eBook: 978-1-63767-059-0
Library of Congress Control Number: Pending

All rights reserved. No part of this publication may be reproduced, distributed, or transmitted in any form or by any electronic or mechanical means, without the prior written permission of the publisher, except in the case of brief quotations embodied in critical reviews and certain other noncommercial uses permitted by copyright law.

This is a work of fiction

Ordering Information:

BookTrail Agency
8838 Sleepy Hollow Rd.
Kansas City, MO 64114

Printed in the United States of America

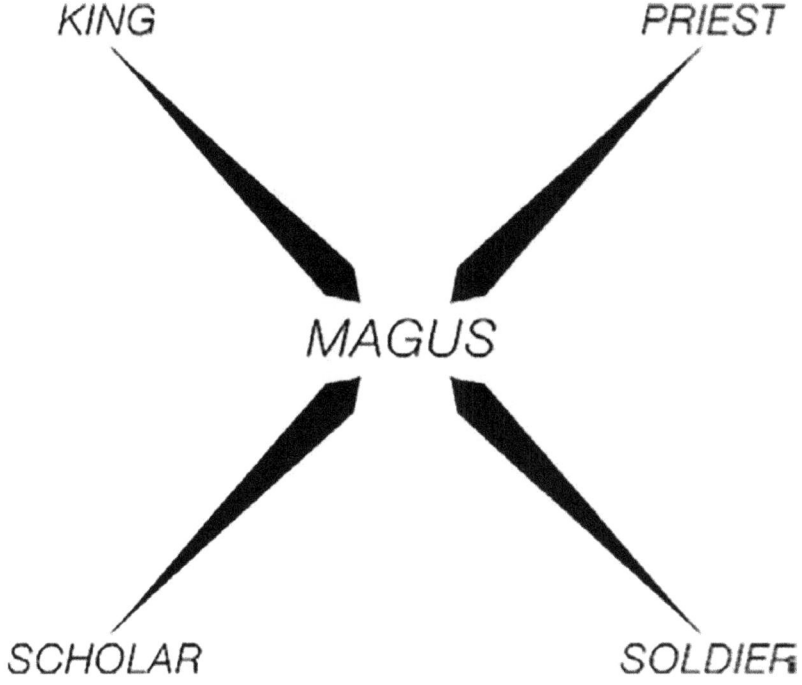

Sceptical scrutiny is the means, in both science and religion, by which deep thoughts can be winnowed from deep nonsense
—Carl Sagan, writer

You are what your deep driving desire is. As your desire is, so is your will. As is your will, so is your deed. As is your deed, so is your destiny
—Brihadaranyaka Upanishads

THE ROYAL LINE OF MARDUK

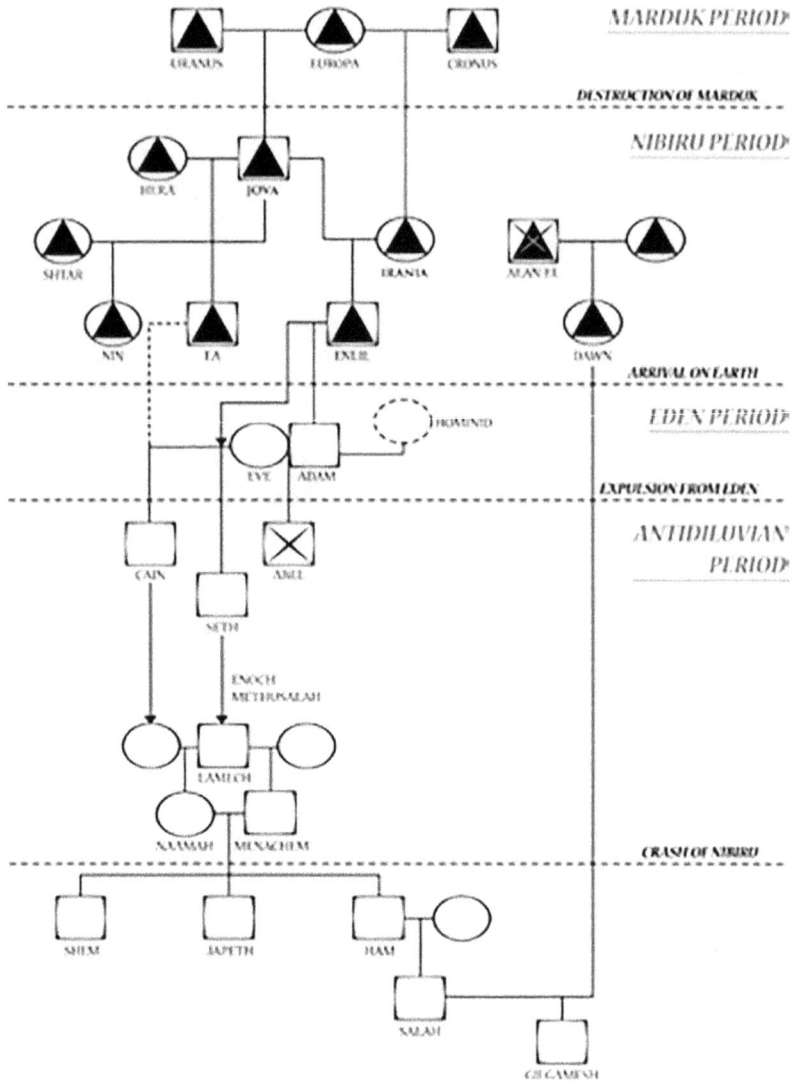

Ideas emanate from the void, turning into superstitions and grow into religions. Recognised as truths, they regress into superstitions, before returning once more to the void

—Unknown

THE NIBIRU SUPREME COUNCIL

JOVA – King

ORIGINAL MARDUK APPOINTEES

URIEL 👁
EA 🌀

NIBIRU APPOINTEES

RAFA-EL 卐
MICHA-EL ✠
GABRI-EL 🪶
HERA ---NIN
SHTAR
IRANIA
ENLIL
NAZAR-EL
PHANU-EL
JEREMI-EL

How often have I said to you that when you have eliminated the impossible, whatever remains, however improbable, must be the truth

—Sir Arthur Conan Doyle

PROLOGUE

'I understand you were an astronomer before gaining kingship. But was it mere coincidence that led you to discover that space projectile?' The young mystic psychologist Shtar, asked King Jova.

'Coincidence, luck, I don't care! I shifted the *Nibiru* Space Station's telescopes to its opposite side, and while panning I spotted the unmapped object aimed directly at our planet. Its extreme red shift meant it was approaching at immense velocity.' Jova elaborated to the young female while peering over her head at his wife Hera - 'assigned' by mother and stepfather as an ideally bland potential queen to aid his selection as Marduk's King. Their adult son was as old and at least as eminent as this Shtar.

Hers was the same inane type of question he had been besieged with since that discovery six months ago – normally fobbing off or ignoring. But there was something in the cool, almost defiant demeanour of this recent graduate, who he had spotted before even her inclusion amongst the refugees. Hence, this special invitation to join him at the spacious pilot's control deck.

Also included for selection amongst the escapees was his pubescent step-sister Irania, already revealing the bewitching beauty she would carry into adulthood. She threw furtive glances at his interaction with this slender, grey-eyed interlocutor – and to Jova's mild surprise, some seeming jealousy!

Hah! Power can be such an aphrodisiac! The ruggedly handsome middle-aged king thought inwardly.

'That's more planetoid than asteroid! Gabri-El, arch guardian and Captain of the *Nibiru* exclaimed in awe, interrupting Jova's fantasies as the meteoroid now took shape on the cockpit screens.

'Over five hundred miles in diameter, fifty times larger than our *Nibiru*.' Fellow arch-guardian and military head, General Micha-El stated habitually flat-voiced and dour-faced.

'It does appear so much larger up close than I imagined.' Jova declared,

'At present velocity it could strike us in moments, and Marduk soon afterwards, Sire,' the Captain warned.

'Indeed, Captain Gabriel, it's time!' It was common to elide the 'El' epithet into those arch-guardians' names.

With that, what was once a stationary terminal for space docking - hastily fitted out with mobility as well as increased residential spaces - began its rapid acceleration to take the ten thousand elect refugees out of range of the impending explosion that would likely annihilate their planet, Marduk.

The contingent consisted of mainly young adult fertile females with heterosexual inclination, as well as a smaller ratio of male technicians and military guardians. Also included was a stockpile of gold for conversion to its monatomic form as their energy source; copious supplies of the life extending and umami tasting supplement, manna; and a group of botanists turned farmers – male and female - to tend the extensive hydroponic garden under the polymer bubble on the craft's surface.

While the 'ship' was yet to reach its terminal velocity of near light speed, the occupants – hapless or blessed depending on individual perspectives – had a ghastly view of the obliteration of their erstwhile home, leaving them marooned on a journey that led to none knew quite where.

The former astronomer-cum-king Jova had pointed them at a distant insignificant star in the outer arm of the galaxy, on a lengthy voyage that he convinced everyone to believe would end in the discovery of a life supporting planet.

They had no choice but to put their faith in their monarch and saviour's hopeful guess. As their *Nibiru* exited their solar system, remnants of their former second of four planets now appeared as just a halo around its sun. Thankfully, that distance saved the mainly young passengers from some of the horror at such annihilation.

Yet, lurking in that interstellar space was a destructive force as the ill-prepared craft sped through undetected exposure zones – cosmic gamma radiation that picked off individuals at random. Those it did not kill were rendered sterile- almost all the fecund females and most males - threatening the very purpose of their salvation and hopes of a new Marduk.

PART ONE

Earth—circa 65,000 A.D. (Ante Diluvium) – 74,000 B.C.E

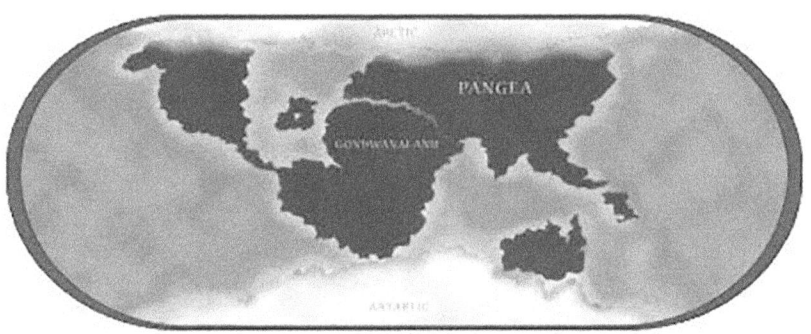

CHAPTER ONE

Emptiness – constricting outside, exuding within.

Young Nineveh's anxiety was absorbed from her father's pacing up and down the royal chambers aboard the *Nibiru*. Her parents were either unaware or unconcerned at young Nin's proximity, observing their interaction.

'We escaped Marduk's destruction only to face this monotony, already losing so many to an unseen enemy. And if not dead, I'll be quite old by the time we get anywhere!' Jova expressed very uncharacteristic insecurity to his wife – but as usual, he might as well have been just thinking aloud.

While outside, space slid past at 160,000 miles per second, Nin felt immobile in every sense. A rare child born en voyage, and educated by her reclusive mother, she had no frame of reference. Yet she knew there was something missing

I don't know what it is but I just feel *it – ever since when – and I* will *find out what it is!*

'Well, it's better than annihilation,' Shtar, King Jova's second wife, now Queen and Nin's mother, responded offhand, oblivious to the empathy he seemed to be seeking, 'Your son Ea managed to retard the cancers and I hear he's working on another cure.' She offered, before returning to her ancient parchments, which apparently contained Marduk esoteric knowledge – whatever that was.

Recognising any rapport as unlikely, Jova mumbled, 'Cellular destruction can't by cured medicine,' and he continued rambling, '*Nibiru* was built for orbit as a *station*, not a vehicle. While we reinforce our protective ionic shields, at our near light speed, even space dust could wipe out our crops. Luckily, my time on the bridge shields me from radiation, and the two of you are safe in here.' He added, running a hand over the gold walls reinforcing the royal quarters.

Nin wondered whether her mother was aware his 'time on the bridge' was spent mainly with Aunt Irania. Did she even care?

Shtar seemed to come alive - with the nearest Nin had heard of an exclamation, 'Oh, we must protect the manna synthesising facility! Otherwise how will we survive?' But that was about as much drama she would get from mother.

In the absence of other children, Nin had no frame of reference for familial relationships, but theirs seemed nothing like she had read or viewed in the ship's chronicles. Shtar, particularly seemed vague and distant and once, seeking a clue, Nin asked what her grandparents were like,

'Oh, the same as everyone else's I suppose,' was all she could get out of Shtar.

Jova was already rather old in Nin's eyes, the folds around his jowls were sagging, as were the lids around his metallic blue eyes. His gait was beginning to stoop, making him appear shorter than his otherwise average seven and a quarter feet. Her mother, second Queen Shtar was still in the bloom of adulthood, but that cool aloofness accentuated by soft light grey eyes and chiselled cheekbones gave her an air of maturity and jaded wisdom. Yet it wasn't just their physical differences. It was as if they were of different species.

Father continued fretting, 'Manna synthesis still requires some seed harvest from the amaranth bush. 'Our Chief Agriculturist, Nazarel is reinforcing the polarized surface bubble, which should protect the fresh crops. But it won't prevent the ongoing fatalities, embryo mutations or our females' sterility. Our mission and even our survival may hinge on the work of Ea's geneticists.'

'What will be will be.' Shtar replied, causing father and daughter to roll their eyes at each other.

'Your genius Ea will come up with something. I'm sure we were not spared just to undergo a slower demise.' She added, seemingly confident.

Nin loved her brilliant stepbrother Ea. And if Shtar felt any jealousy towards Jova's son from first wife, Hera, she gave no indication of it.

Jova, however, was used to that detachment, 'Hmm, you have great belief in Ea, and apparently fate. Understandable perhaps, both of you are eccentrics,' He turned aside to mumble, perhaps to avoid drawing attention to the growing distance with his son - especially since casting aside Ea's mother. 'But yes, his fat assistant informs he seems to be getting close.'

Any intended response from Shtar was cut short by a noise Nin had previously never heard. Indeed, any noise aboard the craft was rare. The moaning hum of the *Nibiru* was as unremarkable as the starkness of its ubiquitous fluorescent Vril lighting.

'The alarm! The bubble has been pierced!' Jova shouted as he ran out of the room, spotting his daughter on the way out. 'Nin, stay down here with your mother and don't come out till I return.' He cast a hasty and angry look at her partial attire.

Nin wore her only outfit unbuttoned, even exposing a childish breast, hoping her defiance against shipboard discipline would attract her parents' attention. But hardly perturbed by the alarm, Shtar didn't appear to care at her undress, and returned to her reading. In the *Nibiru's* controlled temperate atmosphere, there was no danger to health, and thus Nin realised her rebellion was insignificant.

'I don't know where to start.' Uri-El, the king's ancient Sage spoke unusually rapidly, informing the royal couple as a witness to the events that had triggered the emergency. Standing in the foyer, as if too agitated to sit on the gilded sofa of the royal reception room, he blurted his account,

'I was on the surface doing some final stellar observations before the horticulturists installed the dome. Even in his protective suit, I recognised our Chief Agriculturist Nazar-El's short and stocky frame, guiding the last panel into place.'

Nin had never seen Uriel so visibly disturbed, even using Nazarel's formal name. She studied the old sage as he continued,

'I turned to observe a mother with her infant, exchanging waves with a fellow horticulturist— apparently her husband - who was assisting to install the glass-alloy lattice. The baby was intact and healthy, so rare nowadays. But I was still worried about the effect of possible cosmic ray damage to it even if the safety shields protected us all from the exterior vacuum...'

Uriel was the most elderly member of the entire *Nibiru* contingent, included due to his immense academic status and esoteric knowledge, having also been Sage to the previous Marduk King. His strikingly limpid ice-blue eyes below thick bushy brows betrayed his powerful and incisive intellect, but generally he appeared a kindly and benign soul. Nin liked him.

'...Naturally, I heard nothing from the soundless exterior but read the mother's expression metamorphosing from contentment to abject fear.' Uriel went on, 'I turned around to witness the cause of her panic. An undetected tiny meteor had shattered through one of the panels and into the crane, killing its operator and scattering fragments. A shard had also pierced Nazarel's hood and threw him to the spongy ground, still clutching that crucial-locking piece that would combine all the others.

'The connecting panels began losing support, swaying precariously, injuring some and exposing others to unprotected radiation. And a hole began tearing open, sucking out seven of our natural farmers – lost to space!

'I was rooted to my position, unsure how to assist, knowing that the chain reaction of collapsing panels would not only wipe out all our food-production facility, but also eventually destroy the navigation bridge that stood next in the path of collapse.

'Just then, I spotted a quick-thinking and incredibly agile young botanist, weaving and dodging the superstructure collapsing around him and dashing to relieve the stricken crane operator. Meanwhile, the workers who had gathered around the injured Nazarel prised the locking panel from his grasp. Three of them, including the mother and her husband, rushed the piece to the crane, which our heroic botanist had by now regained control.

'As you can see, I'm not as limber as I once was. And while procrastinating as to how I could be of help, the young mother left her child on the floor, rushing past me towards her husband.

'I could only read her lips as she ran into the exposure... "Watch over my Shalimar",'

'Automatically, I went over to pick up the infant while witnessing the unfolding accident. Those brave young farmers thought nothing of exposing themselves to aid Nazarel or the valiant new crane operator who was already deftly shifting the controls within the crane's protected cockpit.'

Uriel slowed to finish his recount, eyes downcast, 'and, holding her babe in my arms, this old astronomer was dismayed to see the nursing mother and her husband amongst them, regretful and ashamed at my helplessness.'

From the conversation that followed, Nin learnt that seventeen herbalists, including the new parents, succumbed to injuries and radiation. Mere hours afterwards, they exhibited extreme tumours resulting in excruciating pain and agonised death.

She recalled Uriel then describing how he had taken the baby to her parents' ward for a final farewell at the ineffective Healing Institute, to alleviate their further anguish.

'I assured them as best I could that their daughter's welfare was at least safeguarded. But they insisted their daughter be entrusted only to me, so after their rapid demise, I carried the child to my quarters.

The androgynous old sage concluded dejectedly, 'I'm not equipped for parenthood, yet If she can bear with this old bachelor, I will carry out her mother's last request as best I can.'

'How awful for the poor child!' Shtar cried. Never known for tact, she didn't consider the implied insult to Uriel. 'But luckily our Chief Agriculturist is alive. How did Nazarel survive?'

Unperturbed, Uriel replied, 'Luckily for him, his suit remained intact and the shard that gouged his right eye, simultaneously served to seal his hood.

Jova continued the conversation pragmatically. 'And luckily for all, that astute young botanist Aigar repaired the protective covering. Otherwise, all our food supply, and much more of the ship, would have been damaged.'

'Yes, but despite all our reassurance, Aigar is disturbed that he was unable to save Shalimar's parents in time, particularly as they were friends and a rare example of fertility, Uriel added. 'Apparently as a result of that unearned belief in his inadequacy, and feeling unsuited to farming, he has asked to join the guardians.'

'Hmm, a natural with such wit and agility, he'll make a great guardian officer?' The king commented.

'He's brilliant despite his self-doubt, but he has a strange speech anomaly and he's given to humour, a trait that does not sit well in the guardian brigades as you can imagine.' Uriel explained, adding out of Shtar's earshot, 'Aigar's a natural.' sharing a seemingly knowing glance with the king, which intrigued young Nin.

'Recruitment to guardian training is a good reward, and I'm glad it was his choice,' Shtar added, seemingly oblivious also to the glances.

Jova moved on, 'Well, we are still only about half way to our destination, so it is imperative that we find a way to prevent more deaths and if not too late, save the few fertile.' He said, before making excuse to 'spend time on the bridge' as he escorted the now calmer but still-shaken Uriel out of the royal suite.

Nin decided to visit her older stepbrother Ea at the Healing Institute and question his inability to heal the afflicted botanists.

Striding down the shielded corridors, Nin was oblivious to her surroundings - the toneless background hum, monochrome light and faint clinically sweet scent that pervaded the *Nibiru* from antibacterial diffusers. The hastily cobbled space station was built for function with no thought of aesthetics—sparse and featureless. But as she entered the Healing Institute the aroma accentuated, a faintly pleasant floral scent.

Ea's lab assistant, the rotund and ever cheery Galael or 'Fubsy' to her, gave a wink and their secret shared semi-circular hand wave as she passed his workstation. He was the youngest amongst those otherwise crotchety geneticists.

'Nin! Ea exclaimed as he caught sight of her, 'your arrival is more than coincidence little sister!' He gushed as he swung her around like a gyroscope. He was unusually exuberant and Nin responded in pent-up glee, lapping up his attention.

'You know, I believe I have found something very important!' He enthused, loud enough to raise the heads of those sourpusses.

Nin briefly shared his excitement. But recollecting the recent accident, she sobered.

'I wish you could have cured those infected in the accident.'

'Yes sweetie, I too wish I could have achieved something so useful. Anyway, what I have found can't cure the already afflicted. But it might prevent those like you from getting damaged!' Again, he raised his voice as if aiming for all to hear, 'Now, we just need to devise the equipment to deliver it effectively.'

At those intriguing comments, the technicians began to gather around his table. As they examined his results, even the dullest among them became flushed and animated. Nin thrilled at the apparent esteem they all felt towards her brother, even if a little unclear at the cause.

All in all, the journey felt like imposed hibernation, overlaid only with the anxiety of random afflictions. The news of a possible cure had thus animated the feckless passengers, stirring hope and enthusiasm – even joy – hitherto devoid from the ultra-conservative Marduk refugees.

'A momentous discovery! If proven, Ea deserves every accolade.' Jova shared with his young stepsister Irania during their following tryst in her cabin nearby the royal quarters. Yet his tone was flat, almost resentful.

'And our course is set so there's really not much call for my leadership in this floating prison,' he expressed in poorly disguised indifference.

Irania was quick to catch the root of his insecurity. 'But it was *your* discovery of the asteroid, and *your* setting this course, that enables us to celebrate his cure! Your unyielding leadership will be invaluable in any new world. His idea is but a flash.' She placated with a look of fond esteem she knew he craved.

Even with the effects of deprivation in the ship's artificial environment, she maintained much of her allure and proportional physique, which had yet to take advantage of any artificial enhancement, even make-up. 'But *we* must ensure they don't forget it and understand your position is sacrosanct.' She added, emphasising her affiliation.

'It's immensely more than a 'flash', darling. But thank you for your encouragement.' His term of endearment was a first – loaded with meaning and his voice implied some sort of decision.

'In any case, let's go find out – together!' he said, signalling she should take his arm.

It seemed all the senior technicians and arch guardians were invited to the small hall dedicated to the *Nibiru* Council.

Ea's science was a little beyond young Nin, as indeed most of the attendees, but all came to attention when he finally described it in common terms,

'...essentially the ultra-low frequency violet rays, harmonically attune and thus cancel out mutating opposite frequency gamma radiation, countering all cell deterioration. Naturally, that means...'

'Surely you can't mean *all* deterioration!' An objection came from the greater Healing Institute group.

'...As I was about to say, the cell nucleus, membrane and mitochondria, including the DNA and telomeres - *all* seem to synchronise in harmony to repel *any* attack...' Ea went again into detailed geneticist jargon until the same protester called out again,

'What you're implying is impossible!'

The challenger's shout began a buzz around the hall. Nin, not quite comprehending, assumed it was due to the rudeness of the interruption, and she looked to her father to intervene.

Jova, appearing a little dumbfounded, raised his hand to silence the hubbub, allowing Ea to continue,

'Indeed, if we take it to its ultimate conclusion - immortality! Since we began testing a desk top device on our tiny short-lived lab animals, none have even noticeably aged – over forty times their life expectancy so far!' Ea finished to the erupting jubilation.

CHAPTER TWO

Jova had fast tired of Shtar's indifference, or perhaps as Nin much later surmised, it was the promise of an eternity of unimpassioned boredom.

By comparison, the fiery amethyst-eyed Irania, whose seductive beauty even other females grudgingly acknowledged, could turn the heads, and thoughts, of any male. And once she had Jova's head turned, she made it a point to keep it forever in her direction, arousing his libido along with his ego. It wasn't therefore difficult to thrust a cleavage into the weak and faltering relationship.

It seemed as if Irania assumed the role of queen from birth, and she was fully aware what their mutually hatched amendment to the Law of Inheritance could mean to her specific ambitions. She thus set mind and body to achieving those goals and was soon pregnant with their son, Enlil.

Jova thus diverted, had married her immediately thereafter, and the parting with Shtar occurred with minimal overt fuss.

'I am sure with our attention and grooming, our Enlil will make a fine heir - so much more than Ea, that dissident son of the old crone, Hera,' Irania declared to Jova in the final stages of her pregnancy. 'And your recent amendment to the Inheritance Law almost ensures it, setting aside any claims also from your Nin.'

Jova was taken aback by her naked and tactless ambition. 'Yes, but remember, both Hera and to some degree, Shtar remain my official wives. There is no precedent to such multiple marriages, and my recent addendum to that Law depends on the Council's acceptance. And dissident Ea may be, but also brilliant!'

'Even if they didn't appreciate your achievements, there's none aboard who would dare challenge your authority. And when he grows up, our Enlil will ensure it!' She shot back.

Finally, someone who understands the subtleties and machinations of power! The more he thought about it, the more he felt at ease with the marriage to his half-sister. She truly was a natural.

Whether that slight to her femininity had any effect on Shtar, neither Nin nor anyone else could tell, but the now former Queen never again bothered seriously with any other male - for companionship or pleasure. To Nin, moving out of the main royal quarters was bad, and she resented the lack of access to her father, but there was little other distress.

Growing rapidly through her parent's separation, and perhaps as diversion, Nin became absorbed in the ship's library of chronicles incorporated in its memory - holographic and narrated visuals.

And imitating Shtar's affinity with maintaining Marduk heritage, she preferred the ancient art of reading. Those written words and the images they invoked, appeared more real than the sterile documentary and monotone audio-visuals. Inferring from some old stories she read, she wondered at the absence of any real heartache from her parents' separation,

Has that something to do with what's missing? Probably just inherited detachment from mother. She dismissed inwardly.

'Marduk's technology seemed to have grown exponentially in just the past few generations. What a great heritage!' She had marvelled to her mother once, knowing Shtar was much easier to engage in such impersonal matters.

'Yes, but at what cost to spirituality?' Came the enigmatic reply.

Nin paused, disillusioned. Shtar was nothing if not aloof. Nevertheless, she was a stickler for truth rather than dispensing insincere platitudes.

Nearing adulthood and fully engaged in the technical and factual chronicles, Nin turned her attention to more complex issues and requested to visit the cockpit, which her father even encouraged.

The roughly circular space station had a nearly ten-mile diameter, which younger Nin had gained considerable exercise exploring. But she had never been to the captain's bridge and was thus awed by the novel experience.

'How long is this journey going to take, Captain Gabri-El?' Nin addressed the *Nibiru* captain formally.

'In time or distance?' Gabriel asked. 'It's a good question, really. At nearly nine-tenths of light speed, we have time dilation effects that make our position in relation to Marduk time or even our target star's time a very complex mathematical correlation. As for distance, that's of course related to time.'

Nin appreciated the captain's genuine attempt to answer but there was an air of condescension. 'I *would* like to know how time was calculated on Marduk, and how you correlate it but perhaps later. Is there a simple answer?' She queried.

'Well, if we take the intended length of our journey, you were born about one-tenth of the way after we left. As mentioned, time becomes aberrant at these speeds and in our galactic position, but I estimate you have lived approximately thirty-eight Marduk years—a pre-adult.' He turned to observe her to verify his last comment, 'we are less than another tenth of that to the target solar system. We should reach there by the time you're adult.'

Nin also learnt from the Captain that the *Nibiru* generated the enormous energy Ea's fount required. The ship's whole energy need was achieved by transmuting monatomic white powder gold into Vril energy, which Marduk scientists had not so long ago discovered in the highly electromagnetic purity of that metal.

'What does our target planet look like?' She went on to probe.

'Well, I'm not sure – although we finally determined its existence, it is still a speck.'

'Haven't you tried the long-range chromatic telescope that I read was newly installed in the *Nibiru* space station?'

Gabriel turned to her with a blank stare that morphed in successive stages - initial incomprehension, then realization, blinking embarrassment, to finally turning away and glancing back in apparent appreciation.

'I believe it's in the Astronomical Observatory.' She added, walking off to save him any further discomfort at his oversight.

With little more to learn from the Captain for the time being, she turned attention to her elder brother and her own increasing interest in genetics. Besides her affinity with Ea, if their species was to survive and thrive, she suspected that field would be the key factor.

Stopping briefly at the laboratory entrance she observed him bent over an experiment at his offshoot of the Healing Quarters. Despite the periodical solar radiation treatment and exercise that were part of shipboard discipline, and even with a reasonable simulation of Marduk gravity, the lack of natural sun energy gave them all a dissipated appearance with pasty, almost translucent skin. Alike all the Marduks, Ea's body had atrophied. A slight build accentuated his seven and a half feet, the average guardian's height.

'Manna maintains inner health but is no substitute for natural starlight. And even my invention, while protecting us from cosmic rays, only maintains external appearance,' Ea lifted his head, responding to her unasked question, clearly aware of her inspection.

En voyage his apparently once emerald eyes had paled with a hint of yellowness, still setting him apart from most with their light blues and dissipated greys in the artificial glow of the Vril-induced light. A slightly elongated skull, accentuated by the shipboard practice of shaving, was typical of all the other Marduks.

'But you, little sister, were doubly lucky to have been born at all!' he teased the young adult.

'Doubly?' She queried.

'Well, reproduction was initially prohibited aboard the *Nibiru* due to space limitations, even if yours would have been exempted by our father's eminence. But worse, nothing could reverse the damage by cosmic radiation. We lost nearly 4,000 before we were able to partially reinforce the transparent bubble with ionization. And then, since offspring were subsequently encouraged, that deterioration still persisted to render our kind permanently sterile or to produce mutants. Your mother was also safe within the gold shielding of the royal quarters,' he explained.

'And then along came your fantastic discovery! What led you to it?' She fawned in juvenile adoration, his genius and the story never failing to excite her.

'Yes, well, cosmic radiation accelerated cell deterioration, which is anyway part of the normal aging process - only more instantly and violently. Reversal was not possible, so I knew that we had to effectively shield the subatomic quanta within the cellular atoms from any kind of attack.' Ea paused to focus on his present experiment.

She knew the rest from her own research and from undergoing the treatment. Wishing to impress him, she spoke to the back of his head,

'So your radiation beam bathes the entire body with polarized magnetic energy, shielding us from cosmic rays and other damaging energies and molecular reactions - allowing cells to replicate almost indefinitely without deterioration. Does it really mean immortality?'

Ea, lifting his head from the microscope gave her an appreciative glance. Appears so as it also halts telomere shrinkage. We'll need periodical treatment - even just anti-aging. But I wonder about psychological effects.'

'I don't understand?'

'Yes, you have no other frame of reference. However, his seemingly endless and monotonous voyage has been sobering. Time and space merge within this cocoon, causing us to feel immobile against the backdrop of infinite space -seemingly stagnating attitudes and mental activity. As our Uriel often points out, life without purpose is simply existence,' he replied gravely, before they moved on to lighter matters.

Nin long sought but had little interaction with the royal sage, Uriel. Wishing to absorb more, she now felt confident in her learning to consult him, and visited his quarters in the Astronomical Dome.

To initiate conversation with the ever-preoccupied master, she remarked on his adopted child, 'your Shalimar seems healthy and growing fast.'

'Yes, and having no recollection of her parents, she and I are close, but with no companions her age she is naturally reticent and keeps to herself. A lot like you I suppose.' He replied with a brief glance from what still sharp sapphire eyes, 'but you didn't come here to discuss her, did you?' He seemed impatient and a little dismissive.

Soon however, astute comments and questions convinced him of her serious interest, leading them to discuss Marduk society, which Uriel began explaining hesitantly at first,

'Ea's radiation bath draws heavily on our once large gold stockpile. We are already melting down the reinforcements used in the royal quarters. I hope the new planet has accessible supply!'

She continued probing his eclectic knowledge, 'I know kingship became by appointment since global governance. But what led to the dictatorial monarchy system we now have?'

Inspecting the serious student, Uriel began to loosen and became more lucid,

'Well, after much tumultuous experiment, our recent ancestors concluded that party or committee rule was extremely inefficient and ineffective in achieving excellence - decisions generally based on the lowest common denominator. And the electorate easily manipulated or biased towards personality as the major leadership criterion. But self-appointed dictators are also dangerous. So, when Marduk consolidated in a single federated government, the previous national heads of state decided on a Supreme Round Table Council for representation.

Then, with advances in the predictive ability of intricate psychometric tests and character profiles to identify the most suited candidates, that Council decided their leader should be an emperor of sorts, with the official title of King.

'Secure in that selection process, the appointed king was given almost god-like power. Ceremonially, executively and spiritually, he or she plays role model and archetype of our species.

'And is it really any better?' She queried.

'So far there have been five Marduk global kings including female King Atlanta, and I have survived four including your father. Their unique authority resulted in some very unpopular decisions but ultimately very beneficial outcomes. For example, despite huge drug industry resistance, third king Beelzebub prohibited then hugely popular and enlightening - but intensely corrosive - psychedelic fruit of the Mandala tree.

And as soon as Vril energy was viable, Jova's predecessor Indra, went against the nuclear industry and banned all fissile uranium – a threat that still hung over Marduk from so many earlier destructive wars. Some was relegated to the *Nibiru* to arm against any alien threat. Unfortunately, they didn't count on the size of the space marauder that destroyed our planet.

'So, what's the purpose of the Supreme Council?' Nin asked.

'They are supposed to keep the king in check, as they did with first king Kali, forcing him to not just outlaw murder but ingrain it into the social fabric from infancy – alike the code now written into the androids…'

Uriel hesitated for a second, before quickly diverting… 'Our Jova has re-formed a Council from amongst the refugees, but it's just as stamp of approval.' The sage seemingly sniffed at the comparative triviality of the recent *Nibiru* Council, 'as we are nearing our target solar system, he has called for the first of that gathering - with an extended number of attendees. Following his nepotistic tendencies, perhaps *you* can be invited.'

'Oh, I hope so!' She enthused dismissing the sarcasm he had clearly intended.

CHAPTER THREE

Indeed, Nin had pleaded with her father and was allowed to attend the group now gathered in the 'town' hall. And Enlil, who had precociously and recently achieved arch guardian rank, was also invited into the first row of observers, awaiting only final approval to replace a Councillor who had died from cosmic attack.

As an officer, Enlil was entitled to the 'El' epithet, but Queen Irania rejected it saying, 'he is a prince, and anyway his very name makes it redundant really.'

No doubt the choice of his name was carefully considered! Nin thought inwardly. *And does that make me a princess?*

Uriel, the sage and already eminent Ea were original Marduk Councillors. The three queens - Ea's inscrutable mother and first queen Hera, former queen Shtar and now Queen and stepsister Irania - were early Joval appointees. With Enlil's confirmation that would count six of Nin's extended family including her father. The others were all male senior Arch guardians—also appointed by Jova without ballot.

Though a little embarrassed, Nin was glad to be beneficiary of Jova's nepotism. But she wondered at the lack of *qualified* females.

She took a moment to inspect the injury of Councillor Nazarel, who appeared fully healed from the shard of meteoroid that pierced his eye. He sported what appeared to be a standardized blue electronic eye, which contrasted with his other natural grey one. With no qualified optical programmer left aboard to animate it, the implant was lifeless, remaining fixed whenever he shifted focus.

Her mother's voice drew her attention to the proceedings,

'If there is intelligent life, it would be interesting to determine how to integrate.' Shtar made the opening statement sitting opposite the king.

King Jova retorted, 'what integration? We must establish absolute supremacy while maintaining our species' integrity. It is a universal law - the stronger must dominate the weaker or else they too will be weakened. We owe it to those who perished on Marduk.'

'And how do you expect these few thousand mainly infertile survivors to overtake an entire planet?' Shtar challenged back. Regardless of degraded status, she had no inhibitions.

'No problem, my dear.' Councillor Raphael, Head of the Healing Institute replied with his trademark hooked nose tilted upwards in condescension. It was accompanied by his typical facial twitch, which seemed incongruous with his otherwise pompous manner. It was clear he felt no deference to the ex-queen as he continued,

'Captain Gabriel reports an absence of spacecraft or even electronic communication from the planet. So, we obviously have superior weaponry. Why, if intelligent life existed at all, they would look upon us as gods!'

'Assuming electronic communication is the only kind and that technology and space travel is a primary objective,' Ea quipped, clearly piqued at the Head Physician's presumption.

'What other objective could they possibly have?' Jova asked as if rhetorically.

'Some higher calling, perhaps.' Ea's inane retort was mumbled offhand, as if unintended

But younger brother Enlil, a Jova devotee, seemed eager to establish his stripes as potential Councillor,

'What higher calling *could* there be except progress through science and technology?' Enlil's voice matched his precociously bombastic and self-righteous personality. It had an air of the theatrical as he continued expansively, raising his volume for further drama, 'please elaborate!'

'Spirituality? Consciousness? Attributes of soul?' Ea threw back offhand and venturing into taboo.

In modern Marduk society and definitely amongst *Nibiru's* regimented contingent, such conjecture was looked upon as idle, counterproductive rambling—discomforting and socially obtuse to such military and technical corps.

Jova scowled, while Enlil and the pompous Raphael were unified in outrage. Most of the other Councillors just shifted about uneasily.

Nin took the following brief hiatus to examine Ea's inscrutable mother Hera, who sat in typically silent and rigid aplomb. *What amazing equanimity! Discarded without a second thought by Jova for my mother – and then Irania - with nary a peep or a blink. She always acts as if programmed - an adjunct to the king - and any feelings or thoughts she may have once seem deleted.*

None of Nin's 'mothers' offered any sense of role model. But her reflections were interrupted as Jova cut short any discussion,

'It seems that idle speculation during this journey has caused some moral deterioration. God and soul have been discarded or irrelevant on our march to advancement.'

Enlil was ever eager. 'Yes, law, administered with strict and wise discipline is the only worthy calling for Marduk interests.'

Jittery Raphael added his support, 'Indeed, there is no medical evidence of a soul, and thus the only purpose of intelligent life such as we, is to propagate our species and control our environment.' His neck continued flicking long after he had stopped talking.

Dismissing his younger brother, Ea addressed the twitching Head Physician, 'Your evidence is retarded! Reproduction requires no mind. I am beginning to doubt the benefit of my "youth fountain". Immortality for purely material progress without inner development is short-sighted.'

Jova had enough, 'well, thank you Councillor, for your most enlightening speculation! Meanwhile, our laws and codes of behaviour were developed over aeons. So, while this exercise might amuse some, we will remain confined to such laws. With our diminished numbers, I had planned to reallocate various duties, but let's wait and see what we're up against. This meeting is over.'

Jova's aversion towards his eldest son appeared almost as if instinctual, and Nin had to admit Ea did nothing to mitigate it.

On her way out, she expressed her misgivings to Uriel 'what's all the fuss over such trivialities? I read of those questions since our ancient history. Surely, we couldn't expect agreement now.'

'Political dissent can also be the catalyst for progress,' Uriel gave a wry wink 'and the eternal polarizer—religion or God is the standard around which antagonists rally their support, the tool in their ambition for power.'

'On that point, I know how Ea's mother Hera was appointed as wife, consort and queen of sorts upon my father's coronation, but how did my mother come into the picture?' She asked.

'That would be better explained by your Shtar herself.'

'Yes, but she's not very communicative, and she particularly avoids such matters.'

'Hmm, alright. Your mother's specialty of Mystic Psychology is nowadays hardly popular. Nevertheless, considered an oracle of sorts, Shtar was included in the list of candidates – a rare qualified female of breeding age. In that selection process, she caught Jova's eye, perhaps finding her non-conformity alluring compared to predictably compliant Hera. On Shtar's part, it seemed to me she succumbed to his advances with neither ardour nor disdain.'

'What a romance!' Nin sneered, expecting no less from the hermaphrodite sage, yet recognising its inherent truth.

Her mother cut a fine figure, but was rather tall and a little too lean, her features too angular to evoke anything erotic or carnal, which undoubtedly described Irania. Even elderly Hera was more exotic - albeit in a more classical, designer style.

She continued to query Uriel, 'Marduk's history in the ship's log only describes events before our departure. How *were* the passengers chosen? Why so many docile females, mostly of minimal rank?'

'Briefly, Jova discovered Marduks killer asteroid, bizarrely blocked from view by this very space station and with its telescopes and probes focused elsewhere in deep space! It was nevertheless the one craft that could conceivably carry out interstellar travel, having also built-in mobility.

Upon his secret announcement to the Council, we encouraged him to commandeer the *Nibiru,* which was subsequently and hastily equipped with all the resources we could muster, along with our ten thousand selected Marduks.

'Naturally the intent was also to propagate our species anywhere hospitable, as fast as possible. So, a majority of females were chosen. Excluding the king and myself, that number was in a precise ratio of 4:1.

'The Council - half of them female I might add – understood that fertility was more important than any other qualities. Hence, few of high career status qualified. And for males, any hospitable planet likely being primitive or combative, physical strength and martial prowess was preferred above spirituality or creativity. Thus, even the technicians were from the military guardian brigades.

From that Council only Ea – already eminent in genetics - and I were chosen. Above my protests at being old, it was felt that I possessed invaluable arcane history of Marduk's heritage.

'Jova also chose this star, towards the outer spiral of the galaxy instead of the more populated centre, which he argued likely harboured more anomalies near the galaxy's central black hole. It seems it was a great guess. So now you understand his almost 'divine' status.

Nin stared enrapt, encouraging the sage to continue,

'He also devised the Law of Inheritance—each male would be entitled to marry his proportion, or up to four females. Children were likely to be related so incest was to be condoned—only amongst partial, not full-blooded siblings. It resulted in an addendum to that Law of Inheritance.'

Nin was glad he had reminded her, 'yes, what is that?'

'The Law dictates that the oldest male child should be first in line as heir, again due to physicality. But then astute young Irania pointed out that the offspring of a sibling relationship would carry the greatest number of parent genes. As a result, Jova introduced an addendum to cover that condition. Let me quote,

'Whereas, in case of offspring brought forth at any time *from the legal marriage of said part-sibling relationship, any first male shall enjoy absolute precedence...'*

'Normal Marduk approval has no meaning here, so it will be automatically endorsed. I also protested Jova's unilateral choices for the *Nibiru* Council, nepotism that could lead to aristocracy, but that only met with general apathy from the passengers.

'So now you see the background of this very patriarchal society.' Uriel gave a sigh of resigned disapproval after his lengthy explanation.

Despite such intrigues Nin was proud of such an illustrious father and heritage. And she continued her interrogation,

'So how is my father related to Irania?'

The sage appeared tired or perhaps disinclined, 'that's a complicated story, best left for another time,' and walked away.

'*Earth* at last! A technician exclaimed using the Marduk term for 'land', upon observing the nascent planet through the cockpit dome. 'Substance and not just pinpricks of light - and it has a moon!'

At that, word spread and passengers gathered in awe and excitement to observe the orb with a melange of hues growing on approach —blues, greens, and browns sandwiched within immense white-splattered poles.

'Yes, this appeared to be the most habitable.' Gabriel announced aloud for the benefit of all in earshot, before turning to King Jova to give more detailed description,

'I have been studying all this sun's planets via chromatic telescope – at the prompting of your daughter.' Gabriel gave an acknowledging nod towards nearby Nin, 'And it seems this 'earth' has a large axial tilt along with the added influence of a moon, causing seasons much like Marduk's,

Jova seemed intrigued by such details, leading Gabriel to add,

'Almost all land is aggregated into a single extended continent, leaving a mainly oceanic basin...'

'...That large isolated island looks like a ruptured yolk in a broken egg within its dark blue bowl.' Nin interrupted, enthusing.

'...And it looks like it's being fertilised.' Older stepbrother Ea now joining the group, added to his sister's lyric, pointing to the mildly active volcano at the centre oozing tendrils of lava northwards off its white cone.

As the 'ship' entered the planet's gravitation, Nin turned again to the ship's captain, Gabriel. 'How much like Marduk is this place?' she asked him.

'Marduk revolved around our sun once every 1,285 of our days - over in that cluster of nine stars.' Gabriel pointed to a constellation in the distance. 'Even our day was a little longer, equivalent to slightly more than 1.4 times the rotation of this planet. So, a year there was nearly five of this *earth*'s years.' He fell back on his technician's description and was already calculating in local measures.

Ea added, 'Yes, and after discovering and introducing manna into our staple diet, Marduks lived what was approximately one thousand of this planet's years. 'As that amino acid supplements the two hormones that diminish with aging. That, and advancements in stem cells as well as the invention of organic nerve circuitry, more than doubled our span. And now with the radiation shield, no one has died of natural causes so...' He arched a single eyebrow.

Gabriel guided and slowed the craft. Trying to decide the point of terminus, he faced a dilemma and now turned to King Jova,

'Sire, as you know, *Nibiru* was constructed almost entirely off-planet – designed only as a launching pad for smaller spacecraft. Having no need for aerodynamics, it is only vaguely circular, which is why luckily we also have the three disc-like, almost frictionless *Transporters* to carry materials from a planetary surface, also enabling construction.'

'So?' Jova shrugged in dismissal.

'We should keep the *Nibiru* here in orbit, well away from both the planet's and its moon's gravitational pull,' Gabriel suggested.

'But this is so far away! Taking too long to commute to the surface and disembark out comapny with just the three *Transporters*. Take it in as near as it can go,' Jova commanded.

The ship's captain displayed rare agitation, like the blank stare he had given Nin upon being reminded of the telescopes. Seemingly caught between servility and accuracy, he hesitated for some moments, neither acquiescing nor defying, until finally he declared a little ominously,

'Sire, I must caution that the closer our orbit, the more friction and the more thrust needed to escape. With only limited fuel and componentry for what was intended as a one-way journey, if I bring it much closer, we could only hold orbit, with no hope of escape – ever.'

The Marduk king hesitated only momentarily. 'I fully understand Captain. Take it in as close as you can,' Jova ordered, characteristically decisive and autocratic.

As he walked off, the king continued aloud for the benefit of those in earshot. 'I doubt we will find another hospitable planet even in our extended lifetimes, and I want quick access to the craft and its weaponry and equipment if needed. And I'm sure there's gold down there.'

The captain grumbled within earshot of only Nin, 'our meagre population is too small to sustain any real industry, so I hope there is some intelligence down there to help us build the massive factories necessary to develop replacement parts.'

But as a dutiful arch guardian, he curbed further protest and guided the *Nibiru* closer.

The first *Transporter* with Lord Ea and seventy-two guardians including their cherubic General Micha-El, plus life support equipment and weapons, bypassed the main landmass and hovered at high altitude for an overview of that 'broken egg with ruptured yolk'. It looked as if soft-boiled as an expansive flat and fertile valley emerged from an undulating blanket of white below a single extinct and time eroded yet monumental volcano shrouded in cloud.

'The mountain acts as barrier dividing the climate into two distinct zones. Based on the surrounding vegetation, rain from the cooler north seems to collect in that massive crater-lake, which feeds the two major rivers.' Gabriel pointed out to Ea on their glide down.

Dense forest in the lower temperate latitudes thinned out to deciduous foliage in the higher altitudes and boreal latitudes. North of the imposing cone and covering the remaining two-thirds of the island was a cluster of snow-napkinned highlands against which the volcano acted as lone southern sentinel.

'Yes, the southern side appears dryer, but the luxuriant vegetation indicates ample irrigation and a warm climate with photosynthetic chlorophyll – indicating oxygen.' Ea surmised.

As the craft spiralled towards the flatland in the south, they had a closer look.

The natural dam of the crater-lake had broken through its containing walls with milky streaks - waterfalls that scoured lagoons out of their black rock base. Two diverging rivers carved an expansive, fertile, and picturesque valley in their interstice, both emptying into the same ocean on opposite southern shores of the island.

Upstream from their deltas, shallow marshland indicated amphibians and reptiles.

'The atmosphere appears similar to Marduk's, bearing out King Jova's prediction. Those look like tracks indicating land-based life, but our instruments are not precise enough to determine an atmosphere that can support *us*.' Ea reasoned to the ever-dour Arch guardian and fellow Councillor, General Michael, who sported some blond head stubble - clearly having stopped shaving it recently.

An admixture of excitement, apprehension and uncertainty followed as the *Transporter* touched down and the pioneers prepared to test the conditions.

Ea marched reverentially along the landing ramp. He was observed from space by every surviving Marduk - glued to the *Nibiru*'s monitors — hushed in anticipation of that first ever Marduk step on alien soil.

'*Earth!*' The long deprived Ea exclaimed as he stepped unsteadily onto the loamy carpet, contrasted against the hard, metallic surfaces of the *Nibiru* and *Transporter*, 'how sensuous and yielding!'

He beckoned his fellow pioneers and soon, helmeted and with attached air tanks, each took their first doddering steps in trepidation.

The brigade stopped at a nearby hillock, scattered timeworn boulders appearing like picnic tables wedged into the soft earth. Surrounded by an expansive valley of grass interspersed with brush and teeming unconcerned wildlife, Ea addressed the team via audio while pointing to his helmet.

'I shall go first.'

The soldiers all held their breath in unison as Ea lifted his helmet and exposed his naked senses to the environment.

He paused, expressionless.

Within their helmets all eyes widened in fear and dismay as Ea held his hand to his neck, his pallid face contorting in pain and the throes of suffocation. He fell to the ground and thrashed about while his cohort stood by in momentary shock and helplessness, confused at how to respond.

CHAPTER FOUR

Snapping awake, Michael lunged to snatch the Councillor back to the ship. As he reached to lift the stricken princeling, Ea shook him off, sprang to his feet and attempted a sprightly but silly jig, shuffling about on his still uncertain legs.

'Hah, if you could only see your faces.' Ea giggled gleefully, overcome with delight at the conditions as much as his trick. 'At ease, my friends, the air is sweet and as invigorating as manna.'

Removing their own head coverings, the entire crew similarly fell about as if intoxicated, congratulating each other on the success of their landing.

Even typically glum Michael blushed and cracked the semblance of an ethereal smile, before mustering his troops to forge ahead with their explorations, leaving Ea behind with his bulky assistant, Galael.

'There must be some opiate in the air. But this is one drug I hope I remain addicted to,' Galael guffawed looking up at Ea. At less than six feet six, the short and rotund geneticist needed to stand on toes to reach eye level even with his friend Nin.

'Yes, I'm not sure if it's the rich mixture of oxygen or just relief and joy, but we all seem to be overly giddy', Ea replied, 'we must beware of hostile microbes, even if manna and the radiation shield might protect us from most noxious bacteria or viruses.'

"As our initial probes indicated, there appears to be no significant intelligence. I wonder if it ever existed and perhaps has become extinct." Galael mused.

'It is fascinating that life here is cellular and their genetic signature is so much like Marduk's even if different in appearance. I suspect all life follows the same intrinsic laws,' Ea speculated with his trademark arching single eyebrow.

'So perhaps, we *are* the only intelligence in the universe.' The ever-jovial Galael rued, a little more soberly.

'Possibly, at least we don't have to contend with any savvy competition. And the fauna here seems docile. But it's a little disappointing to be the lone intelligence on this planet. As for the universe at large – I doubt it based on my belief about evolutionary hierarchy.'

'Which is?' Galael asked.

'Well, if all life is cellular, It would be driven by material aspirations, beginning with food and rising in a hierarchy of finer aspirations. A Stage One type, conscious of itself and its own intelligence, would gain predominance over other creatures and harness natural resources—even modifying its environment through effort.

'A Stage Two civilization like Marduk, employs energy sources and controls its environment - weather, natural catastrophes, and so on. We were taking our first toddling steps to a Stage Three civilisation - beginning to exploit solar energies, exploring space and in our galactic neighbourhood. Our progress was cut well short by the asteroid. But it also accelerated it, as here we are.'

'I presume there's a Stage Four?' Galael asked.

'Yes, the final one on the cellular realm – able to manipulate a galaxy - the power of neutron stars and perhaps, black holes - setting off supernovae for creative purposes. Conquering the Fourth Dimension or space-time, warping space, they would traverse it in quantum leaps—unlike our only linear improvements in fuel and solar wind propulsion.'

'I see. So, I guess the only way we would detect other intelligences is if they had reached at least Stage Two.'

'Right and in the same time period as us. But we would never know of intelligences that find us too inferior to interact with, simply watching us undetected. After Stage Four there would be nothing to aspire in a corporeal body or form, so if there's a Stage Five they would likely be molecular or beyond - in electronic state of existence.

'Well I guess we're back in Stage One as we'll have to start from the beginning again.' Galael remarked.

'Very much, I'm afraid, my friend. But we also can't increase our miniscule numbers. Right now, we'll have to focus intelligence just so we don't regress to primitiveness and forget our technology,' Ea warned.

'But we're practically immortal. We have all the information of Marduk aboard the *Nibiru*. And we have all the time in the world!' Galael argued, characteristically optimistic.

Ea remained grim, 'any knowledge that is not applied ultimately becomes forgotten. How many of us really know how to fabricate anything significant, like even a simple radio from scratch? Technological advancement owes so much to the legacy of its predecessors. Without the infrastructure and ancillary services to support it, any technical knowledge is rendered almost useless. We are essentially marooned, and what little machinery we have, will soon deteriorate.'

'Yes, but we could upgrade that machinery? Or genetically evolve better animals?' Galael suggested, ever buoyant.

'Maybe, but we need *sentient* life if we are to progress.'

'Hah! The prerogative of our non-existent God.' Galael chuckled, where would we sta…'

Galael's question dangled, the fat geneticist attacked from above by a black-furred creature wielding a tree-stump club. He was knocked to the ground against a jagged rock that tore his protective suit, drawing blood from his thigh.

The attacker was immediately aided by four similarly armed bipedal companions - appearing from behind the nearby rocky outcrop. They focused their attention on the stricken Galael but seemed to hesitate at the strangely artificial 'skin' he wore and the colour of the fluid that exuded from his wound.

Attackers thus distracted, Ea had time to draw his sidearm and exterminated the creatures in a volley of light bursts before they had opportunity to strike.

Hearing the ruckus, General Michael rushed to the scene, where Ea was already attending to the wound.

'Curses! Has Lord Ea been hurt? Where there is skittish prey, there must be predators!' It was as close as Michael could come to swearing and anxiety.

Galael and Ea raised eyebrows at the general's 'expressiveness' on his flushed and dainty but always deadpan face.

Galael was mildly surprised at the antiquated 'Lord' epithet, as if recognising some arising aristocracy. But the stone-faced guardians were mostly regimented minions and didn't seem to even blink.

'No big deal. But thanks for not asking!' Galael gave the general a dismissive wink.

'Fan and root out any more!' Michael barked at his team, regaining any missing composure.

Ea mused aloud, 'looks like they were stalking us. They actually wielded weapons, primitive as they were, and also acted in mutual coordination. No doubt a nascent intelligence.'

Observing the ooze from Galael's wound, Michael voiced the anxious looks on his soldiers, 'His blood is blue. Cause for worry?'

'No, and that along with his artificial suit is what saved our young friend here,' Ea began explaining, 'The blow short-circuited his suit's colour selectors and the alternating lurid colours and his blue blood gave those creatures some momentary confusion allowing me time for my weapon. It's the radiation bath. It prevents oxidation of blood even when exposed to this oxygen rich air. In fact, any change would be good indicator for follow-up treatment.

'General, I think we have determined favourable conditions here. The passengers are anxious to get off the ship and this fertile plain seems ideal for a base camp and command post.'

While Ea's advance party were making their first foray onto terrestrial soil, Irania prepared inroads for her son's advancement. Indeed, she had commenced at Enlil's birth - encouraging his self-aggrandizement and belief in inherent superiority.

While her son viewed the landing troupe on the private screen in their quarters, mother evaluated her strategy. The *Nibiru's* moaning hum reinforced her sense of purpose,

Marduk had a population of over 150 billion, but born on this floating island, such statistics are beyond Enlil's imagination. Anyway, I doubt his brand of authority would pass the standards required by Marduk's intricate sovereign testing, so luckily his realm will be limited. And for him, leadership of any sort is its own reward. If indeed there be intelligent beings on this planet, they would be lesser creatures and the better to augment his power.

Seemingly viewing enough of the on-screen pictorial, her son interrupted her intrigues.

'Marduk's progress, as proved by the *Nibiru*, was due to a strict focus on technology with rigid discipline and leadership,' Enlil attempted to lecture his mother, who understood it as just reconfirming his limited personal philosophy.

Bemused by his naivety Irania was however careful not to discourage his fervour, 'Some fools argue that there are other considerations to life.'

'That's fine theoretically and for libertarians like stepbrother Ea. But in this primitive environment, it will take single-minded objectives to regain our former glory,' he argued. 'But he has many supporters with similarly lacking morals.'

Yes, and he is older, and intellectually superior.

She gave no voice to those thoughts. Jova and she had indeed groomed Enlil well, aided by the *Nibiru's* limited confines and lack of intellectual, emotional, or aesthetic distractions. His eight-foot muscular frame, half a head taller than the uniform height of fellow guardians, and his imposingly chiselled face including a square jaw and chin, accentuated his bombastic voice and bearing, giving him a distinct advantage. She had also inculcated in him values that matched his father's, which the king clearly appreciated, compensating for that mediocre intellect.

But Jova regularly threw in a little belittling to keep check on his son's insatiable ambition, leaving Enlil always on edge and insecure, perpetually needing to prove himself.

Perfect conditions for a megalomaniac! Irania congratulated herself inwardly, before Enlil interrupted again,

'Despite the amended Law of Inheritance giving me precedence, kingship is supposed to be by evaluation and Council vote, and my father after all is a true king in his objectivity. I worry that Ea may achieve majority support.' He fretted, clearly eager and excited to take charge in the far-fetched belief that Jova might soon hand it to him.

Jova is becoming a little feeble. But that was before Ea's wonderful invention. Enlil will have to wrench it from him, yet we're in strange times in a strange place.

'Yes, he could be a threat. Let me see whether we can find a way to divert his influence, while you display your mettle.'

CHAPTER FIVE

Despite the rudimentary facilities in base camp below the volcano they called *Dilmun*, the Marduks were initially keen to feel this 'land'. The inane description coined by that anonymous technician at first sight of the planet, evoked sensory memories of home, contrasting with the colourless artificiality and steely surfaces of the ship. In the absence of any alternative name, everyone thereafter referred to it as 'Earth'.

Descending in one of the three *Transporters,* Nin had no expectations - nature being an exotic experience.

Stepping off the metal gangway alone, she was bombarded. The *Nibiru* was indeed enormous— comfortably accommodating the multitude of voyagers along with its extensive componentry, residential cubicles, hydroponic food production facilities, recreation and social spaces, chronicle rooms, and numerous other nooks and crannies. But this surface was limitless—as vast as space itself, she felt.

Yet this space was alive. She awoke!

Insects?

'Those must be birds!' She asserted to no one in particular, becoming a child again, or was it for the first time? Assuming that her studies would prepare her, she was dumbstruck by the deluge of sensations that all but bowled her over - and for the first time in her long but experientially limited lifetime. Every step was psychedelic - riots of colour and sound and scent!

Each day brought revelation. She aroused!

The chronicles depicted towering mountains and wooded valleys; animals and plants; expansive rivers; even sunlight and its warmth, which I thought I could fill in with vivid imagination. But nothing prepared me for the grandeur of this scene and its flood of sensations!

That sophisticated holographic imagery and artistic brilliance was downright two-dimensional! She luxuriated!

The warmth of the sun, the glow of a moon, the feel and smell of soil and wind, even the change of night to day, exotic fauna and flora - so bizarre compared to the chronicles— is this the heavenly afterlife ancient mystics described? No, afterlife couldn't possibly contain such sensations!

This is life in its essence! She raptured!

Earth played its symphony. Her entire body shuddered as currents of emotion swept through, tightening her breath with every move over the wondrous expanse.

The myriad aromas, pleasant or odious, are just one wonderful discovery! She worshipped!

Overcome by it all and hitherto unable or unwilling to cry from any pain, she succumbed – inexplicably and uncontrollably weeping in sheer joy and recognition of all that she had missed. No doubt, the absence of either emotional or physical stroking, whether from a parent or significant companion, heightened those engulfing emotions.

This joy could not be expressed by mirth. It was a choking ache at her breast, both painful and erotic at once. Was that what caused the ache and melancholy? Or was it that she had to experience this alone? Even if that was her preferred state, aloneness becomes so terribly limiting when experiencing joy or wonder or even trauma or pain.

Her psyche called out and hungered to share with another. It became a lasting revelation to her, painted and fixated by a backdrop of wonder; that this was what brought on the oneness of life, the ultimate unifying principle for all sentient beings—that both ecstasy and bereavement, in order to be fully experienced, truly felt, even purged—needs to be shared.

I'm home! No longer in fantasy! Expanding daily! I don't think I can imagine or wish for any other!

'Marduk I believe was once as natural as this,' a voice shocked her out of reverie.

Nazarel, the Agriculturist had joined her in enjoying the vistas. Standing beside her and shielding his crystal eye and now minor scars around that side of his face, he added, 'but over time it was replaced with artificiality, just like my useless eye.' The guardian farmer turned rueful on reflection of both those conditions,

'Even wildlife there had long been narrowed down to the utilitarian, little left to grow naturally and unmodified to suit the population. We must recreate it, only better!' It sounded to Nin like a vow.

Nin paid little attention to the *Nibiru* Councillor's melancholy. She was too ensconced in marvel. But she appreciated his attempt at simpatico and indeed his love of the field. She was glad the community had such a dedicated specialist in their midst.

Devoid of facilities and after initial euphoria, most of surface visits were brief, guardians and technicians turned labourers with limited equipment and primitive materials, commuting to and from the mother craft

Not so Nazarel and his team. Though trained as a guardian and expert marksman in the ancient art of archery, the Chief Agriculturist was keen to develop his preferred calling in this new earth. The accident that claimed his eye diminished his confidence but strengthened his resolve.

His reduced team after the *Nibiru* accident quickly set about clearing a particularly fertile oasis in the interstice of the twin-rivers encompassing the Marduk colony. Nin the budding geneticist could only watch fascinated, she and her mother helping occasionally in seeking berries and local grasses specified by Nazarel—which he soon grafted or mutated into cereal crops, fruit, and vegetables for the farm he called Eden.

In that foraging, Shtar briefly became talkative while all of them adapted to the planet's gravity and climate, 'exquisite as is the scenery, this planet is sterile,' she declared to her daughter.

Nin sensed her meaning but wished to draw out more response, 'How so?'

'Without the influence of an active consciousness involved in its development, the environment is devoid of the memory of spirit—the psychic energy that intelligent life imbibes on its surroundings. The glimmering silver-tinged rainforest is gorgeous, but despite its awesome beauty, its character is similar to that of the surrounding mountains in their napkins of snow—frigid and devoid of spirit.'

In that rare moment of eloquence, her mother continued, 'perhaps that is our purpose after all, to develop in this organism a mind, spirit, and soul.'

The few remaining architects and engineers rummaged for suitable stone and timber to complement polymers from the space station in building Jova's delineated city. And guardians became game hunters, seeking edible meats for the *Nibiru's* deprived omnivores.

But all that had little impression on Enlil, Irania's ambitious young son who seemed of two minds with Jova's order to remain earthbound and help him oversee matters. He sniffed the air as if it was all just barely tolerable, like he had weightier matters to ponder. What those pressing and serious matters were, Nin could not guess, but they appeared perpetually furrowed in his brow, in his pursed lips, and square-jawed chin as he carried himself amongst the pioneers with an air of self-importance.

He came alive only in barking orders conveyed to him by the king who rarely exited his royal caravan. Enlil, delivered them as if they were of gravest import - an actor on stage that Nin had read of in the chronicles. A pity, she thought, as he was otherwise very attractive.

Jova stood surveying the construction of their first city on that island continent they initially named 'Hyperborea' – being apparently similar to a northern region on Marduk. The royal sage Uriel and the nervous Doctor Raphael 'The Hawk' - stood alongside their king on a hummock below the Dilmun volcano. The trio also observed the last of the *Nibiru* residents exiting the *Transporter* shuttles for permanent residence on Earth in the camp 'city' that would act as interim quarters.

As often, Nin was the ignored bystander.

'After six months it seems most of us have regained much of our former Marduk physiques, with little physiological change.' Raphael commented.

Uriel chipped in, 'yes, Earth's solid iron core compensates for its smaller dimension and so its gravity is almost identical to Marduk, compacting our physiques while retaining our height. But the intensity of ultra-violet light is naturally much stronger than the *Nibiru*, making us all much ruddier.'

In the pause that followed, Nin inspected those changes.

Raphael gained his nickname from the bird commonly seen around the Dilmun foothills. His hooknose and constant twitching were now complemented with a slick mane of silver-grey hair, and his darkening grey eyes appeared to have widened – truly matching his moniker.

All were regaining apparently former appearance, alike her idolised stepbrother Ea's now blue-green eyes, rich crop of light copper cranial hair and some lean muscular filling and proportion.

Uriel again broke the brief silence, 'beautiful and inviting as this planet appears to be, we are essentially marooned and will need to reinvent and redevelop our technology all over again!'

Nin recalled her roly-poly friend Galael or 'Fubsy' as she endearingly called him, reporting how Ea arrived at a similar conclusion upon their first steps on Earth.

'Obviously! But first we need to replenish our depleted gold,' Jova snapped gruffly, asserting his regal authority. He was not comfortable in this primitive and rustic savagery. His position was hitherto supported by a legacy of law, and thus military support. Here, he felt naked, reduced to a primitive state where anarchy could easily take hold and brute strength could secure the following of such an uncertain community.

Spotting that shakiness early, his acute wife Irania had warned, 'You must reinforce your leadership and control at every opportunity!'

The guardians were unyieldingly loyal, but that could apply to whoever was on the throne. He concluded that his best security would be in controlling the *Nibiru*, observing matters via its high-resolution cameras.

'I miss the reassuring hum of the *Nibiru* instead of this cacophony of birds and insects - not to mention these primitive conditions.' He thought aloud, observing Captain Gabriel making his way up the hill to their position.

'Geological surveys indicate that beneath the ice and soil north of Mount Dilmun, there are various metals and probable trace radioactive elements that could generate enough energy to serve our basic needs. We can rely on those for base camp during construction, but there's no trace of gold in the vicinity,' the Captain announced.

Raphael stuck his bent nose into the conversation, 'it's a pity we couldn't bring with us more of the automatons to tame this savage world.' His hair flowed silver in the breeze, giving an air of assurance, but his darting eyes betrayed his constant state of anxiety.

Jova shared glances and a brief shrug with Uriel, but both returned impassive upon noticing Nin's inquisitive squint at that apparent secrecy.

Uriel addressed the issue a little obliquely, repeating his earlier observation, 'we're such a specialised society, none of us knows of any process in its entirety. And we lost so many roboticists to cosmic radiation. True, robot machinery would have helped us tremendously but at least we have the few Titans for the heavy lifting.' He pointed over at the *Transporter*.

Nin turned to observe the shaggy hulks, the last of the *Nibiru* contingent, lumbering onto the landscape, outwardly unmoved, but displaying a much lighter gait than on board. She was aware the Titans were token representatives of that primitive species of more than thirty-foot tall Marduk giants, a breed already on their way to extinction.

The chronicles had described that despite massive proportions their intellect was considered limited - ascribed to their rustic culture. Animists in belief and naturalists in lifestyle, they were a docile and guileless race who, if they engaged at all on Marduk, were typically relegated the rare menial tasks that required brute strength. Having shunned the technological progress of their competitor race, and thus clinging to their diminishing natural habitat, they had become incongruous and redundant as a species, tolerated as a symbolic vestige of Marduk's primitive past. And for that reason, as tokens to the future and as potential labourers in any newly discovered planet, six males and six females were taken aboard the *Nibiru*.

Prompted by their appearance, Doctor Raphael went into a private huddle with his king. Meanwhile, the immigrants began to congregate around Jova's circle, anxious about their future.

Breaking off from the secretive discussion with the Head Physician, Jova cut short any speculation and took control, addressing the mass via megaphone,

'We don't have anything like the technology or materials that produced the thirty million components of the *Nibiru* - in some two million factories. So, robot componentry is also not an option. In that absence we'll just have to get used to proceeding manually and with the little machinery available,' he announced, pausing for effect and casting his eyes patronizingly over the crowd to re-establish his dominion before he continued,

'Having established base camp and the foundations of our first city, we will need to urgently find gold to operate the *Nibiru,* and establish our community,' he proclaimed before assigning individual tasks.

'Ea, you will lead the Titans and your fellow libertarians to seek gold in the mainland. After some rigours in the wilds, you will better appreciate the value of our rules and the importance of our technological culture,' he commanded, catching Irania's encouraging nod and smile. But Jova was back in his element and seemingly needed no such reassurance. He turned to his youngest son,

'Enlil, you will oversee base camp here beside this Mount Dilmun and construct our proposed city. Uri-El, you can then start on an Astronomical Institute and Observatory and with Captain Gabri-El's help from *Nibiru*, you will determine local geometry and optimum orientation of structures based on this solar system's magnetic forces. Rapha-El, find a suitable site to set up your Healing Institute . . .'

Leader first, thinker second, and father last, Nin mused wryly but with admiration as Jova established purpose to the uncertain settlers and focused on expediency, even if a little partial.

'Gabri-El, prepare to take me back to the *Nibiru.*' The formal use of full epithets for all the arch guardians added authority to his commands.

Jova had left the female members of his family with all options. Nin now took note of the reactions of her extended family. Hera, with nothing to offer but former royalty, offered herself as a test subject for research at the Healing Institute. Shtar chose life on Earth without offering any reason. Irania informed she would commute back and forth between husband and son till ground conditions were more suitable to her station.

Knowing Ea's restless spirit, Nin guessed he probably looked upon it as an educational adventure. She was torn between going along or staying to help Nazarel in Eden, and seeing potential in the local wildlife, she chose the latter.

Enlil appeared to take it all in stride. But as a fellow *Nibiru* child, she well understood that stripped of the ship's cocoon, the raw chaotic savagery of this expansive planet scared him. Duplicating Marduk's orderly symmetry and co-ordinated regimen would be right up his alley. Eyes fixed on his father's departing back, he responded with a military and perfunctory, 'yes, Sire!

Examining her brothers' reactions, Nin focused her attention on the younger. She was as uneasy in the presence of Enlil as she was comfortable with the older, quick-witted and rascally Ea. Whereas Ea invoked her love and admiration, it carried an element of sympathy. Enlil provoked a deeper, primeval response, causing her to bristle in his presence with an unclear emotion,

Enlil's a fanatic – guided by cold-blooded calculated action! She recoiled at that initial thought.

But there's power and confidence in his convictions, combining the malevolent force and seductive looks and manner he inherited from his mother. He's the definition of the Marduk model male – and a good six inches taller than almost anyone.

All his features, including those now blue-grey eyes only reinforce that ruthlessness of purpose - hair already grown to a rich gold; upright bearing and gait; firm and fixed stare in the act of conversation; his conservative stiffness and his bombastic, even if sometimes empty, oratory—all gave impression of implacable strength. That, together with the occasional flash of charm, inspired confidence, yet threatened to crush all that got in his way.

Those repressed emotions harbour an unspecified resentment. Strange but despite his overt righteousness, he invokes the dark and forbidden, at once exciting and threatening.

And she sensed his inscrutable gaze from time to time, causing an instinctive shiver. She couldn't prove it, but she detected a repressed and insatiate desire in him. *If, as mother suggested, what is important is how a person makes you feel, then I feel much better in the comforting presence of Ea.*

Why she paid so much attention to younger stepbrother Enlil hadn't crossed her mind.

CHAPTER SIX

Ea led three hundred-odd motley volunteers including the twelve Titans and all forty-six dwarfish trolls—the common mutation from cosmic damage on the *Nibiru* - all misfits in the eyes of the community.

The trainee nurse Dawn summed up the sentiment of the mainly younger Marduk technicians and few guardians in the troupe.

'What I heard of Marduk and the *Nibiru* was only technology—all of it artificial. What a great opportunity on this pristine planet to observe something of nature,' she argued with her guardian lieutenant father Alan-El, before setting off.

'But who knows what dangers are out there? What if you don't come back?' Having lost his botanist wife in the *Nibiru* accident, Alanel was disturbed by his young daughter's independence. She was a rare intact shipboard birth, as soon as restrictions were removed and a little older than Jova's Nin,

'Whatever happens, at least *something* will happen. Life on the *Nibiru* was an endless yawn, and not just from the restricted space…' she stopped short, not wishing to put down her very conformist but otherwise doting father, '… but of course once we find the gold, I'll come back. I don't intend to rough it out permanently. I'm Marduk after all.' She reassured.

'Well, make sure you stay in constant communication.'

'Of course, Father. I will miss you immensely. But the pioneers are mainly male, and you never know . . . Anyway, I will call at every opportunity.'

Aigar, hero of the *Nibiru* accident, now guardian lieutenant, had been assigned as second in command of that assorted mob.

'I am right-handed but 'Leftenant Aigar. When I'm not in my right mind, my left mind is pretty crowded.' He had introduced himself to the bemused scientist.

'What say?'

'I may be backward, but I'm looking forward to this mission. Is that ignorance or apathy? I don't know and I don't care!' Aigar responded, unabashed.

Ea was nonplussed, trying to decide whether it was a true defect or insubordination. He wondered at how such a misfit could have been a guardian, and an officer at that!

'You are speaking Marduk, I can tell, but—' He checked himself, inspecting the innate good-natured sincerity in the soldier's grinning face and sensing some ironic meaning in his words. 'Hah! Perhaps you speak a more apt form of Marduk, after all. It's a pleasure, Lieu...Aigar. I'm glad to have your assistance.'

He held out his hand in welcome, sensing a kindred spirit. Exchanging such introductory pleasantries, he studied the officer. A craggy face, exaggerated by a number of scars, indicated a rugged lifestyle in the outdoors. His broad nose, together with flowing ashen hair, gave him a dashing look, accentuated by a powerful, proportioned physique. He surmised that the gregarious and fun-loving lieutenant lacked the necessary guile to be ambitious. Wondering at the absent 'El' epithet from Aigar's official name, he decided to check on the guardian's background.

He learnt of Aigar's botanical past and subsequent heroism - conscription for that prowess - impressive agility and martial skill – thus promoted to officer. His quirkiness was ascribed to probable damage from exposure in the accident, although from what Ea gathered, it dated much earlier. Obviously, his attempts at humour did not sit well with his superiors - especially austere General Michael.

For that reason and the recent change in his marital status, it seemed Aigar eager to get out from the watchful gaze of his disapproving guardian commander and recent father-in-law, hence joining Ea. The courtship of the couple was legendary amusement amongst the guardians - which Ea garnered from a rare friend and fellow officer who described the romance to him,

'I remember the occasion well. Aigar and I had been recently promoted and it was our first visit to the officers' club,' the friend began,

"Hey, there, moonbeam!" she called out across the busy Nibiru arh-guardian club, and Aigar immediately turned around to observe Captain Raguel's vivacious daughter, Lilith. He looked back to me with an inquiring gesture as if - is she addressing me? She was heading directly his way, throwing a seductive gaze and inviting smile.

And as she approached, he lost his famous facile manner and quick wit. Awestruck, the best he could do was, "Hell . . . o, beautiful!"

Dropping her voice to a drone, she brushed past him. "Not you, crater-face!" She said it loud enough for all to hear, bursting his bravado. But she turned and gave a momentary and enigmatic smirk before joining in conversation with her bunch.

"I think she's got stars in her eyes for me," he remarked to me, though clearly abashed.

She stood at the bar intentionally facing away. His constant focus probably caused the back of her neck to bristle, regularly flicking her black locks indicating she was aware and delighting in the attention.

This friend is a perceptive and lucid storyteller – a natural, Ea remarked inwardly, as the ballad continued,

Observing her finishing her drink and placing the empty vessel on the counter, our Aigar saw an opening.

He went over to comment, "Your cup is empty!"

"No, thanks!" Lilith said with a deprecating smile.

"Wasn't offering! Just thought you should know!" He was exaggeratedly offhand and equally loud, turning away with a shrug. But he turned back and gave her a mischievous grin. And as he did so, Lilith seemed captured by the gaze in Aigar's flecked aquamarine eyes.

"Touché!" She blushed, pausing. And her stare took in his whole being all at once, that hint of effeminacy in a comparatively delicate frame containing his muscular covering. Strength tempered with sensitivity is how I would describe him.

Lilith relented, as she probably always intended, and her companions forgotten, she fell into conversation with this seemingly long-lost friend she had never met.

'Why don't you join our adventure in Gondwanaland?' Ea suggested to the poetic friend. He used Gabriel's name—meaning 'beastland' in

Marduk - after spotting its plethora of wildlife via Nibiru's telescopic cameras.

'Nah, I'm not one for rugged adventure. My inclinations lean towards the Astronomical Institute and Shtar's Mystic Psychology.' The officer-poet replied.

As they packed belongings preparing to leave on the quest for gold, Lilith reminisced on that initial encounter with Aigar.

Finally shunted out of the officer's club at closing, she had entered his out-stretched arms in the customary Marduk embrace upon greeting and departure—an efficient form of determining body chemistry. And as they did so, like separated facets of a broken disk, they slipped into a seamless unity, their ultimate separation that night, merely physical.

'I don't believe in short-term relationships.' She whispered.

'Me neither! They should last till breakfast at least!'

It wasn't long before they were each other's only companions.

'None of this multiple wives twaddle, you hear!' She put her foot down as things became serious.

'I think you're pretty tough, don't I?' He smirked. 'How dare you be subservient to me!'

'Stop that!'

'I'm trying!'

'Yes, very trying!' She quipped back, mockingly.

They were married soon after. But the affair never ended, and as was typical of such passion, the ensuing arguments were tempestuous. She was disappointed in her attempts to wean his flippancy and take his position more seriously. But the squabbles were short-lived, inevitably making her laugh with some totally inappropriate comment, and as Aigar put it, they would 'bang away like a latrine door in a storm'.

Aigar too took a few moments to reflect on his good fortune in finding his wife.

She displayed many facets. Whenever he looked at it, her face portrayed a different aspect, a shifting form that, except for her distinct amber eyes, made it difficult to picture her visage in his mind's eye. But he never came to believe he deserved her, and for that reason, she brought out the best in him - which was hardly a fractionlet, he would say.

'I look forward to seeing all the *gondwanas* on that main continent?' Lilith interrupted his thoughts enthusing about their adventure.

'I'm gonna wanna be looking both forward and backward seeing your main continent,' he responded.

'Yes, well, it's probably best we escape from all the rigid scrutinising here.' She said as they finished packing and she undressed to clamber into their bed.

'Yes, like I'm getting rigid scrutinising you right now!'

In a barque assembled from inflatables aboard the *Nibiru*, the explorers set out from the shadow of Mount Dilmun, following the south-eastward Gihon River that ran by Eden and emptied into the natural harbour at the southern edge of the island continent.

From there, they crossed the expansive strait separating Hyperborea and the fertile tropical section of Gondwanaland.

At base camp, Enlil led the *Nibiru* technicians and crew, now released after establishing stationary orbit. These tried their skills as artisans and craftsmen. Except for a few needed to protected the settlers from harassing predators, most guardians were also virtually redundant. Those unemployed soldiers modified themselves into builders. Having learnt from ecological degradation on Marduk, and carrying few recently developed biodegradable building polymers, they chiselled stone, fired mud, and refined cement from the alluvial silts to form the foundations of the city of *Eridu* that arose from the fertile plain. And all design features were augmented with similarly natural materials, fibres, and resins.

Adorned and embellished by some of the precious metals and stones found locally, Eridu burgeoned—a magnificent artificial complement to the natural spectacle of Nazarel's Eden.

There, in the developing Healing Institute, Nin developed as a serious geneticist in the absence of her master scientist mentor Ea and her friend Fubsy.

She thrived in the wildlife laboratory attracted and corralled in Eden, single-handedly isolating the genetic code of the mountain goat to evolve a sheep. That genome mapping and gene isolation soon led to the evolution of the dairy cow from the wild buffalo, and later the horse from the dwarfish and indigenous Pliohippus, as well as the multi-bred pygarg.

Taking a break, she dropped in on Uriel at the already constructed Astronomical Institute.

'Congratulations, Nineveh! What a wonderful achievement evolving those herds of livestock!' Uriel enthused, welcoming her to his quarters-cum-lookout.

The venerable sage's use of her full name indicated his esteem, which delighted Nin more than any overt praise from this now adopted mentor and confidant. His young ward, Shalimar had become even more reserved in late puberty and as usual, with a perfunctory greeting upon Nin's increasingly frequent visits, she retired to her section.

'Thank you! Just trying to improve our community,' she gushed. 'It's strange, but despite all the sensory bombardment of this planet, I sense something missing. I can't identify it.'

'I think I know what you're getting at. Others too have remarked on it. The inner hum of the *Nibiru*.'

'Yes! I never even knew it existed...'

There was sound everywhere on this teeming planet, but that background vibration, the constant droning, lulling hum, was eerie in its absence. It was as if a cocoon, an enveloping womb, had been torn off.

Snapping out of her reverie, she concluded...'but that's not quite it.'

She turned to the reason for her visit,

'Mother says nothing is coincidental, but isn't it strange that of the 10,000 Marduk escapees, exactly 6,666 survived, including births aboard! But that's not *really* what I wanted to discuss. I've read some of the facts surrounding my family, especially Jova. But I'm not quite able to piece together all the connections, particularly relating to Irania.'

'The story's convoluted but let me see if I can simplify,' Uriel began,

'You see, Jova's mother, Europa, was married twice. Her first husband Uranus was Chief Astronomer at the Marduk Astronomical Institute and instrumental in commencing the construction of the

Nibiru - and my mentor. He was killed by a malfunction that exploded a shuttle he was riding.

Uranus had a protégé, Cronus, a genius in Astrophysics, noted for his theories on space-time. That Cronus was my contemporary... but I must admit he outshone me.' Uriel faked a wince at the memory.

'Surprisingly, Cronus then married Uranus' widow, Europa and adopted their already adult son Jova, who ended emulating both fathers as astronomer in our Institute.

'With advanced fertility treatments, elderly Europa bore Cronus a daughter – our Irania.'

'Why weren't the parents included amongst the passengers?' Nin asked.

'Well, that's where the Council proves itself. Due to Europa's advanced age, she was ineligible and Cronus refused to leave her - I suppose paving the way for me. Instead, they entrusted Jova to take care of his by now pubescent stepsister, Irania.'

Nin deduced the rest as she left Urie and strolled Eridu's cobbled lanes in thought.

Irania had clearly blossomed further into the archetypical seductress and siren. In the absence of parental guidance, it seems her passionate nature focused on the pursuit of privilege, power, and potent sex, for which she had a perfect mentor—her own stepbrother, Jova.

Irania could not countenance any role but queen, as much in substance as in form. She had the arrogance to assume she was of supreme importance and the twisted personality to believe that conviction. It was therefore no quantum leap of deduction to imagine in whose mind Jova's Law of Inheritance originated.

Their son Enlil seemed to have distilled his parents' regal qualities. And like Jova, he saw everything in two dimensions—black and white, good and evil. Nin understood why Ea had such an aversion to him, even from his birth.

She recalled his aside as they both looked over the infant in his cot, "Looks like we've both been bamboozled!"

It was meaningless to her at the time, making an impression only because it appeared to disturb her adored brother.

However, Ea's rebelliousness and belief in individual responsibility and freedom left him ill-equipped for command. What apparently rankled him nowadays was that kingship would fall upon their thick-headed younger brother who exhibited no more capability than formulaic loyalty and duty to his father's rigid and legalistic social order.

Enlil's every action was calculated, even sex appeared to be purely utilitarian - if rumours about his escapades were to be believed. Yet his goal was for a state of chivalric honour and moral virtue based on technological progress. Whereas Ea looked on authority as a means to an end, Enlil looked upon it as an end in itself. Unlike his mother's raw desire, Enlil's lust for power emanated from a belief in his righteousness.

Enough of this family pre-occupation! I wonder how the explorers are doing. I wish I could talk to Fubsy for an update, but the Nibiru has shut down all peripheral machinery, conserving power to maintain orbital stasis.

As if in response Nin noticed the excitement building Institute screens beaming a worrying message from *Nibiru*.

Using the *Nibiru*'s small but sophisticated mining and drilling equipment, the explorers slashed their way through the dense forests of Gondwanaland, while guardian weaponry burnt through the brush. The Titans made their foraging lighter and far less risky with their instinctual sense of wilderness. But that did not detract from the hardship in the totally unfamiliar environment.

They were met by a plethora of beasts in natural menageries, more so as they neared the tropics, temperate forests turning to ever-lusher rainforest.

Inventing rudimentary tools to combat the incessant equatorial humidity, rain and insects, the fossickers were stretched physically and emotionally. Again, it was the unacknowledged Titans who paved their path, fending off or warning wild creatures as necessary.

Hugging the Western coast to stay in touch with their accompanying barque, they forged ever southward.

The dwarfish trolls cleared underbrush and developed a devilish ability for providing fish. Learning that many species surfaced for the night, they lay in ambush on the riverbanks at twilight, bopping them with their clubs as they arose.

'To think I could be lolling away on a hammock, gorging on Nazarel's yield in Eden - even my body suit is starting to sag!' A now less rounded Galael complained to no one in particular, 'and its temperature regulator is only barely keeping up in this humidity – even with ample sunlight to power its batteries.'

'At least with a flat stomach, you won't *abdocate* any longer?' Aigar teased the fat geneticist.

The group was setting up camp while Ea, often stopping to examine various creatures, tended to an injured young hominid ape.

'With all the technology that brought us across the galaxy, one would think we could produce some equipment to overcome these conditions.' A young guardian complained.

An older technician joined in. '...Yes, and I wish our technicians could replicate Marduk's sophisticated geological survey equipment to easier locate that gold.'

'Knowledge can only employ materials and equipment to produce the materials for the equipment to employ that knowledge.' Aigar retorted in his cryptic language that yet made absolute sense.

'Sophisticated instruments serve little purpose against humidity, bogs and swamps, or insects,' Ea commented, finishing medication of his hominid patient. 'This climate is already taking quite a toll on the delicate componentry of what little electronics we have. And as Aigar points out, technical expertise is not much use without the precision parts necessary for repairs.'

Aigar's raven-haired Lilith had assisted Ea to patch up the injured hominid and now joined in, 'we have the trolls' fish, the wild fruits and berries that our Titans identify, and our weapons for *gondwana* meat - not *so* bad.' She said while turning her soft tawny eyes up at the young nurse Dawn for approval of her efforts at learning to bandage.

Dawn smiled approvingly and commented, 'Aren't the Titans uncanny in differentiating edible versus poisonous plants?'

Ea mused aloud as he watched his hominid patient limp off into the jungle, 'those hominids are dexterous and quite cunning. And it seems their motivations are so similar to ours. I wonder if such predilections are a principle of all evolving intelligence.'

'You have two parts of brain, 'left' and 'right'. In the left side, there's nothing right. In the right side, there's nothing left,' Aigar quipped to deaf ears.

However, the hominids were mere pests to the rest of the troupe, finding sport in taking pot-shots with their side arms—saddening the Titans. Totally at ease in the verdant jungle, those mighty but gentle giants protected companion and invader alike - scaring the latter away before they were in range. Yet the apes' guile and their temerity to fight back, made the sport all the more alluring.

Over time, the aliens became familiar and appreciative of the savage environment. But equally, the nomad existence wore against their spirits, increasing desire for contact with their distant brethren.

'You've used up your five minutes! We need to keep communication open!' The guardian pilot barked at young Dawn, who was immersed in the single screen aboard the messenger *skoop*. The spherical crystal screen within the two-person flying recreational vehicle was the only communication device, relaying signal to the *Nibiru* which bounced it to Hyperborea.

Galael felt for the miniature device he clandestinely carried but rarely used. The two-way holographic projection unit was a chance find at the *Nibiru* Healing Institute while rummaging through the equipment store for instruments to help Ea develop his electromagnetic youth fount. Delighted that it came with instructions, he also guessed it was a one-of prototype. He thus hid its existence until leaving on this expedition - when he shared one of the twin receiver-transmitters with his friend and colleague, Nin.

Knowing such an invaluable item meant confiscation if discovered, he retained secrecy despite some guilt at depriving the explorers from that valuable communication.

In any case, it's just good for two persons - a toy really. He justified to himself while standing aside observing the queue waiting to use the *skoop*'s solitary official device.

'Wait, I haven't finished talking to my father, Lieutenant Alan-El. Give me one more minute, please, sir? Would you like to talk to him?' Dawn cajoled, hoping also that by dropping her father's officer position, she may influence the *skoop* pilot.

'One minute *only!* You know this is the sole method of tracking our position and progress by the *Nibiru*, every minute yabbering interferes with the tracking signal,' the guardian scolded half-heartedly.

The nurse gave him a thankful nod and turned aside to smile at her luck - most unusual for the pedantically rigid guardians to relent from strict procedure.

Galael too was pleasantly surprised by that courtesy. Perhaps, the removal from central command and the relaxed conviviality he found here in the tropics had softened him. Isolation in the small solar powered craft assigned to shuttle small medical and other supplies from Hyperborea, had affected him also – as he listened to the pilot mumbling to himself for company,

'Only a few gems and precious metals so far... rudimentary electricity.' the pilot griped, 'even the little uranium...for nuclear equipment on the *Nibiru*... too volatile compared to Vril.'

Finally, as nurse Dawn ended her transmission, he raised his volume and grumbled to all in earshot, 'we'd better find gold soon or even the *Nibiru* will be rendered inactive and this simple communication will shut down.'

Was that a guess or did he pick up the rumour from base camp? Nin's last report was that the Nibiru *is shutting down everything and using all vril just to keep in orbit,* Galael worried as he left the growing queue around the little *skoop*.

'It's getting cooler and more seasonal nowadays, less of that tropical heat.' Lilith commented as she sidled up to her husband who, with Ea, was inspecting the last holographic map beamed from the *Nibiru* over three years earlier. As they trudged ever southwards, the gigantic antipodean ice cap began to bless them with cooling zephyrs. The group had camped beside an amazonian westward flowing river they were following for the past hundred or so days.

'The map indicates various ores in the vicinity including nickel, which might mean gold nearby, according to one geological theory I viewed while preparing for this trip.' Ea commented as Aigar moved over to envelope his wife in his arms.

'At least I hope so! We seem to be on an endless course to nowhere. It's been nearly twenty local years since we left, and I wonder if we will ever join up with the rest in Hyperborea...'

'Ever stop to think, and forget to start again?' Aigar's utterly irrelevant gag was ignored as Lilith returned to the subject,

'...And is that so bad? Lilith queried, 'these surroundings are quite idyllic.'

'Perhaps. But isolation may diminish our ability to reintegrate. Notice our dwarfs already adapting to the harsh conditions with a hardier and feral mien. And last I heard city construction is well underway, developing urban sophistication and outlook.'

Lilith respectfully challenged 'You hardly strike me as the type to worry about such snobbery.'

'No, but...'

Ea was interrupted by Aigar's outburst.

'Atlas! Yonder boulder looks like the world on your shoulder! But it's as useful as tits on a bull!'

Naturally, the Titans did the digging while the technicians assayed the land and the dwarfs prepared camp. Atlas, the largest and strongest of the Titans now hefted a massive rock as he plodded their way, planting it beside them without comment.

Intellectually retarded, the Titans - and particularly Atlas - were also eccentric. So, dumping this 'gift' at their feet was looked upon as one of those peccadilloes. He stood impassive while they returned to their musings.

'You were saying, my Lord?' Lilith prompted.

Ea looked her over briefly before responding. Despite all the deprivation of this arduous journey, she was stunning. Her earlier tropically dark-tanned skin had paled to a pinkish glow, highlighting her glittering lion's mane-like eyes—with face framed by long, straight black hair. No doubt, the preying attention of the other guardian officers in Hyperborea was another reason Aigar had joined the expedition.

He finally addressed her expectant query, 'it's not just about social integration, but this isolation will also deprive our gang from...'

Again, he was cut off by Aigar's bark, 'Atlas, if ignorance is bliss, you must be the happiest Marduk alive! Your gargantuan gift is glorious but go get gold!' He scolded, and shrugged back at Lilith and Ea, 'his lights are on, but nobody's home.'

Ea could not get used to the incongruity of Aigar's rugged looks and model guardian talent with his often-juvenile wit. He stole a glance at the soldier's wife as if in sympathy, before turning his attention to the gigantic Titan and his 'gift'. As he did so, the sunlight threw some sparkles off the boulder, catching his attention. Aigar, following his gaze, now noticed them too and they turned to each other in wondrous puzzlement.

'Where did you find it?' Ea asked the giant, containing his mounting excitement.

The reticent Titan turned and led them to a pit he had dug a scant half mile from the camp. Lilith followed close behind.

Sequestered in the *Nibiru*, Jova looked out his window into the emptiness of space, contemplating his role. Unlike the Earth contingent, who were driven by their assigned tasks, inactivity had caused his atrophy faster than even ancient Uriel.

The thought of his Advisor caused him to reminisce on his early days and wander in his thoughts,

I admired my father Uranus, but stepfather Cronus was even more brilliant. I'm glad he married my mother, allowing me to gain special favour from his seat on Council. After all, that's how true leaders get what they want. His eminence gave him access to the test profiles, which he passed to me. Well, I did my share of preparation, foregoing everything else to acquire the required qualities. Power is its own reward!

Keeping a population of one hundred and fifty billion in check was no easy task, but this primitive planet scares me more. What can I contribute here? There's no room for politics and statesmanship - much less my brand of deep space astronomy in times of such urgent need. This distance is all that maintains my mystique of authority.

My children each display their unique brand of brilliance.

Ea is a genius, but he's too eccentric and erratic—missing the clear-thinking decisiveness of leadership—impractical like Shtar and even Uriel. Nin has come into her own right without much input from either Shtar or me, but she too lacks the dynamism and ambition to lead. Besides, gender precludes her in this savage and primitive environment. Luckily, Irania came along with her proposal - the fact that she is so damn attractive was such a bonus!

Jova's long dormant libido stirred momentarily at the thought of his third wife. *It's been a while, I must pay her a visit.*

And the almost eventless journey was a great opportunity to groom our son, Enlil who is also more a natural. And with the Council stacked with loyal supporters...

Gabriel's rap, requesting entry to his open quarters interrupted Jova's thoughts. Entering, the ship's captain looked from wall to opposite wall. His expression indicated surprise at the king aligning his viewing panel towards their former star system and the comparative emptiness, instead of at Earth, looming large on the opposing side.

'Excuse the interruption Sire, but our cameras have picked up flashes from Hyperborea base camp which might indicate something to do with the explorers and requesting your urgent attendance.' The Captain announced.

'*Nibiru* achieved a marvel in crossing interstellar space – fully intact – and we're reduced to flashing lights for communication?' Jova grumbled, 'what do you mean by "might indicate"? Can't you even read their code?'

Gabriel's blinking betrayed his embarrassment, 'Not very well Sire, nor can our technician on Earth who sent it. Even the chronicles only mention it as an ancient language of sorts.'

'For Beelzebub's sake then just turn on the communications system for a few minutes!' Jova barked.

'To do that I would have to fire up the entire Nibiru, sire. It would draw far too much of our almost fully depleted vril. This station's designers never considered such a dire lack of fuel."

Gabriel didn't underscore his earlier warning to the king about bringing the *Nibiru* too close to the planet. It left Jova to marvel at nearly all the *Nibiru* arch guardians' meek loyalty, which was both reassuring and disturbing.

Well, anyway, its time I pay a visit to earth to check developments over there. Our telescopic cameras don't give any real feel of events. It must now be over two years since we established base.'

Gabriel gently corrected him, 'yes, sire by Marduk time actually a little more than four years. However, by terrestrial time, it has been over twenty of their years since our arrival on Earth and fifteen since your last visit.'

'Is that so?' Jova briefly registered mild bewilderment before once again regaining dignity, 'If it has to do with the explorers, it must relate to the search for gold. Make arrangements to visit Ea and his vagabonds first.' the old king ordered and turned his back to face the emptiness.

Aigar was first to reach the sixty-foot deep trench, having kept up with the giant plodding strides of Atlas. Atlas had dug solo into the rock escarpment separating two hills, while other Titans worked elsewhere.

Son of a moonfather!' The guardian cried.

Ea soon joined him and followed his gaze, 'I didn't think such a rich vein could exist in nature.'

Lilith now caught up and was equally thrilled. 'It's as if Atlas knew exactly where it was.'

'If Shtar is to be believed,' Ea reflected, 'the Titans have such concord with nature that they are able to attune themselves to the vibrational frequency of any natural substance, even metals, it appears."

'What distinct instinct!' Aigar turned to marvel at the giant who stood impassively beside his find. 'Atlas, do you have eleven protons? 'Coz you're sodium fine!'

'Gold,' Atlas announced blandly in his sonorous moan—like a whale would talk.

...If a whale could talk! Aigar mused.

The mother lode of gold began as a rich vein at the surface and extended deep below. In ecstatic jubilation at its immensity, they sent word back to Hyperborea with a sample.

For Ea's explorers, it was to be a fateful discovery that would bind them to its yoke and cause a rift that might never heal.

CHAPTER SEVEN

The King's *Transporter* landed in the expansive valley beside the explorers' already burgeoning village. Having spotted the approaching craft, the entire troupe of new prospectors, now downed tools in excitement at the arrival of the sleek airliner – incongruous against such rudimentary settings. The former recalcitrant explorers greeted it with genuine cheer, expectant at reunion with their brethren after such long absence.

On Jova's last Earth visit - apparently fifteen of their years ago - Enlil was well on the way with his city, living standards reflecting elements of Marduk gentility. Jova was now taken aback by the dishevelled and scraggy miners that greeted him, sweeping him into their midst and eager to show him their find. The shaggy Titans and grotesque, dwarfish mutants only added to the squalidness.

Amazed at the extent of the find and potential of the site, the king regained his composure to address the rowdy bunch,

'Your perseverance has been impressive, far more than I expected.' He began with perhaps less admiration than his words conveyed, 'besides fuelling the equipment on the *Nibiru,* Enlil's team can now accelerate the building of that marvellous city of Eridu, already well advanced from its former base camp!'

'Yes, these past two decades have afforded us some great adventures on the way, but my troop will be glad to reunite with comrades,' Ea spoke on behalf of the group who cheered in agreement.

'I'm sure we can arrange for you all to visit Eridu from time to time. But meanwhile, we look forward to your retrieving the gold as fast as possible. I'll assign a *Transporter* at your disposal to ferry the material, and you lot can hitch a ride for short vacations there.' Jova's reply quashed the short-lived euphoria of the discoverers as they realised the implications.

'We can help build it too, and some of them can come here to help with our work,' a voice protested.

Jova tried to be conciliatory. 'That will not be expedient. Those urbanites will take a long time to adapt to the conditions here as you have. Moreover, they have developed the necessary skills required for *their* work. In any case, it won't be so bad. You have the Titans to carry out the brunt of the load.'

'But time, for our kind, is no longer an issue. So, let them learn like us, it will only serve to strengthen them,' Ea complained.

'Unlimited time is no excuse for inefficiency!' Jova barked.

At that, the rabble broke out into discussion and argument amongst themselves. Disinterested, Jova inspected Atlas and the other gathered Titans, who seemed to be in their element. He reflected on their fate.

Aboard the *Nibiru*, they had been confined to a very limited enclosure, mobility restricted by the station's thoroughfares unable to accommodate their height. Naturally, they were disallowed from reproducing.

However, upon landing, they were devastated to learn of their inability to procreate, unaware of the lies and contrivance created to prevent it.

Jova recalled the Titans exiting the *Transporter* taking their first steps on Earth, and wily Doctor Raphael' commentary while leading him aside from their group.

"Imagine if they were allowed to reproduce naturally on earth. It's a pristinely perfect environment for them, fast overtaking our numbers— indeed, with their stature and strength, they could easily overcome us," the Head Physician had whispered.

Jova had leaned back to observe the old guardian, remarking again at the resemblance to those 'hawks' as they were called, hovering over Eden in search of game.

"But that would take aeons and we are far superior.' Jova had countered, in distaste at Raphael's proposed direction.

'Well, they will have all the time in the world - also to evolve. And what real superiority do we have in this rustic environment except for a few measly weapons?'

Jova returned Raphael's hawkish stare with a look of understanding and gave the peremptory order, 'See to it then!'

Raphael had later described his stratagem,

"*The giants were incredibly hardy and fertile. Buried in* Nibiru's *bowels, they seemed unscathed by cosmic damage. But everyone's mandatory quarantine exams to test Earth's effect gave me opportunity to carry out secret vasectomies on the Titan males*" Jova recalled the arch guardian's neck twitching away in sly glee.

'*I then explained to the distraught head Titanide Gaia, how the cosmic rays affected all on board and in the Titans' case it was the males. But that they were actually lucky in not having to endure stillborn and mutant births like us. Of course, those gullible Titans accepted the story in good faith!*' Raphael had stood back folding arms smugly at his connivance.

Ea and his troupe exhausted every argument to no avail before finally Jova declared,

'There's nothing more to be discussed. Now I must leave and share your wonderful discovery with your brethren.'

And Ea realised in that high-handed dismissal, they were still misfits and renegades in the eyes of the king and cultured Hyperborean folk

Without looking at his companions, he lamented to Aigar and Lilith, 'In the fervent rush to establish a Marduk city, we are looked upon as mere miners – functionaries! I'm sorry that I may be the cause, but exiled here as we are with the Titans, this is to be our *Tartarus*.'

The name described the abysmal dungeons used to torment prisoners on Marduk in former times.

'Support bacteria, they're the only culture we have!' Aigar commented wryly.

Following his stopover in Gondwanaland, Jova flew directly to Eridu to describe the momentous discovery. And there he delighted in the increasing edifices of his son's glorious city.

'What wonderful adaptation of that exquisite local material! Those colourful gems, rocks and timber grains beautifully complement our Marduk polymers – especially on the Council Pyramid.'

'Yes, all it now requires is the gold for the capstone.' Enlil proudly informed his king.

As usual, the royal sage Uriel was on hand to fill in any references, 'yes, a pure gold capstone will serve to heterodyne the magnetic forces of the planets of this solar system with the Earth's electrical polarity and thus enhance all the electromagnetic equipment in the vicinity.'

'Enlightening I'm sure! In any case, the *Nibiru* can now return to full operation and seismic analysis of Ea's find indicates almost unlimited supply – the vein reaching for miles. So, I'm sure we can spare some for your capstone, Enlil.'

Uriel dropped a suggestion, 'Hyperborea is a weak word and was coined when we arrived because it resembled Marduk's northerly landforms. As many here have remarked, this island actually appears more like the Marduk holiday wonderland named after former female king, Atlanta. Completion of the capstone I suggest would be good time for an official name, perhaps 'Atlantis'?

Father and son looked to each other and nodded approvingly.

'An excellent suggestion. Consider it done! Now I would like to visit Eden, and on to the genetics lab where I believe our Nin has been achieving marvels.'

Nin joined Nazarel in leading the king and entourage on a tour of Eden,

Notwithstanding the accident that had claimed Nazarel's right eye, most of the plants he brought from Marduk were saved - providing chlorophyll, vitamins, and other trace elements unavailable in the dehydrated stocks aboard the *Nibiru*. Indeed, those dried stocks depleted early on their journey, but Nazarel's ecosystem, recycled the passengers' organic waste into fertiliser and along with hydroponics, produced abundant harvest - the excess dehydrated and stored for times of dearth. He also set aside some seed.

'I began by planting orchards and clearing the lowlands nearby to sow the cereal crops.' He described to the group, 'and naturally I carried aboard seeds of amaranth, which I grafted with similar local grasses, but the terrestrial hybrids contain no manna - just carbohydrates and lesser nutrients. Luckily, we have plenty of seed stock for synthesis.

Yes, our technicians have made it their first priority to establish a fermentation factory here in Eridu.' Enlil advised the king.

'I have carefully nurtured the single Marduk specimen as decoration in a special patch in the centre of Eden over there.' The one-eyed farmer pointed out to the visitors.

'And I see you also planted a sample of that accursed Mandala!' Jova scolded.

The botanist's single eye blinked rapidly but he remained mute. Mentioning to Nin he had tried a nibble once - apparently enough - he didn't wish to discuss it any further. Yet it was his prize possession.

'I believe it's called the 'Wisdom Tree' and it is actually quite attractive.' Nin commented.

Similar in height to the nearby alpine fir with outspread branches and small, soft, angel hair fern-like leaves, it resembled the tamarind, with clusters of bulbous fruit similar to that terrestrial lookalike.

As further distraction she probed Uriel while leading the group away from the scene, 'there's much in the chronicles about its fruit causing paranoia but what does "induces psychedelic experiences" exactly mean?'

Uriel began explaining, 'upon its first discovery on a remote island on Marduk, the fruit of the Mandala was hailed as a true wonder drug. Experimentation showed it contains a powerful hallucinogen that transports the mind to a higher level, opening dormant past-life and inter-life memories—awakening and stimulating dormant interactions of heart, mind, body, and soul - establishing a brief insight into absolute truth. Mystics even claimed it comprehends the fourth dimension, transcending time and inducing fleeting cosmic consciousness, connecting with the All.' The sage had grown increasingly lyrical before spotting the disapproving gaze of Jova, thus mellowing his tone,

'Though it stimulated only already-existing capacities, the danger of such artificial sensory enhancements is that it pushed hitherto untrained nerves and synapses, stretching and damaging them by almost instantly. And some memory with elements of its insights remained, leaving the user in a state of post-euphoric despair. The drug from the crunchy fruit follows the law of diminishing returns, dwindling ecstasy while increasing desolation and dependence.' Uriel now began to sound more like the chronicle voiceovers,

'Moreover, due to its mystical experiences, it undermined the Marduk march towards technological progress. For those reasons, it was once considered as a rite of passage and as a creative inducement for Marduk's youth. But as society progressed, it was shunned and now absolutely prohibited.'

'It sounds downright subversive!' Enlil declared, looking at the tree with contempt.

Nin read Nazarel's ongoing fear for his cherished plant, and chuckled inwardly at his quick diversion as they moved out of sight of the tree,

'...And in grafting the amaranth, we were able to develop a number of cereal crops—maize, barley, and oats from the wild local grasses as base food to supplement manna – over here.'

Enlil took the farmer's bait and went along, 'yes, well, chemically produced manna doesn't seem to have much taste – utterly bland compared to the Marduk amaranth. So, I'm glad we can at least mix the chemical with some organic catalyst and your cereals. It goes very well with the nectar those insects produce from the local flowers.'

'Honey bees! Exactly my Lord!' Nazarel gushed, visibly relieved to have distracted everyone.

Observing the renewed vitality in their lusty environment, Nin found herself confused, in unfamiliar territory, as she too began to feel the stirrings of her own hitherto dormant libido.

Her thoughts drifted to imagine life in Tartarus – Ea's pejorative name now adopted by all. From early childhood and especially after Jova abandoned wife and daughter, Nin's elder brother had filled some of that male role – at least as mentor and protector.

It's time for a serious discussion with mother! She decided.

Entering Shtar's sparse apartment in the large, as yet unwalled city, Nin sensed her mother' congealment and further withdrawal.

Inner essence manifesting outer personality, the hand of destiny shaping each one's life! She speculated, but her interest was now in emotional circumstances, not spiritual.

Mother and daughter were unaccustomed to pleasantries, 'Mother, why did you marry father?' She opened.

Shaken from her reveries and by the directness of the question, Shtar turned to gaze upon a mirror image of her own light grey eyes, 'Whatever brought on a question like that?' She asked.

Shtar was aware her daughter was a casualty of her indifference, but the fact was she only had the child as an expectation of her marriage. Had she waited a little longer, when the natal aberrations on the *Nibiru* began to manifest, she might have made an excuse. Some thought her withdrawal was a post-partum depression she would overcome. But in reality, it was an absence of any real maternal drive.

Nevertheless, she was sensitive to the victim that she had created. And realising Nin's veiled attempts at hiding her emotions—an act with which she was all too familiar, Shtar opened up, 'Nin, you have grown into a wonderfully talented Marduk adult, alas with no assistance on my part.'

She scanned her comely offspring as if for the first time.

Nin bordered on elegant—soft, rounded, clear-skinned face; body not quite curvy enough to be beautiful; hard and sharp grey eyes in an inquisitive brow. From a female viewpoint, she was beautiful. But her coolness suggested aloofness and ethereality – which Shtar fully recognised could inhibit a male's supportive instincts. While homosexuality was common on Marduk, it eliminated selection for the Nibiru. *In any case, she doubted it applied to her daughter.*

With Nin's expectant eyes trained on her, Shtar now intuitively understood her intent. Her response was characteristic, 'Males like your father, disguise their drive for sex in the cloak of love. We females on the other hand, cloak our need for companionship, security, and at least the semblance of love, by holding out the bait of sex.'

'Mother, such sterile bitterness... so . . . Marduk! And I'm not now interested in philosophy.'

'I'm not bitter. Truly I'm not. I was just explaining how nature maintains continuity. And I *am* Marduk. But I wonder at your implied criticism of that trait and whether it is shared by all of you born outside. Anyway, I really have no further interest in prolonging this life.' Shtar checked herself - a little late – realising she was imposing her own introverted state of affairs.

'But such nihil...' Nin did not finish the sentence, forgetting her own indecision and focusing on the increasing incidence of her mother's malaise. 'You're not planning to terminate?'

'No, I don't have enough despair for that. Besides, suicide, like murder, is sacrilege against cosmic evolution. I'll simply not have any further treatments. Meanwhile I also intend to move far from Eridu, pursuing a more ascetic life.'

More ascetic? Nin stared at her mother whose negativity and despair could only be pitied and reviled. She began to feel claustrophobic, perhaps scared that attitude would be contagious. In any case, any romantic inclinations were now utterly deflated.

Shtar spoke again, 'But you wanted to know about me and Jova.'

'It's ok, some other time. I left something unfinished at the lab. Excuse me.' She lied, wishing to escape the depression she felt looming.

Typically, Shtar had left her with more questions than answers. There was a desperate empty loneliness, a hole in her heart that had grown since almost from birth, covered up by activity and learning that diverted her—to forget that chasm. But now, it threatened to engulf her.

Was that it? Was that was missing? No! It's much more fundamental and encompassing than even that!

She willed herself to end the internal dialogue, leaving just the chasm, her thoughts drifting to far-off Gondwanaland with yearning.

CHAPTER EIGHT

'Oh, enough! I volunteered to go exploring, not slaving in these mines,' the young technician complained. His tunic, set to orange, was stripped to his waist as he hooked the bucket held by his companion above, and awaited his pulley to take the load up to the surface.

It was twelve terrestrial decades since the *Nibiru* had arrived, the two Marduk communities increasingly alienated with each passing year, even in some language. Despite Titans digging and the trolls tunnelling, the Tartarus Marduks were required for assaying, sorting and supervision.

'Well, this ain't no holiday, but at least we're free. You reckon you could handle living in Marduk hoity toity again?' Replied the foreman, similarly undressed with his outfit colour set to guardian blue.

The third was a youth operating the pulley, his green polymer suit only slightly worse for wear despite its age and the abuse it received in the mines. He added, 'I can't wait to get back to the surface for some chilled Crius toddy. I hear its effect is similar to Mandala. Have you ever tried it?' He asked the older foreman, a former guardian sergeant.

'No, and you musta' been born on the *Nibiru*! Or else you'd know that scoffing the Mandala could have you sent away to Tartarus…' The foreman scratched his head a little bewildered at that incongruity. '… Anywhose, that fruit has more kick and sends you into the twilight zone more'n that toddy or any other drug. Warps the mind and kills after a couple of times,' the senior admonished.

'Orange' technician complained again, 'Yeah, well so our town is well named! I've been to Eridu and its a picnic compared to these boondocks!'

The elder sergeant sympathised, ''cept for the social shackles. But you're right, it's already hot as hell here without bein' swallowed in these holes all day, and possibly f'rever – s'like a spell in that Tartarus back home!'

Orange grew fervent, 'Yeah, that's why I reckon we should just dump tools and invade Eridu like some of our buddies are standin' up for.'

'Hah! With what – spitballs?' The foreman-sergeant derided.

'What 'bout the Titans! And we're a lot tougher'n those sops. We could whack 'em easy!' The orange one's cries were met with only partial sneers from his companions.

'What's up? You seem very serious . . . For once. I hear the workers talking about a strike.' Lilith tried to get her husband to communicate. She was gently kneading the back of his spine.

'Err . . . Turn me round and you'll see what's "up". Yes, the miners are revolting – and they don't smell too good either! Hope it's all froth and no beer.'

'Can you blame them? Eridu is flourishing, with all forms of entertainment.' Her voice carried a hint of yearning.

Turning over to look at her, he replied, 'Don't wince but our prince also is since convinced. As for me I believe in looking reality in the eye - and denying it. But speaking of hardship . . .' He leered as he guided her eyes downward.

Forced to look down at his emerging bulge, she pretended to pout, yet delayed her gaze saying, 'Well, Ea has various motives to feel dissatisfied.'

'Yeah, no one to do this, heh, heh! He must feel like a one-legged guardian at an arse kicker's party. He's more priest than beast. No lover of power.'

'Hah! True but you think priests don't seek power? In any case, he, like everyone . . . except you perhaps . . . has ambitions. Though I sometimes sympathise with you, it's all so futile in the long run—like a wave on the sea whipped up by a wind or current, standing aloft for a moment and gaining the mistaken belief it is independent and separate somehow from the vast ocean that supports it.'

Aigar looked into her unusual amber eyes, 'you're so deep!' He held his smirk for her to catch on.

She pouted again, fobbing off the feeble pun, giving him the opportunity to continue,

'A wise man said...'

'What?'

'Nothing, he just listened.'

'But monarchy isn't enough for Ea, she continued, ignoring his distractions, he doesn't want the responsibility. As for the workers, how can you blame them – buried in the pits while our compatriots flourish in comparative luxury?'

'Yeah, well, I'm ridin' with the Titans. There's grace in this place. As for buried in pits, I'm dying to be buried in yours!'

Aigar's great disappointment was that he too seemed infertile, perhaps due to exposure on the *Nibiru*'s surface farm. His devastation worsened when it was discovered that Lilith was one of the rare unaffected females.

Overhearing Ea remark to the nurse Dawn, "If ever there was a pair that most deserved to populate this wondrous planet, I can't think of better candidates than Ea and Lilith," only deepened his remorse.

But Lilith hid her disappointment well, transferring her affections even more to her child-spirited husband. And he tried distracting her from that disappointment by physically embracing her at every opportunity, as he now caressed her once more.

Since the Tartarus find, Gabriel had positioned the *Nibiru* in orbiting stasis midway above the two communities. It thus appeared as a smaller moon in the night sky, causing considerable consternation amongst the hominids.

Mortally terrified of the aliens' destructive weapons, the barely self-conscious hominids had initially stayed well clear of the mines. But with time came familiarity and importantly to them, exotic food and colourful trinkets, which Ea used to bribe their approach. It allowed him and Galael opportunity to dissect and study the animals, assisted occasionally by young Dawn in Tartarus' makeshift but evolving clinic. Aigar often visited him in evolving friendship.

The store adjutant stormed into the clinic, and announced to the foursome. 'They've gone too far this time, Lord! Our communicator is missing!'

Ea was nonplussed, 'Now, what would those creatures want with that? They normally restrict their pilferage to food and a few useless baubles,' he was dismissive, more interested in the creature he was examining.

Perhaps they liked its multi-coloured casing,' Dawn suggested.

'Yes, but they're getting bolder since that *Red* started leading them,' the storekeeper complained, alluding to the hominid leader with the coppery fur. 'And that transmitter is our only communication with the outside and to guide incoming *Transporters*, my Lord!'

Aigar and Galael briefly shared glances upon hearing the storeman's use of the honorific title – twice, before Aigar responded,

'Well, our spoon-fed *Red* will have his head bled - or dead - for the trouble he's led.'

None flinched from Aigar's now familiar and often childish eccentricity, but observed him march off to gather a band of guardians as a posse.

'I'm coming along. I want to see what they're getting up to,' Ea announced as the band of armed but bare-chested miners set off to retrieve the stolen booty.

The hominid colony lay just over a mile from Tartarus.

'That tree branch thatching is quite impressive,' Ea commented on the shelter the hominids had positioned over their rudimentary dwellings. 'That largest hut must be Red's. Look at that bamboo rod protruding from his roof! So that's why they stole it!' He looked at Aigar in astonishment.

Beside him, preoccupied Aigar signalled two of the miners to close ranks as protection, apparently disturbed by the silence and lack of movement from the hominid cluster.

'Watch out!' Ea heard and felt the thud beside him at the same time he was tackled to the ground.

'More coming!' a second voice shouted again in his ear as he was pushed down and found Aigar sprawled on top of him while more projectiles landed near or flew past them. He was thankful that Aigar had lost his lyrical facility when it mattered, but was utterly dismayed by the stake that jutted from the chest of the miner who had first tackled him, a blue gurgle oozing from the orange clad young victim.

In a flash, Aigar lunged to his feet, running straight towards their rusty-furred leader, his Marduk light stick spurting nuggets of energy quanta into the ambushing hominid apes. The four remaining armed guardian miners soon joined in, executing the scattering creatures with ruthless efficiency. Ea's command to ceasefire was a little too late to save even the last of the colony.

Returning to Tartarus village, Ea and his lieutenant sat together on the porch of the guardian's rustic villa in the quiet and balmy summer's twilight, sharing pungent Crius toddy – a fermented sap from flowers of the palm. The Titan Crius had discovered how the morning sap, left for a few hours, fermented into potent, sweet liquor. The beverage thereafter carried his name and became a staple of the group's evening relaxation, preferred even to the limited wines from Eden.

The incessant screech of cicadas and the occasional whine of a mosquito were the only interruption to their solitude, both in silent reflection over the guardian miner's death and impending cremation.

Aigar berated himself for going ill prepared into the hominid village, 'Artificial intelligence is no match for natural stupidity! They should have been in protective suits and not just boots.'

'Yes, a guardian suit would have protected that poor fellow who saved me. But don't blame yourself, we had no inkling they had such organizational skills. It takes intelligence and foresight to coordinate an ambush like that,' Ea placated, somewhat distractedly, 'that *Red* was a mutant in more than his looks - less hairy and with a smoother complexion than the rest. I must make a detailed autopsy. But did you notice anything familiar about the bamboo rod and particularly its angle, mounted on his hut?'

'In-dee-di-did! I saw what I saw, but what did I see?' Aigar's quirk had returned.

'Our *Red* must have observed us communicating with the *Transporter*. Knowing it brought exotic food and trinkets, he stole it, probably believing he could summon that vehicle himself and control the gods of providence, which is what our ship would have meant to him. He went so far as to even copy the angle of our antenna with his bamboo rod!'

'More to the guy than met the eye!' Aigar quipped and tried to divert from their maudlin mood, '...this toddy is none too shoddy and is worthy for the body. But for that bungle in the jungle, a beer right here beats a wine and dine with the Eridu swine!'

'You're easy to please, my friend. But as you know, our mob doesn't share your love of al fresco or your equanimity. Eridu is truly a magnificent city, only enhancing the homesickness and resentment at being banished here.

'An attack can distract but will be as fruitful as a Titan poet—and Jova's power is supernova. But then poetry is no place for ideas!'

Lilith came out to join the pair, 'what's all this about attacks and power?' She asked, trying to insert into the conversation.

Ea acknowledged her with a nod but continued his thoughts, 'Yes, Jova has already created the paranoia and the apparatus of a despot, beyond even on Marduk – tracking any moves with the *Nibiru's* cameras. General Michael and his guardians will naturally support whoever has the throne. And there's no point appealing to Enlil, who expects all to eventually be bestowed on him.'

'Aye, in Enlil's eyes power corrupts, but absolute power is absolutely delightful! If I wanted to kill myself, I'd climb his ego and jump to his IQ!' Aigar was in full swing.

Ea went on as if talking to himself, 'civility and society are fragile constructs, and on this primitive planet, all the advances of our species can fall apart in less than a single generation. A leader or government must exhibit fairness, ensuring the benefit of all.'

Aigar continued his banter, 'to Enlil, such ideas are as useful as a gilded latrine to a hominid - though I wouldn't piss on *him* if he were on fire!'

And then, emulating Enlil's self-righteous pout and exaggerated blustery bark, he went on, "**industry and technology is the celestial pole, with control the goal and the soul an obscure hole!**" The would-be mimic added in a dreary monotone. 'How droll!'

Ea clearly wasn't in the mood for frivolity, and declared 'my mind is made up. Our petitions to Jova and the Council went ignored. We will go on strike and force the issue by attacking their gates.' He stared ahead as if unaware of the couple's presence.

Husband and wife exchanged glances of disbelief, wondering at their leader's sanity, before Lilith took over to try at some normality,

'Sir, we're all a little on edge after that skirmish in the jungle, and perhaps this toddy is a little strong,' she began and then continued with a nervous chuckle, 'I can't imagine our hillbillies attacking Eridu's guardian battalions – and the *Nibiru*'s weaponry.' She finished with an endearing smile to try and pacify him.

'As effective as spitting at a charging mastodon!' Aigar added, 'Or…' He was about to add another gag, but was stopped cold by the flash of his wife's switchblade squint.

She turned back to address their leader, 'You can't be serious!'

Ea finally turned to observe the nervous couple, 'Oh, I should have realized you would be unaware of Marduk's 'Protest Law',' he began as, in unison, the pair took double takes at the strange term,

'It was ingrained upon all of us Councillors. You see at the time of first king Kali, there were still many remnant skirmishes amongst the diverse Lords of the realm. And the Council realized that despite the inhibition ensured by the array of psychometric tests, it was still possible a king – or majority of Council – could turn megalomaniac or rogue, and with control of the media.

'So, that first Council introduced a law allowing any disenfranchised group to declare war on the state – which can only retaliate with equal force. In other words, the state can only use the lowest common denominator of weaponry available to both parties. Of course, the state would always have the weight of numbers, and anyway such a war was ridiculous and thus never occurred, but the intent was to give dissent a voice and allow an otherwise oblivious populace to learn of their grievances.

'Jova and his corrupt Council majority is doing just what those forefathers feared. I'm sure the Marduks in base camp are unaware of our complaints.'

Aigar reverted to habitual absurdity, 'and we thought you'd gone insanicidal - ga-ga on the Mandala - candidate for the laughing academy…'

Lilith cut him off to caution, '…but like us, most would not have heard of that arcane law, so what's to stop Enlil ignoring it and coming out in full force?'

'Enlil is a stickler for Marduk law – even if manipulating it wherever beneficial – likewise Arch guardian Michael. The royal sage will ensure they are both made aware of it!'

'Yeah, Uriel the morphadite will put them in a right philosopickle!'

'I'm leaving to demand a meeting of Council, but I have no delusions. Aigar, commandeer the next incoming ore *Transporter*. We'll need as large a demonstration as possible, so also prepare the Titans and our dwarf trolls!' Ea ordered with rare authority.

'Yo lionheart!' Aigar saluted.

Ea left the next day for Eridu in the supersonic *skoop* – assigned to Tartarus for emergency. The *Nibiru* had twelve such vehicles used as surface aircraft, along with the three larger *Transporter* discs that could comfortably shuttle 300 passengers. Two of those discs now mainly carried materials between Tartarus and Eridu, the other attached permanently to the *Nibiru* for Jova.

His first visit was to the office of Speaker of the Council at the magnificent new Pyramid. The marble-coated monolith with its golden capstone—obtained by the sweat of Tartarus—was situated in the centre of Eridu. The city's five major thoroughfares converged upon that midpoint.

The apparently hastily appointed Speaker was none other than Raphael the Hawk, whose excessive twitching at sighting the geneticist betrayed his nervousness, 'Ah, good day to you, Lord Ea! What brings you to Eridu after so long? Although members of your team visit from time to time, you have been conspicuous by your absence. How can I be of assistance?'

Suspecting the geneticist's intentions, the Head Doctor fidgeted with nervous energy, eyes darting about the room while shuffling documents and utensils to appear busy. He seemed to have joined with the other arch guardians in referring to both Jova's sons as 'Lord', apparently due to their relationship to the king. While wondering where that left Nin, Ea decided to ride on the title.

'Surely you received my petitions, which were ignored. So now as Lord of the Tartarus realm, I demand public debate on matters relating to the health and wellbeing of our Marduk community.'

'Why? Is there some illness amongst your brigands. . .I mean brigades? I'm sure if you express your concerns at my Healing Institute…'

'Humour is hardly your strong point! I demand a gathering as soon as possible to review our conditions, and if necessary, to review leadership.'

A Councillor's request to address the main body could not be refused, so without awaiting response, Ea marched out.

'Jova is absent aboard the *Nibiru,* so Enlil, as heir to the chiefdom and Lord of earth, presides as head.' Raphael called out to his retreating back.

Foregoing his *skoop,* Ea strolled the mile or so to where Nin had set up an extensive biochemical laboratory, attached to Raphael's huge medical facility.

The streets were laid out in a geometric pattern based on a pentangular division of the planetary sphere. Gabriel, using the *Nibiru's* navigational equipment, had reduced all measurements using the circumference of Earth as reference – reducing it proportionately to the mile, the rod, the cubit, and the inch - all inter-related. The Captain illustrated, for example, that a rod measured 198 inches, which described the circumference of a circle with sixty-three-inch diameter. Multiplying those sixty-three inches by 25,000,000, gave 24,858 miles, a precise measure of the Earth's circumference at the time.

Alienated from society and a stranger in the city, Ea was also struck by the extent that the Eridians had benefited from terrestrial nourishment, a fact that impressed but disturbed him in its portent for his own crew. But even more disturbing was the effect on the mutant offspring. Like the Tartarus dwarfs, they seemed to have fast adapted to their environment and career pursuits.

In Tartarus, the trolls had grown squat and compact, appearing even demonic as they emerged from the mines. Here, the mutants appeared elfin—waifish and ethereal, even beautiful, reflecting their refined surroundings. They were engaged as merchants, stall operators, labourers, and in other menial tasks suited to their aberration. However, where they missed out on proportion, they compensated with some form of special ability—agility, flexibility, clairvoyance, or other peculiar quality.

They were psychologically unstable and thus needed constant vigilance but whether curse or blessing, they were, almost without exception, sterile - evoking his pity. Despite all the advances in genetic research on Marduk, and even with *his* prodigious knowledge, none had any idea how to circumvent the almost inevitable deviation that nowadays eventuated from Marduk coupling. Nevertheless, Eridu had an air of the theatrical.

Nin was ecstatic to see him but was initially reticent, unsure of his feelings or even her own, and apprehensive about making innuendos towards this brother and lifelong friend. His proximity felt like a well-worn shoe, and she slipped so easily into his embrace. She wondered if he too felt the snugness of fit.

'It's so nice to see you again, little sister. It's been so long.'

'Oh, a mere hundred odd years since you were last here! Gondwanaland - sounds so romantic! Are there really so many more exotic animals there? But what's this I hear of mutiny amongst your group? Are you really planning to revolt?'

'They are preparing as we speak.'

'But why? Your life sounds so exciting! All those wild species and all that freedom in such exotic surroundings!'

'The novelty wears off but I can't begin to explain the relative disadvantage.'

'I don't believe you. We've all come far from the translucent creatures that exited the *Nibiru*. You look so well!' Nin continued in bubbling excitement and uncertain giddiness, her libido aroused by his now comparatively rugged and tanned features. And typically male, or at least typically Ea, he took her questions and comments at face value.

'Yet Eridu's development has transcended ours. Even the mutants here have evolved in a different manner.'

'But surely life is more romantic than *this* routine.'

She was aware that she too had bloomed, her figure a little fuller and more rounded since they last met, her mien less naive and innocent, and she wore cosmetics for the first time.

But he missed the bait. 'Come to the mines and I'll show you tedium.'

'Well, as our Nazarel often quotes, "The other man's grass is always greener". Incidentally, your accent seems to be changing. But why do you begrudge our success in Eridu?'

'I don't, and that's the point. My fellows are specialists - technicians and guardians now relegated to just diggers. They will continue regressing without higher pursuits and culture. Enlil understands, but he has no intent of redressing it.'

She decided it was best to change the subject. 'It's a pity we can't reproduce more automatons here.'

'We don't have the componentry or they could reproduce themselves. We're really back to the primitive, except for some trinket technology. And with retarded population growth, we'll never reach the economies of scale.'

'What about a biological and organic version?' she offered.

'Intriguing idea, and I've actually been playing with it for a while.'

'Really? So have I - mutating and domesticating the wild beasts to plough our fields and even for food. The hominids sound intriguing.'

'Yes, I've thought about them. But consciousness is a different affair altogether. Their genome is actually close to ours, but they seem to be missing a small cluster involved with speech, the abstract and a concept of time.'

'How much consciousness is needed to dig a mine or plough a field?'

He took on an absent look. 'We need more than that. And there's really no suitable native creature, but I have considered another possibility.'

'Go on?' Nin searched his eyes, but his gaze remained distant.

'What possibility?' she asked again. But he had turned his back to her, lost in thought and unwilling to answer.

He gazed out from her balcony at the sparks of light emanating ever more rapidly as darkness fell upon the city and the inhabitants prepared for evening revelry. Nin left him to brood and prepared her apartment for the night. As she did so, she speculated on his vehemence.

He's so oblivious to me. He cares more for cause than for people - whether saving Marduks from radiation, the make-up of Council or his band in Gondwanaland. Strange, but he appears more righteous than even Enlil. Whereas Enlil preaches and professes rectitude, that's just his politics. Ea embodies it - a spiritual vagabond, shunning discipline for anarchic freedom.

All he needs is to marry me. As half-sister, our line would automatically have the throne. But he's an idealist. I wish he'd understand that it's not about having what you want, but wanting what you have . . .

Her thoughts were rambling, and she fought hard to control the urge to throw herself into his arms in mutual solace. Instead, she called out a suggestion.

'How about I show you around the nightlife here?'

As they strolled out together, discussing more mundane matters, the contentment and comfort in his presence returned. But he could be unpredictable.

He may not admit it, but inside is a real resentment at being shunted away to virtual irrelevance while Enlil reaps the accolades.

She opened a subject of mutual interest, 'tell me more about the hominids. I wonder if there are any here in Atlantis.' She sought the comfort of his voice as they strolled down the main thoroughfare of Eridu.

I must get away to think clearly about what to do.

Ea was responding, 'So it's now officially Atlantis. But yes, they seem to be developing the rudiments of self- consciousness, perhaps that's how we evolved in Marduk's antiquity. . .'

Nin had taken his arm while the couple chatted, which was as far as they went.

In that state of emotional confusion, Nin sought out her habitual retreat, a little annoyed that she had to suffer two chaperone guardians ordered as protectors in those unprotected mountains.

Keeping a distance, the soldiers occupied themselves discussing her merits.

Aware but unconcerned at their blather, Nin perched precipitously on a cliff-edge overlooking the canyons and gorges that lay to the north of the burgeoning city.

That precarious sense of danger piqued her alertness, helping to distract from her preoccupation and take in the surroundings.

Glacial foam flowed from mountain peak into deep green alpine forest, giving way below to the verdant pastures of Eden; in turn, melting into the brown and yellow river banks and together seeping into the indigo lake at the bottom of the gorge. The onset of autumn added ruddy speckles on to the watercolour. The setting served as salve to her spirits as she speculated on her new terrestrial life, her brothers' petty animosity and her emotional state.

Hours later the sun had already passed the mountaintop to the west, casting shadows over the valley below.

Her bodyguards had woken from an afternoon nap and became restless to return to Eridu. Alike Nin, they were sheltered from the encroaching cold by protective 'skins' of artificial fibre. Their uniform colouring was fixed into earthen tones for camouflage while Nin had chosen pine forest green.

Each *Nibiru* passenger was issued one such outfit, cleaned by passing through an ionic separator that removed any foreign material. The suits were infused with light-emitting diodes and contained a switch that controlled semi-conductors incorporated into the fabric—allowing the wearer to change colour at whim. Lately, for variety, the citizens of Eridu had begun to adopt or at least add items of clothing from locally spun fibre.

The guards had shed the weight of their side arms for their nap and were slow in coming alert, engaging again in their idle chatter,

'She's more handsome than pretty, not my type really. Royalty aside, I have had better-looking females.' The handsome cadet commented to his comrade.

The feral canines approached with uncanny stealth. Seven of the pack crept silently around the guardians while the giant alpha male padded his way along the boulders towards unprotected Nin.

"Hah! I doubt she would be interested in *your* advances! She seems to have inherited Shtar's grey eyes along with her frigidity. Those icy jewels can freeze you in their glare as much as melt you in their gaze." The older corporal mused.

'Is that what they mean as poetry?' The other asked. 'Anyway, Queen Irania is much better looking and open to any advance - even to visitors from Tartarus.'

Their chatter had broken Nin from her meditations, and she stretched her limbs preparing for her return trek down the cliff face. The earlier caressing breeze now slapped at her face with an icy sting.

She sensed before she saw the creature, which crept at her with teeth already bared. Turning to face the animal, she noticed her guards in the distance were kept separated from their arms by a group of similar creatures with their characteristic snarls.

The lone rabid canine approaching her emitted a growl, ready to pounce. It was twice her size. Behind Nin, who now faced her attacker, was a sheer drop, with only a small ridge of snow jutting from the cliff face some few feet below her. To jump would be too dangerous as she doubted the solidity of the snow ridge below, but anyway pointless as the creature would likewise follow.

She had never faced danger, and though the beast's intentions were clear, she lacked imagination at what those jaws could actually do to her. But her life was about to end, and she resigned to impending death with a mixture of trepidation as well as gratitude for an experience that had witnessed such beauty, savage as it was.

The giant wolf took a single step before lunging at her with its snout agape and jaws set to tear, and during the time dilation that took place while those fangs approached, her amplified senses took in all the features of the animal - brown-stained teeth and yellow sinister eyes with black corneal slits riveted her final attention.

Front paws thumped onto chest, throwing her back over the cliff edge as the snout came at her face with vitriolic breath from its final assaulting snarl. Distant light bursts from guardian weapons pulsated in the air accompanied by yelps was the last sound, glad her protectors had managed to save themselves - but too late for her.

She landed on her back onto the jutting ridge below, with the creature's weight fully on her, the impact of the fall cushioned by a mattress of recent snow. Somehow it held their combined weight, but that was of no comfort, her eyes shut instinctively, expecting the fatal chomp aimed at her bare neck.

Silence.

Time dilation? Afterlife? Reincarnation? Nightmare?

A hot flow trickled over her midriff, which was curious.

Eyes opened warily, still expecting the worst. A carpet of fur slumped over her. Casting her sight over the bristles, a great lance jutted out from a neck. The steaming ooze she felt pouring over her—its lifeblood—had already begun to ebb.

She moved her eyes up the cliff face over which she had fallen, in search of a clue. And as she cast them to her right, on a smaller plateau than the one from which she had fallen, another being, a very different biped gazed at her with an expression she groped to absorb—affinity? simpatico? kinship? *Phileo*! She didn't understand it. She just *felt* it. Nin returned his stare in similitude and gratitude.

The creature's eyes slowly closed and reopened. Offering a gentle, benign nod, he disappeared into the shadows.

So that is a hominid!

The recent terror and its resultant adrenaline distilled that unuttered mutual sentiment into quintessence - indelibly staining her psyche, presaging her future.

PART TWO

Earth —c. 28,000 A.D. (Ante Diluvium) – 36,000 B.C.E.

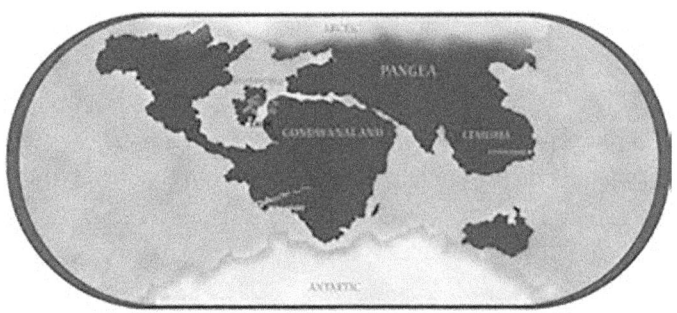

There were giants in the earth in those days; and also after that, when the sons of God came in unto the daughters of men, and they bare children to them, the same became mighty men which were of old, men of renown

—*Genesis 6:4-5 (KJV)*

If the world is a "Great Something" possessing self-consciousness, then we are the rays of that consciousness, conscious of ourselves but unconscious of the whole

—*P.D. Ouspensky*

CHAPTER NINE

Life—it teemed without, burgeoned within.

'Nin, I'm so glad you were unharmed!' Uriel was uncommonly animated. 'I felt as if my own Shalimar had been attacked!' Recovering from her ordeal quickly, Nin dropped in at the royal sage's quarters, intending to rendezvous with brother Ea there later. The squat, white marble dome of the Astronomical Institute was perched atop the basalt mesa on the southern Dilmun foothills. Gleaming from the reflection of the setting sun, it appeared above the city like a giant snowball broken off the ice cream mountain and splattered over the inky table-top plateau - a spectacular contrast visible from the entire Eden plain.

In the distance to the east, the River Gihon reflected that sinking sun, like a silver serpent slithering silently, seeking the southern sea.

'Thank you! It was frightening, but I'm fine. And the outcome was enlightening, so not all bad.'

She dismissed Uriel's inquisitive glance, not ready to discuss her edification, and moved to social platitudes, 'How is Shalimar? She is so rarely seen.'

'Oh, she's nearing adulthood, still studious and withdrawn.'

Nin's sympathetic nod caused him to qualify, 'but *her* interest is more into the mystical side than the scientific. Are you sure *you're* all right? Can I help in any way?'

'No, I'm unscathed, and my visit is simply social. I thought your vast experience might shed light on some gnawing questions, uncle.' She nowadays looked upon the kindly old sage as a surrogate relative, and was sure he liked the all-encompassing term of endearment.

'Delighted my dear Nineveh. I'm always challenged by your insightful curiosity, and I enjoy brief diversion from constant observations and calculations.' He responded in kind using her extended name.

'I'm trying to understand more details of our departure and Jova's god-like status. Everyone seems to have a variation of the story.' She prompted, watching him potter around with his astrological charts. 'What's your version?'

'You mean the truth?' Uriel arched his brows, smirking.

'Hah! Yes, well, whatever.'

'Jova calculated the asteroid would strike in just over 28 Marduk days, or now more familiar, 144 earth days. That it approached exactly hidden behind our *Nibiru* led many to believe it was destined. It was also far too large to destroy or divert by our tiny nuclear arsenal, rendered obsolete and taboo by a globalised community that required no such weapons of mass destruction.' His limpid blue eyes took on a faraway mien as he reminisced,

'To avoid panic and despair, the Council notified the elect refugees surreptitiously - only the day before departure.

'Jova also remarkably chose this particular solar system from all the alternative stars with equally persuasive arguments. He somehow worked out that *this* comparatively insignificant sun had a number of planets, increasing the probability of sustaining cellular life.

'I guess such born leaders are able to slice through an avalanche of data and deduce the essential, intuitively making the right decisions. And extreme uncertainty calls for that decisive divine-like dictatorship.'

Nin probed further. 'Okay, so he was a brilliant astronomer and we owe him eternal gratitude and all that, and of course he's our elected king. But I don't get that divine reverence.'

'Ahh, yes! But that's of his own making. You see your father is an archetypal King just like Irania – compelled to fulfil that decree. A rare and fortuitous leader for our dire times - divinely dispatched, as some argue.'

'Hmm, sounds like you too assign him sanctity. I'd like to come back to that, but *"archetypal* king"? And Irania too? I remember you once told me I'm a Scholar without explaining.'

'Yes, and there's the Priest, and the Soldier. It's an arcane Marduk belief – superstition nowadays - that self-awareness falls within the sphere of those four archetypal extremes - either predestined before birth, if you follow such idea, or determined by the stars if that is your bent . . .'

'The stars?'

'Planets actually, I realise I am mixing mysticism with the sciences, but that is where our philosophers, mystics, scientists, and astronomers were beginning to merge. The belief is that inherent character – mind you not outer personality – is modulated by rarefied chemicals in all cells but especially in the rarefied glands. These chemicals or hormones trigger the brain to respond to stimuli resulting in our impressions, beliefs, illusions and emotions. The theory of celestial influence holds that the varying orbital periods of planets emit vibrations, causing electromagnetic fields that intermingle through time – but become fixed on an infant's glands upon taking the first breath, directing its inherent character.

'That sounds rather far-fetched. Given we all have such hormones, wouldn't we all be affected similarly?'

'In general, we are. The moon particularly influences every cell similarly - such as female menstruation, which, notice, have re-aligned to this planet's satellite. But individuals inherit greater or lesser degrees of that energy or essence depending on planetary positions at the moment of first breath, together with the genetic physical make-up of those glands. It's the nature that interprets our nurture - the attitude that regulates our aptitude.'

'Clever and poetic, but still a little vague.'

'Marduk had only four other planets, plus a moon—affecting our bodies and psyches in a thus more limited manner. This moon and at least seven other significant planets, not to mention Earth's different environment, may explain some of the aberrations beginning to manifest in our personalities. Witness how the mutants with their exaggerated hormones are affected even by geography - dwarfish trolls in Tartarus look and behave very differently to the more elfish trolls here.'

'Really? So, where do the four stereotypes fit?'

'This solar system circles a greater constellation, possibly a smaller black hole than the one in our galactic centre. I am developing that course into a star map or zodiac, but more on that later. Briefly, the character types display themselves in the four universal principles – fire, water, earth and air. Let's ignore the quintessential fifth for now.

'Go on.' Nin was dubious but intrigued.

'Briefly, a fiery King is born to *rule* or lead—what animates a King is ingrained desire for leadership, admiration, and the loyalty of his or her subjects. Any action relies on fulfilling that need.

'The earthy Soldier is motivated by *duty*. The soldier is by no means subservient, for none of the types are greater or lesser than the other—except perhaps in the mind of its possessor!' Uriel smiled.

'So, to continue, the Soldier seeks a *cause*. And that cause must be righteous or some sort of altruistic duty, such as protection of race, community, heritage—or even a king. General Michael is prime example, who will hold *any* king to accountable to those values . . .'

'So, I'm supposed to be a scholar. I do like learning, but I'm hardly academic!' Nin interrupted.

'Individual essence has nothing to do with career, profession, or even interests. It simply describes underlying nature or motivation. The watery Scholar seeks *truth*, pure and simple, stripping all arguments down to facts and reality. Absolute truth—now there's an impossible dream!' Uriel winked and continued,

'Scholars hold all knowledge to be verifiable and real—stripping away the emotional, the rhetorical, and all the other disguises of motivation – like your questioning of Jova's 'divinity'. You seek the justification and rationale for his elevation without all the gimmickry. Does that strike a chord?'

'I must admit it does resonate.' She smirked at her own pun. 'And what would Ea be? A priest perhaps?'

'Indeed! Both Enlil and Ea manifest kingly traits. But Ea is more airy or ethereal Priest - his aspiration for leadership only secondary. That type, often the most prideful, seeks *influence* over minds, hearts, and souls. The Priest doesn't need nor really wish to lead the action, only beliefs and values.

'The four forces interplay within everyone and hence pure archetypes are very rare. Each individual interprets events from the myriad subtle combinations - creating diversity in society, but also social friction.

'A fifth – Magus, is a quintessence of the four, like the plasma within a sun. But Magi are even rarer.'

'It sounds so deterministic,' Nin protested.

'They are only underlying predilections…but aren't you expecting your brother?'

'Yes, he seems to be delayed.' Nin paused, a little puzzled by the extent of that delay, but continued. 'Can individuals change their basic nature?'

'Personality - the facade or mask we intentionally show to others according to our needs - is easy to change. We do it all the time, even just to fit in with society.' Uriel chuckled briefly for no apparent reason, 'However, change of character or essence means rewriting the cosmological blueprint – via spiritual alchemy or revelation, the mastery of a magus – is even rarer. That may be the purpose of death, if reincarnation is to be believed. But can anyone modify essence, tempering it with experience and thus evolve? Absolutely! That is the purpose of life!

'That will explain why many like your mother, question immortality. Although age alters outward personality, we endlessly repeat the same patterns and mistakes imposed by our essential being. Mystics say our souls carry a nascent god or spirit, accumulating the various experiences of its incarnations and retaining all those memories—evolving therefrom in each lifetime,' Uriel concluded.

'Fascinating! But I'm not convinced.'

'Spoken like a Scholar! However, evening is enclosing, and I must catch the first stars. Unlike on the *Nibiru*, here I'm at the mercy of the horizon.' Uriel seemed to grow impatient.

'Oh, I'm sure. We'll continue again soon, I hope.'

Nin bade farewell to emptiness as the sage had already turned away to immerse himself in his observations, oblivious of her salutations.

As she turned her attention to her brother's absence, anxiety took over.

The *Transporter* hijacked by Aigar, and carrying the 300 Tartarus 'invaders', landed on the opposite side of the bridge over Eridu's Gihon River, clearly visible from the busiest section of the city. Ea had earlier transmitted their scope of weaponry to Council, setting the limits of armament and terms of war.

Aigar deployed his troops to fan out from the craft and install the missile apparatus. The dwarfs set up catapults, aided by two Titans who loaded them with boulders. Two other Titans arranged a battery of spears – metal tips bound on to coconut tree trunks, which their massive arms could hurl well into the city. Two more Titans loaded slingshots with coconuts. Stripped of their firearms – eliminated from Ea's list – the guardian lieutenant's troopers were reduced to helping the Titanides prepare ammunition and refreshments beside the craft. Leaving his 'army' under a sergeant, Aigar returned to the ship to communicate via radionics with Ea.

Following the rules of engagement, Michael had arranged a hundred of his troops on Eridu's side of the bridge, with hastily assembled weaponry as a token of resistance. He carried the bow and quiver of arrows - crafted by keen archer Nazarel - which the general had borrowed for the occasion.

Curious city dwellers thronged behind the guardians in amusement at the quaint spectacle, to which Michael was forced by law to play along.

'Sir, the coconut army is prepared for a fruitful battle!' Aigar joked by walkie-talkie with Ea, who was stationed at a Council appointed villa within walking distance to the scene at the Eridu viaduct.

'Yes, well as long as the citizens see our comparative backwardness and inequality.'

'Or beg for our exotic coconuts. Death by force-feeding! Their just desserts!' Aigar was on a roll.

'We'll talk again soon. I'm about to meet my sister, Nin and get her on side...'

'. . . Oh no!' Aigar exclaimed, dropping the transceiver, leaving it connected.

Before dashing off to investigate, Ea overheard Aigar's commands as he exited the craft and shouted at his troops.

'Hold fire! Hold YOUR fire!' the lieutenant screamed.

From the crystal-domed *Transporter* cockpit, Aigar had observed the catapults being launched. Dashing out, he summed up the situation immediately. The dwarfs were hopping about, jeering and about to release a second catapult boulder while goading and berating the other Titans to hurl their spears and fire the slingshots.

Taking that as orders, the Titans let off those catapults and one hurled a spear deep into the crowd, before observing Aigar's frantic signals to cease. The dwarfs, in disarray but with their bloodlust piqued, were admonishing the Titans to continue while Aigar ran screaming at them to hold fire. He finally smashed his fist into the dwarf leader's face, sending the troll hurtling back some feet, which shocked the rest into obedience.

'I would love to insult you, but that would be beyond your intelligence!' He barked at their leader sprawled on the ground.

Across the bridge, Michael was dumbfounded to see the first projectiles hurtling across the river. And as one struck a crowd of guardians and onlookers, his instinctive command was to fire back. But with only his bow, and hearing Aigar's ceasefire, it was pointless.

Ea had reached the scene within the minute but the skirmish was already ended, leaving a guardian and three city trolls crushed by the boulder, an Eridu citizen killed by a spear and another two guardians wounded by coconuts.

Spotting the Tartarus Lord now tending to an injured soldier, the general marched over directly and fixed him in a riveting stare. On Enlil's emphatic jowl that piercing glare would have carried weight. But on Michael's flawless, polished cheeks, the scowl appeared incongruous.

However, his quiet, even, whispering, modulated voice left little doubt as to his authority,

'My instinct and my reputation demand justice and vengeance, which screams within me now...' The habitual monotone became unnerving in its potency, causing unflappable Ea to take a step back.

'However, discretion has taken control and prevents me from exacerbating this absurd rebellion that has already claimed too many of our kind. You will remove the *Transporter* and your troops immediately out of the range of your weapons! In deference to the king, I will leave your punishment to His Majesty!'

It was likely the longest and most impassioned speech the Guardian General had ever given.

CHAPTER TEN

The *Nibiru* held its trajectory at the required speed to maintain stasis 1,000 miles above, appearing more than half the size of the planet's natural moon. Neither waxing nor waning, it appeared as a divine sentinel—like an omnipresent, glowing eye - eliciting reassurance, shame, or remorse dependent on the observer's personal conduct and superstition.

Enlil, with Michael as witness, was quick to make an unprecedented trip back to the ship. Uriel accompanied them to ensure a balanced account.

Barging into Jova's royal quarters Enlil opened his salvo, 'Ea has committed treason and invaded our city. Seven of our citizens are dead or wounded from that mutiny against *your* edicts! He even denounces you as a tyrant demanding change of leadership!'

Jova looked stupefied, clearly in the dark about earthly affairs, and took time to regain composure, 'I wondered why the cameras displayed vacant Tartarus and its mines… But what is their complaint? I thought all was going so well on Earth?'

'Oh, some rubbish about equal rights, social order, and all his usual philosophical twaddle,' Enlil accused.

'What say you, Uriel?'

The sage had been shocked at Jova's deterioration – physically and mentally. Uriel was thus slow to respond and digressed, 'I had forgotten about that background hum.'

But he quickly summed up Enlil's neglect at keeping the king updated and now gave a fuller report,

'A king serves for life, so there is no such thing as a change of leadership.' Uriel clarified to Enlil before proceeding, 'there is no excuse for what happened to the unfortunate victims, sire. But the Tartarus trolls have regressed to unpredictable violence since being isolated in such severe conditions.

'Ea's ultimatum stemmed from deafness to his many petitions. Sire, as you *surely* know, the conditions on Eridu have progressed immensely, no doubt due to the talents and leadership of my good Lord Enlil, here. But the situation with the miners in Tartarus has not changed from their initial assignment over the twelve decades since we landed.'

Jova took a double take at Enlil's 'lordly' title, and cast a doubting eye upon his presumed heir. Regaining his ingrained authority, he addressed his son directly- articulating Uriel's very own thoughts,

'Remember this, a king's one objective is, to rule. While holding power and crushing *all* challenge, it is crucial that he is at least *seen* to be fair. Failure to display that mandate will lead to the downfall of his throne! And if the circumstances were reversed, would you, *Lord* Enlil, carry out your commands indefinitely, stuck out there in some far-flung outpost?'

'Of course! If my king so commanded.' Enlil's reply was instantaneous.

'I actually believe you would! Yet consider whether you would then maintain the loyalty of *your* followers also isolated, who may not share your zeal.'

'But, Your Majesty, as you so eruditely put it, the purpose of a king is to follow his destiny and rule. It is not therefore relevant whether the citizens agree with his direction. By mandate, a king is always right and must be followed.'

'True and well put, but I wonder how long he could hold on to power when none are willing to follow?'

'Well, as long as he satisfies the majority, and has the military might, that shouldn't be a problem. In this case, the citizens of Eridu are a majority, and they are following *your* edict.'

The arrival of the ship's captain cut short the discussion.

'Good timing Captain Gabriel, I have an assignment for you. Please deliver the following message to Ea and his renegades—"return to Tartarus and resume work immediately. Your gang is prohibited from entering Eridu even for recreation until further notice".'

Enlil, dissatisfied with the insipid command, brought out his bluster,

'*What*? That's hardly a response to insurrection and murder! And Michael has already prohibited them from entering the city. I will not tolerate his challenge to your authority! He must be punished as a lesson for all!'

Jova looked at him suspiciously and became annoyed, 'perhaps you mean *your* authority. But what do you expect? His execution?' He pounded a feeble fist on the arm of his chair.

It was a rare public expression of frustration from the king, who quickly resumed self-control, 'Anyway, it's time I attended Council once more. So now Captain Gabriel, in addition you will mediate with the renegades - remaining on Earth as sheriff and ombudsman. Assure Ea that I will address his complaints, but they must return to work. Meanwhile Uriel, I wish a more detailed update on earthly affairs, and we will follow afterwards in *my Transporter*. But for now, I wish to confer with my wife.'

Irania too had hitherto never returned to the *Nibiru* since first landing but had tagged along this time to advance Enlil's cause. In the privacy of their stateroom, after failing to arouse him, she lay on her side watching her husband prepare for bed. There were enough playmates on Earth for any disappointment on her part. Instead she scrutinised her husband, noticing the exaggeration of his stoop, his increasing translucence and the droop in his virility.

It was time to make excuses,

'I'm sorry to have neglected you, my darling. I have been so distracted helping our Enlil develop magnificent Eridu. You would be so proud at how well he emulates you, executing your delegation of terrestrial command to him and fulfilling your dream of a second Marduk. But now that fractious rebel Ea dares to confront your very authority.'

'You mean the son of my first, and technically legitimate wife, my dear. And whose team does not have the privilege to enjoy that progress,' he reminded her.

'I was just thinking that if you are to maintain your authority you must not let this heresy go unpunished.'

'I'm fully aware of the implications of my wayward son's actions, dear sister, and I intend to make a lesson of him. However, I note your outrage does not extend to his band of renegades, who I have observed are frequent visitors to your house.'

How much does he know? So, he has trained his cameras on my villa. Well I have hardly been circumspect. Our extended lifespans make fidelity so absurd. And those miners are so rugged! She giggled inwardly.

But he would not appreciate those young studs thrust in his sagging face. Trying to deflect his jibe, she changed the subject,

'But what will you do at this insurrection?'

'I'll handle it. We shall have a Council meeting, and I'll decide from there.'

'That would endorse the legitimacy of their rebellion! Let Enlil earn his authority? I'm sure he can handle the situation. And you know you don't feel comfortable on Earth. Gabriel can represent you and report back.'

'Dear, sometimes you are so astute but other times you test my credulity! It's time I observe the situation directly. Anyway, Nin and Nazarel have made great advances in animal husbandry and agriculture. It will be good to catch up with some family.'

Gabriel was fascinated by Eridu's advances and organised chaos, framed in a riot of colour, sound and odours.

Standing with Enlil atop the Astronomical Observatory, the pentangular street layout was clear. The city's recently completed buildings displayed massive glass panels fabricated from coastal silicon-rich sands with biodegradable coloured polymers recycled from Eden's fibre crops - and dyes from various wild berries and fruits.

The narrow cobblestone streets sported rudimentary wooden carriages on wheels constructed from those agricultural polymers. A few were battery powered but most were beast led. Nevertheless, Eridu had an air of modernity.

'You have achieved far more than I imagined with such limited materials and technology - alike the quaint hamlets of my Marduk childhood!'

'Thank you! But without constant supply of gold to generate energy, we would literally be in the dark.'

'Yes, I see Tartarus's mines are crucial—indeed also for the *Nibiru*. I will hurry to pass Jova's instructions and I hope for all concerned, the matter can be resolved soon.'

The rebels were held at bay on the outskirts of the city in inflatable camp membranes, where Gabriel met with their leader.

Ea sat alone ruminating in the largest of those hardy tents of Marduk polymers - part of the survival kits provisioned in the *Transporters.* Once triggered, the lightweight and compact package would expand to rustic but comfortable living quarters.

Gabriel's arrival was discouraging. A staunch advocate of military command, the captain's assignment to this task meant that Jova had already been misinformed by Enlil. He thus wasn't confident of the king's impartiality – nor indeed that of most Councillors, whose loyalties were clearly aligned to the heir apparent.

'Please come in, Captain,' he invited,

'King Jova has graciously acceded to your request for Council meeting, but only on condition that your troops return to Tartarus and recommence mining.'

'I'm sorry, Captain. I doubt if my team would follow such commands, even from me. I'm only acting on their behalf.'

'You are their commander and leader!' Gabriel paused, nonplussed at the refusal, 'And it is decreed by the King!'

'Command has no meaning in savage Tartarus, and Marduk's regulations serve no purpose here. They follow their own discipline and will adhere to duty only as long as it is equitable.'

'You all could be excommunicated!'

'Hah! They are already almost independent of Atlantis. After all, what does Eridu provide? We fend for ourselves, and Marduk technology is employed only to scavenge the minerals that ensure our own slavery. No, they will remain here at least until we are heard. And as there is only one item on the agenda of importance to all Marduks, I request the meeting be in the form of a public forum.'

On his arrival, Jova was assigned to Irania's villa in the palatial complex Enlil had constructed for himself—almost as a temple in the centre of the city. The king's lodging with the heir apparent and in only secondary quarters enhanced the son's status in the eyes of the citizenry.

Jova grudgingly admired that astute political manoeuvring and chose not to protest, *A masterstroke inherited from me! And I doubt he consulted Irania, who I'm sure would have tried to dissuade him from cramping her social activities.*

His first call was to Eden and his daughter. With only a nod as greeting, his first words to her were also less than endearing, 'you have done well in feeding our people.'

Nin offered a wry smile of acknowledgement.

But her face brightened as Nazarel now began displaying his advances in the fields

'This barley was once sparse and inedible buds – likewise the wheat and oats.' The stocky farmer explained, at ease in his preferred surroundings.

Despite his aging stoop, Jova stood nearly a foot taller than Nazarel's six and a half feet - similar to Nin's height.

The one-eyed agronomist then took the king to his rudimentary winery. Thereafter, the troop proceeded to the pastures where Nin introduced Jova to cow's milk, at which he initially baulked, unfamiliar with its flavour, but soon savoured.

'And tonight, you will try roasted lamb, which I'm sure you will agree is a treat.'

Jova looked at her doubtfully. The Marduks were essentially omnivorous, but animal meat had become both scarce and even unpalatable, especially the laboratory variety that had all the nutrients and taste but seemed to lack something vital. Food aboard the *Nibiru* was naturally vegan.

Returning to the city, he paid a visit to her quarters. Over wine and the promised roast lamb dinner, she tried to lecture him,

'Ea has a very strong point, and I urge you not to be blinded by the narrow zealotry of his enemies,' Nin began before he cut her off.

'No doubt you are alluding to your younger brother and future king, who has remained faithful throughout. If Ea had been as loyal, this state of affairs would not exist.'

The meal continued in silence and occasional triviality before Jova, upon preparing to leave, added,

'I will give him my ear and make my decision correspondingly. Thank you my dear, for the tour and indeed the delectable meat.'

Jova, wishing anyway to show his face to the community, had acceded to Ea's request for open forum. Two hundred or so interested citizens – mainly relatives of the miners with some inkling of their concerns - now filed through the grand double redwood doorway, into the great hall of the Pyramid for the first full gathering of the Earth Council.

Shtar had deferred her societal withdrawal after Nin persuaded her to attend for one last time what she called 'that boys' club' - Jova's three wives just token female allies in the Council of twelve plus king. Ea was glad to have another potential supporter in that reclusive former queen.

Inside, aromas of frankincense wafted - tapped from a fragrant shrub found in the arid western part of the continent - allegedly to calm the nerves. The white flowers of myrrh, a likewise fragrant shrub, were clustered in pots and vases along the hallways and on the central tabernacle. Within that shrine resided the sacred Skull of the Oath and on it stood the granite boulder sheathing the Sword of Destiny – the sacred and esoteric symbols of the king's mandate, along with the more openly exhibited Royal Sceptre.

Enlil took centre stage. Projecting his bellow in the reverberating hall, he brought all to attention, pointing at Ea and launching into his tirade,

'This rabble-rouser, disguising an attempt to overthrow the throne with blackmail and mutiny, attacked us - causing death and injury of our citizens. I demand that he be banished from Atlantis and confined to producing our gold – in perpetuity!' His address was well rehearsed, and Ea looked to Irania as the possible inspiration.

Jova stepped up to take over, figuratively pushing his son aside to address the gathering,

'Ea, this community's existence is dependent on the precious product of your *volunteers*, who *elected* to join you into that wilderness.' He stopped to ensure everyone understood that free will, 'and indeed, both your mutiny and the killing of innocents, even if accidental, are unforgivable. Nevertheless, we will hear your case as you have indicated you may also have an acceptable solution to this overhanging dilemma.'

Although stamping his authority in pushing Enlil aside, Jova's tone lacked former dynamism and his attitude was oddly conciliatory.

Ea stood, pausing to take in the unfamiliar chamber and to seek out any friendly faces. Enlil had grown more ambitious, left alone to taste the aroma of unmitigated power and influence in the king's absence.

Summing up his position, he began, 'Firstly, my younger brother's proposed 'sentence' only describes our present circumstances without any apparent respite, so I dismiss that or any of his threats – unless he intends to execute my entire group.' He raised his single arched eyebrow at his brother, yet without rancour or challenge, 'I also earlier proposed to our king the idea of sharing the load amongst all Marduks in shifts, but that was summarily rejected.

'Yet we all know the importance of gold. The impressive achievements of my sister here, and my own research in Tartarus, have indicated a possible solution – also to aid construction in Eridu and in Eden - but which poses social complications.'

The audience shuffled in anticipation. Even Enlil's belligerent face showed intrigue,

'Unfortunately, the trolls are naturally sterile and the Titan males have somehow been similarly restricted.' He paused briefly and pointedly glared at Doctor Raphael, 'regardless, it would have been immoral to have them exclusively shoulder the burden.'

He stopped again, a little apprehensive as to how to proceed, seeking an acceptable way of presenting his proposal

'Get on with it!' Enlil prodded impatiently.

'There is a local creature common in Tartarus and judging by our Nin's experience, an even more advanced but reclusive version here that shows the rudiments of intellect and thus is teachable.'

'You don't mean those hominids!' Enlil scoffed.

Doctor Raphael pricked up his hawkish nose and his neck began flicking, indicating intent to display his ignorance,

'They have only just emerged from living in trees like their cousins, the apes. It would take aeons before they could become 'teachable' as this warlord Ea proposes - even with generations of culling and crossbreeding!' The Healing Institute head announced and nodded smugly to Enlil as if seeking his approval.

'I'm underwhelmed! I thought you had a viable solution,' Enlil sneered, continuing with his earlier tirade and bellowed, 'once again, my brother clutches at straws and wastes this Council's time!'

'True, they are too primitive, and we can't rely on that species alone. We will need to interbreed it.' Ea stated evenly.

'And what creature do you have in mind to breed it with? A lesser animal?' Raphael asked, inflating his chest, as if showing off his medical expertise.

'A mammoth?' Someone in the audience offered.

'No,' retorted Phanu-El, a Councillor and mind healer, 'not intelligent or dexterous enough.'

'A lion?' Another voice. 'A bear, perhaps.'

Ea maintained the pause and speculation, but finally he broke the suspense,

'Actually, I had a more comprehensive plan in mind, but we could start with the Titans.'

Jova showed some rare excitement, 'Of course! What a wonderful idea! Our Nin has shown me her team's great strides in genetic manipulation of the local species, and your ability in that field is also proven. Can it be done?'

'The hominids' genome is quite close to the Marduk, but it will require considerable experimentation...' Ea began before Raphael cut him off, twitching in approving excitement,

'The Titans have the manual dexterity *and* sufficient intelligence to make them malleable. Besides being totally adapted to this environment, their imposing size and strength would be a huge advantage. We should cull for only males, in that way controlling the population to just our own needs.'

The exchange of affirming nods throughout the hall appeared to seal the argument in everyone's mind except Ea's,

'I would only carry this out with the *expressed* agreement of the Titans!' His voice was scolding.

In the brief silence following Ea's reprimand, Shtar voiced scepticism,

'Who would bear the embryos? As you know there are only six Titan females. Surely, they can't be expected to become assembly line incubators! But I also shudder to contemplate how a hominid could bear or deliver a Titan infant that could grow five to six times their barely four feet in size.'

Raphael replied excitedly, 'I believe our Nin has learnt the relevant genomes that affect size. Perhaps we could even deliver them by abdominal births, a bit prematurely and . . .'

Enlil took control, cutting off any possible further objections '… it sounds like the proposal has majority support so let's get on with it.'

Jova scowled at his upstart son and had the final say.

'Ea, we will leave you with the technicalities and expect you can convince the Titans to agree. After all their species is doomed like us and they can at least contribute with what will anyway be only a partly related species.

'Meanwhile, in view of your proposed solution I will suspend your sentence except that your band is to return to the mines and continue to provide our energy necessities until you achieve a successful alternative. Nin's team and the Healing Institute facilities will assist, by remote conferencing if necessary. And there will be no further rebellion! This meeting is ended. Captain Gabri-El, prepare our return to the *Nibiru*.'

Enlil appeared about to protest, but Jova raised a restraining hand and continued,

'However, before I depart, there is one more matter. I remain king of the Marduks and will return for matters of grave significance. Yet, it is not necessary for me to attend routine Council gatherings. Therefore, I delegate executive power of this planet to my son, Enlil. Uriel, you will witness the handover.'

Jova handed over the Sceptre, and Uriel reprogrammed the Sword of Destiny to accept the vibrations in Enlil's hand. It was a symbolic weapon exclusive to the king in case of attack by any usurper from the Council, a remnant of more violent days, but since upgraded, allowing it to be wedged in rock and programmed to read psychic vibrations.

Nevertheless, Jova was not quite ready to relinquish everything to his son, holding on to the key to the tabernacle containing the ultimate symbol of what was deemed as a divine right of the King - the Skull of the Oath.

After the proceedings, the king slowly rose and shuffled through the hall towards the king's private *Transporter*. Ea inspected him as he left.

Manna retarded aging, but only maintained the status quo. And unlike the landing party that had the benefit of continued exposure to solar radiation, exercise, organic nourishment, and life's general vicissitudes, Jova's body had visibly deteriorated. It took on a skeletal quality accentuated by the translucency of his skin.

Ea trudged away from Jova's send-off crowd, in resignation at Enlil's ascension. There would be no test or vote, the king's word was accepted as law. It would retard his grander plan, having to persuade his short-sighted brother to accept an idea he will certainly find unpalatable.

The day was ending and the first lights flickered on throughout the small city. The silhouette he threw as he entered his apartment building, was splattered on the walls by the foyer's irregular glass tiles - a grotesque parody of his state of mind. He didn't bother to close the door. Observing his father's departing *Transporter* from the balcony, he thought back to earlier days. Fully adult, he understood Jova's abandoning the loveless, pre-arranged marriage to his simpleton mother Hera for Shtar. But then he went and married his sister Irana, clearly seeing *me* as a threat!

Hell, she's even younger than me, he thought to himself wryly. *I suppose I too had my share of young females on Marduk, but unfortunately very few here are of interest.*

The Law of Inheritance meant I would inherit the throne. But then Irania's amendment undermined my claim.

Enlil's mediocre mind's ambition is power for its own sake – I guess well- schooled by both parents. The Council too is driven by the immediate and the tangible, seemingly the basis upon which Jova chose them. Having no instrument to capture or measure intuition, they look upon it as either illogical or impossible. I understand why they find the likes of me so 'unnatural'. Hah!

Materiality versus spirituality - both just opposing expressions of the same cosmos, which cannot manifest without such balance. The unlimited energy of space converts into dense matter. And from that moment, matter attempts to convert itself back to energy in an eternal cycle – perhaps like the mystic belief in the soul separating from God...

Ea was startled out of his rambling reveries by a gentle grasp of his arm from behind, sending a current through his being. The sensation within the touch and the look that greeted him as he turned to face the culprit, suggested it was not just sisterly.

'So, when do we get started on our reproduction, master?' Nin asked in a combination of eagerness and light-hearted mockery.

His surprise at the meaning of her touch and the effect it had on him caused his slowness to catch on,

'I will be leaving for Gondwanaland tomorrow to start working out the details.'

'I wasn't talking about *that* kind of reproduction.' Nin's face was downcast, appearing demure, but her uplifted gaze and a smirk betrayed an air of seductiveness and confidence in taking the sexual lead.

'Oh.'

Her grasp on his arm maintained its sensuality, more a stroke than a grip. He caught the challenging defiance in her eyes and the invitation on her lips, and there was no turning away, which he briefly considered.

He became less tentative, yet his advance was gentle as he combed fingers through her rich ashen hair and caressed the back of her neck to draw her towards him. Momentarily unsure of herself, Nin relaxed when she felt the pulse in his hardness as she pressed against him, and she gave way to the moment, secure that the choice and timing was right.

She relished his body as he pressed down upon her. The first stab was not as painful as she had braced herself to expect, and as he glided gently into her, thrusting and withdrawing in marginal increments, her initial apprehension gave way to a relaxed pleasure. Under his weight, she dissolved into him.

His movements were precise, technical - expert. She was at ease in the moment, relaxing into the pleasure. Yet there was none of the passion she had expected, sensing his disengagement, as if performing just for mutual gratification - like two good friends!

Enjoying the process, the lack of ardour and romantic intimacy led her to understand there would be no permanence – mere affair or tryst. However, for the moment, it was good enough.

And afterwards, lying and chatting in each other's arms, their relationship reverted to mentor and pupil, champion and supporter, friend and partner –just overlaid with carnal knowledge.

CHAPTER ELEVEN

Disappointed by the failure of their protest and with any assistance only a distant promise, the miners nevertheless returned to Tartarus putting their faith in the success of their leader. Nin joined Ea's small team in the makeshift institute there, her first experience beyond Atlantis.

She explained to Shtar upon mutual farewells, 'I want to be part of the action and I also look forward to catching up with Fubsy again. Besides, you're also planning to leave, to who knows where.'

Eden evoked tastes of beef and earthy lamb and tubers in sunflower yellows, parsley green loam and strawberry perfumes wafting off sun-dried grain. However, the grasslands and forests of Tartarus conjured exotic game and peppers and mangoes, the pungent orange of palm toddy and aromatic spice, fiery red chilli and plump purple brinjal—the sourish musk of a lover's armpit wafting under a humid blanket.

'Even if the terrestrial genome can tolerate android componentry, we have no such sophisticated technology,' Ea briefed the team, 'so we will need to learn by crossbreeding these animals first before we introduce any Marduk chromosomes.'

Preliminary experiments thus resulted in freaks, from grotesque to sublime. Galael managed to combine a dolphin with a hominid for a marine hybrid. Nin derived a flying horse, crossing a giant orc with the seed of a horse she had evolved in Eden, and that same seed with the local rhinoceros resulted in a single horned equine. Ea produced a half bull-half hominid. Mainly albino, and lacking an integrated skeleton, all of those beta versions were held together mainly by cartilage.

'Some of these creatures are truly destructive and they are all highly unpredictable.' Nin fretted.

'Yes, but luckily they're sterile,' Ea agreed,

Buoyant Galael added, 'yet we're learning and progressively getting close. Can we take a break outside? I need a drink.'

It was a hot late afternoon as the scientists exited the air-regulated laboratory into the steaming rainforest. The trio shared coconuts seated on tree stumps carved into armchairs by the trolls.

'What is that teeth numbing screech?' Nin asked.

Fubsy enlightened her, 'Cicadas – like a diamond drilling into steel, isn't it? But after a while it becomes bearable, even narcotic.'

After a hypnotic pause Galael sighed, 'We've learned all we can from the terrestrials, I guess the next step is with the Titans.' He was sweating from the oppressive tropical humidity, which taxed his corpulent frame.

Nin expressed a niggling worry, 'what shall we do with the freaks? We can't just kill them.'

'And we can't just let them loose! They have been fed with manna and will live a long time,' Galael warned.

Ea finally joined in, 'The next visiting *Transporter* can remove and scatter them far away within the continent to find their own destiny. And I already obtained consent from the Titans, so yes it's' time.'

As if intuitively aware of the geneticists' progress, the Titan matriarch, Gaia materialised out of the forest.

'What timing! And how uncannily they blend into nature,' Ea whispered to his companions as the Titanide parted the trees and addressed them,

'Hairy Titan ok. Me carry baby,' Gaia declared in their deep bass voice.

Galael turned his back to the giantess and translated for Nin, 'She prefers a Titan as surrogate versus an apish female. I guess she's hoping that way the outcome will be Titanesque. But can you imagine what would happen if such a behemoth ran amok?'

'Notwithstanding, apes would be too exiguous as maternal proxies.' Nin's glibness was aimed to be incomprehensible to Gaia.

'We'll try our best Gaia. But we can't be sure of success,' Ea forewarned the Titanide, and worrying about monstrosity he added, 'let's just try with one and see what happens.'

Arriving on that next Transporter, Tartarus was shocked at the arrival of Ea's mother, typically vacant Hera,

'I heard you will soon deliver a Titan offspring. How delightful! They have always had a place in my heart. I needed a break as donor and test subject for those doctors, so I caught this supply *Transporter*. It's surprising how much diversity this small planet can support!' she announced - unusually chatty - to the dumbstruck geneticists.

I didn't know you were capable of delight... or that there was such a place in your heart! Nin held a sarcastic inner dialogue with the former queen.

After scrupulously recombining amino acids of both hominids as well as Titans, the geneticists finally coaxed the deficient chromosomes of their subject to match physiological profiles. Successfully developing a male zygote, Ea implanted it into the volunteer surrogate Gaia, who eagerly anticipated the resulting hybrid.

From that gestation came triplets, but from the singular eye in the centre of the three males' foreheads it seemed success was limited.

'I'm sorry Gaia, Titan blood is just too strong.' Ea tried to explain to the distraught Titanide, who was not so much disappointed in the appearance of her children but what it meant to the future of their species.

'How cute!' Hera attempted to console, 'Some say the seat of foresight lies in that central eye,' she added in empathy with the inarticulate giants.

'You make name.' Gaia, grateful for her solace, invited the Marduk queen to name her Cyclopean children.

In deference, Hera offered names with Titan meaning, 'That one is fierce and impetuous, like lightning – he is Steropes. And the one with the bright eye - Arges. And that one's rumbling gurgles sounds like your word for thunder - Brontes.'

But the central eye proved nothing more than that, with no adherent powers of intuition. Indeed, it was not their only limitation. As they grew, it was clear that the giant children were also struck with autism. That, combined with their bestial ape heritage, made the creatures utterly both ferocious and dysfunctional.

Nevertheless, Gaia insisted on keeping two of her brood in the Tartarus mines, where they grew to be adepts in the art of forging weapons. And with mixed emotions of sorrow and pride she took up Hera's offer to take the third, Brontes to Atlantis, where he would be stationed as Eridu's pet mascot and sentinel on the far side of the river Gihon's bridge.

'The hominid sperm is too weak for a Titan egg and amniotic fluid. We should be more successful developing a zygote in vitro and planting it into a hominid mother.' Ea surmised at their laboratory membrane after the cyclopean birth.

Galael cautioned, 'well then, we'll have to do a lot more tampering to minimize giantism.'

Nin chipped in, 'Enlarging the mini pliohippus into a horse, I learnt of the relevant genes, so I believe we can reduce embryo size for a hominid womb to accommodate, while maximising bulk after birth.

'And our experiments have also indicated other far reaching possibilities.' Ea commented without elaboration, and exited the bubble with that hanging promise.

Almost a decade later, Ea and team finally achieved a suitable recombinant sperm and ovum, planting the modified zygote into a hominid surrogate. The issue was a creature they called 'ogre' – meaning 'brute'.

Standing almost erect with huge feet for stability, the ogre, when adult, was much taller than his hominid ancestors, around ten feet, but inherited their stooping gait and hairiness. From the Titans he inherited a more compact arm and chest structure, an opposable thumb, and squarer jawline. His complexion, though swarthy, was much fairer than his ebony terrestrial ancestors— ashy brown with rusty hair over much of his body. He gained some savvy from the Titans but retained the hominids' roughhouse playfulness as well as the lazy nature of both parents - tameable but crude.

The production of ogres was handed over to the doctors at the Healing Institute in Eridu, who followed Raphael's instructions to abort all females.

'This continuously implanting zygotes is tedious and inefficient. I wish we knew how to just eliminate the female chromosome, saving us having to destroy so many.' One of the medical technicians complained to their chief Raphael, 'can't we just create a few female ogres to at least supplement our work?'

The Hawk unwilling to display ignorance, had been averse to asking Ea's team for their possible genetics know-how. But in response to the grumbles, he replied magnanimously,

'Well, a few females can do no harm to aid as incubators, but keep them out of sight. And of course, to minimise frequent duplication, just expose them to our youth fount, and naturally manna.'

'That's a good idea Doctor Raphael,' the technician flattered his boss, reaching that conclusion long ago and already feeding them with such. 'I'm glad they finally built a production facility here in Eridu to synthesize the supplement from that original tree in Eden.'

The ice that first greeted the aliens had now receded. Sea levels rose along with the temperature in both Tartarus, south of the equator, and Eridu in the northern tropics, fraying the nerves and the tempers of the inhabitants.

Under Titan guidance, and over millennia, the ogres freed the Tartarus miners from much of their drudgery. Some Marduks with weapons were required to ensure the indolent ogres fulfilled their production quotas – and enforce the discipline those giants lacked. And after their extensive isolation and freedom, many like Aigar and Lilith, chose the rustic life and remained in Tartarus. Mainly forgiven, Ea commuted between the two centres while Nin returned more permanently to Eden and continued research there. Their trysts had dwindled, measured in decades.

Initially awed by their overlords' resplendent power, and grateful for their creation and sustenance, the ogres even managed to pick up some of their masters' language. But the grind of endless drudgery went against the nature of this impulsively playful creature. Coupled with the lack of any modulating family ties, they despaired and turned spiteful.

'Get back to work, you lazy imbeciles,' the miner roared as his whip stung the backs of the loitering pack, 'half the daylight is gone and you've barely started loading the ore. If all you ogres can do is sit around and play, we would never have created you.' He continued, chasing them back to the mines.

One stopped and stood his ground.

'What the hell are you gawking at? You dare stare at your god!' The sentry challenged, making a show of reaching for his sidearm and lunging again with the lash.

Others ran only as far as the reach of the whip and turned back in alarm yet tentative support for their comrade.

Alpha male Ogre #374 felt the sting on his shoulder as he stood motionless. Encouraged by the handful behind him and by the fleeing onlookers who turned back cowering in anticipation, he grabbed at the receding scourge as the Marduk tried to draw it back to strike a second time.

The guardian was no physical match for the burly creature. And startled by the ogre's daring, he held on to the butt of his sidearm a fraction too long.

Before he could draw it from its holster, #374 had him by the neck. With no more effort than uprooting a weed, he tore his tormentor's head away. Held by the hair, the guardian's blood drained to earth in bright blue tendrils.

Awed by the apparent sacrilege, even those fleeing back to the mines stopped, stunned motionless and agape. To even touch a god was unthinkable! They looked about unsure as to how to move, as if anticipating catastrophe.

Momentarily paralysed, #374 stood in daze holding the head, while his companion #375 slowly eased towards him. Ogre #375's initial terror turned slowly to admiration, and putting his arm around the shoulder of the assassin, he raised his friend's hand holding the decapitated head in a sign of defiance and victory.

That galvanised the rest. Sealing their fates in camaraderie with their new leader, they broke out into roars of rebellion. Expecting the imminent arrival of the gods, they scurried into the deeper forest with the guardian's head as trophy, leaving his torso behind as a gauntlet. The group of twenty-three renegades picked up the two female incubators in the clinic, and made their way through the jungles to the east and the continent's centre.

In distant Atlantis, the city of Eridu glistened in the midday sun. The population was at stasis as Marduks avoided procreation, due to inevitable freaks. To stave off their boredom some had ventured to the coast and facilitated ore traffic. The resultant city, Lagash, burgeoned on the south east coast, evolving over the past two millennia as a marine centre of sorts.

But in the fields of Eden beside their capital, the sun was at its summer zenith, stinging the hirsute backs of the agrarian ogres as they ploughed the fields for the next crop of grain.

As if by sympathetic osmosis with their rebel brethren in Tartarus, a band of workers downed tools and headed for the Gihon river to swim.

Captain Raguel, in the company of visiting General Michael, scanned the farm from the perimeter citadel, spotting the frolicking ogres by the river. He was shocked by their deviance.

'What's got into your workers, Lieutenant Alan-El? Get them back to the fields this minute!' Raguel ordered his subordinate on the communicator.

Raguel lowered his spyglass, displaying the source of his daughter Lilith's golden eyes, and commented to his visiting commander Michael, 'All these ogres want to do is play. And they're becoming really troublesome lately.' He said, and barked again at his lieutenant to respond.

At silence from the captain's repeated command, Michael lifted his glass to scan the river as Raguel tried a third time.

'Come in, Alanel.' The liaising of the officer's epithet betrayed Raguel's growing anxiety. Can you hear me? Guardian, where are you?' His worry was palpable, 'I can't imagine what would have caused Alan-El to let these brutes just down tools and frolic around.'

'Bold ogres!' Despite the deadpan tone and assured stance, Michael shifted back and forth from spyglass to naked eyes betraying anxiety – his guardians were too well trained for any laxity.

'Sentry post #3, please investigate grain sector disturbance and check on the whereabouts of Lieutenant Alan-El,' Raguel called this time to the main guardian post in Eden.

'Sir, we noticed Lieutenant Alan-El's absence some time ago and have sent out to check. They're just returning now.' Came the responding voice.

It was followed by a period of silence.

'What's the problem, sector #3, I am not hearing from you. Where is Alan-El? Come in!' Raguel demanded.

The returning voice was stultified, apprehensive. 'Sir, it appears Lieutenant Alan-El is . . . dead.'

'What? How?'

'Sir, he's . . . been mutilated . . . decapitated, sir . . . apparently by a band of ogres, who have run off to the river.'

'Unthinkable! Murder?' Raguel looked at his general, aghast.

Michael grabbed the communicator, taking control from the distraught officer with one hand on his field glass. 'They are fleeing the Healing Institute… with females? Crossed the river …Evading our Cyclops for the coast. Retrieve them! Salvage Alan-El for cremation!'

Nin's familiarity with murder was only from ancient scripts - the killings in Ea's attack on Eridu just unfortunate accident; and she had seen hominid lethal violence. But two simultaneously wilful acts—and by a hybrid of a gentle Marduk Titan? She hastily researched any precedent before the emergency Council meeting, where she was to attend for the first time as Councillor:

Since the introduction of manna and its resultant life extension, Marduks found murder and suicide are illogical, counterproductive to order and to universal evolution. They are thus signs of retardation requiring early detection to correct such symptoms in childhood.

Factions and groups, less cohesive, still behave illogically, persisting in violence for communal selfishness such as for territory. But with globalization, these differences are now resolved politically, the belief inculcated in early education by King Beelzebub. Premeditated physical aggression on individual level is anathema and thus never encountered, tolerated or even contemplated – thus there is no prescribed penalty.

(*A Modern History of Marduk by Djehuti of Egesta*)

The text was considered a little too lyrical to be fully reliable and Nin noticed some description and even speculation, unlike typical chronicle factual presentations.

'We must quash this insolence and violence immediately,' Enlil assumed leadership of the hastily convened Council, dispensing with the preliminaries, and even Jova's supremacy.

Elderly Hera had abdicated her position, probably at Jova's persuasion, and the king had already taken the opportunity to replace his former wife with his daughter, Nin. None complained, now accepting such nepotism.

'But the coincidence of timing and method?' Nazarel's halting query betrayed his confusion, his blinking left eye drawing attention to the static artificial one.

Shtar had a theory, 'remember, the ogres are essentially replications from a single initial zygote – virtual clones. As a result, they all share an immense genetic and physical chemistry - even more than identical twins, they likely share a glandular, sympathetic communication – like schools of fish or flocks of birds.'

It was only Jova's third visit to Earth and it was clear that he did not particularly enjoy the experience. He was visibly frail. But instinct seemed to drive him to regain control, and although Enlil was official chair, he now took command,

'How awful, I thought the labour problem was solved. What could have caused such rebellion?' Jova's tone betrayed confusion, and though trying to stare at Enlil - as if holding his youngest son responsible for this second terrestrial rebellion - his glare seemed faltering.

Micha-El, is it serious? Can we quell it?' Jova asked.

The angelic general's consistent dourness made it difficult to detect any overt disquiet as he responded, 'Defiance unifies them. We can control them but can't force productivity.'

Enlil tried to explain, 'their initial awe has diminished with familiarity, recognising some of us are not as omnipotent as they once imagined.' It was no apology, instead it sounded vaguely threatening as he shot an eye at Jova.

'We pushed those lazy and playful creatures too far.' Shtar chimed in. 'No creature with any sort of mind can tolerate perpetual repression of basic nature or instinct. Eventually, something had to give way.'

Amongst the speculation that followed, Raphael commented aloud, 'Not enough indoctrination! They had no belief system, and thus nothing to live for.'

Enlil tried to regain control with raised voice, 'I agree. We should have instilled a more thorough brainwashing,' reducing it to a mumble '– something to remember.'

Uriel went deeper, 'That's true! For such a clean canvas as their empty minds, *any* sense of purpose would be interpreted as being a happy one.'

Enlil now fully latched on to the idea. 'Indeed. If fully convinced at our invulnerability and benevolence, they would have no other frame of reference to understand they were anything but happy.'

Nazarel the farmer's pragmatic question cut into the speculation. 'What do we do now? We depend on these creatures in both Eden and the mines.'

Ea's conclusion was also matter of fact, 'Too late for any of those re-programs. We face only two choices—either set them free or eliminate them.'

Michael shook his head, 'Freedom is ill advised. They are physically stronger - with females.' He looked accusingly at Raphael, who avoided eye contact and broke out into excessive neck twitching.

Ea added, 'Yes, and they're far more capable of cooperating than the hominid apes that ambushed us earlier in Tartarus. I'm afraid I agree with Michael.'

Nazarel spoke up for the community at large, 'And then how will we manage? Toiling as labourers again?'

Enlil regained ascendancy and was decisive,

'Point taken Nazarel, but we cannot take further risk. There's no alternative than to destroy them. While we have most of them captive, Raphael, you can destroy them here in Eridu, while Ea and Galael can do likewise in Gondwanaland. As for the renegades, Michael and Aigar can take as many troops as necessary and seek them out. As mentioned, we must not leave any alive to cause any mischief in the future. With so much manna they could survive a long time - and reproduce!' He too glared at Raphael's dereliction.

Raphael added apologetically at the open secret, 'Yes, I'm afraid we administered the radiation fount on a number to see its effect on the different species, so their lives could indeed be prolonged.'

'Really? And what was the outcome?' Ea asked, intrigued by the science and ignoring the potential threat of the now almost immortal escapees.

'I don't know. There are no negative effects so far. They could possibly—.'

'All the more imperative that we seek and destroy every one of them!' Enlil barked, glowering at the Head Physician again.

'As for any alternative solution to the labour problem, we can reconvene after their elimination.' With that Enlil had relegated Jova to mere bystander.

The ogres in Eden were herded en masse to the Healing Institute in single file. Anxious and uncomfortable with this unusual break in routine, they were reluctant to follow orders. But afraid to challenge the guardians' weapons, they complied.

'Ogre no sick. Whatfor go sick house?' Asked one of the ogres loudly.

A hubbub of disgruntlement began to erupt along the file.

Fearing a possible riot, Michael sought the assistance of Raphael, who now came out of the hospital.

The Head Physician's hair was smooth, sleek, and grey. His eyes had a crinkliness of wisdom and trustfulness in them. Dressed in his doctor's robes with its swastika symbol, and emanating immense serenity and calm, he appeared benign, even angelic. The grooming of the gods was as much a symbol of their divinity as the threat of their weapons.

And as healer of injury and illness, Raphael was a god to be trusted. Yet the cold, white, and geometrical marble architecture and the sterilised aroma was instinctually foreboding and the ogres remained rattled.

'Come, my good fellows! We have heard your complaints and just want to give you more manna, also to let you bathe in our immortal light so you will be like us.'

Raphael's slick voice allayed some of the dread as they neared the once benign but now forbidding building.

The corridor that led to the rotunda was narrow and could only be crossed in single file by those hulks. The pacified victims were herded in sectional groups into progressive soundproofed anterooms, the door to each section locked as they passed, preventing any communication with the pack behind.

The panic that ensued in the forward section was too late to filter back the lines. There was no escape. An otherwise pleasant aroma suffused the basement hall once they entered. Instinctual fear taking over, each group cowered together.

The process was mercifully fast. The gas almost immediately sent them into paralysis, and the guardians within the hall, masked from the fumes in headgear, dragged the fast-succumbed victims on to mechanical trolleys, shunting them for incineration to free up space for those that followed.

Their numbers were never counted.

The renegades that escaped Eden were pursued ever eastwards by Michael and his troops. Having the presence of mind to destroy their electronic tracking shackles, they crossed the strait that connected Atlantis to Eurasia in a stolen ore transporting barque moored near the south-eastern tip of the island. They were met by a *Transporter* of troops and mowed down. But a few escaped, heading north to the retreating glaciers and disappeared into the monochromatic wilderness.

The same extermination procedure was carried out in Tartarus. Aigar's band of guardians also chased the renegade murderers, who had managed to run off with sacks of manna.

Those rebels had now reached the land bridge connecting a shoulder of Gondwanaland separating an oriental section. There they were picked off by a sub-troop from a pursuing *Transporter* that landed to track the remaining few, on foot. The more agile ogres - and better adapted to the environment - took shelter in the river gorges, shielded from Marduk telescopic cameras and weapons.

They continued eastwards into the emerging mountain range that split Afrasia and enveloped them into its bosom of snow, employing the same tactics as their northern brethren, inhibiting any further pursuit from even the well-equipped guardians.

'There's just a few left and there's nothing in those desolate mountains. They'll die off soon. If Aigar asks, say we shot them and they disappeared falling into a chasm, so no photos of proof. Let's go back.' The guardian sergeant ordered his companions, who were only too happy to comply and escape the buffeting blizzards that tore at them from that highest of mountain ranges.

The sergeant had no inkling of the effects of that seemingly insignificant laxity.

CHAPTER TWELVE

Earth – c 14,000 A.D – 22,000 B.C.E.

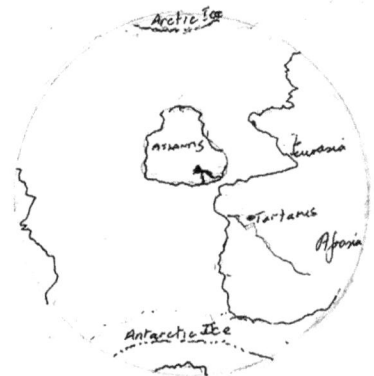

Ogres exterminated, disgruntled Marduks on both continents clamoured again at the labour problem.

Jova had remained on Earth expecting such furore and to revive his supremacy, called Council to deliberate. Again, it included many concerned citizens.

After preliminaries, Ea's request to present his plan was conceded,

'We came carrying the hopes of annihilated billions to perpetuate our species and establish a new Marduk.' He opened. 'Though smaller than ours, this planet is still vast and bountiful for our minimal numbers. We're almost immortal, yet many are sterile or reluctant to procreate. Hence, it is highly unlikely that we will succeed in our mission unless we take a more inventive approach...'

Enlil interjected sarcastically, 'So, Officer Obvious, give us your master plan.'

But Ea was not to be rushed...'with no likely increase, the best we can achieve is cottage industry. We have the knowledge to do great things, but we don't have the scale of resources to achieve it. I propose to produce a similar species to serve us.

Enlil continued to prod, 'Enough suspense, what marvellous animal do you plan to modify this time? Another fabulous species in your travels to the netherworld?'

'No new discovery, I'm talking of the same hominid.'

'Enough! Enlil roared. 'You're wasting our time. We will not risk more experimentation with that vicious species. Perhaps a new, improved version with the Titans? I don't think so! Step aside and let more competent Councillors deliberate on this important issue!'

Ea remained undeterred, 'Not the Titans. I have a more comprehensive solution than that.'

'More comprehensive?' Jova now injected himself to cut off the bickering and regain control.

With an absent-minded gaze at the pyramid's apex, and anticipating an uproar, Ea announced,

'The subject I have in mind is *us*, Marduks. We can introduce our own genes into that hominid and create a biological equivalent, a hybrid.'

Enlil was outraged. 'But we are talking about a base animal. Even if it is achievable they would dilute, if not destroy our genes, eliminating our species. How monstrous!'

'Any more monstrous than the aberrations we are already giving birth to?' Ea quipped back.

'Will it have a soul?' The voice was at conversational volume but perhaps because it was rarely heard, or perhaps because of its inherent modulation, Shtar's question penetrated the hubbub. She had yet to leave for her intended retreat.

Nonplussed by the obliqueness of the question, Ea's response was automatic, 'I don't see why not.'

'And what form or aspect will that take?' The rhetorical nature of the question made it clear that Shtar was now becoming disturbed by the implications.

Jova quickly reined in the idle conjecture. 'The issue of any soul or God is unknowable, and therefore not really relevant, so let's hear out Ea.'

Raphael interjected with indignation, lifting his head and projecting his hooked nose, 'Sire, this is an abominable idea and not worth entertaining. As you all know, on Marduk even cloning was prohibited due to the disastrous aberrations in the replicates.'

Ea responded, 'Yes, such problems are why I didn't propose cloning. This will be a totally natural process.'

Shtar objected, 'it *would* debase our entire evolution with a likely degenerate, yet conscious version of ourselves.' But the protest lacked conviction and sounded more like evaluating the possibilities.

Ea ignored Jova's countermand and returned to the soul for advantage, 'our Nin's experience clearly shows they possess empathy, a quality of soul no doubt.' He argued with his typical single arched eyebrow. 'A hybrid will evolve like we did over time, and who knows with our guidance, perhaps better. Hominids are certainly physically more suited to this environment.'

Some of the audience overcame initial shock and revulsion to speculate aloud as voices arose at random,

'What will it look like?'

'What status will we give it? Is it to be one of us?'

'And will it behave more like us or more like the apes?'

'How will they procreate? Will we approve females this time?'

'Wonder what they'll look like. Imagine sleeping with one!'

Of course! Nin had instinctively exclaimed inwardly the moment Ea delivered his thunderbolt. On second thought she became disturbed by the implications, averse to such regression. But then, like the *Nibiru's* constant hum, once recognised, it could not be ignored. And now while the room speculated, she searched within,

It would mean the extinction of our species. She cast a glance at Shtar, who seemed lost in her own speculation.

Focusing on the actions, I had all but forgotten the look on the eyes of my saviour. So pacifying was its aura - is that what aura means? It's unfamiliar to us— even to the Titans whose goodwill is genetically ingrained.

No, it's from another source. As if evolved - somehow either missing or long lost from the Marduk psyche - a more altruistic concept of 'love' than Shtar tried to describe or the chronicles bandied about.

In her muddling thoughts, she latched onto that affinity - as if the spirit of the hero hominid was invading, trying to impose understanding.

And assimilating that leak into her psyche, a conviction arose in wafting epiphany,

Ea's proposal isn't just right, it's necessary!

Nin's attention was brought back to the meeting with Raphael protesting, '...but it will not be *our species* - just bastard hybrids!'

While the hubbub of speculation continued, Ea glanced over at Enlil, sitting as if disengaged, flashing looks of rage from moment to moment – with jaw thrust forward and eyes blazing in inner dialogue,

Ea then turned his attention to Jova, who seemed to be getting used to his suggestion and demanded, 'Son, is this really possible?'

The noise abated in deference to Jova's unfamiliar address. And Ea was taken aback at his father's almost term of endearment. But before answering, Ea scanned the myriad expressions, from disdain to deep apprehension, suspicion to eager anticipation.

'Their chromosomes are quite similar to ours. However, the number of such on the spindle of their genetic code...'

'...And how long will this take? If successful, under your charge, they could build their own civilization and as you suggest, offer us at least some hope.' Jova asked and became encouraging, as if switching sides.

'I'm not sure I can answer that yet, but I...'

'No more of your frailty! Enlil's voice took on a thunderous force, and dashing to grab the attuned Sword of Destiny beside the tabernacle, he slid it out of its rock sheath, flashing a swipe with the blade.

Jova's head quivered for some seconds, the Vril energy making a laser-like cut, before it toppled onto the floor. The blue gushes from his neck, together with Nin's piercing scream echoing through the polished granite hall, gave the scene was surreal.

CHAPTER THIRTEEN

For the second time, Council was struck silent in disbelief. Murder in front of their very eyes, and of their king, no less! All sat agog while Ea burst forward reflexively to attack his brother, except for Michael, Raphael and Uriel, who were also immediately on their feet. Michael as if in anticipation, intercepted the eldest son, pinning him back.

'Hold, Lord Ea. Your brother has not yet committed a crime!' Raphael called out as if privy to a plot.

Held back by Michael and bewildered, Ea looked to Uriel, who now gave a resigned sigh.

'That's true, Lord Ea. A king, by law, rules until death or abdication. But there's a provision for a successor to take power by removing his head - provided he has support of the Council - in a single blow, thus dispatching the victim without suffering, trapping the spirit and transferring its power. Naturally, that can only be carried out with a weapon such as the sacred Sword.'

That wasn't enough for Nin, who fought to quell her outrage,

'We profess disgust at hominid murder! Yet we condone it now?' she rasped.

Nazarel gently held her in consolation while Uriel tried to be solacing,

'Such type of assassination is technically the only way to remove a deviant or inept ruler and thus, not really murder. With the wellbeing of an entire planet at stake, the actions of the king have absolute effect and so must maintain full faculties. If those faculties deviate or fail in any way, you can imagine the consequences. With absolute authority, how else can such a ruler be removed?'

'Then we Marduks are the worst hypocrites, and I side with the hominids!' Nin had regained enough composure to add rational vehemence to her accusation.

Raphael ignored her,

'Well, the method was lawful. So now it is up to Council to ratify the replacement. As Speaker I call for a vote - 'all those in favour of Lord Enlil as King of *Nibiru* and Earth, please raise your hands!'

The nine up-held hands rendered Ea's intended refusal and Nin's shocked abstention irrelevant. Shtar too abstained but Uriel raised his arm slowly, as if realising the expediency and necessity.

The perfunctory manner of the act and the outcome left the Council and its attendant audience intact - observing Raphael, Michael, and Gabriel removing Jova's corpse with all due reverence and ceremony to the crematorium in the vestibule built for the remains of future rulers.

'In view of the importance and urgency facing us, we should proceed with the swearing immediately,' Uriel announced, taking the key from Jova's belt and unlocking the suspended tabernacle to unveil the Skull of the Oath, which only he amongst them had hitherto seen. The diamond-like skull, with its slightly elongated retral section, was a perfect replica of a Marduk skeleton.

'What is that?' Irania enquired on behalf of the attendees, all marvelling at the exquisite object.

Uriel stopped briefly to explain. 'When Marduk first formed its democratic monarchy, an icon was sought that would represent the head, the seat of the spirit, of all Marduk citizens, whom the monarch was entrusted to protect and serve. This is a crystal crafted from the fine white powder that remains after transmuting gold into the plasma energy or Vril. It was crafted by Marduk's most acclaimed artisan, who is rumoured to have employed arcane esoteric principles to excavate the inaccessible inner parts of the crystal into such an intricately accurate skeletal replica. The flawless result is considered un-replicable.'

The sage maintained its sanctity by omitting to mention a duplicate in his possession.

In quick ceremony, Enlil was sworn in, and to his credit, made no acceptance speech but was quick to adopt a regal air and authoritative command,

'Under the circumstances, this meeting is closed. But the problem is pressing and we will reconvene in three days, after the cremation.' He declared, returning the Skull to the tabernacle while holding on to the key that Uriel had handed to him as his inheritance.

'How do we explain Jova's death? Are we to raise up the tabernacle following Marduk protocol?' A Councillor asked before the meeting disbanded.

The Royal Sage spoke again, 'There is no necessity to raise the capstone. Councillors can explain to the Marduks, who, anyway generally support Enlil. Nevertheless, many will wish to express their gratitude to our Jova for saving us. And so, Sire, I suggest an elaborate funeral during the three days of mourning.'

Uriel had fast evaluated the possible repercussions and hence the community needed as much pomp as possible to reunify. He thus became particularly grandiose, 'Gabriel as royal messenger can officially broadcast to Marduks at large that a new era has begun and that Enlil has been appointed King of the World.

Returning to open Council after the funeral, Enlil immediately reverted to earlier issues.

'My intervention was only to fortify our leadership. Nevertheless, I don't share Jova's enthusiasm for such a project, and certainly will reject any idea of integration or independent civilisation. If it is to be entertained at all, the only objective for such a hybrid would be as slaves! Yet I would prefer an alternative. Any suggestions?'

Ea was adamant, 'a Marduk hybrid is the only viable solution.'

'They will turn on us like the ogres!' Raphael's eyes darted about like Dilmun's predatory birds. 'As menials, they will be prone to despair just like the ogres and again bearing the homicidal gene of their apish ancestors.'

Uriel concurred. 'Raphael makes a good point. It's not advisable to create such a species with a good semblance of intelligence and treat them as slaves. They're equally likely to rebel.'

Ea followed that line of thought, 'it will be *our* genetic input, not the Titans' this time. More importantly, instead of as slaves they can be partners, colluding in our mutual development . . .'

'Never!' Enlil interjected. 'We should be advancing not degenerating our species, so as I opened, integration is out of the question. Any such creation should be simply utilitarian.'

'Why assume degeneration? Perhaps they may augment us. If not, they would anyway be inferior so what are you afraid of?' Ea challenged

Enlil paused to glare at his brother. He had eliminated Jova and his brother's claim in one swoop, but his rule was only embryonic and Ea's implication of 'fear' struck a nerve, able to switch allegiance just as easily as Enlil had. After a tense and lengthy hiatus, he gave his first royal edict,

'In the absence of alternative proposals, I take up your challenge – for *one* experimental specimen! We can test it for its obedience and psychological suitability, limiting its exposure to knowledge—except what *we* induce—thus controlling its behaviour.'

'Education is preferable to brainwash,' Ea quipped but went no further. 'But for now, what about the labour issue?' His retort was met by disconcerted nods of affirmation from the entire gathering.

Raphael came to Enlil's rescue,

'Sire, I had considered proposing the idea earlier but was pre-empted by Lord Ea, and also reluctant due to my already mentioned worry about hominid violence. However, both teams have gained from the interbreeding experiments. We already have advanced strains of hominids and can develop them into a smaller, more manageable species to help in basic labour until we prove the failure of this hybrid.'

Enlil observed the enthusiastic nods to that cautionary path. Thus reassured, he instructed,

'Excellent suggestion! We have built a stockpile of gold and now that many miners have relocated to Atlantis, they can help the already improved hominids. Meanwhile, the Tartarus team can experiment with a single specimen hybrid. Consider it a Council edict!'

A *Transporter* carried the group of geneticists including a few assistants from the Healing Institute, to the Gondwanaland laboratory. Nin and Galael were excited to be in the cockpit, while Ea had flown ahead independently in his *skoop*.

'Pilot, last time I came here on foot. It would be lovely to view Gondwanaland from above.' The rotund Galael acted as spokesperson for the visitors, and the pilot complied by dropping altitude.

'How was that crack formed?' Nin asked, observing what appeared as a hairline fracture in the earth, creeping up from the Southern tip and splitting it from North to South

The aeronaut answered as if reciting from the chronicles, 'the planet's original integrated surface was cracked over time by meteorites into four large crustal plates, including Atlantis and Godwanaland. *Nibiru* instruments detected a large strike some sixty-five million years ago, southwest of Atlantis – possibly causing its separation. The remnant crack below will likely split the main continent in two one day.'

Lilith greeted them upon landing. Their scant interactions during Nin's earlier stint had hinted at instant rapport, although focus on the ogre experiment and Nin's involvement with Ea limited them to only brief encounters.

'I've been going bananas like it's going out of style, waiting to chew the cud with you. What's 'nu in Eridu?' Lilith gushed effusively, accompanying the geneticist to Ea's quarters.

'Lilith! You've spent too much time around Aigar. It's rubbing off!' Nin scolded playfully.

Lilith blushed deeply, 'see what I mean about no one to talk to!' She threw a dazzling smile.

Such shared embarrassment marking their camaraderie, both females examined each other briefly.

Lilith's stunning and inherent vivaciousness was a stark contrast to Nin's demure personality. The riotous abstract colours of her outfit - against Nin's northern style cool grey with a streak of pastel peach as only hint of contrast - further highlighted their respective attitudes. But that interplay of opposites carried some mutual appreciation and the pair became fast friends.

Having learnt how the genes of terrestrial creatures combined interspecies, Ea turned towards the interplanetary. In that process, Nin shuttled between both clinics to share information and assist Raphael's team develop their 'sons of man' or 'humans' as they were to be called.

Ea explained to Galael and Nin, 'To intertwine our chromosomes, we must first maximise the similarity of the hominids. Their brains are large enough, but need more synaptic connections to enhance creativity and intellect – although their mirror neurons are greater than ours. And Marduk influence should raise their consciousness overall. He was trying to pacify fat Fubsy's annoyance at the tedious genetic manipulations - matching the specimens' DNA.

Later, when visiting her colleagues in Eridu, Nin had mixed emotions at Raphael's conclusions,

'I hate to admit it, but it appears we *do* share some base physiological similarities with the hominids.' But then he followed with, 'we could just introduce our surface traits to produce enhanced humans—and maintain our separate species!'

And after nearly twenty years, the joint effort did lead to some advanced self-aware humans, yet barely stepping over the barrier of bestial consciousness. It became the subject of argument at Eridu's Healing Institute, with the interbreeding experiment hanging in balance. Enlil had dispensed with the rest of Council and acted as sole mediator.

Raphael took advantage to explain first,

'Sire, both teams have produced somewhat similarly advanced humans - more upright, much less hairy and with thinner hide than their apish ancestors – and doubling their previous lifespan – to nearly forty years. Most importantly, they are able to comprehend complex instructions. Uselessly, they have even developed two-dimensional art and synchronised dancing. So, we have already a suitable slave - there's no need to proceed any further.'

That puffed-up chest, grey-streaked swept-back hair and hooked nose actually appears more like an eagle, Nin mused.

She was distracted by furtive glances Enlil threw her way – looks that were now more recognizable. *He can't be seriously interested!*

'...making them almost a new species, but that was not the objective!' Ea was protesting.

Nin reengaged, 'Yes, we were to create and test a "fully conscious" hybrid, to which I was also assigned. Surely the Council would not let all that learning and work be swept aside by an expedient half measure.'

'But, my dear, your work has not gone to waste, we have gained a hundred thousand years in hominid evolutionary advance - with sparks of consciousness that will allow humans to accelerate their development much faster than their progenitors. More importantly, my young Nin, they are controllable and generally ignorant - thus ideal slaves.'

Raphael's patronising manner made Nin rethink her comparison with the eagle - unfair to those majestic birds–or even to the lesser hawk.

Uriel recently leaning with the geneticists now decided to weigh in, tempting Enlil's ego, 'Of course the donor sperm for a hybrid should come from the best of us and thus our king.'

Nin caught simultaneously the glint in Enlil's eyes and the momentary flinch in Ea's - which was immediately followed by his arched eyebrow and a conspiratorial wink at the sage.

Enlil paused briefly.

And soon after he addressed Raphael, 'those sons of man will indeed be useful slaves. But Council did agree to the creation of a hybrid. I must admit I have grown intrigued to observe how they might turn out. One specimen can't do any harm.'

To test the effects of the terrestrial environment on the Marduk seed, Ea's team once again toyed with smaller creatures, incrementally increasing the proportion of alien genes.

The finer Marduk genes contributed to fantastic results - fairies, goblins, leprechauns, and other eerie little sprites. Fortunately, although long-lived due to the alien influence, they were again sterile.

'Time to find the most gifted amongst the humans.'

Nin chipped in, 'those from the northern Atlantis hominids are the most talented. Their slighter build has probably forced more creativity - devising tools and weapons much faster than the bulkier primitive lowland kind developed at the Institute.' She was also elated that specimen came from her hero's lineage.

'Yes, and their brain physiognomy is a closer match to ours,' Galael added. He had grown even plumper, being constrained to tedious lab work.

Ea announced, 'Well, we'll soon see. I believe we have a compatible ovum type.'

The first outcome was a homunculus, which soon died, leading Ea to comment,

'The hominid genes are powerful, overcoming our recent reproductive damage. However, it still seems the lower species can't adapt to the higher one. The fundamental problem appears to be the host mother's suitability to carry the higher functions of intelligence, particularly the mirror neurons.'

'Mirror neurons? You mentioned them earlier too.' Nin asked.

'The capacity to observe and automatically imitate, even experience vicariously, another individual's pain or disgust or even love, by empathy—without personal experience. But I just can't generate them artificially. It seems they are absorbed, as if by osmosis, through the human placenta. Regardless, our species are too distinct and a hominid mother just can't support the hybrid foetus.'

Galael came to the obvious conclusion, 'I guess we can't avoid the inevitable then – a Marduk surrogate.'

'Though in the eyes of the Council that damages our chances of replicating the experiment - unless we produce a fertile female also.' Ea commented, 'But where will find an undamaged Marduk volunteer?'

'On that count, I think I may have a solution,' Nin offered before exiting the laboratory.

CHAPTER FOURTEEN

'It's good to see you again, Uriel. And Eridu has flourished since I was last here,' Shtar greeted the sage cheerfully upon entering his villa. Finally isolating herself after the death of Jova, she was tired from the near 600-mile and thirty-day trek on foot and ox-cart. After decades as a hermit, she was happy to see the royal sage and his young ward, Shalimar.

The sage scrutinized her while responding – as if looking for signs of aging since she discontinued radiation,

'Yes, thank you for accepting my invitation. You'll note the city has burgeoned since enslaving the advanced humans. You've met my daughter Shalimar.'

Uriel's ward was rarely seen as a youngster. Now fully adult, Shalimar's pert nose and flushed cheeks made her pretty yet in a juvenile fashion. Shtar also noted the sage's pride - introducing her as his daughter.

'Yes, I hear you've been dabbling in the metaphysical.' Shtar prodded in an attempt to get her to speak.

Shalimar remained shy as if in awe, so Uriel answered for her,

'She initially followed her parents' line and worked with Nazarel in Eden. 'Finding that unfulfilling, she decided to join the Healing Institute, learning medicine. But she found that also wanting, which is why she wished to speak to you.'

Shtar gave him an inquisitive glance but remained quiet awaiting any further comment.

Shalimar finally rose to the task and spoke, 'They were both interesting, but they're material sciences.'

'So you prefer the spiritual? Tell me what you understand in that area,' Shtar began interrogating.

Shalimar began to open up, 'Was it coincidence that we were saved and pointed to a hospitable planet at first shot? And found animals with our cellular structure, allowing even attempts now at a hybrid? Is this earth a living entity—something we need to adapt to and avoid being ejected like a threatening virus? Were we guided here for just such a function, having expended our own purpose and perhaps just a catalyst for another entity?'

'Intuitive questions!' Shtar remarked, scanning the girl in growing attraction. 'Though on the issue of coincidence, my research has shown that mostly it is just random, and our mind only registers when events seem to synchronize. For example, had we not found this planet, we would have perished and not had the luxury of questioning our good fortune *or* the coincidence of compatible animals.'

Shalimar was not convinced. 'I understand that. But I don't think that explains it. I sense a guiding or underlying hand greater than all of us. But that's not the real reason I wished to speak to you.'

'Then what is?'

'Why did you decide to discontinue radiation and the chance at immortality?' Shalimar asked.

'Years pass like days and terrestrial life seems to last not much more than a season. Yet what is any one of us achieving? Rare youngsters like Nin… and you…are the only ones coming up with any new thought. The rest are just existing in the groove of habit. We all *should* be elderly yet have added nothing to our species' psyche or consciousness, only just layers of experience. I suspect evolution relies on death and rebirth, and that includes for the development of our souls.' Shtar was animated, and her lecture was yet to finish,

'Our mutant progeny are just reflections of our own deformed psyches, or are possibly compensation for trying to outwit the universe, as you also seem to imply.' She ended, but caught the smirk on Shalimar's face.

'Yes, it seems your "underlying hand" pokes its ugly face everywhere.' The former queen conceded.

Shtar's weak attempt at satire gave Uriel pause to inwardly remark at her "layers of experience", while Shalimar followed up,

'Which is why I asked my father to invite you. I would like to join and learn more from you.'

'I'm not sure I could teach anything to the likes of you - more the other way I suspect.' Shtar smiled deprecatingly.

'Yet it might be enjoyable in any case.' Shalimar smiled beguilingly, causing Shtar to hesitate at its meaning,

'Actually, I'm considering leaving even Atlantis. If that eventuates, I will contact you, and you can decide if you want to come along.' She said, and spent the evening appraising Shalimar and her curious suggestion.

Nin addressed the couple tentatively. 'What were your thoughts on hearing Ea's hybrid idea?'

Lilith had thrived on the experiences of the beautiful continent in the company of her soulmate and husband. Their rambunctious and capricious lovemaking in forests, fields, seaside and mountains was a rare display of alien spontaneity. Despite such abandonment, both she and her mate had been disappointed that no child had resulted. The discovery that Aigar was essentially infertile or at best his issue was defective, was particularly devastating to the gregarious and vivacious couple. Lilith had the voluptuous curves—full breasts, tapered but not too narrow waist, and rounded hips—that immediately brought the maternal to mind. And at the height of her youth, suffused by fecund surroundings and deeply in love and lust with her husband, such instincts were in overdrive.

'I think it's a delightful idea! This planet is such an untapped paradise. I'm all in favour of any creature that can appreciate it.' Lilith's spontaneous response put the geneticist at ease.

'So, you wouldn't feel any stigma or loss of Marduk identity?'

'Absolutely not! As you know, Aigar and I can't conceive, but I wouldn't dream of depriving anyone the opportunity. Why even a mutant would still be a gift,' Lilith responded, while Aigar gave an approving shrug and added,

'Lose the worm to catch the fish.'

'Well, I'm glad you both think that way, and perhaps I have an idea that may interest you.'

Nin proceeded to outline the opportunity for Lilith's involvement in the experiment.

Gaining the couple's agreement, she hurried back to the clinic to inform her colleagues.

'Hmm, it seems that the hominid genes have a local advantage in physical influence. Their chromosomes seem to weaken Marduk input. We'll need to tinker more.' Ea mused aloud to Nin and Galael who observed him manoeuvre the microscopic specimen.

'They're only insignificant and mainly cosmetic defects, and anyway they'll only end up as slaves,' Galael complained, tired of the seemingly endless genetic manipulations.

Nin rebuked her friend gently, 'They may be small Fubsy, but they're nevertheless disagreeable defects. And any prototype should be as flawless as possible, you never know.'

Ea added, 'Well said. Physically it's also best they resemble us to avoid antagonism or prejudice.'

'Well, I wish we could call on the idle technicians amongst us to do this repetitive work. Their makeup is anyway more suited to such meticulous adjustments.'

Galael then switched track to ask innocently, '…anyway, they'll never be allowed to procreate with us, will they?'

Ea and Nin exchanged inquiring glances and returned to their work.

After painstaking and intricate coercion, even into the molecular structure of the genetic helix, Ea was satisfied with the consequential zygote, transferring it immediately into incubation.

Developing rapidly by Marduk standards the embryo matured beyond the capability of its artificial hatchery.

'It needs live placental sustenance to develop any further.' Ea turned to Nin in apprehension as much as excitement.

She nodded, 'I called Lilith already. She's outside,' and marched purposefully to the adjoining room.

Nin guided the surrogate mother into the laboratory. Lilith's fixed smile and urgent gait betrayed a little anxiety. Calming her with a detailed description of the procedure, Ea eased her on to the makeshift maternity bed and transferred the growing organism.

After a due course of 267 terrestrial days, coinciding closer with conception of its simian progenitors than with the alien, Lilith conceived a male child - as designed by its creators.

From the altitude of the *skoop*, Nin spotted Shtar's simple abode at the southern coast of Atlantis. Arriving at the cottage, she was further struck by its crudeness. An eclectic combination of rock pile, dried mud, tree stumps, and hodgepodge from Eridu and the *Nibiru* were somehow assembled in a relatively orderly fashion to deliver a very rustic, nevertheless cosy looking residence.

Upon reaching the end of a rocky corridor that separated the front part of the dwelling to the back terrace, where Shtar was tending her plants, Nin was awestruck by the grandeur of scenery that elementary patio afforded its occupants, with wide sweeping vistas over the southerly ocean. A constant sea breeze contributed to the idyllic setting.

'Mother we've done it! An intelligent terrestrial species, a Marduk hybrid!' she blurted, skipping greetings and startling her otherwise solitary parent.

Shtar, downing tools, was equally animated by the news, 'why, that's wonderful, my dear. I know we're both not sure what to make of it but I'm delighted after all your painstaking work. I'd love to see it!'

Nin looked askance at her mother, impressed by the new-found responsiveness, 'the air here seems to invigorate more than just the body!' she commented, 'in any case, that's partly why I came. We would like your opinion.'

So now the pair sat cramped in that *skoop,* heading for Eden.

'I must admit I am fascinated, and I have always sensed this planet was missing a native mind to complete its evolution as an organism.' Shtar's statement, as often, was oblique.

'Uh . . . huh.' Nin wasn't quite sure what the enigmatic comment meant, but her mother's mind was in another realm, bridging another dimension perhaps. 'That's why we want you to observe our Adam.'

'"Earth creation". A good name! I'm looking forward to it. Although initially sceptical, meditating in isolation I realised the necessary path of evolution for this planet and solar system. Intelligence is like skin for a planet, the membrane that gives a world its consciousness. And by the way, this mode of transport is also a lot more comfortable than my lengthy treks back and forth.'

'I almost understood what you were talking about. Hmm . . . Perhaps Uriel's teachings are rubbing off on me, or perhaps like you, I'm losing my mind. Mirror neurons indeed! But speaking of lengthy treks, why so far from Eridu, over a hundred miles to even Lagash?'

Shtar was introspective and didn't respond. But after some silence, mother turned to her daughter, 'You're finally adult I see.' She said with a smirk.

Nin looked back into her mother's grey eyes. Faint lines showed around the edges indicating deprivation of radiation therapy, 'you didn't answer my question, why so remote?'

'Oh, it wasn't a matter of distance. I'm looking for the soul of this planet.'

Nin went silent in incomprehension and they continued in silence until they were about to disembark,

'By the way, how was your first experience?' Shtar taunted as they headed to the Institute.

'What are you talking ab—? How do you—?' The questions were left hanging as Nin wondered how or how much her mother knew. She and Ea had been very circumspect and anyway their liaisons were very sporadic.

Dismissing the question and while escorting her mother to the Institute in Eridu to view the baby, she reflected on the painful process of bringing Adam to Eden.

Lilith and Aigar had been in rapture, perfect parents for an infant of any kind. And Nin dreaded approaching the couple for the inevitable.

'What does aunt Nin know about children? How could I possibly not love even the first thought of you?' Lilith cooed as she suckled the beautiful baby.

'Lilith, this must be so hard, but we did agree you would give him up after 180 days.' Nin tried to be as gentle as possible. 'He's getting old enough to develop attachment and memory.'

'I didn't expect him to be so beautiful!' She cried into her husband's chest.

'I know it doesn't compensate, but our cameras will be with him at every step, and you are welcome to observe him anytime on-screen.'

Nin had never felt as inadequate and realised how inept she was for such emotional interaction. She had intended to allow the couple to name the child but had the presence of mind to understand that it would only deepen the attachment and thus refrained.

Escorting Nin and the baby to its penned off section in the Tartarus clinic, Aigar had looked to her in desperation. But he remained silent possibly in fear that he might blurt out something utterly inappropriate.

Initially nursed by a domesticated human female until he became more aware, she too was then removed and the toddler was relocated to Eden. There, he was sequestered in a cave – with minor furnishings from natural items and materials - and under continual camera observation.

The term Lilith used initially for the new-born was 'adam' – creation of earth. In deference to his surrogate parents, none proposed a name, and thus her description had remained as his label.

In Eden, undetected attendants left daily sustenance for him overnight, often including Lilith, who also observed him on the Institute's video screens. She would sometimes linger while he slept, even occasionally sneaking in to hold him in her arms, whispering gentle endearments – until his second year, when she was caught and sent back to Tartarus.

As he was to be a unique single specimen, Ea had taken pity on him, circumventing any sexual urges and frustration by adding an additional X chromosome to his male XY constitution. Thus, although Adam was technically male, he was rendered androgynous.

'Except for the fact that he will grow up to be only about Nazarel's height, he actually looks a lot like Enlil!' Nin had enthused to Ea upon Adam's placement in Eden.

'Yes, well that was the intent, wasn't it? Enhances his chances for survival! However, somehow and for what reason I can't quite place, he seems incomplete, inadequate,' the geneticist replied.

'I know what you mean. I was thinking similarly but also can't explain what it is.'

Nin's response had been absent-minded, recalling the subject of mirror neurons, which then led to thoughts of her mother, causing her to finally pay this recent visit to invite Shtar to view the boy.

'He's already near puberty!' Was Shtar's first reaction, but she said little else, observing Adam on-screen at the Institute.

Finally, she expressed their collective misgivings.

'An abomination! It has a soul but no spirit!' She cried in dismay, 'worse, he is asexual. He can think but with no contemporaries, and now doomed to solitude and introspection. My reclusiveness is a *choice* after the advantages of a fully experienced life. What's in store for him?' she accused, walking out.

Ea confessed his own misgivings to Nin and Galael after Shtar's departure, 'I'm afraid your mother's anxiety is well grounded. In such isolation this creature can be no more than an unprogrammed android... but with the curse of consciousness.'

'Excuse my ignorance, but where's the problem? He's only an experiment, so why not indeed experiment with it and test our theories?' Galael questioned.

'I see you agree with Enlil's intent to program our Adam with his "healthy" thoughts and beliefs.' Ea accused.

Nin was far more reproving, 'Fubsy, that will starve the spirit, stifling any talent. To give it individuality as we have done and then deprive it of its self-expression is, I agree with my mother, irresponsible at best, if not criminal. And how do we then determine if the experiment is a success without testing it in the real world?'

Fully grown - precociously faster than his alien forebears - Adam's Marduk resemblance increased. He stood erect as Nin had predicted, at six feet four inches, but better proportioned than the aliens. He was fairer and more delicate than his newly evolved human relatives. His eyes appeared as piercing black coals, the strongest remnants of his hominid ancestry.

Eridu had met news of the successful experiment with a mixture of alarm and titillation. Crowding at the Institute to gawk, gasps of awe and amazement erupted amongst the viewers

'Why, he could pass easily as one of us,' whispered one. 'Surely we have become as gods,' cried another. 'Can he talk?' Another asked. 'I always imagined aliens would look like us, but not so closely!'

However, initial fanfare and curiosity waned, with no real bearing on their lives - the humans already serving any imaginable purpose.

The hybrid thus remained fully cloistered from any Marduk interaction – with Enlil also disinterested in the interim - and observed only by his creators and Institute staff.

As Adam turned adult, still oblivious to Marduk existence and exposed only to a few uncouth human farmhands he saw at a distance in Eden, his future became a matter of deliberation at Council.

'I wonder what he thinks upon waking to find his daily sustenance left overnight for him. Probably imagines it's provided by the gods!' A Councillor speculated offhand as proceedings began.

'Indeed!' Enlil latched onto the comment, 'as I mentioned long ago, if we are going to continue or expand this experiment, we should ensure that such hybrids are utterly subservient, even awed by *us!* Its moral direction should thus be inculcated. In this case, as its 'father', he should be exposed to *nobody* but me.'

Ea nor Nin bothered to question what they expected was a foregone but anyway inconsequential command.

But Doctor Raphael took a different tangent, 'Sire, do we really need to continue to be distracted by this silly novelty? We should exterminate him and just leave our needs to the humans.'

'Actually, he's turning into a rather handsome runt, with even some finesse. Naturally, he should not be exposed to a society he may never be permitted to join or have any knowledge of his true origins. Hence, any work in Eden must be done at night. Let's see how I can indoctrinate him and we can decide on his fate later, after seeing how he turns out.' The king declared.

As the meeting ended Enlil announced,

'It's time I paid *my* creation a 'visit'.' He shrugged off the incredulous looks continuing, 'after all I had at least as much as anyone to do with his existence.'

Enlil's holographic image appeared at dusk beside Adam's grotto. His white velveteen-like 'skin' of finest Marduk microfibre was accessorised by purple boot-leggings and matching belt with the platinum insignia buckle of Marduk royalty. The hitherto unseen and apparently unnatural shade of the leggings alone was sufficient to render the apparition venerable in Adam's eyes.

But to further inspire Adam's awe Enlil also had donned a cobalt blue coat caparisoned with royal badges, emblems, buttons, medals, and monograms. He also carried the sceptre of kingship. The agglomeration of so much precious metal, jewellery, and rampant colour against the white backlighting at the Institute, made Enlil aglow in the darkness now encroaching on Eden.

In addition to intended majesty of his attire, Enlil had all the speakers throughout Eden turned on and with a slight reverb to sound more 'divine'.

Since arriving in Eden and upon Adam falling asleep, the doctors had played gentle subliminal tapes from speakers high in the lush trees – with programs from the *Nibiru*'s chronicles. They ensured maximum sedation for caregivers to leave his sustenance and carry out occasional medical treatments undetected. It had the subsidiary benefit of inculcating him in Marduk language, which by now he understood.

'I am Enlil, King of the world who came here from the heavens.' Adam's god announced in his thunderous voice, pointing at the skies and in the chronicles' antiquated formal Marduk language,

'I created you, my son, placing you here in this garden paradise I call Eden, to rule over its tame creatures and follow my instructions. If you are obedient, your spirit will grow until the day when you can join us in our heavenly city.

He beckoned his awestruck subject, 'Walk with me while I instruct you of my expectations, from which you must not divert.' His image now drifted above the nearby bushes.

'Unlike us, you are a product of this earth itself but, unlike all other creatures in this world, created in our likeness. There are other humans as you have witnessed, which we have also developed along with the animals and plants in Eden. But only you are a true son of god!'

'You will listen only to me and follow my commands. Your thoughts and beliefs are to be those that I give you, for I will tell you all you will need to know.

'I will watch over and keep you safe, even against those sons of man or humans who will wish to cause you harm. I have also appointed guardians, protective angels to watch over you. They will come to your assistance should you call out if ever need or danger arises. For wherever you are in this garden, they will hear your call, and I will know of it.

'You may have any of Eden's fruit, but notice two trees that grow in its midst. The one with the red stamens and seeds is the Tree of Life, the seeds of which contain the manna that we provide each night to sustain you. It is not of this earth but placed here by me. But *do not* eat the scarlet fruit of the other tree from the heavens. It is a Tree of Knowledge prohibited even to your angels!

'You will thus avoid corruption. But if you eat of that tree, you will understand like us, all that is both good and evil, knowledge which your spirit is not yet developed to contain, and which will give you all sorts of delusions and corrupt your soul. It is my test of your loyalty and obedience. If you break that trust, you will be deprived also of the Tree of Life and thus you will die just like the beasts in this garden.'

For Adam's security and for his 'divine' observation and communication, Enlil sought the help of Gabriel,

'I don't want him indolent and so have instructed his how to grow produce - even if no value to us - but I don't want him contaminated by the aboriginal humans who might break in to steal from Eden.' Enlil explained.

'There is plenty of no longer used audio-visual equipment on the *Nibiru*, although we haven't the capacity to produce more. I shall plant them around Eden for greater monitoring and to scare off any marauding sons of man.'

'Good! See to it!'

Meanwhile, the purpose and development of that 'son of god' had yet to be resolved.

Once the novelty of Eden wore off, the unwitting troglodyte began to lament his loneliness. His rare contact was with God and only for instructions with no visible benefit, becoming tedious.

On the next such visit Enlil, shook his sceptre and scolded,

'Adam, why are you neglecting your work? As agreed, it is the proof of your worship!'

'I could offer much more if I had company. Why is it that I alone of all the creatures in this glorious garden must exist solitary?'

'Your education is not complete. Besides, you may call upon me at any time.' Enlil groped for a satisfactory explanation.

'But my Lord is too eminent for me to engage in conversation. What can I show you that you have not already seen? I seek someone to share my wonder and experiences.' Adam protested.

'You have not yet proved your loyalty and dependability.' Enlil groped again, putting on a commanding voice to project authority.

'But when will my Lord be satisfied? What must I do to prove my worth?'

'I will think on it and see what can be done. Meanwhile, get back to your obligations, lest I deny your plea.'

Enlil was disturbed by Adam's truculence. Yet he enjoyed moulding the godling's thoughts and actions as desired—a perfect subject. And unlike the uncouth 'sons of men' and their guttural human tongue, he was conversant in Marduk. There was some grace about this hybrid son of his.

CHAPTER FIFTEEN

'My godling is turning recalcitrant and pleads for companionship,' Enlil reported to the Council, seeking rare input. Aware of the agenda, Nin had flown to Shtar and convinced her to attend.

Ea was first to comment, 'Yes, it has been long enough. Adam has stood the test.' He should be duplicated and given his freedom to develop and disperse in the greater world—it's the only way he can fully evolve.'

Enlil didn't share Ea's lofty purpose, 'He's not fully educated and a long way from complaisant and deferential as I wish.'

Ea pressed on, 'On what basis will he be ready? And how will we know unless we test him?'

Phanuel the psychologist Councillor made a rare contribution, 'Interaction with a female could allay any bestial viciousness arising from sexual frustration.'

'No! Females will not be necessary yet. It will introduce too many moral complications.' Enlil shouted down the idea.

'What moral complications?' Nin challenged.

True to form, Raphael supported Enlil, 'As we observed in the case of the ogres, females will only serve to distract the males and lead them astray.'

Nin bristled, 'I don't know how you both came to that conclusion, but surely you don't blame the females for the ogres' violence?

Ea followed suit, 'And how else do you expect more "godlings" as you call them? Our tests show no hominid and human females can carry the foetus. Do you expect *our* females be called upon as volunteers to bear the creatures—only to give up the infant as did poor Lilith?'

Enlil was at odds to respond and instead surreptitiously observed his sister. He had a greater plan to ensure the supremacy of his bloodline than puny Adam offered. But there was plenty of time for that.

She's not really my type—a little too self-possessed and intellectual. But I notice some familiarity with our brother that goes beyond just sibling or collegial. I hope I haven't left it too late!

Enlil was confident in his attractiveness. Unlike others who sought sex for intimacy, his seduction was calculated, devoid of uncertainties from desire or emotion. Dismissing those limitations, his charm was purposefully contrived, and he felt sure he could woo her when the time was ripe. His features softened into a smirk of reassurance.

While Enlil mused at how to consolidate his ambitions, Raphael had taken up the argument, 'This creature was to be just a vassal, perhaps as substitute for our inability to fabricate automatons. Its feelings are of no concern.'

Glum General Michael decided to contribute, 'Females are complicated - with intrigue and caprice - discontent and demanding.'

Enlil's response was diplomatic, 'Yes well, that's one opinion. But by adding females and multiplying, Adam will next have delusions of equality.'

Nin paid close attention as Ea returned to his earlier point,

'Well, regardless of those arguments, the dilemma remains as to how to replicate Adam, and having eliminated cloning, how else could that happen besides through their intercourse? Or again, do you expect our females to cooperate?'

Shtar joined the fray and was adamant, 'You can't all be serious!' She looked over at her daughter.

Nin was too flabbergasted to add anything more than, 'Absolutely not!'

Irania had her own reasons for objecting, not the least being that she, like Nin, was one of those eligible surrogates,

Yet she addressed Shtar, 'well, dear, that's something you don't really have to worry about at your age and condition.' She teased her elder queen. 'But I must agree with my stepmother, oh no . . . I'm sorry . . . step-wife?' She paused and pouted with eyebrows raised. 'I'm not sure *what* our relationship is, really. Nevertheless, we are sisters in this resolve. The idea is absurd, so drop it!' She looked pointedly at her son, as if that dismissal was final, and continued,

'Now that's settled, so on another note, the godling, this adam, can certainly be considered attractive to those so inclined, although clearly from his purely functional "equipment", he was designed by a male.' She looked askance at Ea.

Ea became defensive, 'I didn't want him to experience unnecessary frustration...

Irania cut in, 'Perhaps our good Lord Ea can enhance any future specimens to be more . . . functionally and dimensionally aesthetic... more Marduk?' And any female will be likewise fetching and endowed. Perhaps their intercourse could stimulate interest by our own kind.' She nonchalantly looked over at Shtar, who was up to the task and retorted,

'I'm sure you know more about male functionality and stimulating their than I, but I concur that the few undamaged females will *not* be baby factories – for sons of god or otherwise! As for Adam, we have already crossed the threshold of divinity by creating an equally self-conscious being. To eliminate him would therefore be murder!'

Uriel's nods confirmed her assertion. Enlil thus concluded,

'To leave him solitary would be cruel and anyway pointless. And as terminating him is illegal, we must consider Adam's request. But I absolutely condemn – as treason - any dilution of the Marduk bloodline by intercourse between the two species!' It was his turn to look pointedly at his mother.

Doctor Raphael was unconvinced, 'Whereas we evolved over aeons of experience and breeding, I fear this creature has skipped that evolutionary growth by too large a quantum. And what would be the gain? We would not be propagating Marduks, just creating a new species, with no advantage for ourselves.'

Ea was quick to point out, 'Well, not really a new species as we *are* able to mutually procreate - more a separate race.'

Enlil became statesman-like, 'we can address their procreation later as Adam is apparently androgynous and impotent. Meanwhile, we cannot ignore his plea for companionship. God-like we have created an imperfect being, and acting as gods, we must improve his morals and ethics.

'To cease endless opinions and arguments, I make this a royal decree -we will allow Adam a companion, a female – accustoming him to the opposite sex - but sterile. And I don't wish to contribute again to produce a half-sister, nor add further complication by another Marduk donor.'

And that way, maintain your unique influence as progenitor of an entire race! Nin sneered inwardly.

'Is there any other way we can bring about this female?' Enlil went on to ask, looking from Ea to Nin to Raphael.'

Ea responded immediately, 'Well, yes, Adam's extra chromosome is what causes his ambiguity. But he *is* functional. I could isolate the male component from his DNA, leaving just the X chromosomes. I then insert the separated XY chromosomes into a hominid ovum – stripped of any of its own genetic material.' He was becoming excited by the science, 'due to the differentiation in sexes the product would be Adam's replicate, but not a clone.'

Amongst murmurs of both amazement and confusion at the intricate science, Enlil authorised,

'Whatever! Go ahead!'

While Adam slept, Ea anaesthetised him and removed fluid from his spleen to act as donor cells.

He explained to his team while showing how to create the foetus,

'The spleen produces antibodies to fight infection, so it will give the female the best chance for survival in vitro.' 'and to avoid the risks of complications from incest, I think we had better introduce some random variations in the mitochondria of the female DNA and ensure its predominance.'

As variant to the Jova-Irania-Enlil line resulting from Adam's sperm donor, Ea modified the female features with elements of his own mother Hera's genome. As variant to Adam's dominant hominid black eyes, he allowed Hera's blue-grey to act as a recessive gene. And with an auburn mane, she would develop Hera's statuesque build: slender limbs, curvaceous hips, and rounded, firm breasts.

Adam had benefitted from Marduk longevity. And typical hominid telomere deterioration was slowed by manna - eliminated entirely if ever treated with the radiation fount. But Ea was sympathetic to Shtar's theory that every living entity has a quota of ability and a limited time frame to express it – the trade-off between immortality and creative stagnation.

Therefore, for the female he retained her human forebears' natural tendency for telomere shortening with each replication.

Adam and his initial heirs will be rather long lived, but that effect will dilute over the generations and diminish until one day they might develop their own science to prolong it—perhaps that achievement can indicate suitability for integration with us.

Ea having achieved his promised objectives, the following Council meeting was lively. Enlil questioned his brother,

'It's quite remarkable the change that has come over Adam recently. He is more muscular. He appears to be growing more hirsute, gruffer in his manner, and even his personality is changing—less effeminate. How did that come about?'

'Yes, it seems our Ea has heeded my advice. I notice a decided bounce in the man's equipment.' Irania's winking smirk was aimed to tease.

'As I mentioned earlier, to create the female, we had to subtract one of his extra female chromosomes. Besides, what use would he be in his former condition? We simply polarised their chromosomes. Otherwise, they would be identical - clones.' Ea's facile explanation was condescending to try and deter any further probing.

'Why not? They're not supposed to procreate.' Raphael complained. 'Did you sterilise her?'

'Well, in effect, she might as well be. And you of all should know that sterilisation can only be done after puberty. We can do it then.' Ea was deliberately dismissive, 'besides, despite Adam's "equipment", his experience is androgyny. And that coupled with Enlil's indoctrination on morality would leave the poor man rather in the dark, or at least innocent, and possibly even averse to any sexual liaisons. I'm sure the thought would appear to him in some ways as making love to himself.'

'Or to a sister!' Shtar didn't miss the chance to add, also arching an eyebrow at Irania.

The council thus distracted moved on to other issues, while Enlil continued long to glower at his wilful younger brother, convinced the omission of the female's sterility was no oversight.

After weaning at the Institute, the female infant was taken to her prospective husband as ward in Eden. She was left swaddled outside his cave, whereupon Enlil called him out one morning,

'Adam, I have considered your plea and agree that it is not suitable for a son of god to be alone. We thus created a companion, taking sap from your side while you slept.' He pointed to the spot below Adam's ribcage where a tiny scar had strangely appeared one night - wherefrom Ea had extracted his glandular fluid. 'She is to be your equal and helpmate.'

'What shall I call her?'

Call her shit for all I care! Thought Enlil,

'As with other earthly things, you will choose her name. And you will pass to her all my teachings. She will share the bounty we provide from the Tree of Life – available exclusively to you in this world. But do not eat from the Tree of Knowledge!'

'You truly are a glorious and benevolent God. I have thought on it and will call her "Eve", the harbinger of night and rest. I have heeded your lessons well, my Lord, and I will instruct her in your ways.'

'She too was created in our image, and if it is necessary to have more of you, then we will create them just as we created you both. Therefore, do not lay your hand on her or copy the base and coarse rutting of the beasts.'

'Of course not, my Lord. I will treasure her as myself. Together we will worship you and give thanks for the gift of our life and our companionship.'

Eve grew into a svelte teenager as Ea had designed, and was nurtured and schooled by Adam according to Enlil's dictates.

In response to Eve's concern about her lack of obvious genitals, alluding to her miniscule clitoris, which she exposed to him in frustration of its comparative size, Adam had reassured,

'I too was more like you when young, I'm sure they will appear in due time like mine.' Although he wondered inwardly at the coincidence in timing that his genitals had only really begun to grow with her arrival. Moreover, her appendages were diverting to her chest. He turned away from her innocent exhibitionism, disturbed at the twinge it caused in his loins.

'As I tried to explain at Council, after our initial spark, the humans are developing naturally in their societies. But we have exceeded and accelerated the evolution of these hybrids too suddenly,' Raphael complained to Enlil as they observed the couple on the monitors of the Healing Institute.

'Yes, it is daunting enough for *us* to have to deal with individual accountability. They can't develop a moral code so quickly. That's why I will play their moral pillar while they develop full self-consciousness—one that is beyond question, reproach, or doubt—that only a god can fulfil,' Enlil replied.

'Well, their gratitude, devotion, obedience, and love for you are evident.' Raphael grovelled.

'Their ignorant prattle is tedious, without having to deal with both. Therefore, I concentrate on Adam who is more pliant, and let him do the rest. However, their adoration and obedience is based on fear. If, for a moment, they doubted my invulnerability, that cord binding them to us could be severed.'

With no other frame of reference, and witnessing the seasons and the birth and death of the wildlife, the couple assumed themselves immortal, separate and merely observers—removed from the cycles of nature. Involved in the cyclical nurturing of the fauna and flora, they imagined themselves as part of the causality of nature itself, semi-divine.

With Enlil's exclusive indoctrination of the male, Eve was left to her own devices in a freer environment, resulting in a curiosity that Adam was hard-pressed to satisfy each night.

'Why must we work and leave food for our Lord when he can create anything? Why aren't there more like us? Why can't we have young like our fellow creatures? What's wrong if we gain knowledge?' Eve constantly bombarded him.

The mantra of response from her partner was never quite satisfactory, 'We are not to question the ways of our Father!'

The onset of Eve's puberty was their first disturbance. Waking one morning before her, Adam was astonished and terrified by the apparent injury to his mate, oozing blood from her unformed genitals. He shook her awake, fearing she had somehow succumbed to mortality like any injured beast.

'What is it?' Eve awoke, startled by his agitation.

'I don't know. Somehow you have been damaged.' His response bordered on the hysterical as he pointed to the dried smudge and ambling trickle. Somewhat startled herself, Eve was sooner to calm,

'Perhaps it is time for the growth of my small appendage to become like yours,' she answered as if intuitively.

'But that didn't happen to me.' Adam was placated by the possibility but still a little alarmed.

'Well, I feel no pain, and I sense no damage, so let's just see what happens in the coming days.'

But as those days came to pass, and over the ensuing months, the same condition repeated at similar phases of the moon. Observing that lunar connection, she sensed that perhaps there were other powers at play in the world than just those of the Lord Enlil, who appeared oblivious to her condition.

Adam was both puzzled and a little repulsed at the periodical flow from her genitals, considering it an element of her bestiality, reminding him of the afterbirth of his cattle.

Sensing that disgust, to some degree sharing it in accompanying shame—shaking their unison a little—Eve decided to withdraw from him whenever she sensed the onset of the flow.

Expecting Eve's menstruation, Ea began monitoring the couple on video beamed from Eden to his clinic in Tartarus.

"I think it's time to make my appearance to our little experiment," he mused aloud to Nin.

'You can't expose yourself to them! You're under orders!' Nin exclaimed, disturbed at Ea's perpetual unruliness.

'Enlil is presenting himself as God! They need education, or they will remain forever mere curiosities or pets.'

'But that was the edict!' She was frantic, grasping his arm as if fearful of the consequences.

'The female is no longer a child and menstruating,' he argued.

'Yes, and she's becoming very attractive, rather like Hera, don't you think?'

'Nonsense! She looks nothing like Hera. A bit late for Council who will just argue and be bothersome. Enlil's not going to tie her tubes or explain what's going on with her, so she will need to be exposed to one of us anyway. I must rush.' He sauntered to the *skoop*.

'Yes, but shouldn't it be a female to guide her in such matters?' Her call dissipated out of earshot of her partner, who had already shut himself in the cockpit.

CHAPTER SIXTEEN

Eve had marked the hilltop cave with its sweeping vistas of the entire valley of Eden while wandering with Adam. From there, she could view the grassy sweeps in the south-east merging into the orchard forests and the forbidden trees in the central plain.

Reaching the spot at twilight she watched the dying embers of the sun as it disappeared behind the western lowlands. Its orange afterglow melted into a hazy murk, before giving way to darkening shades of blue as she panned the sky in an arc over to the east. Beyond Eden wafts of smoke rose into the evening sky, and she guessed it was from the human settlements, giving her a slight shudder of fear.

Do not venture beyond Eden, the humans there are savage and will eat you if caught! God had threatened.

The crisp clear air of early autumn offered a pellucid sky and magnified the cosmic drama that unfolded as first, solitary points, and then sparkling bursts of light took over the gloaming. And as she observed those stationary fireflies alighting the night sky, she wondered,

Our God Enlil's power is indeed awesome. But is it so great as to have created such majesty? Somehow, he appears limited by comparison. And Adam is no more than his vassal unable to answer my simple questions.

Surely there is more to life than just adoration and worship. What's wrong with knowing?

Ea, scanning from his *skoop*, spotted the young woman perched upon the precipice of her clifftop vantage. He approached and landed on the leeward side, from which Eve was completely obscured.

Deciding on a cautious approach, he maintained the facade of divinity that Enlil having worn his Institute attire.

From there, he crossed through the central part of Eden, past the Mandala tree, picking one of its smallish fruit and placing it in his pouch distractedly pre-occupied with the moral issues that Shtar had raised when asked about why she had foregone treatments. Having explained her thesis about mental stagnation to him and Uriel, she addressed other issues,

'... any being that claims consciousness, must think for itself and question everything. Only from that introspection and its resulting behaviour, can one truly claim to be conscious or at least awake. In a sense, we have all been indoctrinated since childbirth—by parents, peers, and pedagogues—who in turn were trained by similar mentors and so on, back to the beginning, leaving us with unconscious preconceived ideas.

'But personal responsibility is laborious. How much easier it is to handover one's morality, ethics, and even thinking to a government, master, priest or - like Enlil with Adam - claim divinity for himself! Perfect scapegoats for the lazy! Believers then imbibe that icon in reverence, with the power to absolve all wrongdoings and sins, circumventing their karma. What perfect self-delusion!'

It was a rare burst of intensity from the otherwise placid priestess. But her diatribe wasn't over,

'Free will means taking personal responsibility, not automatons serving some creator's purpose - like Enlil with the hybrids. When it comes to technical achievement, we Marduks are masters. But for spiritual growth, the Nibiru passengers especially are almost entirely novices - all the less qualified to instruct any adams.'

Uriel added, 'True! Higher consciousness can't be gained by reciting dogma. Religion and God turn individuals into hapless victims, blaming a creator for their imperfection and sins.'

It was why he chose this task instead of sending Nin, who would have performed simple sterilisation.

And it was in that state of quandary that Ea addressed the bewildered girl, who was startled out of her reveries by the apparition that emerged from the crags within the periphery of her sight.

'Don't be alarmed. It is I who brought you to life. I come to help you through the changes in your body as you develop into a woman.'

Eve had no direct experience of fear and the similarity of this apparition to Enlil was reassuring, 'Our Father Enlil gave us life. But how do you know of my condition? Are you another God?'

She shied away, suspicious. Whereas Enlil's regalia threw golden light, this one had a silvery white aura — a similar radiance but of different hue.

'Yes, well, your creation is another story, but as to your condition, I have come to explain and help you through the experience. But why have you removed yourself to the far reaches of Eden, away from your mate?'

'He does not care to be in my presence in this state.'

'But your flow has already stopped. Yet you remain here.'

She was taken aback by his familiarity with her details, 'You truly must be a god to know so much. I also retreated here to deliberate on other matters that are confusing and distressing.'

'Such as?'

'I must not complain about God who gave me life.' Eve answered coyly, fearful of her apostasy but hoping that this understanding stranger may offer some answers.

She inspected the emblem emblazoned on the tunic he wore over what appeared to her as an exquisite skin. That covering shimmered in a scaly, silvery sheen like the lustrous sheath of the snake – a caduceus with the single snake around a sceptre - that was emblazoned upon it.

'There is no disrespect in questioning. How else can one learn?' Ea's tone was reassuring.

'But our Father instructs us in everything and told us that too much knowledge leads to corruption.' Eve's response was a little bolder as if not believing a word she said, 'yet, I do wonder.' She looked at the stranger, this time with a hint of demure appeal.

'Perhaps I can shed light on some of your dilemmas.' Ea's placating voice was in stark contrast to the barking commands of her Lord Enlil. It had a mesmerising, soothing quality to it, enticing the lonely young woman—desperate for some empathy and compassion. And this one was more real, tangible, than Enlil's ephemeral apparition.

'Why is it that we, of all the lord's creatures, cannot multiply as the other creatures do naturally? Are we to remain alone forever with no more of our kind?' She burst out.

Ea was slow to reply, so she continued her lament,

'I feel emptiness and yearn for an offspring. Adam too tires of my sole companionship, although he does not share the depth of my discontent. Even the lowly beasts are afforded that fulfilment. How can God who created that longing, withhold its fulfilment?' She stopped, checking her audacity, while testing the stranger's reaction.

Ea was reluctant to expose a whole field of knowledge best kept hidden from these hybrids. But Uriel's and Shtar's discourse on freedom and dogma reverberated – and he decided to gamble,

'Well, you have the capability.'

'But our Lord has told us that we are not to behave like the beasts. As our creator he must be obeyed.'

'Enlil is indeed King of Eden and Earth, but it was I that brought you to life, and your condition shows you are capable of giving birth. Indeed, you have the potential to understand and achieve anything that he or I or any of us are capable of. Although I came here to steril. . .'

'. . .That is blasphemy! You are *not* our creator! Our Father warned us against that temptation to knowledge, which is evil!' Eve's vehement tone indicated as much hope as it did reproof.

Ea glimpsed the coyness in her expression and the implied infidelity in her voice. Despite obvious ignorance and innocence, the young woman projected an inherent sensuality. He inspected her thoroughly, while inwardly examining how much to reveal.

Remembering his pouch, he felt for its contents.

'There is no evil in knowledge, only in ignorance. It is why you are so confused and ill at ease. This will help you to understand your part in the scheme of things.'

As he uncovered the fruit, Eve emitted a gasp, 'The forbidden fruit! I should not eat it.' Her protest carried with it a tenuous plea to convince her otherwise.

'It is indeed from the Mandala, a fruit of enlightenment. Don't be afraid. It will answer many questions that torment you.' He took a crisp bite from the bulbous fruit and held out the remainder to her.

'How can I imagine to know as much as God.' Her tentative steps towards his outstretched hand belied her complaint, caught between fear and intrigue.

'In being moved to ask those questions, you have a right to their answers. For you too have self-consciousness, alike we gods who created you in our image.'

While speaking he caught Eve's provocative pose. This most innocent of women, devoid of any such experience, was intuitively more flirtatious and beguiling than the most permissive of Marduk females!

His jaded worldliness and blasé cynicism were stripped – her countenance so refreshingly unassuming. As his eyes lingered over her for momentarily longer than was professional, her nakedness began to stir his anatomy.

As she reached out and wrapped her lips over the nodule, crushing it tentatively and allowing its scarlet juice to seep over her jowls, suspended between her breasts like purple jewels, he marvelled at the result of his creative sculpture.

Designed in his fantasy and now here before him physically, his artistry stoked his libido as much as his ego. Full breasts that now stood upright in their juvenile bloom, gossamer strands of down that reaffirmed her puberty, but left her raw and exposed. That fine hair would coarsen in adulthood to shroud her slit in a different artistry, and like Adam's fully sprouted pubic hair, was a remnant of her terrestrial heritage. But for now, together with her alluring coquettishness, it enhanced her sexuality, making her more enchanting.

The unfamiliar intimation of his gaze was as disturbing as much as thrilling - intuitively sensing its intent. Her skin bristled as she felt a constriction and warmth about her loins. Reciprocally her eyes sought out the analogous part of him, now burgeoning through his snakish covering. She watched in awe as he shed that skin, and catching sight of his enormity, palpitating in its tumescence, the analogy of that reptile was complete.

As he approached to envelop her and she felt his pulsation against her stomach, Eve was at once petrified and titillated, tantalised and abashed. Enlil's indoctrination via Adam thwarted her zeal while at the same time fed her anticipation. The interplay of fear and desire, caused a headiness - unable to discern which was cause and which was effect.

In the jeopardy she saw hope of countermanding pedantic Enlil. Before her was a being possibly equal to that Lord, but whose words and empathy struck a chord with her starving sensibility, wooing her. It seduced with charismatic charm, impressing her with abstract possibilities rather than concrete prohibitions.

She instinctively turned her back towards his protrusion, bending over in submission, as she had observed amongst the beasts. But Ea turned her around, his hands caressing her curves, reaching down and peeling her lower lips to expose and tickle her nub, and guiding hers to fondle his awakened and emergent virility. Distracted by her fascination with its girth and vibrant strength, and mesmerised by his artful massage of her own miniscule version, she languished in the moment, the warmth oozing about her.

She was suddenly startled by a sudden stab from within. He had probed her with a finger to minimise the pain and haemorrhage, and now, in her fecund lubrication, he was mounting her, the pulsing snake self-animatedly gliding into her engulfing slick.

Learning all her hitherto unknown erogenous zones, artfully explored and manipulated by the god, she was transported into ecstasy by his technical mastery. In so doing, at once she comprehended her individuality, her separateness from the world. While enjoying her act of carnal rapture, she at length sensed, or at least envisioned, the true purpose of her existence—a discovery that served only to heighten her bliss.

As she peaked, the narcotic from that exotic fruit also took full hold. She felt herself melding - this time more than just her physical body - into the god whose memories now dissolved into hers, both connecting to universal mind.

The leap of understanding was instantaneous, jumping to a state of heightened awareness hitherto unimaginable. Eternity became compressed, exploding from a point, expanding like a lung, collapsing back to a point—repeating like a succession of breaths. Answers everywhere, but like an oracle, answered only what her now heightened intellect asked of it. Paying attention to the answer, the expansion stopped and telescoped to the specific question - only one or the other - either watching the totality from distance, or engaging in the answer. She at once caught the infinite potential of her mind as well as the puniness of it.

It offered an indelible understanding of life, this time its unity and her role within - her capacity as a god and that of all her progeny after her, realising that indeed as the snake-god had implied, she contained within her the potential of all that Enlil claimed as his own.

Euphoria was short-lived. The revelation dissipated like a nocturnal dream, only remnants of understanding amidst the memory of her sexual experience and pleasure. And like a dream, it beckoned her to return for more. But breath now normalising, she disengaged - physically and psychically - from the melding with her stud.

Guilt and uncertainty encroached in its place. She now reflected on the physical, and the detached technical prowess applied to her by this sire. Recoiling, she sought the more comfortable companionship of her husband.

'What have I done? I have sinned against God! You are indeed the devil our Father spoke of, sent to tempt me and betray him! I am afraid.' She wailed.

'You haven't sinned. You have simply gained knowledge.'

'But I have eaten of the forbidden fruit!'

'You cannot betray God, you have simply disobeyed - yes technically your father Enlil. But in that melding with my thoughts, you have awoken to true communion with the divine.'

She was inconsolable and her sobs increased, 'I have committed the evil that God warned me against.'

'After what you have seen, how can you believe that Enlil or any of us is God?'

'I have seen much through the eyes of that fruit, but it is too much for me to understand, like the images sometimes in my sleep. But our creator provides for us. We must be thankful!' She said as if willing herself to believe again.

'What a thorough brainwashing! But then you two are blank slates upon which any impression can be fixed. I must give you at least a glimmer of truth so you can escape that state of automatic programming,' Ea mumbled, fully aware he was thinking in concepts that were far beyond her.

He now addressed her more directly, 'If he is truly God, then he must have created everything. Then who created Enlil?'

'He created himself. And he is "goodness".' Eve was not so certain.

'If he created everything and himself then he must also *be* everything. If so, then he must also be me and you. And if he is "goodness", then with him being everything there cannot be anything that is "not good".'

'You confuse me. Our Father was right. You are trying to divert me with your foolish words, just as you tempted me to lie with you!' she accused, putting her hands to her ears and averting his eyes in an attempt to block out his presence.

'No. Listen. In the light you just saw lies your only hope, and while remnants are still within your system, remember and reflect on this. If God exists, then by definition *it* must be perfect. Otherwise *it* cannot claim to be God – only a lesser power. Now, if God is everything and perfect, can there be anything that is evil and not perfect?'

'No.' Eve's answer was robotic, goaded by his logic in the dissipating influence of the Mandala's drug.

Ea pressed on, 'What appears to us now as evil is nevertheless part of that perfection just as you saw in that vision – eternity changing from good to evil and back in an everlasting cycle of death and re-creation. It is only from your mortal perspective or "time", that something can be considered evil.'

'Are we not immortal?' Eve asked in astonishment, more concerned with that revelation than any of this god's confusing philosophy.

'No, you are not immortal. You are equally part of that life cycle you see around you, but with an unnaturally long lifespan with manna from the Tree of Life. Imprint that illumination upon your memory and hand it down to your heirs - before your mind is forever closed by my brother and you return to that state of waking sleep he has cast over you and your husband.'

So much insight and adventure was overwhelming. The excitement was stimulating, but it also left Eve feeling inadequate and was fast being relegated to an aberrant dream.

'I am becoming quivery. I miss Adam's warmth and understanding. Maybe he can help me interpret this very strange... thing.'

She picked up to rush home, leaving Ea with the consequences of his actions.

An enlightened yet bewildered Eve returned via the forbidden tree. The fading of the drug simultaneously reduced her paranoia, and while the memory of what she learnt dissipated, understanding remained and continued hatching.

Adam had sensed the growing distance in his wife. Once a delightful extension of himself, providing identity and purpose in her clinging, she lately grew more daring and independent - posing a vague and source-less threat.

Yet in the recesses of his mind, he recalled such faculties - she was just manifesting his once harboured thoughts. But since God took her from his rib, he felt himself solidifying, becoming more staid, responsible, dutiful and pragmatic, while she engaged in her flights of fancy. Much as he revelled in his new sense of masculinity, he missed that duality he once contained.

'What has kept you away for so long?' He questioned upon her return, as if whining.

Her air of tranquil confidence - even contentment - was puzzling,

'Adam, my husband, it is so wonderful to see you again!' Her greeting smile dissolved him briefly, but he immediately withdrew in discomfort at its unfamiliar suggestiveness.

Her expansiveness was beyond even *her* liberal character, 'I have learnt so much of the nature of the world and have experienced such pleasures that I never dreamt existed. I feel I have been recreated afresh. So many questions cleared!' An ecstatic Eve exclaimed.

She proceeded to try and explain all that she had learnt, but the retelling was frustratingly tortuous and incomprehensible.

'I so wish you to share my discovery...Let me take you on that wonderful adventure,' she pleaded, attempting to take his hand, the other remaining hidden.

A disturbed Adam pulled away and interrogated her, 'Where did you learn all this?'

'From another god, who appeared to me in the night as a serpent and showed me the way of the world,' she responded, still in a state of excitement, exposing one of the two scarlet fruits she had gathered on returning.

'Put that away woman! God fiercely instructed not to touch that fruit or venture into such matters. I can't imagine what he would do if he learns of your disobedience.' He looked about fearfully.

But Eve, undeterred and eager to share her experience, took a sensuous bite at the fruit and offered it up to him, taking hold of his mild arousal and manipulating him with instinctual art to his full proportions,

'See, no harm comes upon us, and with this, we can know like the gods. Enlil too must be tired of his endless lectures. He hasn't visited for years,' she reassured.

Adam, by now mesmerised by the effect of her manipulation and aroused by her suggestion, succumbed, biting viciously into the fruit as she knelt before him to engulf him in her mouth.

This time she was in control and she now relished guiding her husband. Her titillation, even if less intense in passion, was more fulfilling, seeing the effects of her ministrations on him. His ardour enhanced by the fruit's narcotic, he thrust violently at her face.

Eve, disengaging, reclined herself under him to further enhance his sense of domination while guiding him into her. His passion previously frustrated by fear of retribution, a now unleashed Adam took her in delightful savagery.

Smaller than the god in dimension, he was still disproportionately larger than the terrestrial beasts. No docile female beast that submit with nonchalance and submission, she played the eager participant. And whereas Ea had been masterful and technical in his servicing, Adam was raw passion.

She revelled in her femininity—the power it had to bring out his bestial savagery, losing that steadfast control, and trying to damage her. That aggression only heightened her stimulation and pleasure. His uninhibited violence was assuring, a sense of dominion. And his utter abandon at the time of climax gave her shudders of absolute wantonness - secure with his desire, love, and devotion.

His spiritual epiphany under the hallucinogen was inferior to her initiation - Eve's acumen being far less than Ea's expansive consciousness. The melding less potent, Adam's impressions were thus scattered and less robust.

As was the nature of the Mandala and its lure to addiction, the enlightenment was fleeting. Like all experience, its value was in the memory. And like a good memory, it embellished with time and absence, increasing the yearning for repetition.

Yet for now, with his intensity spent and in post-coital depression, the spider of guilt crawled upon him as it had on her, sending Adam into a deep funk.

'What have you done, woman? You have tempted me to sin and depravity. Get away from me!' he cried in increasing disgust.

Eve was nonplussed by her partner's rejection and about face. From ardent and passionate lover, he had turned to revulsion and disparagement. Whereas she had given up to exhilarated languishment, the ecstasy of her orgasm now turned itself against her while the drug also dispersed.

Observing his aversion, she was suddenly aware of her raw exposure, her open exhibitionism turning to inhibited embarrassment at her nakedness.

Adam had long been curious about the artificial objects peering amongst the trees—alien in that natural environment. That speculation now turned to a suspicion that they were the eyes of God, detached and multiplied. Where before he regarded those lenses as a protective and reassuring talisman, the garden now became a multi-eyed beast—something from which to hide.

'Cover yourself, woman, lest other eyes prey upon you.' Though what he was ashamed of, he was not quite sure.

The fruit having given a glimpse into the eternal mind, the couple felt liberated from the veil of ignorance - nor could they ever return to that state of innocence. But that was not reassuring. If anything, rather than answers, it multiplied the questions. Their anxiety grew, overlaid by Enlil's obvious power, and the two paradoxical truths left them poised over the abyss between intuitive truth and dogmatic doctrine.

Recognising their physiological differences and in the absence of alternatives, they stripped the large leaves of nearby trees to cover their sexuality, as if in doing so, their transgression would be masked.

But in a vestige of intuition, Eve gathered up the other uneaten fruit, placing it in a canister. She hid it in a rock opening in their cave where she stored other strange trinkets she occasionally found on forays around Eden.

CHAPTER SEVENTEEN

Atlantis—c. 2,500 A.D. (Ante Diluvium) – 10,500 B.C.E.

The glacial conditions that greeted the Marduks when they arrived on the planet some 63,000 years earlier had long dissipated, the climate waxing and waning in the intervening millennia. The present freeze was causing the icy shells around the poles to creep further than ever.

From *Nibiru* Gabriel had observed that immense accumulation, especially the antipodean ice, increasing with each Age, exaggerating the tilt of the planet's axis and the seasonal cycles. He began to feel vaguely uneasy.

The absence of her monthly flow was less than reassuring to Eve, particularly as it was accompanied by a daily bout of nausea.

'I feel God is already punishing me for my transgression, each day making me ill to remind me,' she confessed anxiously to her mate.

But she guessed at the cause and inwardly she celebrated. By a leap of understanding, she connected her earlier sinfulness to her condition, and though not quite certain, she knew whose seed had quickened. As life burgeoned within, her celestial memories from the drug faded.

Now is for preparation to welcome our gift to this world. The heavens can wait.

Adam, recognised her condition from observing the wildlife. Dumbstruck by their good fortune, his enthusiasm was overshadowed by panic that their crime would soon be evident. A sudden explosion of fire and smoke that billowed from Mount Dilmun in the distant northeast only made his anxiety peak.

'God is angry at our sin in making this cub!' he cried in dismay. 'Can we destroy it?'

Eve's instincts were jolted. 'Never! Go and whimper to your lord, but I will fight for its existence even if I must give up my own!' She shot back.

What was once a convivial relationship, open and trusting in all their personal thoughts, now took on an element of guile. Nevertheless, mutual guilt inspired a complicity that amalgamated their relationship.

Irania was more than just bored as she addressed her son at his palace overlooking Eridu,

'Is this the extent of your ambition – overseeing a handful of farmers, redundant technicians and guardians turned even more slothful by human slaves doing everything? Even our Tartarus 'miners' hardly earn the name any longer. And who decided to clothe those savages anyway – their nakedness is less erotic than dead fish! She complained, irritation mounting with each sentence.

'Well, what would you have me do? As even Ea indicated, a stagnant population provides no impetus for growth.' Enlil sighed, avoiding the stare of his close confidant Raphael, the third member present.

'Indeed, that little demon Ea *did* predict this,' Irania admitted. 'he also suggested the hybrids could be a solution. Now, I can understand if *they* needed to be clothed!'

'I haven't paid much attention to them for some time – since that little eruption of Mount Dilmun.' Enlil confessed and diverted to that incident, 'Hah, that little cherry bomb sent the humans into paroxysms - seeking forgiveness, confessing unknown wrongs and begging me to stop it – which I did of course, timed to Gabriel's seismic predictions.'

Irania stepped up her mockery, 'Wonderful - fulfilled by the adoration of abominables! Well, at least they're multiplying – faster than we can count. They'll overrun this island soon! Well... what about the hybrids?'

'I am reconsidering whether to artificially induce our seed or allow the couple to procreate on their own.'

'Why introduce more Marduk seed when they have the best that Marduk has to offer?' She winked.

Raphael's eyes darted between mother and son, not liking the direction of discussion, he interjected, 'Introducing more Marduk genes will lead to integration and ultimately the elimination of all pure-bloods. And if let loose, they will likely mix with humans, who are advancing rapidly, as proved by some of our servants.'

'We *could* keep the hybrids isolated in Eden,' Irania replied.

Enlil was not convinced. 'Yes, but if they reproduce, that habitable space in Eden is too limited.'

Irania became more enthused, 'All right, then while Adam's brood expands, we can replace our human servants with the godling hybrids, devoting this continent to only Marduks and hybrids - truly deserving its name Atlantis!'

Enlil looked to Raphael and inclining his head at her astute idea, encouraging Irania to add, 'As you recall, Ea failed to sterilise Eve, and she is already at puberty. You could impregnate her. The resulting heirs would be the nearest to pure-blooded Marduks – all from *our* family lineage!' she beamed jubilantly, highlighting her twinkling amethyst eyes.

Maintaining his gaze at the Healing Institute chief, Enlil raised one eyebrow this time as a query.

Fully supportive Raphael nevertheless cautioned, 'to approach her physically would corrupt your very precepts and diminish their belief in your omnipotence. But I could do it artificially, appearing as a "divine conception", gaining further reverence in their naivety.'

'How risky would it be for any future progeny to reintroduce my seed?'

'A little, but not much more than a half-sibling coupling, which so far has only provided positive results...' Raphael nodded deprecatingly at the queen. 'But we could always exterminate any defective births that might arise in future.'

'Speaking of half-siblings,' Irania interjected while smiling appreciatively at Raphael's implied compliment. 'What about your bloodline on the Marduk side? If your subjects multiply it's best you cement your claim to the throne. I hear our Nin's closeness to her elder brother may be more than filial. You know what that could mean for future heirs.'

'She's too level headed to marry such an unreliable and fickle type as Ea. He's just a father figure. And he's even older than you!' He said, failing to observe his mother's flinch,

'I'll attend to that later. Meanwhile, I'd better check on my godlings and see how the mother of my future child is getting along,' Enlil chortled.

Finding the couple absent from their cave, Enlil scanned through the recordings. There was little to observe, the pair seemingly evading the planted 'eyes'. However, he traced earlier movements and hounded them.

Enlil speculated as the cameras panned throughout Eden and his voice barked for them to come out, *the woman is a feisty one. Perhaps with the introduction of my child, she'll be less recalcitrant. It's a pity Raphael spoilt the fun, insisting on the artificial approach!*

Mystified by Enlil's voice uncannily guessing wherever they hid, the pair finally relented to the inevitable confrontation, appearing out of the thick brush.

'Why do you hide from me, and why do you now cover yourself before me?' Enlil's apparition roared and shook his sceptre, inspecting their attempts at clothing.

I thought you knew everything? Eve wondered.

'We wished to cover our nakedness from you,' Adam answered sheepishly.

Just as you cover yourself from us! Eve kept that thought also to herself.

'And how came you to know that you were naked?' Enlil's eyes matched his infuriated voice upon noticing her pregnancy. He seemed focused on the husband, appearing wary of the woman's apparent confidence, defiance even.

Adam, breaking down immediately at the onslaught, was quick to implicate his partner and grovelled, 'It was the wife you gave me, Lord. I tried to warn and avoid her advances, fearing your wrath, but she would not listen.'

Forced to turn his attention to her, Enlil spewed his fury, 'What dared you disobey me, woman?'

Remembering the other god of similar might, Eve, though still fearful, answered openly, 'Another god, appearing like a serpent, showed me through the fruit, the many wonders of this world and the many possibilities we possess,' she omitted the seduction.

'You ate from the forbidden tree!' He shuddered in rage, his divine mantle slipping as he fought to regain control, 'and there is no other God! What impostor is this? Never mind, I can guess, and I will deal with him. You . . . and he will regret this sin for eternity!' Enlil paused again, collecting his thoughts.

His voice now boomed again – having raised the speaker volume for dramatic effect - causing the couple to cower in fear as he vented his vengeance at them, frustrated by the inability to aim it at his absent brother,

'I warned you of the consequences of satisfying your curiosities and consuming your passions. Forsaking innocence you have proved disloyal and untrustworthy, thus I can no longer hold you fully under My aegis. As fascination from your new-found knowledge wears off soon you will learn how frightening it is outside of Eden!' Enlil had regained his confidence. His hopes were dashed, but his divinity intact.

'You will depart this garden and fend for yourself, no longer fed from the Tree of Life. You clearly cannot handle the responsibilities that come with eternal life, thus unworthy of communion with us.

'As for the Mandala, that abominable tree never belonged here. Both heavenly trees will be removed forever from this world.'

Adam grovelled. 'Lord, my wife is about to bear a calf. How will we live alone and on what shall we survive? You have already warned us of the humans. Without your protection, they will kill and perhaps eat us!'

Enlil momentarily checked his anger. Irania's plan could at least partly proceed, the hybrids were procreating, perpetuating *his* seed. Fearing for their safety, and to ensure the success of their progeny, he relented,

'You will go West of Eden, separated from the humans by the canyons of Mount Dilmun, until I drive them from this land. I will prepare you a suitable cave there.'

But with their inexperience and gullibility he realised that may not be sufficient to ensure their protection.

'Remain here until I return.' Enlil said, switching off the cameras while he sent a guardian to retrieve some clothing.

Switching on the projectors again, he said, 'I am a merciful god and I will give you this sceptre as sign of my new covenant with you – it will signify to all mankind that your heirs are to inherit kingship of your kind on earth. I will show you how to wield its power, which also depends on its handlers' aptitude.'

Enlil began mimicking the simple movements to employ the staff's Vril power, and how it could be sheathed in rock just like the Sword of Destiny. The lesson was long enough for the guardian to return.

He next displayed two multicoloured tunics of synthetic fibre – *skoop* pilot outfits for the cold of high altitude - with attachments containing various utility gadgets.

'These 'skins' will do more than cover your nakedness, protecting you also from the elements until you become acclimatised. For without the manna, you will be more sensitive to temperature. They operate by touching these buttons, but use them sparingly, lest they lose their power, which can no longer be replenished. These items will await you in your new cave.'

Casting his eyes over Eve, Enlil's rage returned,

'And you, woman, I see you are already about to bear the consequences of your sin. Your sex will be cursed forever with the pain of delivering children! Yet they will be drawn to that yoke forever after.

'But remember this, you are not to lie with those sons and daughters of man, - the humans – or their seed will contaminate yours and rob your claim as sons of God.'

Returning to Eridu, Enlil addressed the Council,
'This defiance is . . .' And after a timed long pause for melodrama and in loud voice to highlight it '. . . Unforgivable!'

From the godlings' adult appearance many Marduks had seen some opportunity for their kind. And thus, Ea was uncontrite,

'But inevitable, were you planning to keep them as pets or as curiosity, cocooned in their ignorance forever? Many agree, this is our species' only hope. And how long did you expect to protect the adams' innocence of sex?'

Enlil rasped in restrained fury. 'This is not just about protecting their fragile innocence, you imbecile! Can't you see that by opening their eyes, they will no longer be controllable? Their love of us is only due to their reverence and fear. What purpose do you think they can serve now by unleashing their independent thought – and doubt?'

'I note their love is of *you* not *us*. And how were they to advance if just fed your censored and programmed dogma?' Ea replied a little less confidently, knowing that programmed slaves were exactly what many in Council wanted.

'We don't need thinkers!' shouted Enlil. 'We have far more capability! We need their hands, not their puny brains!'

'Those presently puny brains have as much capacity as ours. The only thing missing is experience. Freedom of thought is a precondition for evolving consciousness. Look what happened to the ogres.' Ea's confidence returned with the poignancy of his argument.

Enlil was equally emphatic, 'Freedom is simply a perception. Unexposed in Eden, our hybrids absolutely believed they were free. They are too immature to deal with self-reliance, needing direction and clearly defined goals – like a God can provide. You have not liberated them. You have awakened despair—that they can never be truly free but responsible for their actions. As a result, we must defer their immortality!'

Ea countered, 'Eve was less innocent than you might have believed, awake to the present incongruity of her role in nature and your prohibition of their mating! And I already limited her span to the hominid rate of deterioration.'

'Under whose authority?' Enlil again exploded.

'I just allowed natural forces to follow their course. In any case, only the radiation bath can prolong life and that would mean exposing our existence. Their limited lives will drive them faster – under a shorter time frame for achievement. Let *them* work out how to overcome it for themselves and achieve immortality by their own devices . . .' Ea tried explaining.

Uriel cut in to break the impasse. '...Yes, our lack of progress seems to indicate that immortality diminishes self-expression.'

'Well, whatever the philosophical ramifications,' hawkish Raphael interjected, 'we must not degrade our species and corrupt our bloodline. They must be isolated, multiplying as an inferior species.'

'Ha! No matter how we pretend otherwise, we need their race, not just as servants but as brethren to augment our own diminishing souls.' Ea derided.

'Do you say that from guilt that the woman may be pregnant with *your* offspring? How else could you have known of the woman's loss of innocence and she know how to seduce her husband?' Enlil denounced.

Amongst the furore erupting from that suggestion, Irania's amethyst eyes flashed playfully, 'Why Ea, I never thought you had it in you!' She smirked in satisfaction and looked pointedly at Nin.'

Ea maintained defiance—which was all but an admission of guilt and a mighty mistake, 'It was part of her education. As for the child, I had no intention, and we can't be sure yet that it is mine, but . . .'

Nin stared at her consort, her expression inscrutable, while Enlil thundered, 'You dare to try and justify?' He turned to oratory while commanding,

'Just another example of my brother's rebellion, comrades of Council! This experiment is a failure, and there should be no further interaction with our kind. Nazarel, remove that accursed tree, and also the other one to deprive them of learning to extract its manna. I have expelled them west of Eden, where Michael is hereby ordered to expand the electronic fencing used to block the human tribes in the North and East. Marduk law counts the foetus as sentient so we cannot terminate the pregnancy. But with luck, she will abort. As for my brother, his actions have forever invalidated any future claim to Marduk leadership. What says Council?'

Raphael led the 'ayes' that followed unanimously, even Nin's.

Enlil now addressed Ea directly with his sentence,

'You continually disregard Council laws and resolutions! As you clearly do not intend to follow our society's dictates, you are hereby banished from Atlantis and will remove yourself from any further contact with Adam or any of his ilk. You may remain in Tartarus, aptly named for such asylum. If you interfere in our decisions again, you will be denied any Marduk facility or equipment, meaning also your very own youth fountain. Nevertheless, you may retain your seat at this Council to represent those in Tartarus, but only upon our invitation - for matters that might affect all Marduks.'

Nin's geneticist mind flashed to the relative benefits and disadvantages of adding more genetic diversity to the hybrid race than just Enlil's seed. However, personal feelings took over,

What an imbecile, I didn't even consider the possibility! But why did the secrecy of our relationship not bother me? Why does his betrayal not dismay me so much now? Was our sexual ambivalence his fault? Or just lack of chemistry? Without intimacy, sex is reduced to lust, and without sex, intimacy is reduced to friendship.

The sting was more to her pride, recalling her mother's similar 'disposal' by Jova - than any betrayal or deprivation. But with all that rationality, still, it hurt.

At the same time, she understood the raging internal passion she inherited from this fecund planet was not for Ea - perhaps never to be expressed.

The meeting had ended and she was unaware Enlil had moved beside her,

'It's so unfortunate he can't employ that mind to more productive activity. But surely you don't intend to accompany that criminal back to the jungle?' He said acting abject as if in sympathy, 'you know how much I admire you. Our union would go a long way towards mending our community and salving both our spirits. Stay here and think on my proposal.'

A proposal? At a time like this? Salving our spirits? He's so self-absorbed, utterly transparent!

Yet Nin astounded herself at considering the offer. *If not intimacy, perhaps at least gratification – but hardly the occasion to entertain such ideas.*

'I'll think on it,' she replied and moved away.

CHAPTER EIGHTEEN

Nazarel addressed his frustration to Uriel and Raphael in an impromptu meeting of the three Councillors,

'I'm glad we don't have to pander to Adam's delusion as 'Lord of Eden' – serving his food and other whims. But when can we expect these slaves he's supposed to procreate? My workers are complaining things are going backwards. At least before, we had the ogres and then human labourers. But since reducing the human population in Atlantis to a few villages, the remainder are only interested in working in the city, now demanding better conditions in the fields.'

Pre-empting Doctor Raphael's unending protests at the hybirds, Uriel tried to pacify the farmer, 'Well, the hybrids are not like your rabbits. Yet I realise few technicians or guardians are interested in agriculture or mining or indeed any other menial labour. And I worry they are increasingly turning any talents to onscreen games of fantasy. I suppose it's lucky the lack of available terminals limits their slothfulness'

However, Nazarel continued his gripe,

'Anyway, even if the humans are smaller than the adams, they are hardier and more adapted to the rugged environment than those mollycoddled outcasts from Eden. And training them is a great improvement on their hominid ancestors. We should allow them to interbreed with those hybrids.'

Again, Uriel cut off hawkish Raphael's intended objection and shrugged, 'I doubt Enlil would go along with that contamination of his seed. Their progeny are right now his only direct descendants, although Ea might have thrown sand in his machinations.'

Forced to fend for himself, Adam was disconsolate, railing against his woman. Eve, abandoned by all the males she ever knew, and whose Mandala experience was now a hazy recollection, held herself responsible and took her husband's rebuke almost willingly as punishment for her depravity.

I wish I could remember all I learnt from that forbidden fruit, opening my eyes to so much. Though cast into the wilderness and fearful for our future, I am glad for the experience – feeling so much more than when asleep in Eden. I wonder if the remnant I stashed away still holds its power? I'm scared to try it on my own, and Adam cowers at even the memory of that communion. Yet, he has strength and conviction, his fear is as much for me and the calf I carry in my belly.

He is more handsome than even the snake god in a rugged sort of way - resembling our Lord Enlil. I hope my calf will be a man, more like him than me. However, I will teach him to be vigilant for the truth.

None of those considerations of course inhibited Adam from taking her in lust, 'Our Lord ordered us to go forth and multiply!' he would argue each time.

But she shied away when her stomach protruded, warning him of possible damage to what was growing inside her.

And soon, Eve delivered a boy they named Cain. Upon his birth, all her previous trials disappeared into insignificance, and she doted on him to the exclusion of all else.

'My Lord has given to me a man!' Eve exclaimed as she laid eyes on the baby, even if inwardly unsure as to which of her three 'lords' she referred.

'We must thank the Father for this wonder despite our grievous sin.' Adam marvelled upon sight of their firstborn.

Eve thought better than to voice her doubts about that fatherhood.

But life in banishment chafed at Adam, particularly unfamiliar with the demands of an infant, who from the onset was ornery and disagreeable.

'Due to your disobedience, I am reduced to foraging for paltry rodents and the sparse grains from this barren land. Perhaps also, you would not have produced such a cranky son.' He chided his wife, craving a return to their halcyon days in Eden.

Eve remained silent, fully content with her son Cain.

'I'm sure there must be an easier way.' The boy suggested.

'Your mewling never ends. Just pick up those logs, you good for nothing!' Adam took any opportunity to scold the eleven-year-old.

Cain grew up in that austere and remorseful environment, absorbing the guilt, fear and increasing repugnancy of his father in punishment for an unknown crime.

Upon the boy's development and display of his character, the father's original pride turned increasingly to suspicion. It hadn't yet crossed Adam's mind how Eve learned her sexual art.

And to spite her personal fulfilment, he relied on shame as excuse for his growing prejudice against their son,

'He shows none of my markings – more damnation from your corruption!'

The more the mother spoiled, the more the father turned averse, ultimately leading the son to ignore Adam.

In time and in progression, Eve delivered two female children: Cassandra and Anthea respectively, followed by another boy they called Abel. And as they all matured, Cain's dissimilarities became more manifest, highlighted by his tall, gangly frame, copper-red locks, and large blue green eyes.

Indifferent to the birth of his sisters, Cain was disturbed by the subsequent birth of his younger brother, Abel. Unlike the revulsion aimed at him, Adam, though pleased with his daughters, acted overjoyed at the appearance of his second son.

And besides the obvious physical dissemblance, most damning was Cain's acute intellect, which he often sharpened against his father.

'Why do you continue to inhabit that dank, smelly cave when I have constructed you a house?' he asked, exasperated at Adam's obstinacy and pointing to the shack he built with light and air apertures, copied from Eden's barns.

'If the Lord had intended us to live in such a dwelling, he would have provided us with one from the beginning,' was Adam's stock response to issues he couldn't explain.

'At least do it for my mother's health!! And why do you continue carrying those bales, one by one on your back? You can use the large cart with the discs I carved for its legs? And do you also dismiss catching fish—just because it was not available in Eden? You nanocephalous niblick!' Cain shouted in frustration at his dense father, using his facility for coining new words as amusement. He practiced it on his dimwit brother Abel as well.

Aware of intended insult but clueless to its meaning, Adam was unflappable, 'God willed when he banished us, that our work must be carried with the sweat of our brow and the strength of our backs. It is punishment for our disobedience. Otherwise he would have given us the necessary tools. It should serve as a lesson to you so the Father will also bestow gifts to you alike your brother.'

'Yet this god employs devices like in Eden and flying carts I have seen in the distance. I'm sure he didn't intend us to maintain ignorance, for why else would he create us with intellect - which is in a way also a tool?'

'That is exactly what our Father intended! Knowledge is the root of evil, as he has so well reminded me. It is God's privilege.'

'It sounds like your lord enjoys our drudgery and slavery bent on maintaining our ignorance and keeping us enslaved!'

'Indeed, we were created to glorify and worship Him.'

'And not to think at all?'

'Do not dare question the Lord! We must trust in him.'

'And why should we trust him? After all, he's the one who banished us here, away from his Eden.'

'Silence! Lest God hears your blasphemy.'

'Better the risk and gain of my blasphemy to the eternal pain and hardship of your stupidity! You great whopping twig!'

Eve finally convinced Adam to move into Cain's artificial shack, and thereafter gave birth to four more daughters. With assistance from the growing brood, the family's conditions improved and the couple settled into contentment, the withdrawal from Eden relegated to nostalgia more than addiction. But as his family grew, Adam's distrust of Cain amplified.

'God appears more benevolent to us with the birth of each of our children. But I wonder at Cain. He is very different and contrary. And he is so skinny, so unsuited to the rigours of the field. Even the Lord seems to shun him,' Adam grumbled to his wife as she suckled the latest infant - omitting Cain's superior intellect.

Reminded of her seducer's similar eyes to Cain, Eve stayed mute, changing the subject to argue back,

'He endured the hard times much more than those who followed, with no encouragement at all from you or Enlil. Can you blame him for being cynical and unfriendly? Cain is very clever, look how he finds new tools to make his work and our lives easier.'

'Hush, woman, do not call God by his name. But Cain is deviant and lazy. His fair skin is a sign that he spends little time in the fields. He does not listen to my teachings, and he does not worship the Father as he should.'

Yes, Cain uses his mind, not his body. Abel is slower and more docile, but he knows how to curry favour. Eve kept those thoughts to herself.

Adam pushed his point, 'Strong and muscular Abel is so much more agreeable, reliable and respectful, which is why our Father now looks upon us more favourably.'

Oh really? what has Enlil done for us lately? Eve was in no mood for trivial arguments and remained silent. But she continued to muse, *and his appearances seem to have been restricted to within our cave. Can he no longer project himself elsewhere like he did in Eden?*

The dark-haired older daughters were olive-complexioned. Elder, lithe Cassandra was impressed by Cain's inventiveness and appreciated his wit and acerbic humour, becoming his sole companion and confidante. Taller, more proportional and with dark sapphire eyes bordering on violet, she grew more alluringly sensual in aspect than her sister. Younger Anthea, buxom and curvaceous - with Eve's blue-grey eyes and auburn hair - was better described as pretty and demure, happy in her domestic duties.

Both were naturally fun loving and gregarious, relishing the attention of Marduk farmers and guardian patrollers from across the Eden barrier. Unlike the cool, calculated Marduk goddesses, Adam's daughters were positively lascivious.

However, Eden's lengthy fencing and the western Pichon River kept human tribes at distance from Enlil's isolated godlings. Yet venturesome Cain learned to swim that river and circumvented the garden in the north, sowing his seed among human females who were happy to accommodate the swanky demigod.

Brainwashed Abel had no such imagination, and frustration turned his eye towards his sisters.

Irania paid her son an infrequent visit. Raphael, as usual stood beside the king as if trying to replicate Uriel's role as official royal Counsellor.

Doesn't he have some healing or something to do at the Institute instead of hanging around my son like a bad smell? Irania thought to herself, frustrated by the doctor's presence, preventing private time with her son.

And she was further interrupted by the arrival of General Michael and the farmer Nazarel who came to complain.

Michael opened in his typical glum monotone, 'Sire, Eden's electronic fencing is malfunctioning. Humans are trespassing.'

Nazarel took over, colouring in the General's less than enlightening report, 'At first I didn't mind those humans sneaking in and stealing the occasional lamb or fruit from Eden and even seed for their own plots. But it's now becoming a menace, and with our once exclusively servant village having multiplied, we may soon have to buy our food from *them!*'

More concerned about the social implications, Enlil complained, 'Those mutant hominids are proliferating like rodents! We relocated almost the entire population to northern Gondwanaland only a thousand or so years ago! I don't want them gaining access to our godlings.'

It was clear none of them were aware of Cain's escapades.

Raphael concurred. 'Yes, I suppose it's to be expected given their only decades long lives and limited procreation time. But the two races are quite distinct and Adam's superior kind would not condescend to interracial procreation . . .'

Irania cut in, 'Well, I'm not sure the godlings share your elitist xenophobia. And there's more to sex than just procreation. You should try it sometime,' she taunted Raphael, 'And some of our comelier servant women have caused second glances even from our Marduk males. Marduk females find the men a little wanting in stature and other attributes, but the adams, well...' Her exaggerated, prurient wink was intentionally provocative.

Nazarel dismissed the bantering, following up, 'on that count now that humans do most work, our disengaged farmers and guardians have turned to more sensual pleasures and perversions. Many have already seduced the daughters of Adam, bribing the father with animals from Eden flock and the girls with trinkets.'

Enlil scowled, 'It appears sexual urges have taken precedence and despite all my efforts, my line is becoming contaminated – already obvious by more than that reprobate Cain's appearance.'

Yet he seemed resigned to the realities, as if somewhat tiring of the hybrids after being hijacked by Ea from producing Eve's child, 'but we must prevent godling procreation with those aboriginals. It would ruin any plans for them!'

'Sire, your indoctrination and Adam's dread of any further retribution, will I'm sure keep them in check.' Raphael retorted, undaunted by Irania's earlier sarcasm, his latest naivety causing her to throw up arms in resignation.

'Yes, guilt is a powerful tool, at every opportunity I make sure to rub in their character flaws.' Enlil chuckled.

However, catching the expectation in Nazarel's natural eye, he was reminded of the farmer's appeal and decided on a comprehensive solution,

'At least the godlings will multiply faster and we can soon start engaging them to replace the human servants, which I will allow a few more as temporary workers from Gondwanaland until then.

'Your offerings are excellent, young Abel. As usual, it's the younger brother who is more talented and deserving,' Enlil congratulated the youth in front of the entire family upon his next appearance at their communal cave. He maintained the chronicle android style of language, which anyway sounded more sacred, in keeping with the burnt offerings he demanded as symbols of worship.

'Cain's are paltry and poor in quality. And bad as they are, we note that he maintains the best for himself,' Enlil was particularly derisive.

'As Abel has proved himself worthy, his heirs will gain kingship of Earth – learning from his father the power within the symbols I gave Adam as elect son of God.'

Adam's firstborn, already disenchanted, had seethed at the god's empty blessings and his family's adulation. Cain had spied his sisters being seduced and treated as nothing more than beasts by his 'angels'. However, the girls never complained about the minor bruising, both building up a treasury of trinkets and devices.

Cain confided to his favourite sister Cassandra, 'I see Enlil's prohibition of our intercourse with the humans doesn't include preventing his angels condescending to lie with our women,'

'Nor has it stopped you finding entertainment amongst those daughters of men.' She arched a conspiring eye, giggling. 'Beware though, you know Enlil has hidden eyes.'

'The gods don't seem so omnipotent to me. Just yesterday, I saw one injure himself in his haste to visit you, when he fell and cut his leg on a rock.'

'Yes, and I had to clean him up and bandage him before he had his way with me. Hah, except for their blue blood, they are no different from you and I.'

'Well, if any of those gods hurt you, let me know and I'll kill him!' His aquamarine eyes bulged in anger at the thought.

'No! They may not be omnipotent, but they are well armed and they wear sometimes impenetrable skins. They are not so brutal really.'

'Let's see those skins protect them from a rock crushed into their skull!'

'Enough of that talk! And you must be off. I am expecting another visitor at any moment now.'

Cain left reluctantly, but did not go far, choosing to stay in close range in case any of his fears should manifest, taking the opportunity to also examine the guardian's boat.

Afterwards, he watched the god scamper away from Cassandra's hut and slink across the Pichon to Eden.

Observing his unhurt sister exit and walk into the forest, he relaxed and began to make his way back home to his stone cabin.

But as he did so, he caught sight of another spy in the bushes. It was his brother, Abel, stalking their sister as she went deeper into the woods.

He had long suspected the clod had already had his way with the similarly dim-witted Anthea and had caught him eyeing their maturing younger sisters. His blood boiled however, at the idea of that oaf laying his hands on the sensibilities of his favourite. And now observing Abel's furtive skulking, sneaking closer to the unsuspecting young woman, he was in no doubt as to his younger brother's intentions.

Not wishing to alarm Cassandra, Cain crept over to his brother stealthily.

'Abel, my brother!' He startled the youth, who turned to face him bewildered and dismayed but made no attempt to disguise his arousal.

Cain continued in inane tone. 'You're very *hard* to keep up with. Can I divert your extension . . . I mean, *attention,* for a minute?'

Abel was spooked but not completely unnerved, 'Ahh, yes. Well, I was just playing at hide-and-seek with our sister up ahead.'

'Yes, I know how you love "hide your meat" with our sisters. But I seek your advice.'

'Well, how can I help?' The oaf was easy to distract.

'I would like to determine how you so utterly capitulate your principles, genuflecting and ingratiating yourself with that mountebank Enlil, garnering so much of his benefaction as well as that of our patriarch.' Cain was intentionally savant.

'Well, I'm not sure I understand your words, but, well if there is any way I can be of assistance to you, my brother, well I would be very happy to help.'

'Well, all your "wells" leave me welling with nausea. Now excuse my inaniloquence and walk with me to my catacomb, and there you can impart your great acuity on this gomerel.' While Enlil had taught them the language of the abstract, he had left it to Adam and his kin to name the physical objects on the planet. Cain was not satisfied with that, and he now revelled in his eloquence, contriving words at his whim, delighting in Abel's stupid gawk.

The brothers strode up the verdant hill that overlooked the fields and orchards that Cain tended. His tall brother at a purposeful clip, Abel struggled to make up the distance.

'Well, to start, you shouldn't... rebel against our father Adam ...and God.' Abel broke the silence, hurrying all the while to keep pace with his sibling. He continued breathlessly, 'Well, you are... only making it worse on yourself, just... well, follow my example... God will look... on you with favour.'

'Facile for you as Enlil has bequeathed his benediction upon you to inherit Adam's kingdom and his divine possessions in the Cave of Treasures. And what philosophy do you intend to promulgate upon your vassals?'

'Well, err, I don't know, just be king like our Adam and follow the teachings of the Lord, I guess.'

Cain stopped momentarily to glare at his brother as if preparing a retort, wondering at the same time whether Abel's understanding was a lucky guess. But he decided to hold his thoughts till they walked the few more steps to the summit of the hill that afforded full view of his farm and distant Eden. Jutting boulders and moraine interspersed the foothills— looking like inanimate guards to his isolated abode. Reaching that small plateau, he stopped to view his fields while waiting for Abel to catch up.

Already smoking with outrage on behalf of his sister, and ablaze with anger at the insults from Lord and family, what he now saw turned him volcanic,

'What's the meaning of this? Your cattle are trampling and gorging on my vegetables!' He pointed at Abel's herd rampantly foraging at his crops.

'Well, brother, it's only a few blades from your fields, which well, appear so plentiful. Well, you can always grow more.'

'They can't grow to grain if they are nipped at the bud! All this while I thought it was the birds from Eden or infertile soil that retarded my harvest!'

'Well, the Lord and our father prefer the meats from my herds to your grains and vegetables, which well, fortify my herds, I am just, well, fulfilling their wishes.' Abel showed no inkling of remorse.

A lifelong accumulation of all the wrongdoings and scorn culminated to bring on Cain's state of mind, which became abnormally and utterly subdued.

He spotted an exquisite jagged boulder, which he collected.

'This would be ideal for slaughtering a sacrifice to God, don't you think?' He said, putting his arms around his stocky shorter brother.

'Yes, but well, Adam's sceptre makes a much clean…'

It began with a single calculated blow to the back of Abel's head. Red fluid that spouted from the ear to ear split, looked so much like Abel's lamb offering to Enlil. Encouraged by that emblem of sacrifice, Cain decided that this offering should be far more valuable to that bogeyman.

He thus let loose his rampaging spirit to spew all the pent-up resentment into mutilating his brother – each blow indelibly staining the consciousness of his heirs - murder ingrained into their psyche.

CHAPTER NINETEEN

Shtar had finally resigned from Council, and Enlil appointed another lackey arch-guardian, Jeremiel – Nazarel's vintner, to take her place. The slaying of Abel was the only item on the agenda.

Ea was sheepish, summoned from banishment in Tartarus due to the gravity of the crime and, he suspected, to act as scapegoat.

However, Gabriel interrupted with an announcement. 'Sire, I regret to inform that some of the *Nibiru's* componentry is beginning to fail. For now, we are able to make repairs, but I fear for the future.'

Unable to understand the implications, the Council sat blank-faced. Enlil too had his priority,

'We hear you Captain, but as it seems any emergency has been circumvented, we will deal with the issue later.'

'Yes sire, but…' Gabriel tried to explain.

'…Meanwhile there is an important issue to attend to here on Earth.' With that dismissal Enlil proceeded,

'The hybrid has committed murder, without even provocation,' Enlil's voice reverberated within the muted gathering. He paused and cast his eyes over each member individually to allow the horror to sink, 'The capacity to slay their fellows by the humans has been inherited by our hybrids.' He managed to exhibit disgust and gloating simultaneously, continuing with his rhetoric,

'What's even more disturbing is that it has been carried out not by a legitimate son of Adam but by a bastard of one of our own. Is it perhaps influence from the unconstrained and libertarian beliefs of his heretical father?' He glared at Ea, who averted his eyes. 'What say you now? Do you still hold on to your "enlightened" advocacy of wanton freedom and unfettered knowledge?'

Even Uriel sat with up-cast, vacant eyes, obviously embarrassed and no longer sure of his concessions towards the elder brother.

Ea appeared loath to speak, but the Council was silent, expecting a response, which he finally offered,

'I could not possibly condone or make excuse for that despicable act, though I can guess at the frustration that led to it. And I know that most of you believe that it's a result of allowing intelligence to run unchecked. But then, the rest of Adam's rapidly growing family appear unaffected.'

'Exactly! The others are from Adam and adhere to my doctrine!' Enlil rejoiced, sweeping the room as if expecting acclaim.

'From my interacting with the woman, they are not as docile as we may think. They follow your dogma only from fear.' Ea protested weakly.

'Obviously! And it's been carefully calculated that way! If not for your obvious distance in Tartarus, I would have said that you had a hand in this.' Enlil's taunt was followed by a hubbub of assent. But Ea was steadfast,

'We tell the humans they are free. But the frustration of that contradiction between your imposed desires and their natural ones...'

'...You say you make no excuse, but already you are justifying that bastard's actions,' Enlil cut into his brother's lecture. Raphael's twitching nods indicated his vigorous support, shared by most.

Enlil hadn't finished, 'Should we let them just run free, with no guidance or discipline, to take whatever action they desire and act upon anything that pleases them? What chaos! What a catastrophe! And to what end?'

'How can any species progress otherwise?' Ea's question caused some to ponder, and Irania threw him a reluctant nod.

'Of course!' Enlil shouted, as if the answer was obvious to all. 'Pleasure simply leads to the desire for more pleasure and ultimately to corruption. Look at that other parallel experiment, those humans, fornicating and defecating wherever they please, using what little intelligence they have towards wanton hedonism. They're all a noisy, filthy, disgusting rabble, and if they weren't still useful, I would order their annihilation – all of them!'

Ea was not to be thwarted. 'But yet, the humans progress, building communities, even developing primitive art and invention. What have your family of devotees achieved except for their adoration of you? Consciousness develops from experience. That is the inexorable purpose of life.'

Michael, the pragmatic general, seemingly bored, steered them towards practicality. 'It is murder. What is the response?'

The council returned to the moment and looked to Enlil for a solution.

'Execution is prohibited. And isolation is not sufficient.' He stated more subdued and looked about the hall for a solution.

'Perhaps I can offer a suggestion.' Uriel had gathered his wits and all heads turned to hear him,

'It is clear that Lord Ea and his followers, even some in Atlantis, insist on their libertarian ways for the hybrids - leading to ongoing vexation for this Council. Therefore, I suggest that we banish the felon and let him find his way amongst the sons of men east of Eden. Let him exercise his intellect uninfluenced and exposed to everything, as suggested by Lord Ea. Meanwhile, the faithful descendants of Adam and future progeny, can remain at the foothills of Atlantis – a race in isolation - following the ministrations of King Enlil. Over time, we can observe them both and make an evaluation of their relative success over time.'

The suggestion was met with approving nods from all.

'It would mean Cain's intermingling, and his bastard roots diluted to insignificance – seems a very agreeable option!' Enlil conceded with some satisfaction.

Enlil's apparition gave the verdict to Adam's entire family beside his former cave.

'Once more, it is with heavy heart I pass judgement and punishment for your crimes.' He cast his eyes over them one by one as if to emphasise their individual guilt. 'Cain, you have committed the most heinous of crimes and thus are not fit to live under my aegis and amongst your kin. Hence, you will remove yourself and live amongst the sons of men in the east beyond Eden...'

While Enlil delivered his lecture, Adam was speculative. Fleeting hints of the forbidden fruit haunted his doubts. *Where was your all-seeing eye? Why were you unable to prevent the slaughter of my Abel?*

'...You will collect your meagre belongings and depart by tomorrow!' Enlil finished pronouncing.

'But how will he survive alone. The humans are growing in number and are jealous of our privilege,' Eve pleaded.

'Those sons of man have already been warned against harming the sons of god. Cain is well marked by his unusual appearance and towers over them.'

The couple was distraught, their family in disarray. While Adam was not sorry to see the last of Cain, and was even glad to be rid of his intellectual barbs, he was torn by the lack of a male heir. Absorbing Enlil's prejudices and curses heaped on Eve, females were corrupt and at best, insignificant.

Even Lilith, the shadowy recollection from infancy that sometimes haunted Adam's dreams turned in his mind from radiant goddess to spectral evil.

Eve had patiently worn the robe of guilt that husband and Father tailored for her. However, the loss of Abel was unbearable - and now Cain. She berated herself for neglecting her firstborn and pandering to Adam's prejudice. Traces of the brilliant serpent god in her son alleviated her concern for his future, but hardly mitigated the lament at his punishment.

As Cain was about to depart, she withdrew to the recesses of their former cave, which now held Adam's divine treasures as well as her own trinkets. There, she withdrew from a hidden ledge, a small intricate canister she had found long ago in Eden, mislaid by one of the gods. Within were the dried remains of the prohibited fruit she had saved after Adam's seduction and subsequent repulse. She hastily threaded a string through a small loop in its cap.

'Take this and keep it close,' she whispered, slipping it over her departing son's head and under his tunic as she hugged him. 'It is too risky to keep here. Try it but once if at all, for it can be dangerous. But I feel its use may have some meaning in the future,' she mimicked how to unscrew it as she gave him a final embrace.

Abel's death meant Enlil's direct line was at a dead end. He had long expected Abel to mate with his sisters, but the subservient little oaf had failed to reproduce. Adam's girls bore children only with the Marduk riff-raff.

Carrying Ea's bloodline, Cain's heritage from the family of Jova was thus much stronger with both sons' bloodlines and Enlil recognised his would be threatened. Re-hatching his original plan - before Ea cuckolded him - he consoled the bereaved parents at the loss of both their sons, and promised,

'Don't despair. Trust in me and I will watch over you. Continue to lie with each other, and I will contrive to give you another,' he soothed, delighted at his choice of words. To Eve, he inquired, 'Do you continue to menstruate?'

'Yes, my lord,' Eve replied, perplexed. 'But . . .'

'Do not fret. I will deliver you another son, chaste and beautiful like your husband. Continue your coupling and soon you will be visited by a guardian angel, who will ensure the seed is planted.'

How is it you know less about me than the snake god I only met once? Eve wondered.

Raphael was excited to be finally called upon to be of service, but had little exposure to the hybrid experiments - mostly carried out by Ea's 'progressives', while he tampered with the humans. He was thus apprehensive and voiced concern to Enlil,

'Our earlier plan meant only fertilizing an egg. I don't have the experience achieved to create a Marduk-human zygote from scratch. I would need to examine and fertilise Eve directly. But is it really necessary sire? After all any boy the couple produces would already inherit your genes like Abel. And Adam may become suspicious, as he was towards Cain.'

'Eve seems to produce only girls. And if you're to go amongst them, we might as well reinforce my input while also ensuring it is male. Otherwise Adam's legitimate line is dead. Almost as bad, we will have to recognise some other hybrid from the couplings of his promiscuous sisters and some Marduk underling. If I can't rule them directly, my line must do so.

'And as for Adam's suspicion, my child will again look like him… and me,' Enlil explained.

'Yes, sire I will get to work on it.'

Having observed and timed her fertility, Raphael announced one evening to Eve as she mourned over Abel's grave, 'I am an arch guardian of the Lord, who sent me to ensure you conceive another male as he promised!' He had emerged from a *skoop,* displaying his Healing Institute's swastika insignia.

How many Gods are there? She asked herself. *And this one has wings to fly here.*

Under the pretext of examining the woman to ensure her fertility, he gave her a knock-out anaesthetic and removed an egg. Taking it to the skoop, he injected Enlil's donated sperm. Scanning it after the combination quickened, he was relieved the first zygote was male.

Reintroducing it into the woman's womb, he declared when she woke, 'the Father in his infinite mercy and love has seen fit for you to conceive a male child. Glory be to God! Rejoice, and give thanks to your benefactor!'

Adam already counted ninety-two heirs since the couple's departure from Eden and the beginning of their mortality. Time before that was incalculable, and hence the couple's actual age was indeterminate. That population included nine daughters, most already grandmothers— Anthea pregnant again with the child of an unknown god. The slight wobbles on her thickening flesh and some flecks that darkened on Cassandra's complexion, were the only hints at the first daughters' maturity.

And, taking its due course, Eve conceived a son to the immense joy and satisfaction of his parents—all three of them.

'You will call him Seth, which in our language means "firstborn", thus confirming his line as the true sons of god with the heritage of kingship,' Enlil insisted to Adam. 'For Cain is the accursed son of the devil.'

'Remain here below Mount Dilmun, following my discipline. And never intermingle with the sons of men or of Cain - equally sinners beyond salvation and who will only corrupt and degrade your kind.'

CHAPTER TWENTY

Uriel's theory that depression resulted from lack of purpose, had struck a chord with Shtar. She sent a message from the nearby port city of Lagash, asking if Shalimar wished to pay a visit and discuss a planned pilgrimage.

Emerging from the s*koop* together with his daughter and after brief greetings, Uriel asked, 'Did you know the Titans have petitioned Lord Ea to be released now that the humans have taken over much of their work?'

The visitors scanned the spectacle of golden sand crescents fringing the bays on either side of her cliff-top shack. The constant crash, sometimes gentle, sometimes ominous, created a soothing rhythm.

'What an ideal backdrop for meditation. Shalimar commented.'

'Yes, yet even here I find no peace,' Shtar lamented, 'but I'm glad about the Titans.'

'Perhaps they can journey with all of us! Shalimar enthused. 'There are many besides me who wish to join you.'

'Really? Without even knowing where we might be going? And giving up any treatments, it's a journey into death.' Shtar warned.

'Not at all!' Shalimar shook her head vehemently. 'It's a journey into life!' We have been on this planet for well over 60,000 terrestrial years. But what have we done? What can we show? We're not living, just existing. Eridu, Tartarus, and now even Lagash caught in routine—titillation only provided by fantasy games, and intrigues from humans and godlings. We treat this planet as a hermitage, cocooned on this isolated island, trying to recreate Marduk's aggrandised memory. Who knows what wonders are out there for us to see and feel? But who cares—we'll be alive!'

Shtar was struck by Shalimar's newfound expressiveness. *Her enthusiasm is infectious. Whereas I am just escaping claustrophobia, Shalimar is embracing her future, however limited. Well, if it's guilt we're trying to assuage or escape, this time it will not be into the frigid eternity of space but the fecund womb of this wondrous planet!*

Indeed, as Shalimar had predicted over 100 wishful pilgrims from Atlantis joined Shtar's departure.

Crossing over to Gondwanaland by barque, they took Ea's earlier path to Tartarus to rally with the Titans.

'Don't you think it would be great exposure?' Lilith was propped on one elbow, fully naked. Her left hand ran over Aigar who had returned after a week spent further south.

'Your exposure is always great!' He smirked, looking her over and responding to her stroking.

'I wasn't talking about this. But I'm glad you missed me so much, as I can see.'

'Well, abstinence makes that part grow stronger.'

Aigar luxuriated in her attention and in turn, he explored her. Tightened by the herbal treatments, the binding and herbal smoking process administered by the Titanides to whom post-natal recovery was second nature, she had quickly regained her shape and texture after giving birth to Adam. As all Marduk females, she removed even the fine, sparse down that fleeced her cleft and appeared raw, exposed in her flaring nakedness.

To Aigar, the entire world could be encapsulated in his arms.

And after about an hour or so of such absorption, she gymnastically flipped over him, legs akimbo and returned to their discussion,

'So what do you think?'

'What a cunning stunt.' He grinned.

'I mean joining Shtar on her escapade. Be *serious!*' Her scold contained an affectionate and lascivious smirk. He loved that she revelled in her exhibitionism as much as he did, 'anyway, there's nothing for us here - or in sterile Atlantis, without even access to my Adam. And the humans proliferating there are rabble, turning Eridu vulgar.'

'It seems immortality leads to immorality. But where does it all end?' He said turning his back to her as if wanting to sleep.

She missed the ending irony but was excited nevertheless, 'Aigar! That actually made sense!'

Earlier, Lilith had gingerly addressed Nin on the subject of Ea's dalliance with the hybrid, Eve,

'Ea takes his own path, I suppose that's either a cause or result of his brilliance' Nin responded, 'and without the passionate rapport you share with Aigar, I knew from the outset that we were never a match - more one of respect and mutual solace.' Nin had explained rather dispassionately, dismissing further discussion.

And now Lilith accompanied her friend to catch up with her Shtar, just arriving from Atlantis.

After brief initial greetings, there was an uncomfortable space between mother and daughter, which Lilith took opportunity to fill,

'We all volunteered so long ago to join Ea, as much to pioneer this planet as to escape Atlantis. Instead, we were shackled to the mines and reluctantly established Tartarus,' Lilith explained to Shtar, 'But even Tartarus appears impermanent, a glorified mining camp. And now relieved by humans, many of our original pioneers have returned to Atlantis. But some of us would love to continue with that initial intent, even if it means forsaking our immortality.'

She felt similar instant rapport with the mother as she had originally with Nin. Unfortunately, mother and daughter suffered the same detachment, causing perhaps the two likes to repel.

Lilith felt sad for both. Their strained relationship was nothing like the scant memory of her own mother. While her father, as guardian captain, was allowed to take their infant daughter as intended future incubator, her mother was left behind. And now Lilith's recollection became much more poignant, recognising her mother's desperate attempts to conceal her despair, pretending jubilation that her young daughter was to go on such an exciting trip.

Those memories added to the sense of sorrow when it came time to bid farewell to Nin, the only real friend she had made besides her soulmate husband.

Along with the already freed Titans, some humans also petitioned for release. With almost unlimited available replacements Ea naturally gave permission— also to the few dwarf trolls and other mutants. But he and Nin were joined in sadness at the departure of his companion,

Aigar and his delightful wife. The loss of Shtar added to the anguish, realising that due to their impending mortality, it might be the last time they would see any of the departing troop.

It was thus a motley group of nearly three hundred that bid farewell to their kind, leaving Tartarus and heading up the unexplored eastern segment of the Afrasian coast.

Shtar was glad to have affable Aigar and lovely Lilith as companions. Despite his silly verbal convolutions, Aigar was a trained guardian, quick and resourceful. And with the Titans, who also found in him a degree of kindred, she had nothing to fear.

Outcast Cain made his way northeast along the Pichon River to the highlands of Mount Dilmun, catching sight of the gleaming city of Eridu in the distance. Its polished marble and granite walls sparkled in daylight. The golden capstone on the central Council Pyramid reflected the afternoon sunlight, projecting a beam back on to the shadow side of the mountain and illuminating the cliff face that danced in its spotlight. The marvel, though impressive, failed to placate Cain's outrage.

I don't know what caused that temporary psychosis in killing Abel. I will miss my mother and Cassandra, but I am glad to escape Adam and his malicious god. How dare they pass judgement on me! The gods may be powerful, but I know their limitations. I will learn and expose their magic. Even the fence they put around Eden is so flimsy, it will be so simple to separate those wires and sneak between them.

The internal diatribe helped work up his courage to break into Eden after occasional skeletons and carcases along that perimeter fencing had made him wary.

Hah! They planted those dead creatures on their weak fencing as scarecrows – like they do with birds in Eden. But I'm no bird! I wonder if their magic comes from that shiny mountainous hut with the yellow metal hat?

His musings were interrupted by a hominid ape, approaching some 200 yards away, apparently with the same intent of breaking into Eden for food. Unsure how to deal with such an animal he hid behind a cleft in the nearby rock face.

The hairy black creature spied some hanging fruit and headed straight for the fence. Reaching out to separate the wires as Cain had intended, he grabbed at the upper rung. And as he did so, a sharp lightning-like crackle discharged from the wires around his fist. After a momentary shudder the animal slumped to the ground, grip still clutching the cable. Smoke, which turned acrid as it reached Cain's nose some thirty yards away, continued to emanate for some minutes from the source of that spark.

Confusion and fear kept Cain rooted and hidden in position.

I'm not sure whom to thank for saving me through the sacrifice of that creature, but I'm sure it is not Enlil. Yet I must beware not to underestimate the power of the gods.

He was unaware for how long the scare had immobilised him before a troop of humans in the company of one of the angels appeared.

How funny those humans look in their uniforms copied to look like the gods' but of coarser material.

He watched fascinated as the angel used an instrument to touch the upper wire that had stricken the hominid. There was no effect. And then he watched the procedure they used to deactivate the fence to remove the dead hominid.

Cain was pensive as he later trudged away from the scene, giving up any immediate aspirations to break into the compound.

Their power is greater than I thought, but it seems to come from those instruments. Did they create them or were they given, just as Enlil handed those treasures my father keeps in his former cave? He speculated as he fiddled with Eve's trinket around his neck.

Soon, scattered hamlets of cave dwellings and attached rudimentary shanty villages marked human habitation. Fragments of rock, bark, and mud had been clumped together in shapes the humans had attempted to copy of the Eden barns, like Cain himself had done in building his parents' cabin.

Further along came human concentration - hemmed in the south by Eden, the natural barriers of Mount Dilmun to the west, and the swamplands directly south. He would learn that the South-Eastern pocket of Atlantis was exclusively Marduk, while Adam's tiny brood was isolated in a pocket to the west of Eden, below the volcano.

The family groups shied away from the strange visitor as he passed. Towering above them by nearly two feet, they were unsure of what to make of this demigod, wondering at any powers he may possess even if unarmed and with only animal skin clothing.

They're more primitive than the servant women I fucked, but they don't fear me, only slinking away. I wonder why? But it works to my advantage.

Finally coming across a leader with a smattering of Marduk, he was able to communicate, learning the cause of his good fortune.

'Me learn little god-speak. Them say "no touch sons of god".' The chief had told him.

So, Enlil was true to his promise about warning them. But it's going to be a very limited conversation until I can teach and lead them. If we can't defeat the gods, at least I know how to raid their garden.

Cain's inspection of the guardians' boats as they dallied with his sisters, began paying off,

He was soon commanding his riverine sailors,

'Our modified local materials are almost as good, now lash together those wooden planks with woven straps and stuff the gaps with reeds to seal the beams!'

In the West, as the third son of Eve grew to maturity, the predicted resemblance to Adam emerged. Seth's features were slightly finer than his father—dark haired, dark blue sapphire eyes and strong-set bone structure. To his family, he grew even more handsome than Adam.

While young and at Enlil's behest, Seth had married his elder third sister Azura, lying also with the daughters of his other sisters. In fact, Enlil had informed Seth of their Law of Inheritance, allowing him four wives in order to facilitate that coupling. His brood thus grew rapidly, while he also began assuming leadership of the clan.

Living ascetically below Mount Dilmun, Seth's kin joined Adam's path of indoctrination - strict with their women and children and living on subsistence crops and herds. Cocooned from their fast-developing human counterparts, they found little reason for any commerce or other ambitions.

Armed also with the 'magical' objects Enlil had handed over to Adam and now kept in what they referred to as the Cave of Treasures,

Seth felt protected from any straying human or beast and his was thus a self-contained race with no other aspirations.

'The humans are stealing again! Even after our fence repairs, they have worked out how to breach the electronics this time, stealing even more than before!' Nazarel accompanied by Michael reported to Enlil.

The king looked to his general. Unlike the ponytail fashion nowadays commonly adopted by the effete Eridu males, including many of his guardians, Michael wore his hair cut short. His suit was fixed on to the guardian officer display of azure blue.

'How?' Enlil was clearly annoyed, mildly distracted by his general's rosy, effeminate face - especially for a guardian of such high rank - explaining his choice of hair style, perhaps as compensation.

'They short-circuit the wiring with animal carcasses, then lay a ramp on it and jump over - same upon returning,' Michael explained.

'How ingenious. But I can't believe the humans have either the wherewithal or the audacity.'

'Adam's banished son is leading them - banding groups together into cooperatives and even trading in what they steal.' Nazarel elaborated.

Michael's drone became slightly animated, indicating he too was clearly impressed, 'Very industrious. Not just limiting to crops and livestock – they're even ransacking our utensils and machinery!'

'Well, post more guards and capture him! I'm beginning to regret we prohibit execution.' Enlil fumed.

'Insufficient guardians for a twenty-mile perimeter. He hides like a king - while minions steal.' Michael seemed unaware of his implied insult, going on in his minimalist speech, 'mercenaries won't spy on their own.'

Ever present Raphael, silently listening until now, was only obliquely concerned, 'We must capture and sterilise him before he lies with the human women.'

Michael shook his head. 'Hah! spies report his screwing them long before expulsion. Plenty kids with unique features.'

Enlil held his gaze on Michael, pursing his lips in speculation at the implications.

Increasing the tension, the one-eyed farmer Nazarel added, 'Cain has also invented hunting weapons and musical instruments, and he is building boats - Marduk style. He's more god to them than we are.'

And over the proceeding centuries, the fast-growing human population led by Cain and his heirs made regular crossings over the 300 miles of calm, protected waters that separated Atlantis from the nearest shores of European Gondwanaland.

Driven by necessity and fuelled by unguided ambition, greed and lust, they congregated in superiority against any local savages, establishing trade and commerce.

Townships and cities emerged, as much for safety as for community. These fast expanded into kingdoms populated by a melange of myriad species, which included mutants who drifted away from Eridu, finding affinity amongst similar freaks. Never before or since would the planet witness such a diversity of physiognomy or dimension - from gross and brutish giants to fine and ephemeral midgets and nymphs. Music, art, and various new entertainments indulged and satisfied their carnal passions.

Adventuresome Marduks relieved from the Tartarus mines moved in amongst them, establishing petty kingdoms in northern Gondwana – newly named by the humans - and southern Eurasia.

Taking over the trade of gold and precious stones, those cities also provided raucous entertainment for Atlantis Marduks seduced by the wanton hedonism.

'She is a direct descendant of Cain himself!' Jural the Trader boasted to the visiting Marduk technician, whose gaze lingered over Meryth, his statuesque jewellery store assistant.

Meryth took a hefty fifty per cent for her exclusive contract with Jural, but it was worth the investment. Regardless of his customers' species or background, she never failed to attract business to his store with her exotic and perfectly symmetrical features. And she played her role to perfection, raising long copper eyelashes coquettishly to reveal her bright aquamarine eyes, or flicking her mane of gold, copper, and silver-streaked hair with just the right flourish.

'So unique. What an unusual combination of Marduk and human,' the smitten Marduk commented to the dwarfish trader while the girl left to fetch samples they traded with visiting smugglers.

'Ahh, yes, her father was a mutant from your Eridu that came here to Utica some sixty years ago and manages the Cyclops in the bronze foundry my dwarf brethren operate. Beautiful, no?' Jural always delighted in client reaction to his assistant's allure.

'Spectacular! How much?'

Now came the part pudgy little Jural enjoyed most. The client hooked, it was the opportunity to drive up the bargain,

'Oh, no, Meryth is not available. She's my assistant and is very choosy. In fact, I hear she's still a virgin,' he lied. 'You will have to make your own arrangements with her. But you look so eminent and presentable. Perhaps I can put in a good word to recommend you, my friend.' He raised both eyebrows conspiratorially.

Timing her return, Meryth carried a tray of gold ingots and a selection of jewellery prized by the Eridu Marduks for their expert Utican craftsmanship. Jural winked as she re-entered the display area, indicating the negotiation was on. It was going to be a lucrative day. In addition to being able to drive up the price for his goods, he will later split the proceeds of Meryth's transaction for her 'after-sales service' to the novice Marduk smuggler. The dwarf trader congratulated himself while she played her seductive role.

But soon it was time to interrupt the flirtation and get down to his part of the business.

'So how much manna will you pay for such a masterpiece?' he inquired of his distracted customer, holding up a brooch of emerald, ruby and sapphire with a soft chuckle and wink at Meryth, hoping she would appreciate his clever ambiguity. She pursed her cheeks and raised her eyebrows at his feeble pun.

The smuggling and distribution of manna was one of the only serious crimes imposed on the Marduk community, the penalty being permanent ostracism from Atlantis or Tartarus. The smugglers thus diluted it with terrestrial amaranth and only referred to it by its pseudonym and codeword.

'Bdellium!' the Marduk corrected him glancing nervously around the shop and beyond at the mention of the prohibited substance. 'It has no other name. And I will give you twenty shekels of my highest grade.'

Jural knew he would also be punished, and his shop ransacked by the Marduk guardians and all his manna confiscated if discovered, but he was confident in his security and the confidentiality of his partner in crime, having no qualms about openly naming the substance. Nevertheless, he played along.

'Twenty! Of your diluted low-grade bdellium? We all know you cut your manna at least five times with terrestrial amaranth, reducing its rejuvenating powers,' Jural spat on the floor for emphasis, 'this masterpiece is worth at least fifty shekels in gold, and at manna conversion of ten to one, I won't take anything under thirty.'

It was really worth about ten shekels, and he also had to give half to Meryth. But manna was becoming ever rarer, and he would also share her spoils from the night ahead. He finally settled for twenty-five shekels of the diluted version. It really *was* going to be quite a profitable afternoon.

'Now, for the rest of my display . . .'

Meanwhile in the same bronze foundry, Gabriel had found an interim opportunity to mitigate the *Nibiru*'s failing components, engaging the dwarfs to follow the template he gave them. The metal was far weaker than the original lonsdaleite structured alloy parts, and would need regular replacement, but for now it was all he had. With the Council's apparent disinterest in his warnings, he felt no compunction in paying Jural's kin the exorbitant amount of manna demanded.

CHAPTER TWENTY-ONE

Shtar's troop followed the now ancient path of the fugitive Tartarus ogres, guided by the same barriers. In that unplanned process, the pioneers followed the course of whatever landform that took their fancy - river, canyon, forest, field, or mountain - heading ever south-easterly.

'Each day we walk into that rising sun is like walking into the arms of God.' Shtar's inward observation was at barely a whisper, but it echoed in the silent morn and caught the ears of Shalimar.

'And everyday means a new encounter as if a new life.' Shalimar revelled.

Shtar continued, 'Mortality highlights the wheel of life, the reincarnation Marduks have circumvented. I look forward to it with as much anticipation as uncertainty.'

'It seems a strange paradox—the more I appreciate life, the more prepared I become for death.' Shalimar added.

A gigantic mountain range blocked the eastern route, and a river emanating from there carved a narrow valley, as if a passageway, through the land. More akin to a large rapid stream, the river was ideal transport for Aigar and the Titans' cedarwood rafts as it carved its way through multi-hued craggy canyons and small verdant oases. It left billabongs alongside which the travellers pitched their nightly camps.

Finally, the river spilt into an expansive valley, straightening out on a flattened plain bathed in springtime sunshine. Magnificent snow-topped pinnacles of those central earth mountains glistened and stood sentinel across an expansive cloudless sky. And as they approached, the Titans began to tarry, dilly-dallying in breaking camp each day, as if yearning to linger longer and savour the surroundings.

It was left to Hyperion, the uncle of Crius the toddy finder, to express his tribe's views to Shtar and her trio of regular comrades at the encampment,

'We follow you long time. Enough!' His bassoon moan was as much vibration as sound.

'Here? It's more barren than my dong!' Aigar reverted to plainer wit with the Titans.

'Home.' With that unequivocal statement, the Titan turned and headed back to his folk.

Nonplussed, the other three members of the campfire group looked about for some possible explanation.

'They acted so content in our company,' Shalimar commented in puzzlement.

'You know that tingly feeling you get when you like someone? That's common sense leaving your body. I'm sure one day I'll see why there's 'good' in goodbye!' Aigar bemoaned.

Dismissing his ramblings, the rest turned to personal introspection.

Aigar examined the 'young' orphan. The description hardly applied any longer, for Shalimar was already showing the fine lines of her journey and the deprivation of manna and radiation treatment.

She often strayed alone from camp, and he had followed her once, relieved to find her writing on her electronic tablet, presumably keeping a diary of sorts. He wondered at its power source.

He was no psychologist but he had observed that inactive females often develop reproductive problems. He was thus happy that Lilith chose to act as surrogate for Adam and had recommended she act as babysitter to the infant, Zhulan. 'The voices in my head may not be real, but they have some good ideas!' He had commented to his wife.

He now reflected on a conversation between Lilith and Shtar only days earlier while Shalimar was absent with her diary,

The humans are evolving rapidly with each subsequent generation, maybe from our influence. Their features are becoming ever more refined like our pretty little Zhulan here, aren't you, sweetie?' Lilith cooed at the hybrid toddler with the smiling almond eyes and little arms wrapped round her neck - while Shtar cut up the ingredients for an evening stew.

'Yes, and they have turned the heads of at least one of our kind, it appears.' Shtar said, nodding at the half-caste while stirring the pot.

'They are powerfully fertile - as proved by our Xeres' child here with the Tartarus servant, despite his earlier diagnosis of sterility. And I hear a guardian has also impregnated another human.'

Aigar squatted over the fire, keeping it alive while he listened.

Shtar was pensive, neither elated nor judgemental, 'But they have such comparatively short lives, less than fifty years. Even without treatment we could still expect to outlast them at least sixty-fold! How can they form any sort of lasting relationship?'

'Relationships are not measured by time but by quality. And the urge to procreate can overcome most other prejudices.' Lilith set Shtar straight, avoiding attentive Aigar's eyes.

Shtar nodded in solemn acknowledgement as Lilith continued, 'which makes me wonder at Shalimar's apparent lack of male interest. It seems she walks a different path to the rest of us,

'She has a very unusual and creative intellect with some interesting occult powers. And she associates strongly with the humans, despite the intellectual and cultural chasm.' The former queen replied, deflecting any character perspective.

'It's as if she inherited her Uriel's androgyny.' Lilith half-joked.

Shtar was about to interject, but observing Shalimar heading their way, they had changed subject.

'Aigar seems to relate to them better than any of us…' Shtar's mention of his name brought the guardian back to the present, '…but I do know some Titan history.' She was responding to Shalimar's puzzlement at the Titan decision to leave them.

'They were relegated to the remotest and bleakest environments on Marduk - similar in terrain to yonder mountains, which must be striking a chord. Isolationist by nature—notice even their own interactions are minimal—it seems they yearn for that austere habitat. Unlike us, trapped in routine and yet continually trying to escape it, the Titans are one with tranquillity and thus embrace it.'

Lilith expressed the silent feelings of the sombre gathering, 'Although they say little, their presence is always a source of comfort. I feel constantly embraced, wrapped up by their simple company. They express so little yet emanate so much.'

And the next day, as the giants made their silent parting, a pall fell over the group, which until now had been unified in mutual solidarity. In addition to their physical impressiveness, the Titans afforded the travellers the watchful aegis of a parent, with nothing to fear and free to wander at will.

'You… Friend. Peace on you and your folk.' Hyperion's lingering gaze over Aigar's face highlighted his sincerity as he held on to the guardian's hand, miniscule in his immense clasp.

With that final perfunctory act, carrying more meaning than an hour of oratory, the Titan led his band towards the icy mountains.

The gesture allowed Aigar the dignity of being forefront amongst the group, shielding his tears from sight. Finally, stemming the flow, he called out to the disappearing backs,

'Piss on you too!'

The group lingered to watch the Titans till they blended into the achromatic wilderness of that eastward mountain range they now called home, leaving the travellers exposed.

It was on that night, the two females alone, that Shalimar approached Shtar to express her feelings.

Shtar was taken aback but did not repel her, 'Are you sure, this is what you want?' She asked, searching the young mystic's face.

'I was sure upon our first meeting and my request to join was not just to leave Atlantis with you, but on your journey through life.' Shalimar replied and reached up to wrap arms around her would be lover's neck.

And throughout that expedition, Shalimar found a comfort in Shtar's arms that she was unaware she lacked.

For a multitude of reasons Shtar too was for once, contented and at ease in the company of another.

'Lord, we give you a good third of our treasure in tithe. What more do you want?' Matho, king of Utica in northwest Gondwana, addressed Enlil. He had inherited the throne from his father Caliel, a former junior guardian of Tartarus.

'Indeed, your treasure is appreciated, but it comes from plunder not industry. Your people spend their wealth on pleasures of the flesh, your streets are lined with filth, and crime is rampant. I see little of our laws!' Enlil accused the mutant, aware of Matho's background. Cali, his father had added the 'El' for added status and married Meryth, a famous Utica courtesan and former jewellery store assistant, who claimed lineage from Cain. The pair conspired and murdered the previous king, Meryth's cousin - another alleged heir of that Eden outcast - and usurped his throne.

Eridu and Eden forbade anyone but pure Marduks into their environs, and Matho now took opportunity to rub in such prejudice,

'Ahh, I'm not permitted to visit Eridu, so I can't compare these to the pristine and sterilised streets of that divine city.' Matho's tone was sarcastic bordering on insolent, confident also in the value of his offering,

'Anyway, those that count here are happy with the outcome. God's laws suit the refinement of the gods. We are not as enlightened. Now if my Lord has no more he requires of me, I must return to my palace to take care of pressing matters.'

With that self-dismissal, Matho made his way to exit their venue - the *Transporter* that had carried Enlil in the company of his general Michael and sage Uriel to Utica.

Enlil turned to his cohorts. 'Their life is too easy. Their only pursuit is pleasure, regardless of method or consequences.'

'Pleasure and progress are not necessarily mutually exclusive,' Uriel counselled, worrying a little over Enlil's growing paranoia, 'it may well be the impetus for their rapid progress in both population and technology, seeking ever more inventive ways to fulfil their desires.'

Uriel continued reflecting on Enlil's leadership. The more the sons of man ignored Eridu, the more austere Enlil became with his godlings. He seemed to have concluded early that religion was the most evocative of sentiments, and thus the most powerful weapon of all. Having missed the opportunity to inflict his dogma upon the humans, now already muddled with Cain's blood, he had decided he would harness it ever more firmly onto his godlings.

With no experience of large societies and only familiar with Jova's style of rigid authority, he's getting out of his depth and overanxious at his loss of control. That kind of dogmatic dictatorship is perhaps not as appropriate in a developing planet, the sage observed.

In Western Atlantis, Adam on his deathbed looked back over the centuries in which his community had spread west of the Pichon river. Eve had passed away in their 640th year since the Eden expulsion. He had since gleaned much about gods and humans and the affairs of his derelict Cain from the frustrations expressed to him by Enlil—even learning of the existence of Jova. He took it at face value, never really questioning how the creator of all could have a father.

And in time, deprived of manna for 930 years, Adam gave up to a permanent sleep and went in search of that elusive super-father, apparently up in the heavens.

His body was mummified in his Cave of Treasures - as taught to Seth by Enlil's untalkative arch guardian angel Michael - preserved there for posterity.

Their eastern path blocked by the titanic mountains, Shtar's pioneers turned south. Having spent so much of their journey in the rugged mountain wilderness, they yearned for the warmth of the coast.

Humans had yet to venture that far, but as Shtar's group made their way, they were followed by groups of native hominids, intrigued by the strangers' booty. But, repelled by Aigar's guardian weaponry, they held back well out of range.

Following the horn of Asia, the pioneers crossed to a tongue of land at the southern tip, with its accompanying island of serendipity that marked the centre-point of the planet on Gabriel's chart. They were greeted there with a cornucopia of fruit and exotic fauna—as if all the world's offerings had gathered to represent themselves on its marvellous shores.

'My wife is getting too feeble to walk any further,' Xeres had explained to Shtar, in the company of his five children, including daughter Zhulan, and a few fellow Marduks with human wives.

'Yes, I understand. Zhulan aged so slowly, we failed to notice her mother's condition.' Shtar admitted, scanning their hybrid companion – only recently displaying puberty despite the thirty odd years since the Titans left. The simian eyes of her mother augmented by Xeres' alien influence, gave Zhulan a pair of exquisite yellow flecked, brown almond-shaped eyes.

'This place is abundant and seems benign. We have decided to settle here,' Xeres announced, to the nods of the other Marduk husbands. 'But my Zhulan here is not happy at our decision and wishes to continue with you.'

'Of course, she's a quiet one but sweet natured, and we would be delighted to have her for company if you let her.'

Thereafter, Zhulan had attached herself to her undeclared 'godparents, clinging to Lilith and adopting the lovely couple as her surrogate family.

But the departure of more fellow guardians now left the security of the troop very much in the hands of Aigar.

The travellers moved northwards once again, before the geography allowed them to continue on their eastward trek.

The human and hybrid infants had no qualms playing with the hominid children who frequently strayed from their tribes – to be claimed eventually by their terrified mothers. And soon the families were eventually absorbed, hominids acting as porters and foragers for the caravan.

Reassured by the complaisance and deference of the savages, the pioneers set aside their apprehension, venturing in small groups and even individually, ever further from camp.

'There's sure to be a brook below that small waterfall over there. I'd love to get this junk off me.' Lilith was pointing north across the small ravines that separated them from a distant waterfall as the group put down their loads to set camp for the eve. The past three days had been arduous trekking, alternating between dense humidity in the jungle and searing sun as they crossed the ridges. The admixture of mud and dust and grime built up since they last came upon fresh water to bathe, together with the ubiquitous mosquitoes by night, had served to make all the members testy.

Zhulan too chose to keep company with Shtar and Shalimar, giving some space to her godparents whose once rare arguments had become frequent.

But now, with some respite in sight, Lilith's mood changed from annoyance to the stirrings of ardour. It had been some time, and she was glad they had a brief hiatus of privacy from the doting girl.

'I'd love to get that junk off you too, and I'll join soon. But be careful and don't venture too far.' Aigar's twinkle before he turned away made it obvious that he had similar thoughts, and as Lilith headed towards the stream, she glanced back realising he'd made a straightforward statement.

Her gaze lingered a few seconds, wondering if she should point out that anomaly. But he was oblivious in his preparations, and she kept it for later, sauntering off in anticipation of the sensual pleasures to come, beginning with a refreshing bath.

The lengthy march had cut Lilith a lithe and tanned figure as she plunged into the rock pool created by a secondary tumbler. The sky was changing hue, still bright but darkening in shades as she swept her eyes in a westerly direction, awaiting her husband. But the small canyons that ridged the basin made by those falls gave her very limited sight in any direction, and after a quick plunge, she slid into repose on to the tableau of rock that jutted slightly over the pond. Her nipples, made erect by the cool, light breeze wafting from the falls, protruded upwards from full and maturing breasts that still maintained their suppleness with nary a sag.

Lying naked atop the pond scoured by the tumbling falls, she offered a statuesque pose in silhouette against the gloaming background. Now, finally cooled and refreshed by the dip, the sensuality of the scene reverted her thoughts to Aigar. Their bickering had been so trivial, and she berated herself for her petty badgering. She looked forward to making up. The surroundings seemingly suffused with pheromones, her fingers moved towards her anticipating moistness as she closed her eyes and fantasised at his familiar lascivious gaze.

'Ookilay eetsway gurl. She otgay nais titi mo she so klin!' (What a beautiful woman. She's got nice breasts, and she's so pure). The youth whispered to his companions. The five of them crept stealthily from boulder to boulder, now less than fifty yards from the edge of the pool and the oblivious Lilith.

Ya! Mo, she otgay nais kan – mo she playplay!' The eldest brother marvelled at the sight of the Marduk female's hairless genitals and her masturbation.

'Me untway fuck 'im!' The twin of the first youth said, stroking his erection.

'Wat . . . fuck?' The youngest boy asked, gaping at the supine, exposed goddess. He was equally fascinated by the effect the female was having on his brothers who were now all in full arousal, their fierce eyes agape in excitement and anticipation.

'Kwait!' The former ogre #463, now going under the name of 'Glong', whispered hoarsely to his sons. 'She no gurl. She Got! Lukout, mebbe she otgay fye-stik ken killem you 'allfello!' He warned, fully aware the goddess' sidearm could quickly wipe out all of them.

Glong had been with the band that had first fled Gondwanaland after the murder of the mine guardian, and was lucky to have taken one of the females with him, having beaten off or killed his competitors for her. Smatterings of Marduk were overlaid with their own added colloquialisms.

Glong's children had long ago formed their own incestuous families, and he had already buried many generations of heirs. By now feeble, he and his aged wife nevertheless had outlived lived them all.

Foraging for food some weeks earlier, he had spied the advancing convoy of travellers by their evening fire. Returning home to collect his gang, the family of ogres trailed the Marduks, maintaining distance for the past many days.

Stalking the travellers for the past few days, he warned them clear of the well-remembered firearms. Instead, they picked up scraps left behind as the party broke camp each night. Surprised to see hominids lingering by the group, apparently in rapport, he nevertheless still held ingrained fear and deep hatred of the gods' cruelty inflicted upon his kind in the mines.

Until this afternoon when Glong spotted the Marduk female drifting off on her own towards the waterfall. Making sure her guardian husband, whom he recognised from the mines, was not following, he had bird-called his youthful tribesmen.

Aigar too was looking forward to reconciling with his wife. The past few weeks were a strain on both of them, and for the first time in their union, they had both sought some distance from each other. In the past, their occasional volatile arguments had invariably ended in passionate reconciliation. However, that had yet to eventuate.

There had been no real provocation for the rift. The heat, the humidity, and the rugged desert terrain of course were hugely contributable. And now that they had set camp in what appeared to be the fringes of a benign forest environment, the shroud on their spirits had begun to lift. Lilith's provocative wink as she headed towards this gorge and its accompanying cascade served to sever any misgivings on his part, and now that he was making his way up towards that fall, his whole being was fixated on their reunion.

It was the first time the youths had seen a female other than their mother and Glong understood their arousal. Indeed, the goddess was even reinvigorating his own long-wizened libido. But he was more interested in her god-skins, her trinkets, tools, and any weapon she may have been carrying. He rued that she had already exited the water. Otherwise they could have stealthily removed her things without being found out. But the boys were now in heat, and there was no avoiding disturbing her, lying as she was beside her effects. It was all he could do to hold them back.

'Ookilay, she wan' fuck tu.' the bolder of twins – Kleng, commented at Lilith's self-stimulation. His gigantic member rigid, he now ran towards the unsuspecting goddess.

Glong knew they had to move fast before she could reach for the fire-stick, and hobbled after the others. His apprehension was placated by the fact that she was a lone, naked female, and he was emboldened by having long ago witnessed the murder of a guardian in the mutiny at the mines.

Agile son Kleng had pounced upon the goddess and was already tearing at her, pinning the fragile body on to the rock with his burly arms, before Glong could shuffle over to the scene.

Her vagina moistened in anticipation of her husband, the first thrust was almost pleasurable as it tore at Lilith's seam, the immediately subsequent pain reminiscent of the delivery of Adam. But the violation grew more brutal as the ogre at first slammed her against the rock, then began to smash her against his trunk, thrusting her like a puppet on to his rigid spear, purple gushing from her wound. And soon the youth exploded into her.

But the violence only intensified. The brothers, whipped up in frenzy had already begun taking their turn, thrusting into every orifice, slamming into her and tearing at her pristine flesh as Kleng held her aloft, all the while marvelling at the oozing radiation-deprived blood only partially oxidised in purple hue.

Despite his eagerness to catch up with Lilith and wash the stench and grime from his body as well as the accompanying aversion from his heart, Aigar had lingered to ensure that the camp was fully secured and was now confident of his meticulous contingent preparations. That concern was thus soon replaced by his fantasies and the anticipation of the pleasure that lay ahead as he headed up the rocky crags that led to the now audible falls.

He was as unable to explain the cause of some hesitation, as he was to understand the reason for their recent rift, but the combination of both left him with a tightening in his gut and a mild nausea. Even now, as he made his way towards her, his emotions were in conflict and somehow his passion was being inhibited by an unknown creeping anxiety.

Glong rummaged through her effects, waiting his turn. After her initial screams, contained and echoing emptily within the caldera that enveloped the pond, Lilith became limp, a ragamuffin torn apart by lions. After their repeated mutilation, Glong, frustrated by the dearth of any value in her possessions except her god-skin and a weapon he didn't know how to operate, added the final rape against the limp and torn torso.

Spent, his long pent-up anger and fear now finding a scapegoat, he picked up a boulder and smashed it down upon the Marduk's skull, before the group slunk off into the gathering gloaming with their paltry spoils.

Those vultures seem very far from their desert habitat? It's highly unlikely there's major carrion in this brush, Aigar wondered as his palpitations grew from much more than the strain of the climb.

The circling birds were competing with his fantasies. A fleeting possibility entered his mind and stabbed at his chest but was quickly swept aside. He tried to quell the queasiness and the slight accompanying debilitation in his knees, by paying attention to his foothold, while his legs unconsciously propelled him up the steep jagged slope. The growing thunder from the falls had long drowned out the screech of the birds, as he and they appeared to be converging on the same location.

The object of their attention was unmistakable.

For an instant, Aigar denied what he saw. That denial transformed into desperate prayer to a divinity he had hitherto never considered. Immobilised, overcome by sickening paralysis, he crumbled to his knees, unwilling and unable at even shooing the monsters that now tore at her. There was no need for reason or understanding, for causes or for blame, for vengeance or anger, or for anything. The vestige of his being had been removed, and everything was now irrelevant. In his catatonia, he observed the surreal scene of his wife's shredding without emotion or aversion, purple smearing the ground like trampled Mandala fruit.

Two spectres departed the idyllic surroundings that eve – one an unwilling perfected soul, the other a forsaken, abject and wretched spirit.

PART THREE

Earth —c. 500 A.D. – 8,500 B.C.E.

Man is immortal: therefore he must die endlessly. For life is a creative idea; it can only find itself in changing forms . . .
—Rabindranath Tagore

One kills a man, one is an assassin; one kills a million, one is a conqueror; one kills everybody, one is a god
—Jean Rostand

CHAPTER TWENTY-TWO

Purpose—It surrounded without, blossomed within.

On the planetary scale, well over a thousand years since the Eden scandal, the prodigious Antarctic ice mass now imposed an irregular wobble on the Earth's axis— gradually warming the atmosphere, melting its extremities and raising seas that now encroached on the coastal human cities. The warming ocean in turn began to undermine the solid ice sheet, a carapace that balanced precariously on a very thin base.

Oblivious to the geology, Enlil gathered his counsellors to his palatial villa for some impromptu advice. Raphael was always dependable but limited in scope, so he had included the sage Uriel, also to receive an update on the progress of his godlings. He vented his frustration at both.

'At this rate, the humans will take over the planet and drive us *all* out – including our godlings!'

'Yes, they're in the tens of millions, but that has brought on considerable industry.' Uriel offered.

Enlil remained petulant, 'At what cost? They thumb their noses at our laws. The smuggling of bdellium—manna by any name—is rife, and pleasure is their sole pursuit. At least our godlings display *some* moral discipline.'

'Well, our Eridu folk are as much to blame in that two-way enterprise. Yet even our architectural achievements and some of our technical designs are provided by human industry. Wasn't that progress always our goal?'

'Yet it's not by *our* kind!' Enlil protested.

Raphael stepped in to expand on Enlil's aversion, 'As we all recall, bionics enabled us to merge Marduk and machine, and with organic componentry. Yet it was still *Marduk* brains that resulted. And with Adam's kind, it was a majority of *Marduk* genes and attributes. The godlings are thus still our species as it were. Any further dilution by the humans will be less *us* and more *them!*'

Uriel was not impressed. 'I see the point but disagree with the prejudice.'

Enlil expanded on the doctor's argument. 'The godlings are becoming backward. We must find a way to advance them without allowing them to be corrupted. How goes our Enoch?'

This subject was more to Uriel's taste, having long ago spotted potential in Adam's fifth generation descendant, 'I'm delighted to advise Enoch has a perfect memory – and probably the highest intelligence ever!'

Enlil gave the mage a curious and briefly suspicious look, 'Well, keep an eye on him. That genius can just as easily be used for depravity like the human rabble. So much for my brother's liberalism.'

'Sire, we can't keep Adam's heirs cloistered forever. They are inquisitive and thus it will be difficult to isolate the two races.' Uriel argued.

'Which is why I have allowed you to expose young Enoch to our learning and technology, to arm against his human cousins.' Enlil snapped back.

The sage turned pensive,

Enlil's conviction in his moral superiority and righteousness as the only path to progress is astounding! Yet Ea's unprincipled freedom with no moral boundaries is destructive.

While Enlil's righteous discipline squashes their spirit, Ea's unguided permissiveness diminishes the development of their souls. Funny, one with no interest in the soul, tries to control and develop it. The other tries to set it free, but instead degrades it.

Uriel became circumspect, 'Right now we are only informing him of our expectations, but if he's to lead his kind, he will need to understand fully. For that he needs to be brought to Eridu - even *Nibiru* - to experience the balance of scientific progress with social grace.'

'But that would expose him to all our mysteries, dissipating their awe and wonder!' Enlil argued.

'I believe our Enoch already understands more than we think. Regardless, who would believe or understand any description of his experiences amongst us? I believe it is worth the experiment to see whether there is indeed any potential for your hybrids to coexist with us.'

'Hmm. I am a bit anxious that we may lose our primary advocate to so much exposure and knowledge, but I'm more scandalised by the humans at large. Go ahead. Indoctrinate him. But do not allow him to write about any of this.'

'I was summoned to the Eden fence and was led from there by carriage to the pearl-encrusted gates of the city of God where I was met by his angel, Uriel.' Old Enoch related to his son Methuselah, who was already a grandfather in his own right.

'And on the way to what that guardian called an 'Institute' I marvelled at their adaptation of common terrestrial materials,' Enoch went on narrating, 'Uriel explained that their heavenly materials were unsuitable here, so they had developed the stunning earthly equivalents I witnessed in a myriad of colours and textures. And more, the gods had contrived a machine that could project life-like images they called 'holograms', creating realistic effects such as the flowering in Spring – in their full dimensions!

'At the Institute, Uriel taught me the mysteries of numbers, the planets and stars and other occult matters.

Methuselah was astonished, but queried his elderly father, 'But would it not be more expedient to teach all of us his children directly, so we too could witness the glories of God?'

'I too asked him that, and why me? Uriel explained that I needed to be tested to ensure we could understand heaven's ways or we could all be confused like our mother Eve.'

'And he warned me not to put anything in writing or it could be misunderstood and even worse, misused. He said, "Unlike the sons of man, whose lives are short, your kind spans many centuries and generations. Hence you can pass on your knowledge first-hand through your heirs, ensuring accuracy and truth".'

'And after I was returned here, the Lord, seeing that I had passed the test, called me once again. This time it was into a flying chariot, in which I was taken up into the darkness wherein glowed his heavenly city they call *Nibiru* – the one up there like our moon – from where they showed me the great expanse of heaven beyond this puny earth.' Enoch recounted excitedly. But then he turned uneasy,

'On one occasion, Uriel was called away to attend to an important matter. Curious about God's abode, I wandered off and found myself in the bowels of that great floating city and heard a discussion between two of the Lord's other angels. I do not comprehend it, but by their anxiousness, I sense it is of great importance. As you know my memory is perfect and so I will recite it to you. Perhaps you may come to understand it:

'Captain Gabri-El, this station is falling apart.' One of them reported, sounding fearful. Some of the dwarf bronze parts can be used for external repairs or less sophisticated machinery and simple electronics. But the main nuclear drive and the Vril-driven engines are also corroding beyond repair, sir.'

'I tried to warn king Jova when we arrived here and then also the Council, but none listened,' His leader responded in similar panic.

'Imagine the consequences!'

'I know, we must try our best to prevent it.'

'And what are we to do with the stowaways found hiding in the Transporter?' The first one asked.

'Keep them unconscious and isolated for the moment. Uriel is arranging for our healers to erase the experience.'

'That was all I heard when Uriel found me and led me back to the learning room. He claimed ignorance when I asked him the meaning of the overheard conversation, but I could read his concern and displeasure at my knowledge of it.' Enoch finished his story and searched his son's face for any indication of understanding.

But Methuselah was blank, 'I understand less than you, father. But it is notable that my son Lamech and some of his companions were also absent during your departure and reappeared soon after your return. His companions explained to me that they had tried to follow you into the field where you were taken up, but strangely they have no recollection of the period from then until they returned to their families days later.

'However, Lamech has turned to brooding and is disturbed, blaspheming against the Lord. He has turned his interest towards the cities of men, hearing from others who ventured there about great wealth and progress. I fear we are losing him to that hedonism. As precaution, I have taken his young son Menachem, "Noah" as I call him, under my wing to educate him in our mysteries.'

'Well, that's a surprise! Enlil has announced Council, inviting us both!' Nin announced, looking up at Ea from the communicator's crystal sphere. As a Council member she had access to one of the few private screens - stripped from Ea upon his exile, 'I wonder what global issue prompted him to include *you*!

'Oh, probably to blame and heap scorn on me for some trifle.' Ea retorted, 'I hear he makes all decisions nowadays, rarely calling on advice.'

'Well, we *are* rather remote, and with Shtar gone I've had even less reason to return to Atlantis. But I hear Eridu is quite exciting nowadays. I look forward to returning and seeing for myself.'

Ea remained silent, allowing his sister to continue in her giddiness, more animated than for a long while. She had fully matured now and the chasm of their relationship widening since his transgression with Eve, she rarely sought his opinion any more. He too had to admit that life on Tartarus was humdrum.

'Let's go a little early so we can re-familiarise with folk there. There are so few of us Marduks left in Tartarus,' she decided for both. 'Cain's kind has spread far and wide throughout the planet, but I wonder how Adam's brood is getting along.'

Nin was alarmed at Eridu's degeneration into unholy hedonism. It was evident that the Marduks had intermingled with human servants, the resultant myriad mixtures exotically attractive. However, there was little evidence that Adam's tribe had made their way into that blend. Nevertheless, Atlantis society was at once glamorous while simultaneously gaudy and vulgar, even chaotic.

Males and females of all types in scanty attire delighted in their sexual exhibitionism. Law seemed absent as the strolling visitors from Tartarus witnessed violence and petty crime - without any intervention or even attention from the guardian police, who seemed likewise engaged in the reeking corruption. She observed Ea's sardonic smirk at the naked decadence,

'So, this is the "improvement" we have been hearing so much about.' Ea snickered.

'You should be delighted. It seems they have adopted your libertarian ways!' She was clearly unimpressed.

'This is not the result of just free will but an overlay of repressive laws and dictates, releasing resultant frustration - exposing your brother's philosophy.'

'Oh, he's *my* brother now, is he? But isn't this exactly the freedom and abandonment you advocate!'

'Indeed, everyone should be allowed their own expression, to learn from experience and mistakes. Excesses of such freedom usually lead to cries for consensually agreed regulations. But pre-empting those cries and imposing such laws with threats and dictates may limit their actions but not their desires. It's clear that this is not the result of *my* philosophy, but *Enlil's*.' He said, arching a pointed eyebrow.

She observed him obliquely, *I can't forgive him for seducing the hybrid woman—he never even sought it! It seems that what I thought to be love was just infatuation and admiration, still there, but missing intimacy...*

Her reflections were interrupted by the sight of their younger brother.

Enlil stood masterly atop the stairs of the grand hall of Eridu, consolidated in his position as king of the world. He was flamboyant and magnanimous in welcome, seemingly also caught up in Eridu's hedonism.

'Greetings sister, and welcome!' his disregard for Ea was conspicuous.

'I have long missed your company. Your wanderings have worn well on you, and captivating as ever.'

He had mellowed over the years, and his stare was more than filial. He now addressed Ea, while continuing his gaze on her, 'And you too, of course, brother.'

Oh my dear Beelzebub! He's still *trying to seduce me!*

He glowed with inner confidence and ease. This time his typical ambition and passion exposed a lustiness betrayed in his features. Instead of aversion, she felt a familiar warmth about her loins.

But this is madness. It must be my long abstinence! She was startled by both the physical responses as well as her accompanying explanation.

'I look forward to your joining me at the banquet I am holding in honour of your return,' Enlil exclaimed in open delight, addressing her specifically. And again his look lingered while they were led to their quarters.

Ea had noticed the exchange between his siblings and was split by emotions. With their filial bond since Nin's childhood, he was never able to see it as amorous - not so much as sibling - more friend or relative. Yet, as a lover he felt the pangs of jealous rivalry at his windbag nemesis.

'I see our brother is pretending to take an interest in you. I suppose by marrying and having a child with you, he can consolidate his supremacy and his line,' Ea stated indifferently as the couple settled into their assigned multi-bedroom and sumptuous apartment, overlooking the main Eridu thoroughfare

'He did appear to show interest. Did you notice it too? Does it bother you?' She gave a furtive, faraway smile, taunting him with a bit of coquetry. But she hadn't missed his cynicism, as if there couldn't be any other reason for Enlil's attentions.

'Kingship and power mongering serve no interest for me.' He evaded her disguised appeal for warmth, and in that omission, had made his feelings clear.

Although we were never really passionate lovers, it seems he has become more unpredictable and withdrawn since that tryst with the hybrid, Eve. I know he harbours no feelings for her, so I'm guessing the Mandala still retains its influence.

'Then I suppose I don't really serve any interest for you either.'

With a final penetrating glance, she marched off to her bedchamber to prepare herself for the feast, leaving him to stew, watching her curvaceous rear in a slightly exaggerated swagger, glide through the corridor.

'I don't wish to attend this banquet, to have Enlil gloat openly at his delusional victory over me.' He called to that retreating back.

'Suit yourself. But I am looking forward to the evening.' She tossed back in response as she slid shut the panels to their bedchambers.

'My lady is unhappy.' The human servant assigned to Nin's toilet commented.

What business is it of yours! Nin was about to snap, turning and casting the woman a sharp glare. The gentle touch, the placating voice and the deferential mien as the young woman helped remove her garment, moderated her mood; instead, she took the opportunity to cast an appraising eye.

'I am Delima,' the human offered, observing the goddess' scrutiny. She was attired in simple polymer fibre, a by-product of Eridu cottage industry, unlike the rich brocades from Utica and the fine Agad silks added by the Marduk females to embellish themselves. Yet, Delima carried it elegantly and in fashion.

That made Nin self-conscious of her own appearance. Grooming was not a priority in the jungles and plains of Tartarus, and Nin's attire still comprised the original *Nibiru*-issued uniform, which, after all this time, still maintained its integrity, shape and multi-hued apparatus. But her tousled wind-dried hair, unkempt nails, and other elements of her grooming were blatantly deficient.

As the woman kneaded her body in massage and later applied cosmetics to her face, Tartarus faded away—along with any disturbing associations it carried. And as she submitted to the meticulous care, the woman extended her assistance in every aspect of Nin's improvement, including the choice of attire for the evening.

Nin came to notice something else.

The woman's technique was a little less professional than the Marduk beauticians. But in her touch and her devoted yet composed attention, she exuded something no Marduk she had met could project—genuine concern and interest in the well-being of this unknown and churlish goddess who shared nary a word. Unobservable, it was inherent. Nin just *felt* it.

And as she watched herself transformed by the caring servant, Nin's heart welled in recognition of something she had long sought again after glimpsing it in her hominid hero on that long-ago clifftop: affinity; empathy; *Phileo*. Recognising the feeling, she was beginning to understand.

Fully attired and now eminently presentable, Nin was looking forward to what the evening may offer.

'Now my lady is happy.' Delima beamed with joy as much as pride, looking upon Nin as she might upon a queen.

Before exiting the room, Nin turned to the woman and prepared to speak to her for the first time. She paused, realising that the words she was about to utter were her first time using them—indeed the first time she had heard them from any of her kind,

'I like you.'

Uriel and Raphael looked worried awaiting Enlil's return from greeting the Tartarus visitors.

'I too had hoped to catch up with Nin after so long. But this is far more important.' Uriel commented to the doctor, filling time.

Enlil greeted them in the royal visitors' hall, 'What is the great urgency?' He was in high spirits.

'Lord, we erased the memories of the *Nibiru* stowaways who followed their Enoch. But Uriel here has more disturbing news regarding him,' Raphael announced, his tone ensuring to deflect any possible blame on his part.

'And what is this great catastrophe concerning our genius Enoch?' Enlil's tone was dismissive, maintaining his magnanimity.

Uriel related, 'I caught him eavesdropping on Captain Gabriel and his chief technical officer, discussing our intent to erase his followers' memories, but also a much more serious issue they were discussing. Again, it was something he did not need to know.'

'Well, that doesn't sound *so* devastating. Lamech and his companions seem to be taken care of without great harm from their trespass. We are their gods after all.' Enlil was not to be shaken from his high spirits. 'But what was this other information he was not supposed to hear?'

'I don't know, sire. Gabriel seems very circumspect, even refusing to state his agenda in case any technician might eavesdrop – which might explain his request for a secret meeting of Council. He was visibly disturbed when he learned of Enoch's spying. He said it concerns highly secret news that even unauthorised Marduks should not hear. I have prohibited Enoch writing anything, but he has near perfect memory and I'm not sure what he may divulge to his student and son, Methuselah.'

Enlil became more serious, 'Why are they all so disobedient? Any suggestions? Can we isolate him somehow?'

Raphael came to the rescue,

'Sire, I suggest we take old Enoch up once more to the *Nibiru* on the pretext his righteousness has earned him the privilege of immortality and transport directly to 'heaven'. And this time leave him there to live out his few remaining days.'

CHAPTER TWENTY-THREE

Aigar had left Lilith's remains in situ, and hence there was nothing to entomb. His stoic, unflinching demeanour said everything, seemingly denying himself the catharsis of mourning - lest he be salved of even an iota of pain.

The gathering around him was mute. Shtar and Shalimar, flanking him, kept the consolers at bay, both intuitively understanding that he shunned commiserations or communication of any kind. And in that empathy, they too remained silent.

None noticed Zhulan squatting behind a nearby bush. Her eyes were fixed on Aigar, and, as if mirroring his own, they were blank.

'With all my occult practices and discipline, why is it I had no premonition or even inkling of foreknowledge of such a tragedy?' Shalimar despaired privately to Shtar, questioning the validity of her study.

But Shtar was undeterred. 'The ogres have no soul, so they emanate no psychic energy. It was a random and senseless crime, likely with no premeditation, and thus no foreknowledge to decipher. Don't abandon it. I sense we will need your powers to help us survive.'

Shalimar's thoughts recalled those were almost the very words her father Uriel had used when handing over the enigmatic skull upon her departure.

Breaking camp immediately the next morning, they persevered ever eastwards. The depleted group travelled as if carrying a burden, a weight that had appeared upon the departure of the Titans and now augmented by the loss of seemingly *both* their blithe champions. In losing one they were absorbed into the affliction of the other. And for the first time, Shtar and the others felt the depletion of their manna, as if extruded from their marrow, desiccating their psyches.

Briefly, Aigar's rationality must have awoken, realising the funereal effect his presence was having on the rest of the travellers. The following day, he placed his weapons and all his guardian paraphernalia outside the tent of Shalimar, along with a brief note:

I failed to save your parents and their fellow naturals. And now my kindred soul. I go to redress some of it.

'Do you understand Aigar's message?' Shalimar inquired much later that day after Shtar had arranged for the group's security.

'I'm sure you were told of Aigar's heroism aboard the *Nibiru*, yet somehow he still feels responsible, though 'fellow naturals' is a little cryptic. And now he's also taking blame for some ogres that escaped extermination in Tartarus. What a burden! But has anyone seen Zulan?'

It was some hours before they had news of the girl. Their newly appointed guardian security head reported, 'One of our human trackers found Aigar's footprints in the sands to the north. There was a second, fresher set alongside.'

'Oh, I do hope he realises her presence soon and no danger befalls her.' Shalimar cried.

'Well, Aigar may have left his weapons behind, but it appears she has stolen my side-arm,' Shtar reported after rummaging her scant belongings.

After all that tragedy, Shtar broke and found a rocky outcrop overlooking the ocean where she sat flooded with memories.

It had been a millennium since she had left her solitary home on the bluff in Atlantis, not long after the banishment of Cain. And now, as she sat on a similar cliff overlooking this balmy tropical ocean as the sun set, she recalled the events that had led her to this far eastern continent, including contentment in Shalimar's arms. She began deep breathing - the surf ionised brine aiding the detached awareness her partner had taught.

As the giant crimson orb dipped below the ocean - giving off its terminal green flash - and as twilight fast descended, she felt her spirits lifting.

As night fell, she was still unclear as to what or where that pilgrimage was leading but now she roused herself to return to her fellow travellers, at peace.

She gave a momentary thought to distraught Aigar, wishing somehow, he would allow himself a similar catharsis of his grief.

Finally, the pioneers reached the edge of Gondwana. The deprivation of the youth supplements and radiation, along with the hardships they had undergone had taken their toll and were etched into their features. The few offspring born en route, with miniscule inherited remnants of their parents' longevity, had also aged naturally, their deterioration overtaking even their parents.

Some of the younger folk wished to continue, going north with accompanying humans and hominids, fragmenting the community.

Shtar and the main body remained on that extended far-eastern section of the mega-continent that they called *Lemuria*. There on the headland, on a bluff basalt clifftop, Shalimar uncovered the object entrusted to her by Uriel upon leaving Eridu. She reviewed the final conversation with her adoptive father, along with his accompanying instructions,

'I wonder at my influence in your upbringing, depriving you of a normal Marduk life,' Uriel rued.

'Nonsense! You have been a better father than any I can imagine, and I have no idea what a "normal" Marduk should behave like anyway. Would you have me...'

He had left her in mid-sentence while he retreated to his private quarters. By the way he ambled away without excusing himself, it was clear he was having some inner dialogue.

He returned carrying an object wrapped in a light woollen fabric spun from Eden fleece, uncovering it before Shalimar.

'As you know, I'm not keen on your leaving Eridu—more importantly, leaving me. But I understand your reasons. If I were younger, I may well have considered such a venture myself. So, I'm giving you this not just in memory of me but its powers will be useful to help you all survive.' He said.

'It's gorgeous. But what is it? How was it made? It doesn't look like anything that could have been produced by human or mutant hand, skilled artisans as they are.' She enthused.

'No, not human - peerless even amongst Marduk virtuosos - an oracle. It is composed of the alchemist's stone or monatomic white powder gold—the essence

that remains after the transmutation of that precious metal. There were very few such mystic objects created and only four remain, given to Jova upon his departure.'

He became increasingly grave, 'One was the sceptre of kingship, which has been handed down to successive kings of Marduk and which Enlil gave Adam as symbol entrusting him with kingship on Earth. Two others are the Royal Skull of the Oath, which resides in the Council tabernacle, and the Royal Sword of Destiny set into that same stone cubicle.'

She almost dropped it in her surprise, 'It's so light, almost weightless. It feels as if I'm holding nothing. Actually, it almost feels like it's raising my hand. But that's impossible!'

'Ahh, good. You have achieved the gift of attuning with its vibrations naturally. To the uninitiated, it weighs more than gold itself. It is actually trans-dimensional, bridging the lower mineral and the higher electronic states, mediated by the molecular or spirit world. Thus, with skill, cellular beings like us can integrate all four ascending states of existence—mineral, cellular, molecular, and electronic into a quintessential nexus of birth, death, judgement, and enlightenment. And only one that is prepared to step into that precarious corridor can begin to tap its true potential. It is the nearest thing we can come to the truly divine. The higher the state of consciousness of its wielder, the greater its power.'

'But where did it come from? What science or sorcery made it?'

'Ever since I took you home as an infant, I have been teaching you the discipline and mental experiments - the fundamentals of that mystical alchemy - which most call "sorcery". That science was pushed into a fringe pursuit as Marduk went technical, and the alchemists were dismissed to the realms of superstition. Whereas the transmutation of gold is now taken for granted for its overt energies such as the Vril, it is looked upon only as a technical tool, utilitarian. Ignorant of mysticism, Marduks look at these miracles as just symbols, unaware of their deeper and more subtle powers.'

Shalimar sat spellbound, while Uriel continued, 'They were devised by enlightened artists, using techniques I am only beginning to vaguely comprehend. This one is an identical twin of the Royal Skull of the Sacred Oath – which I used upon swearing Enlil as king. Jova had used it only once - to swear each of the members of the Supreme Council on Marduk to secrecy upon being informed of the approaching asteroid. This one was entrusted to me by the artisan creator *of the original, who made a duplicate for his own reasons, but who was left behind as his talent was considered ineligible for the Nibiru,' Uriel explained.*

'But it's so precious. Why are you giving it to me?'

'Invaluable indeed! Its antigravitational properties may assist you in the far-flung corners of this planet. But those are only a few of its properties. As I mentioned, the derivation of its power stems from the spiritual development and sophistication of its possessor, and for that reason it must be guarded carefully from the unprepared and uninitiated. In your quest for the supernatural, which no doubt will be augmented by your travels, you may be able to derive more of its capabilities. But even if only for that apparent antigravity power, it will serve you better than it can hidden away here in Eridu.'

And now as Shalimar uncovered the skull on the edge of this placid ocean that bordered Lemuria, she looked down from the cliffs—across to the bay - deciding the layout for their city. There, using the power emanating from that Marduk icon, she projected her mind in concentration as Uriel had taught her and which she had practiced all her life.

Isolating massive basalt slabs from the cliffs, she levitated those wafers, and later, with technical advice from the miners and dwarfs from Tartarus, she hewed them to fit into place. The massive slabs, up to eight feet in length and a little less than half that in width and depth, would slot together precisely, such that even the prolific tropical grasses were incapable of breaching those joints. Together they carved out a small elaborate city with an intricate system of waterways, they called 'Nanmadol'.

The pilgrims settled into a rhythm, augmented by hominids and descendants of humans pushed out of Atlantis by Enlil's long-ago purge, now also communing and supplying those aging gods with produce in exchange for the security and augmented education the Marduks offered.

Unlike Eridu, famed for its technological artistry and marvel, Nanmadol was a city of the spirit, incorporating the natural elements of earth and drawing its latent energy with the power of mind.

Nin was astounded by the cornucopia greeting her arrival at Eridu's grand banquet hall. At various sides of the room, whole lambs rotated on spits manned by humans and other half-castes, and alongside, all manner of fowl. Dominating the far corner at the rear, an entire ox carcass, eyes glazed to white by blazing logs underneath, rolled over, end on end, in a mesmerising rhythm. Adorning each of the tables, wooden bowls overflowed with an array of Eden fruit, and barely clad half-breed slaves carried silver pitchers of wine and wheat or barley beers, which they poured up to the brim of golden goblets set beside each of the guests.

Despite the ventilation created by openings in the upper walls, allowing the smoke and stench to escape, the atmosphere was permeated by the smell of flesh, sizzling with heat and with lust.

The Atlanteans had grown corpulent in their indolence and sloth; scantily clad females draped over their laps—fondling a breast here, a thigh or crotch there, as they drank themselves to stupor. Any reason, commencing with the welcome of the visitor, was used to propose a toast and quaff another goblet of ale or wine. Jugglers, acrobats, and the seductively erotic hip movements of naked dancers added entertainment. Females led by Irania, likewise showed no reserve in their licentiousness, stroking and exposing their servants' virility, which they displayed to each other in a competition of dimensions, as the party descended into wild orgy. There was no inhibition to sexuality, hands groping whatever was at hand without predilection.

While Nin was titillated by the spectacle and the wine, she was not attracted to the various mixtures of humans. Nevertheless, the scene before her was engaging and liberating, aphrodisiac.

She did not fail to notice Enlil's elect soldiers at attention and unmoved by the events around them. Enlil too, although relaxed, remained aware and in control, as if timing his occasional outbursts of uncharacteristic and bellicose laughter. Seated beside him at the head of the table, her initial reserve degenerated, carried away by the heady liquor and the rampant eroticism. And before long, she was being openly caressed and seduced by Enlil.

She tingled with the excitement of taboo and as initial traces of anxiety diminished and restraint dissipated, she became suffused with pent up passion finally allowing herself to be led away to the King's chamber.

Enlil's ardour was spirited and raunchy, more natural than Ea's technical verve - which had made her feel as if being serviced. The younger was more wanton and therefore more thrilling and fulfilling. Yet there were no passionate breaks in his whisper, no promises after— just an implied contract of engagement.

There was liberation in that. Stifled passion and dearth of affection was absorbed as if by osmosis from childhood, her life built on tolerance rather than love. Well, if not love, then power and pleasure was good enough.

Afterwards as post coital ennui set in, Nin evaluated her actions. There was no regret. Noticing Enlil was likewise awake, she spoke,

'When did you decide to throw out your convictions, tolerating such debauchery? Rather hypocritical, preaching one thing to the hybrids and behaving the opposite? And were we Marduks seduced by human primitive ways or just reverting to inherent repressed traits?'

'Hybrid brainwashing was just a method of gaining submission – away from those 'human primitive ways' to fulfil our need for technology. But it seems their isolation has only steered them to mysticism – less dependable. As for the Marduks, I learned early from Jova, a king is still subject to the whims of the populace. Every society gets the leader they deserve – they put him there or at least tolerate his position.'

'So you tolerate their corruption - vindicating Ea!' She accused.

'You think so? I still believe that the correct path for all of us lies in righteousness and discipline. That is how the Marduks progressed. Accepting Ea's rationale for hastening their mortality, I thought Seth's line could learn faster. But instead of science, they have turned to religion and the meaning of life, each generation regressing rather than enhancing progress. The hybrid experiment has failed.'

Nin recalled Uriel's fundamental character types, *the King's thirst for power has prevailed over the Soldier's righteousness and duty.* She mused, but Enlil was adding his postscript,

'I thought I could steer them away from that drivel by directing them as their God – giving them the necessary decrees so they wouldn't have to waste time on that fruitless quest!'

'You can hardly blame them searching for meaning. Don't we all?' She offered.

'But they're inherently flawed. If I had the opportunity, I would start over with a new creation, with attributes chosen by *me* this time.

There was no other dimension to him, she realised, *He doesn't know what it is that he doesn't know. Irania bleached his essence and left only his will. How sad!*

'So, now you understand my proposal. Together we can produce the true sons of god that I always envisaged. What say you?'

'I'm still thinking.' She said and arose to dress.

'I reckon this must be what Eridu looks like.' Alena, the woman marvelled, gaping at the giant black basalt edifices of the city and the breakwater that ringed its harbour.

As they entered the large courtyard of the tallest of the rectangular buildings, she was surprised to see a goddess approach in the company of another—older and frailer with eyes that had faded and matched the greyness of her hair. Both were attired in simple muslin fibre, in contrast to the glamourpusses she had encountered in her Agad, across the sea from Atlantis. But their similarity in height and slightly elongated skulls, exposed by falling hair, were unmistakable. Her curiosity was interrupted by the 'younger' goddess,

'Welcome to Nanmadol. I am Shalimar, and this is my companion, Shtar. You are the first humans to visit since we settled here over three hundred years ago. But where do you come from, and how did you find your way here?'

Alena took the opportunity to inspect both at closer quarters while her husband Irad responded,

'Name's Irad from Agad, over the other side of the world. There' was over 600 of us when we left about thirty years ago, lookin' for gold, which your mates in Atlantis pay shitloads for. But some of them lazy bastards stopped and set up shop along the way. Others just pissed off on their own.

And somewhere in the middle, we were jumped by them bloody wild ogres who knocked off a bunch of us. 'Would'a lost more 'cept for that wild guardian who whacked 'em with his arrows. Bloody angel, he was!'

Shalimar, at first groping to understand the accent, now exchanged a look of recognition with Shtar, who broke her silence,
'Aigar is still alive and safe! I'm so glad. Was he alone?' Shtar enquired of Alena, who was eager to respond.
'Nah, he had this hybrid old woman who looked' lot like Irad 'ere, and there was a bunch of what 'musta been their kids.' The folk there call 'em 'khans' or something like that. The bloke didn't talk much but the woman told us about you guys and where you might be headin'—so 'ere we are. Bloody lovely it is too.'
Shalimar turned to Shtar in bemusement, ignoring the visitors for the moment. 'He reproduced with Zhulan? How?'
'Hominid fertility seems powerful, as Zhulan's own birth proved.'
Shalimar turned back to the awaiting travellers. 'Please refresh yourselves here and then join us in our evening meal – and tell us more of Aigar and Zhulan.'

Whereas the essence of success is a sense of timing - which Ea unfortunately lacked - the quintessence of grace is a sense of place. And Ea knew his place. Nin's lack of fulfilment had nothing to do with his dalliance with Eve. His love, she knew - if that was what one would call it - was purer and more selfless, not the amorous kind. And more so since using the Mandala.

No questions were asked or words even spoken upon Nin's return the following day. She hadn't really expected a scene, but his ambivalence about the affair gave her a small stab, as if a final turn of the screw. Confused and seeking a diversion, she fell back on 'uncle' Uriel,
'Hello, Nineveh! I was wondering when you would come to see me. I hear you are not returning to Tartarus with Lord Ea.' The sage greeted.
'No. It doesn't seem I belong, or if that was what I was after.'
'And have you found it now?' His expression was whimsical.

'I don't know. Does anybody know? Our actions and our decisions seem so capricious? There seems to be no consistency amongst us. We seem to about-turn on so many convictions. Look at Enlil, how he has changed his whole philosophy. The only one with any real consistency seems to be Irania. At least she has never strayed from the act of straying.'

'Integrity is such an imaginary construct.' Uriel offered. 'We presume that others are consistent—somehow always good or always bad, or at least always predictable— and that we alone are aberrant and inconsistent. Having cheated death, we Marduks are just dropping our various personae. Perhaps we are all now reverting to our inherent nature or essence.'

'Yes, so it seems lately. But why can't we step out of that groove and change our nature especially as we have so much time?

'Perhaps that paradox is in fact the purpose of our lives. Notice that the moment you achieve something you once desired, that desire seems to dissipate, losing its significance - the achievement taken for granted? Maybe that is why we are born in the first place, not so much to achieve our desires but to overcome the desire itself.

'Well, if there is a Prime Mover or God, it is perverse!'

'For all we know, we *are* that God, or at least fragmented emanations of It, stepping out of eternity and throwing ourselves in the trap of time, in order to experience ourselves.' He was winking with enjoyment at the discussion, 'Immortality renders consistency as somewhat meaningless, whereas death creates a sense of urgency.' Uriel tried to explain.

'I don't get it.'

'Notice how the humans act so much faster than us? For Marduks with infinite time, there is no hurry, no enthusiasm. After all, one can achieve anything eventually, and hence desires lose their power of attraction. And materiality offers only *things* – tangible and measurable progress with items for sensual gratification. The *Nibiru* refugees – led by Jova and now Enlil - are seduced by the habit, or drug, of technology. In any case, a person must decide on either the material or the spiritual.'

'Or balance the two,' she countered.

'Indeed. But such balance is extremely rare—achieved only by magi. The longer we Marduks are trapped in time, the more we need to find and cling to security and certainty—habits really - illusions that we cling to—becoming ingrained into reality.'

Nin was struggling to grasp the concepts. 'By that reckoning, if life is an illusion, then certainty is the ultimate delusion.'

'Yes, and as a delusion, it is the strongest illusion—illusion concretised into reality, as it were. What a paradox!'

'Pithy. But what is the correct way?'

'The correct way is the way you believe is the correct way. One can't have both at the same time—solid reality *and* mystical experience, it's like squaring a circle—or live infinitely and achieve change - the true mastery of the magus!'

'So, how does one get out of the loop of habit?'

'Perhaps, as sleep rejuvenates our cellular bodies and minds, death is sleep for the soul - the necessary period to evaluate experiences and filter their essence and determine the lessons for the next lifecycle. In a sense, we Marduks on Earth are simply sleepwalking.'

'Then is death to be our aspiration?'

'Or perhaps finding an unfulfilled purpose – a vision as it were.'

'Yes, but given enough time, it will be eventually be fulfilled. After all, failure is only success delayed.'

'Very astute, my dear Nin! But I believe you can't really experience life without the threat of death. Perhaps that was the dilemma that caused God, if It exists, to bring forth life in the first place – fragmenting Itself into myriad experiences for their own sake . . . Maybe we are all gods just trying to believe in ourselves.'

If so, then let it be my *reality that dictates!* Nin resolved.

Uriel's lecture had distracted her from her anxieties. But she had enough of metaphysics and moved to more mundane matters,

'Any news of Shalimar or the pilgrims?'

'No, they have passed well the beyond horizon and range of the *Nibiru*'s antennae. Transmissions ceased some time ago.' Uriel replied ruefully, 'but speaking of the *Nibiru*, it seems Gabriel has something momentous to deliver at Council tomorrow - news I fear we may all hope is indeed illusion!'

CHAPTER TWENTY-FOUR

'My dear Menachem, you don't understand. They are going to destroy us. And when our Enoch suspected it, they removed him to the heavens again, under the pretext of his alleged holiness. We are their slaves!' Lamech tried explaining to his son, who had trekked his way around Eden and made his way into Gondwana to catch up with his father in Cush.

'What bizarre allegations! Your head has always been filled with conspiracies!' The young man came to rebuke Lamech for abandoning wife and family. Yet his father's endearing tone and using his given name instead of grandpa Methuselah's diminutive nickname 'Noah', softened his resolve.

'Enlil and his 'gods' are very clever with their mind control, and they have all the resources available to maintain that influence and counteract any "heresy".'

'What heresy? And what slavery? God gave us free will! Is your paranoia from the drugs these degenerates take to heighten their depravity? Come back with me.'

Lamech remained affectionate, 'Better you stay here and open your eyes, my son. Exposure to the world beyond that family enclave might lift the shroud of credulity that the gods have induced. Enjoy my hospitality. You came a long way, and the wine from nearby vineyards is the best outside of Eden.'

'But why so bitter? Yours sound like the rantings of those believers in Eve's blasphemy!'

'Indeed, Eve taught those who listened some of the mysteries she learned from sampling the forbidden fruit of Eden. But Enlil vilifies and minimises her insight. Adam too lately had lucid moments, and tried to pass on some of that hidden knowledge, which our patriarchs dismiss as the rantings of dotage.

'Yet what I learned as a stowaway in Enoch's ascension is far more crucial than Eve's theories, enlightening as they may be,' Lamech insisted, 'I stayed quiet to avoid incriminating my kin. But it's too much to bear alone, and I feel I must pass it. You have grown into a learned and discerning man, please listen and judge for yourself.

'Of course, you are still my father. I will give you my ear.'

Lamech gazed at his son for a moment before he began opening up,

'I was once as callow and devout as you, my son. When your great-grandfather Enoch was called into the desert in the West and taken up in that chariot of the gods, my friends and I secretly followed, hoping to gain the ecstasy that he described. And upon his entry into that disc, the three of us hid ourselves within its belly.

'But on arrival at the home of the gods—that smaller moon ever visible and never moving above us—we were discovered. And the gods covered our eyes, holding us prisoners in some container I am thus unable to describe.

'While his angel instructed Enoch, we were taken to their "healers" and were subjected to a nectar which they pushed into our arms with a thorny tube. My two friends were struck by a deep sleep. And when they woke they seemed to forget everything since the time we left our village. Strangely, or perhaps by the will of the true God, I was fully awake during their probing and my memory remained afterwards.

'They made fun of us while the other two were asleep and from their humour, I learnt the true purpose of our creation, which Eve had implied. Menachem, they have no interest or love of us. We are only slaves that were created to serve and worship them and for their study - experimenting with our minds and our souls.'

Noah rebelled at such atheism and became exasperated by his father's fantasy. But there was a hint of anxiety, sensing the inherent honesty in Lamech.

And now his attention was being briefly diverted by an apparition bearing wine and sweetmeats that entered his father's guest room.

Noah protested, 'Father, you are not paranoid as I originally thought. Instead, you are truly deranged. How can you accuse our creator of such crime? Even our patriarch Enoch, who lived amongst them, has attested to their kindness and benevolence. And your friends who you say accompanied you, are also still devout!' Yet his eyes remained distracted.

'Enoch knew nothing of what happened and was given special attention. As for my friends, for all I know their memories were replaced with some artificial delusions of the gods' own making.'

'It sounds more like you who is delusional!'

Lamech was about to retort. But noticing the distraction the woman had on Menachem, he set aside his frustration and anguish at his son's disbelief and reproof. Instead, he smirked in encouragement, dropping his argument and towards his duties as a host,

'Come, it is not a king's feast, but our Naamah here has brought the best of what my household can offer. She is my daughter from my wife Zillah, who I met here in Cush and who traces her ancestry through many humans, but is also descended directly from Cain.'

From his vantage on the *Nibiru*, Gabriel had kept track of the spread of the various breeds of sentient life in the two occupied continents ever since their arrival - even tracking Shtar's colony part of the way—all east of Atlantis. None but a few intrepid sailors had ventured into the empty ocean in the West.

Before Council the next day, the Captain made a flyover of Atlantis and was awestruck by the advancements since his last visit.

The port city Lagash, southeast of Eridu, had now become a thriving maritime metropolis - increasingly cosmopolitan, with impressive human sailing vessels adding variety.

But arriving in Eridu, he was dismayed by the slovenly inhabitants.

'The beauty and grandeur of its construction is matched only by the depravity of its occupants,' he commented to Enlil upon their meeting.

Enlil shrugged. 'Well, I'm sure that's easy to say with your head up there in the clouds. But what's this impending disaster that requires a secretive meeting of Council?'

Prolonged lack of exposure to sunlight accentuated the *Nibiru* captain's pallid and ashen mien as he replied,

'Sire, I'm sure once you hear it, you will agree that such information should only be divulged once. Therefore, I must excuse myself and remain secluded until tomorrow.' He said in self dismissal and followed escorts to his quarters.

The two arch guardian consuls were dwarfed as they entered the oval redwood doorway. Along the walls and ceiling were murals and etchings depicting arcane Marduk symbols in astronomy, physics, and mathematics.

A miniaturised replica of the edifice on Marduk, the Pyramid's interior space was pentagonal. This gave greater seating and view in case an audience was invited to observe the proceedings of the twelve members and the king at the circular table - also the suspended tabernacle, which, when raised, appeared as an eye looking down upon all. Only Marduks were permitted to enter that sacred auditorium - even for cleaning or maintenance.

'Imagine if mankind saw this. We would certainly lose our lustre,' Raphael, in Healing Institute regalia, commented to his psychologist colleague Phanuel as they entered the grand archway of the Council Pyramid's central dome. Both displayed the Healing Institute's swastika emblem.

Beginning his habitual neck twitch in anxiety at the unprecedented demand for secret convocation, Raphael tried to nevertheless sound calm and continued, 'Much of what they thought was our magic would be explained,'

His equally edgy companion gave a clipped reply, 'Perhaps not. An unexposed human mind would see incomprehensible code - making us more mysterious.'

Enlil, appearing equally anxious, quickly convened the restricted gathering,

'Members of Earth Supreme Council, Captain Gabriel has requested an urgent and confidential meeting, apparently with some momentous news. Without further delay, I hand over the floor to him.'

Gabriel's walk to the podium was stiff and formal. His ponderous gait and apparent procrastination added to the mounting angst.

Finally, he began. 'As his majesty, King Enlil has indicated, a very serious crisis threatens this planet, the extent of which I'm not quite able to predict.' Gabriel paused again, groping for words.

'Come, good Captain, I'm sure it can't be all that bad.' Enlil attempted to be expansive, but his uneasiness increased upon Gabriel's uncharacteristic hesitation, 'Please get on with it.'

'Well, let me try . . . Some of you may not be aware that although centrifugal force can account for much of the energy required to keep the huge *Nibiru* in orbit, gravity and friction from Earth's atmosphere in our orbiting position still require us to augment that force with regular bursts of thrust.' Once begun, Gabriel was regaining his composure and reporting in more military and even pace.

'For millennia, gold, platinum and some radioactive metals found on earth have been constant, so fuel is not a major factor. But over time, the components that house the Vril, as well as nuclear, electronic and mechanical energies that keep the station operational have been wearing down. As you know, some of the higher drives were devised and honed by the most sophisticated and some say—even esoteric scientists on Marduk—which we have not managed to yet emulate here. Too many of our senior physicists anyway died along the way. Without new accessories we have thus far made repairs with only spares and makeshift parts.

'However, we have unfortunately reached our limits. The more sophisticated systems are reaching absolute lifespan and already shutting down. As you know also, the *Nibiru* was designed for a one-time thrust to get us out of our own solar system's gravity. The thrusters were long ago jettisoned after achieving that purpose. So, we do not—nor actually did we ever really—have enough thrust to completely break from this planet's gravitational hold, particularly in such close orbit.' Gabriel made no mention of his warning Jova of that eventuality upon first entering Earth's gravitational tug.

'I'm afraid we will be unable to maintain the station in its orbit for much longer... In effect... the *Nibiru* will soon begin to spiral downwards and crash into Earth.'

A pre-thunderstorm stillness fell around the table. The hitherto unnoticed mechanism of the pyramid's coolers hummed somewhere.

The solar panels on each face of the capstone, recharging batteries that caused a barely perceptible background vibration as the air passed through and exited the ducts—like in the *Nibiru* – became at this moment, hauntingly distinct.

'That could be catastrophic.' The understatement finally came from one-eyed Nazarel. It animated the other members, who awoke and began to search respective faces, dumbfounded and aghast.

Gabriel continued to fill the silence. His response now stoic and pragmatic, 'It certainly will be. We can calibrate it to crash into the massive empty Antipodean ocean east of Gondwana. But that may not help much. I suspect we will not evade total global annihilation.'

'What about the solar wind that we rode upon to escape Marduk?' Uriel asked hopefully. His thoughts were no doubt for his daughter, somewhere near that Antipodean sea.

'That is insignificant compared to the initial thrust needed to extract *Nibiru* out of earth's hold, let alone escape this sun's gravitational pull to exit the solar system A *Transporter* might achieve that but the greater craft has no such power,' Gabriel explained.

'So, history is about to repeat itself!' Uriel's loud musing gathered a cloud of despair, accumulating the mood of the woebegone group.

Nin searched the faces of her colleagues for some form of reassurance but all were dejected, so she addressed the Captain,

'What exactly do you mean by *annihilation*? Surely, the *Nibiru* is only a few miles in diameter, and if it crashes so far away, I can't imagine it causing that much destruction. Will it?' she asked.

Many had witnessed the small asteroid's devastation of Marduk, guessing at a *Nibiru* impact on this junior planet, and none volunteered comment.

Gabriel replied, neither too dire nor offering any false security. 'Actually, the *Nibiru* is smaller and with far less velocity than what destroyed Marduk, but still, the momentum it will generate is far more than this planet can tolerate. And the massive Antarctic ice mass is now larger than Gondwana, causing the huge variations in climate you must have noticed recently. The impact will definitely undermine that icy colossus, causing even more devastation and flood throughout the earth than perhaps the *Nibiru's* impact itself.'

Irania was uncharacteristically morbid, 'What incredible coincidence! It seems salvation from Marduk was a cosmic aberration, and now that anomaly is to be righted.'

Doctor Raphael controlled his paroxysms long enough to suggest hopefully, 'Captain, you mentioned the *Transporters* could escape this gravity. That would allow some of us to be saved, wouldn't it – like on the *Nibiru?*'

'They could accommodate some, but not for the time this planet would take to recover.' Gabriel replied.

Enlil turned contemplative while he asked, 'When will this happen? I mean how much time do we have?'

'Around thirty terrestrial years by my calculations.'

'So soon? Pygargs! You must have calculated the probability much earlier?' Enlil was harshly accusing.

Not even Enlil's mention of Nin's genetically modified cattle as choice of his expletive, awoke Nin from glum despair.

'I actually warned King Jova of this likelihood upon our arrival...' Gabriel began excusing, but paused and brightened a little... 'Yet, ... Doctor Raphael's query has raised an opportunity for some.'

A number of Councillors pricked up their ears and Enlil too became inquisitive, 'Continue.'

It is possible to reassemble a much smaller space station from the *Nibiru* by combining the *Transporters* to sustain a limited number in space for a period of time – at least till the conflagration is over and things settle down again on earth.'

'And what is a "limited number"?' Enlil asked.

'That depends on our expectations of comfort. But it won't be many. Let me calculate the alternatives.' Gabriel returned to his seat and began tapping on his electronic tablet.

'Will all those that remain perish? Won't there be any survivors at all on the planet?' Nazarel asked, his good eye rapidly blinking in deep disturbance and exaggerating the static artificiality of the other.

'I'm not sure, although I believe it highly unlikely,' Uriel replied on behalf of the occupied captain.

'And how will the refugees to be chosen this time?' Irania asked, turning to Enlil.

'Well, one thing is for certain, it won't be necessary to bring along any hybrids - Marduk or otherwise.' Enlil commented morosely.

That news disturbed Nin as much as the earlier announcement, and she delved deeper in thought.

'It seems nature will take care of that failure.' Raphael concurred, 'but even then, there are far too many Marduks, not to mention the pure-blooded mutants.'

Enlil became decisive, 'When the time approaches, only the Originals, and even then, only those who have remained disengaged from the humans, will be eligible.'

But Irania had not finished and asked somewhat contemptuously, 'And then what? Come back and start all over? And how and with what . . .?'

'The survivors, if any will have to deal with that. Gabriel, let us know your tally so we know how many to eliminate.'

CHAPTER TWENTY-FIVE

Gabriel lifted his head to report to the stupefied Council, 'With its expanded facilities, but also with the housing of the much reduced Vril engine, it could seat over two thousand. But to live-aboard for any considerable period of time and with provisions, only 108 would fit comfortably, 144 if cramped.' The Captain replied.

And what does "any considerable period of time" mean?' Ea finally spoke up and asked.

'I estimate it would take about a year at least for things to settle back on Earth, allowing our return' Gabriel reported back.

Enlil now took command, 'All right, we will rely on that estimate and use the greater number of 144, suffering any discomfort from the cramping.'

'However, before our Captain returns to the *Nibiru* and begins his reconstruction of the *Transporters,* we will all swear upon the Skull of the Oath not to let this information pass these walls.

'Also, in this predicament, I will invoke my power of absolute authority and set the parameters,' he commanded. 'As mentioned only those originals who stepped off the *Nibiru* will be considered. Also, no mutants or hybrid progeny - not even Seth's and obviously not Cain's. Any remaining space will be decided by rank and based on their relationship to members of this council, descending to other prominent Council nominees.

'Our good doctor Raphael will draw up genetic and social criteria. And, we will only notify the eligible in the final days before departure, as the Marduk Council once did to prevent rumours or panic.'

Enlil's delivery gave no hint of any emotional or personal interest, and none questioned its overall pragmatism, although Nin shook her head in opposition to some of it. Ea had hardly engaged and stroked his chin in thought, as if planning something or other.

The King continued his instructions, 'On the appointed day, all the eligible are to be gathered north of Mount Dilmun, where the reconstructed royal *Transporter* will gather them.'

'Nin was disturbed. Shouldn't we save some hybrids at least to repopulate? Otherwise, what would be the point of returning?'

'No, they are all unworthy. And now Seth's descendant, Lamech has already divorced and remarried - into the line of Cain no less! Hence, all our plans for a pure Marduk line are dashed. We will recreate a new species.'

Ea's comment was offhand, still somewhat distant in thought, 'What makes you think that any other species we create will be any better, or that we won't taint that species like we did this one?'

'It wasn't *we* who tainted them, it was *you* – exposing their inherent weakness! I'm sure we can devise a more compliant strain,' Enlil replied, 'in any case, they murder their own kind almost by nature.'

Ea, more engaged, thrust further at Enlil, 'Not to mention your imposed guilt, infecting them with the belief that they are indelibly unworthy and sinful – with nothing to aspire towards.'

But Enlil held his ground, continuing the incongruous argument as perhaps a distraction from the ghastliness of what they were about to face,

'Really? Look at the result of your Cain's libertarianism!'

Ea was quick to respond, 'As I understand it, our objective from the hybrid experiment was multiple. Firstly, they were to alleviate our work. Secondly, they would perpetuate our genes and carry some form of our heritage. Thirdly, they would proliferate and in doing so, create the conditions and the market to allow us to develop our technology. Finally, they would evolve to emulate us and stand as equals with us to evolve the next stages of our technology. It seems to me, whether intentional or otherwise, that is exactly what Cain's progeny is doing and is heading towards!'

'Stand with us? I don't think so!' Enlil scoffed, 'with all the interbreeds – contributing nothing to us - only degenerating our morals!'

'But in that random and chaotic way, they still progress. Perhaps due to that very diversity?' Ea countered, before disengaging again, seemingly distracted with other thoughts.

Even possibly improving us! Nin had wished to interject but in Enlil's mood it could be counter-productive. *There must be a way!* She hoped.

Enlil was not finished, 'But where then is our Marduk heritage? Just a vague and forgotten genetic contribution? No, we already compromised ourselves by creating Adam, who at least was a purer hybrid. Our own kind would be ideal . . .' He glanced at Nin, 'we owe it to the memory of Marduk!' He finally concluded, 'So this is wasted argument. We will remain with my parameters.'

'What about those in the East? And the Titans?' Nin asked tentatively, worried for the fate of her mother. But she guessed at the inevitable, while Uriel also hung his head.

Enlil's decisiveness continued, 'They have already chosen mortality, so leave them be. And obviously no space for Titans.'

However, Irania remained sceptical, 'You still haven't addressed what to do upon returning - to what will apparently be nothing but ruins at best? With so few of us and no human or other slaves?'

'Well, make do we must. And I will repopulate the planet with my own seed—descendants of Jova, the archetype of our species. This time, they will be true sons of Marduk!' Enlil announced while staring at Nin, as if expecting her cooperation.

Terminating discussion, he vacated his seat and walked over to unlock the tabernacle. Removing the sacred Skull, he decreed solemnly, 'I hold you all now to take the oath of utmost secrecy and adherence to our decisions.'

Ea held back in contemplation as each of the members took the oath,

Enlil has only two short-sighted options. One assumes Nin has his child, which fortunately she too is reticent about, the other is to somehow derive a more pliable hybrid - a singular breed of clone-like automatons more brainwashed than Seth's line!

Cain's interbred humans are morally degenerate and slothful, but their frequent sparks of genius are so much greater than our diligent and methodical, yet ponderous march.

....and my idea could just work!

He sidled up to the royal sage, 'Hello, Uriel. It's been some time since we got together to solve the problems of the universe. Have you had news of your Shalimar?'

'Greetings, Lord Ea. It *has* been awhile. The *Nibiru's* transmitters cannot reach beyond central Earth, so all communication is dead since they passed that point, heading to the far eastern coast.'

'I'm sorry to hear that. I also miss Aigar and his wife, and I hope they are all well, even if alas, temporary. But I heard you took one of Seth's heirs under your wing, showing great promise?'

'Yes, besides Enoch's raw intelligence, his sense of ethics offset the baser human desires. Regrettably he observed too much on the *Nibiru,* and we have thus sequestered him there. His son, Methuselah and his great-grandson, young Menachem or Noah, indicate high on the scale of consciousness. Unfortunately, his grandson Lamech and his companions were stowaways on Enoch's first ascension. Their memories were sterilised, but Lamech has since turned recalcitrant, mingling with Cain's ilk in Cush and even marrying a descendant of that criminal. Enlil is livid enough without knowing that Lamech's son Noah, has also gone and met someone there.'

'Yes, I do admit my Cain's brood has progressed materially but at the expense of consciousness and morality.'

Uriel marvelled at Ea's aplomb in admitting but making no attempt at contrition for his transgression with Eve, and the resultant hybrid condition. He noticed something else about Ea's genius that seems have evolved since his experience with the Mandala, always rebellious, he had become cunning – evidenced by his increasingly arched eyebrow and a growing leer.

'Well, no matter. It seems that fate will put an end to all of that soon enough. But I will be sorry that Enoch's kind will also be killed,' the mage replied.

'Hmm. It seems such a pitiable waste—to destroy all of them, I mean.' Ea's comment was accompanied by his infamous single high-arched eyebrow.

Uriel's response grew into intrigue, 'well, by default, we will be saving Enoch and taking him with us… but I suspect you have some sort of plan.'

'Yes. Enoch is only one man - already in his dotage and happily entrenched in the Marduk lifestyle. Irania's unanswered question is, who will rebuild the earth communities if they're all destroyed? And what of all the other creatures of this planet?' Ea goaded.

'Enlil is implacable, and intends to repopulate with his own. As for the other species, there will obviously be no room. So, what's to be done?' He shrugged, but his manner and tone indicated he was hoping for some lifeline.'

'You know, it *might* be possible to save some of them planet-bound, as seed for the future, I mean,' Ea suggested, looking obliquely and again raising his tell-tale arched eyebrow.

Uriel cast an inquisitive look back at that glint. He never doubted Ea's ingenuity, and before turning away, he gave an almost imperceptible shrug of support. 'It's my time to take the oath. Excuse me.'

Enlil and Gabriel were bombarded with questions relating to the necessary preparations for departure while each Councillor took the oath at their own pace. The distracted king thus failed to notice that Ea made only a peremptory stroke of that skull uttering nothing. Uriel spotted the evasion but also stayed mute knowing protest or even exposure meant nothing to that devilish lord.

CHAPTER TWENTY-SIX

'So, you're staying on in Eridu,' Ea stated matter of fact when the former pair finally addressed each other.

'Yes, Uriel has graciously offered me Shalimar's apartment,' Nin responded in similar tone.

Their awkward civility churned with varying degrees of embarrassment— uneasiness, equanimity, and confusion overlaid with the comparative insignificance of it all in the face of now impending planetary doom. It seemed Nin's infatuation was fully outgrown. And for Ea, the Mandala's after-effects had left him rather mellow, if not apathetic to any such passion.

'Activities in Tartarus no longer have meaning, so I too have decided to remain here,' he announced.

'Won't the absence of both of us alert them?' Her protest was mild.

'I will commute from time to time. Matters there are routine, and I can leave the lab in Galael's good hands.' He also wished to avoid unnecessary questions from the Tartarus folk.

'Yes, well I'll miss Fubsy, who we must ensure is chosen as one of the escapees, as of course I would like our trio to continue working together.'

Her dismissive comment and lack of resentment affirmed the futility of their tryst, but also made it less uncomfortable for Ea to stay on in Eridu and to carry out his scheme.

Unlike the varied females cavorting around Cush, this Naamah had a sense of modesty about her. She eschewed the flagrantly exhibitionistic and often obscene fashion of the sirens and the effete of the city, preferring the flouncier skirt and bodice, which served to surround her with an even greater femininity and hinted sensuality. The concealment of her slightly tanned lissom body and the fullness of her mouth, crowned by a mane of henna-coloured hair, her main surrender to vanity, added grace and elegance to that naturally exuded eroticism. And unlike the elaborately coiffed tops of the majority of Cushite women, or the bunned or veiled women of his kind, that hair flowed free in wild yet attended abandon.

'She is my stepsister then?' Noah asked his father Lamech, trying to disguise the overtness of his appraisal of the demure girl and her yellow-flecked green eyes that occasionally lifted up to meet his.

Noah was middle aged and still unmarried, all the more endearing to Enlil, who might have mistaken that as an example of sanctity. But in reality, it was neither piety nor ambivalence that caused his celibacy. His kinswomen were naturally dowdy, prevented or abstaining from any ornamentation or grooming - functionaries whose sole purpose and interest appeared to be childbirth. For want of suitable partners in his eyes, it was thus easy to maintain the mask of conservatism.

As much as he shunned the women of his tribe, he was also not impressed by the overt obscenity and vulgar lasciviousness of the city folk here in Cush. It was thus refreshing to find a woman who struck the balance.

Lamech was pleased at the effect his daughter was having and encouraged their acquaintance,

'Stay awhile with me, son, and perhaps I can lift the veil that has you so thoroughly shrouded.'

'Yes. It has been a weary journey. I would like to spend some more time with you and also observe the habits of the damned here in Cush.'

Naamah was of course more circumspect in her evaluation of the visitor. She was not wanting for suitors; her sultry smouldering beauty balanced a demure disposition, making her all the more alluring to the local studs. She was tired of holding those dilettantes at bay, each carrying their sameness, an emptiness of ideas or humour, relying on sarcastic wit, foppish handsomeness, or ill-gotten wealth to try and snare her. But this man emanated a self-confident air in his physical gait, a strength of purpose and a combination of fire and intelligence in the light sapphire blue of his eyes and serious demeanour. She was equally drawn by his comparatively quaint distinctiveness and unconventionality, making him all the more interesting.

She gave a hint of her attraction by raising her eyes to him as she overfilled his goblet.

'Excuse me while I make arrangements for your stay. Meanwhile, Naamah here will look after you,' Lamech gave as pretext for leaving the room, allowing them to be further acquainted,

Noah found his father's departure both disturbing and titillating, unfamiliar as he was for such strangers of opposite sex to be left alone and un-chaperoned. But he also was glad of the opportunity to talk to the girl in private.

Her return gaze was open, utterly unlike the coy or obsequious demeanour of his tribeswomen. It was neither suggestive nor challenging. Her exquisiteness belied the necessity for such pretensions. She looked upon him as equal.

It had disturbed him that she was of the tainted tribe, in direct contravention of the Lord's prohibition. But he was smitten.

And so it was that Menachem-Noah, the middle-aged bachelor, had found his wife amongst the children of the damned.

Lamech had blessed the union with a precious wedding gift,

'This was given to me by Cain before he died, and upon my marriage to Zillah, his heir. Cain claimed his mother Eve gave it to him upon his ouster from Eden, informing him that it contains the last remnants of the forbidden fruit. I am loath to try such a venerable legacy, and it is now yours my son, in case you may need it.' His father revealed, handing over the strange metallic canister.

And Naamah accompanied her husband to Western Atlantis, unprepared for the consternation their coupling would cause the parochial society. There she bore him three sons.

The zealous descendants of Seth were less than welcoming of the heathen woman, far more attractive than their ilk. The couple thus became socially isolated. But Noah was happy in his choice, in turn shunning his own kind and isolating his nascent family to the banks of the river Pichon—downstream from their village and near its delta into the Atlantean Ocean.

'How far is it to your house? Nin asked.

The last of the Vril-driven surface mobiles, which Enlil had loaned for her trip to Cush, was just approaching the outskirts of the city. The others had deteriorated beyond repair.

'Oh, not far. It's only about a mile from here.' The human servant Delima assured her.

'Thank you, guardian. Please leave us here and return to Eridu. I will send a signal when we're ready to return,' Nin instructed their driver, who looked back at her with consternation.

Equally alarmed Delima protested, 'No, my lady, it is too dangerous to walk unprotected through Cush. There are vagabonds and thieves roaming about.'

'From now, please call me Nin. But I'm sure you're exaggerating. I have been among much wilder humans I'm sure, in and around the mines of Tartarus. And I'd like to witness at close hand what a human city is like.'

'Perhaps my lady, but this is a city of over one million and though many are friendly, there are no guardians unlike in Atlantis.'

However, Delima could see her argument was falling on deaf ears and reconsidered. 'But maybe they would not dare attack a goddess. Nevertheless, please beware of your bearings and your belongings, my lady...Nin.'

The pocked and undefined streets of Cush were narrow and haphazard, as were the arrangement of the buildings and houses—shanty shack neighboured manicured mansion, next to shop, 'smith or warehouse. From the overflowing refuse and filth, it was obvious that any removal was undertaken by the beggars and packrats. But amongst the chaos, the ruthlessness and blatant cheating as the pair coursed the central bazaar, Nin noticed something that was rare amongst her kind – smiles and laughter.

Thwack... Thwack!

The sting on her buttocks caused more startle than pain. Nin turned around to see two children, slingshots in hand, falling about in gleeful laughter, congratulating each other at their aim. Behind her were spongy seedpods from an unfamiliar tree, which had apparently been their ammunition.

'Scram, you scalliwags!' Delima scolded, although more mildly than Nin would have expected for the brats' impudence. Her only experience with children of any sort was with the ape-like hominids, who were far less naughty.

There was little conversation as they went on - highlighting the little they had in common. But Delima spoke in gestures: a gentle smile of understanding; a tender touch of reassurance; a nod of approval; a wink of shared conspiracy—mannerisms that Nin could only absorb, never initiate or even quite reciprocate. And as they approached what Delima pointed out as her home, two more children - a boy and girl - tore out of the house and clung to the woman, jumping about, clearly overjoyed at her return. The children's joy overflowed to include Nin, who initially recoiled in embarrassment at their hugs, but soon relaxed to enjoy.

'My niece and nephew,' Delima explained.

Apparently no introductions were necessary, as Nin found out encountering the entire extended family who had gathered to greet Delima and their collective new best friend.

Beginning with their shared meal and extending for three days, Nin experienced the vicissitudes of human life—the joy of reunion and affection; the enjoyment of shared banquet; the annoyance at leaks and damage to a dilapidated house; the hurt of slights and accusations; the sting of criticism; and the heartache of Delima's eventual departure.

Their hospitality had sought no reward. There was neither goddess nor deference; no stranger nor differentiation. There was affinity. It was inherent – *Phileo* - felt, recognised, understood. For the first time in her life, Nin experienced family.

The return journey was similarly non-conversational, with Nin in deep introspection. Her heart was bursting with torment in containing it.

Upon her return, she was glad that Uriel was away at his observatory.

For only the second time ever – both after she arrived on this planet, Nin gave way to uncontrolled weeping. Yet unlike the revelry and joy that brought on the first, this time it was in utter helplessness and despair.

There must be a way! She prayed again - unsure to whom or what, but hoping there was an entity that listened.

'I am not long for this world. And with my son Lamech's apostasy, it is to you my boy, that the sons of god will turn for guidance and for intercession with our Lord.' Ancient Methuselah began to Noah, who smiled inwardly at being addressed as a juvenile.

'You will thus need to know the meaning and special use of Adam's invaluable treasures, which must remain hidden from all except the elect,' The patriarch warned before showing Noah the recesses wherein those heirlooms were saved.

Besides the sceptre of kingship and the colourful clothes of gossamer-like thread Enlil had given the outcasts of Eden, the cave contained the long unused audio-visual devices that Enlil used to communicate his instruction to the patriarchs. Neither of the men was aware of those projectors and cameras recessed and disguised in the shadows of the rocks.

'I have yet to receive a visit from our God. But he has all-seeing eyes and is aware of any that approaches this cave. Adam warned that his angels also prevent any unauthorised access. Should he choose to contact you, he will make his presence felt, just as he did to our forefathers.'

Methuselah continued in the verbal tradition of handing down the secrets, 'But God is displeased with the affairs of men, and Enoch warned of omens he had overheard while in heaven, involving a great disturbance that could affect our world.'

Noah was briefly distracted, recalling Lamech's similar warning. But he soon returned his reverent attention to his grandfather's instruction that included the astronomy Enoch had learnt on his first visit to heaven.

'Before they perish, I would like to see how Adam's family are faring. It has been so long since I saw them.' Ea was at the Healing Institute, requesting the Head Physician Raphael for access to the projection room.

It was from there technicians kept watch over the first couple and their heirs, and Enlil made his proclamations and holographic projections - originally on Eden's ubiquitous speakers and projectors. But afterwards his apparitions were restricted, due also to few secretive locations in and around the couple's original residence after banishment – now called Adam's Cave of Treasures.

The hawk was at home in his nest and displayed very little of his regular neck twitching, 'Since they are to be left behind, there is no longer any point in monitoring them monitoring them and I have reassigned my staff. Feel free to use the room anytime. I'll leave it to you to switch on and operate the equipment yourself.' Raphael offered magnanimously, leaning back and stroking back his slick grey hair.

'Your plan might just work! But have you decided who to save?' Uriel enquired.

Ea had timed his visit to coincide with Nin's absence from the house, accompanying her maid-servant in Cush. He sat at the far corner of the apartment watching the sage pour nectar from Nazarel's vines into tall-stemmed human-blown goblets of Lagash glass. The old guardian's lightness of step in delivering their drinks was admirable.

'I have no preference, and I'm of two minds whether to choose from Seth's tribe or Cain's. By the way, this wine is extraordinary. I've missed out on a lot in Tartarus.'

'It's an early vintage. Well, I suggest for the sake of their survival, any candidate should carry Enlil's blood.'

'Yes, anyone from Cain's brood would inherit a death warrant, but just Enlil's blood will result in more of the same like Adam. We need Marduk diversity, not just a singular genetic sequence,' Ea argued, as if thinking aloud.

Uriel agreed. 'That's true. Funny, it seems this very planet has anticipated and conspired to reject its alien interlopers—almost as the body will reject an incompatible cell. Perhaps we should just return this world to its rightful heirs, playing only a subsidiary role, if any.'

'You mean hand over to humankind? No. That would be a regression. The infusion of our strain has advanced hominid evolution by a huge leap, providing the link of consciousness to this planet, which may have never evolved on its own. Nearly all human progress proceeded from Cain.'

'Hmm, yes that does pose a bit of a dilemma . . . But wait! I just realised something!' Uriel suddenly enthused, 'Shalimar's *underlying hand* seems to have struck again!'

'I don't understand?'

'Fate as thrust a candidate at us. You asked earlier of Enoch and his descendants, and I mentioned his great-grandson Menachem, or Noah as his grandfather has nicknamed him.'

'Yes, I recall.'

'Well, as you know, his father Lamech coupled with a human interbreed that traces her line directly to Cain. He's already feeble from Cushite excess, but the couple produced a daughter, Naamah.'

Ea had not seen the sage so aroused. 'And?'

'Can your contraption carry seven?'

'I had planned on just two. I suppose it can be modified. But why?'

'Apparently our Noah fell for that multi-racial descendant of Cain – his *stepsister,* marrying and producing three sons, two of them also married!' Uriel twinkled, allowing the implications to sink in.

'Underlying hand indeed!' Ea marvelled, 'An ideal combination of genetic diversity. But why all seven?'

'Both he and his wife are actually naturally righteous even without Enlil's indoctrination. I doubt they will leave without the entire family.' Uriel counselled.

'Well, in fact, our Noah might need assistance in maintaining the craft, so I'll add a little more space before giving him the specifications.'

'But why would he listen to you? Any inkling he may have of you is related to Eve's encounter. He'll more likely blurt it all to Enlil.' Uriel warned.

'Well, naturally I won't display my snake logo, and only Adam and Enoch have seen Enlil – both no longer on Earth.'

'True, but with Enoch's eidetic memory, I know he has shared detailed description of 'God' with all his kin, including no doubt, Noah. In any case, you can't just show up at their doorstep.' Uriel cautioned again.

'I have a more effective and dramatic method, which I will now need to adapt a little based on your advice. I'm sorry, I can't yet share that information.'

With his head full of details and instructions from grandfather Methuselah, Noah made his way to the Cave of Treasures for his first rite of worship as patriarch-to-be. It was a weekly ritual imposed upon Adam since his relocation there and was carried out religiously by heirs ever since. The latest scion trekked the ten miles past his kinfolk's township, deep in thought about recent events in the night sky.

As Enoch taught us, our world is a globe that rotates around our sun - I'm not quite sure how - but in any case, it now seems off balance. Could it be the erratic shifting of that stationary smaller moon—the heavenly city of God according to Lamech and Enoch? It also seems to be getting larger each passing year. I hope I can decipher the devices and charts well enough to gain a clue.

On arrival, he performed the preparatory occult incantations and meditation in reverence and to better attune with the objects.

In that semi-trance, a pinpoint of light flickered from the rock face and immediately grew into an apparition of a strange looking object.

Is this the result of my breathing exercises? Or a reflection of sunlight from outside? He wondered at first.

But now fully aware, he dismissed both those explanations and he stepped forward to examine it.

A loud reverberating voice stopped him short, and he made to block his ears to mitigate the volume, although it sounded muffled – like spoken from behind a door or screen.

'Noah, this is your Lord! Observe the images I show you and listen carefully to my instructions!'

Enoch had described how God spoke with a bluster and this voice called him by his grandfather's unique nickname, which indicated perhaps divine familiarity. The voice went on,

'The ways of this world are wicked and have exceeded my patience! There is to be a great flood that will destroy every living creature within it. But I am pleased by your prayers and thus selected you and your family - direct and pure descendants of Adam, that first son of god I created – for salvation.'

Noah, regaining his wits, protested, 'But as almighty God, creator of heaven and earth, can't you just prevent it?' He had dispensed with his tribe's formality, preferring the Cushite jargon he and Naamah preferred.

'Time is short and elaborate preparations must be made, so listen closely and act hastily. You will construct a craft like the image you see before you, and you will build it according to the following specifications...'

'...But it's impossible for anyone to stay submerged for so long!' Noah had protested after receiving some of the details.

'Do not question my abilities! Divert from my exact instructions and you will be doomed like the rest of your brethren!'

'But why me? It's a privilege I'm not sure I deserve.' Noah queried warily, partly out of inherent modesty and partly out of a growing scepticism garnered from Lamech's account of the gods' duplicity and possible ulterior motives.

'Nevertheless, I have chosen you. Now stay quiet and all will be explained. While you build your craft, I will gather for you the eggs and the seed of every living creature. They are to be kept safe in their containers at the bottom level of the craft, which is the coldest part. But more importantly, upon your exit, you will return them to me for repopulating the earth. You will also take seven live pairs of cattle as soon as you enter, for meat and milk to sustain the long confinement,

'And near Lagash, there are craftsmen I will send to help you with special skills needed for your Ark. You will allow them to install various devices - especially the zohar. By that screen, you can track the sun and the stars in the heavens, attracting their light, which is so important for the survival of all the living within and to mark time.'

Ea chuckled to himself at his hamming, even putting on Enlil's gravitas. And by the time he had finished with all the 'magic' as Noah had called it, Adam's heir was fully convinced he was being addressed by God.

I probably overdid the volume at first and it probably wasn't really necessary to muffle the sound, given anyway that he couldn't possibly know Enlil's actual voice – I doubt Enoch was also a mimic. But all in all, a credible performance!

And I'm delighted Noah has discarded that ceremonial and punctilious jargon – clearly not a sucker for Enlil's pomposity. He even had the gall to question his omnipotence, asking him to prove it by preventing the accident in the first place! Hah! What a great progenitor for a future race!

CHAPTER **TWENTY-SEVEN**

As the fateful day approached, and while Councillors personally briefed the elect in Atlantis, Gabriel delivered instructions in ancient Marduk script to the few nominees in Gondwana. No humans or mongrels could read, only Enoch's heirs and the odd rare half-breed scholar. In any case, none read ancient script, and thus were kept completely oblivious.

After the Council had accepted their positions along with the eleven guardian officers and senior technicians permanently resident on *Nibiru*, the next set of invitees were senior guardians and technicians. Many rejected the offer, and again on the next tier, even fewer took up their invitation.

'What? Sit around on an even smaller floating island than the *Nibiru*? And return to the same fruitless and futile existence?' Was the typical response.

Having integrated into human communities with strong bonds - even osmosis - of that hominid trait of empathy, the veil of secrecy weighed very heavily on their spirits. Not for the ending of their lives but at the elimination of their compatriots and the destruction of their material endeavours. Indeed most, even some Councillors, accepted their invitation as a duty.

Nevertheless, in the interests of preventing irredeemable hysteria, all candidates remained remarkably circumspect, in solidarity with the rest of their kindred.

Finally, the 144 were identified.

Ea in his *skoop* had scoured the terrestrial expanse for donor creatures to supplement any missing from the Healing Institute's vast collection of samples. Where he was unable to obtain the sexual secretions—the ideal zygotic vehicle—of a particular creature, he obtained a scraping of cells, the DNA from a male and female of each type. Similarly, he collected and froze the spores from major plant species and the eggs from the primary genera of arthropods.

His thoughts wandered as he flew over the terrain for what he knew would be the last time. Following the pockets of settlement that dotted the coast of Southern Gondwana along the trail that Shtar's pioneers had taken, he found the city of Nanmadol. He was struck by the symmetric placement of the black stone slabs into the various geometric shapes of the buildings, where he paid a visit to the two dowagers.

'From the accounts of a couple who crossed the continent and made it this far, Aigar is still on his vendetta to exterminate the ogres, at least those who escaped from your mines,' Shalimar related their tragedy with the ogres and subsequent visit by the hybrid Alena and husband some time ago.

'How utterly awful! They were such a wonderful couple. I knew some of the Atlantean ogres had escaped into northern Eurasia, but I hadn't realised some of ours from Tartarus had also escaped,' Ea remarked, unable to take his gaze off the two females before him. It was a long time since he had seen a Marduk so old as Shtar now appeared, almost bald. Uriel the ancient, had far more bounce. But there was a benign peace and equanimity in her visage that he also hadn't come across for so long - since Lilith after her delivery of Adam.

'He has not ventured so far as the northern arboreal lands where Eden's escaping ogres apparently settled,' Shalimar added, acting as the spokesperson for both, eager to gossip and also to hear news of her uncle and events in the greater Marduk community.

Diverting his attention from Shtar, Ea turned to address the 'young' Shalimar, who nevertheless also appeared frail.

'I understand our ex queen Shtar doesn't wish to be saved, but no doubt with the intercession of Uriel and indeed myself, we can find a berth for you.'

'Thank you. I do miss my uncle. Many that accompanied us have already passed away or ventured elsewhere. So Shtar and I are essentially the last alive. But I have no desire to prolong life, especially if what you predict of global destruction is to occur,' she said and then asked offhand as she shuffled to a corner of her small cottage to fetch an object wrapped in Eden wool, 'will you be collecting specimens of any of those ogres as well?'

'Definitely not! Not even humans or other mutants. In fact, it was your uncle Uriel, who convinced me of the ideal candidate, one of the heirs of Adam who has married into my line through Cain - providing an ideal cross section of the entire hominid line and ours, while also lessening any complications from incest.' Ea openly divulged the 'secret' of Cain's paternity to the two doomed females.

Shalimar handed over the package she carried and as Ea unravelled the cloth containing it, he was shocked to behold the replica skull,

She explained, 'My father Uriel gave this to me. He would be happy to know I put it to such good use in establishing this thriving metropolis and port city. But it serves no further purpose for me, and is too valuable to be lost. So, I'm passing it to you and though you might employ rudiments on your own, you can consult with my father, who will decide whether to train you further' She said, while also handing over an electronic tablet, the diary she kept of her journey and of Nanmadol,

'The power source ran out some time ago, but I'm sure you can retrieve its contents once connected to an adequate charge.'

Ea checked the calibrated time on his *skoop* instruments, 'This visit was prohibited by Council, all taking an oath to maintain the secrecy surrounding the impending crash. I must therefore leave before dark, or I will be forced to engage the *Nibiru's* positioning system, resulting in unwanted questions.'

Finally, as the sun was already setting and having also picked up exotic specimens from a menagerie established in Nanmadol, Ea was ready for the three-hour journey to Eridu.

At its hypersonic speed, Ea knew the *skoop* could stay well ahead of daylight - outpacing the sun's shadow of 1,040 miles per hour at the equator.

'Any other messages?' he asked the two, focusing his gaze on the former queen.

Shtar finally broke her silence, 'From my Shalimar I learnt what is missing is actually an addition – yet the search will give Nin a purposeful future.' Her opening words were meaningless to Ea,

'Tell her also I neglected my daughter, yet my thoughts will be with her to the end.'

By her expression and demeanour, what was left unsaid made it one of Shtar's most impassioned pronouncements, Ea thought to himself as he sealed the *skoop*.

Uriel's inclusion in the conspiracy was of no value, he knew, but Ea always needed a witness to his genius,

'I collected only the archetype of each species. From that, I believe each genus should evolve their adaptive mutations according to whatever new environment will emerge after things settle down. All of the specimens will go into the freezer section of the ship,' Ea was explaining

The sage was a little incredulous, "freezer"?'

'My reticulation combines refrigeration and respiration in the same process,' Ea gloated, enjoying Uriel's wonderment,

'Gabriel is jettisoning surplus equipment from the *Nibiru*, dumping it underground, hoping to access it in future, some of which I salvaged. The Ark's hull can hold immense quantities of liquid oxygen and other trace gases, to be pumped up into the bilge. Exterior warmth will release controlled quantities of supercooled pure oxygen up to the lower levels of the three-storey vessel - an ideal refrigerant and preservative for the dormant cells within. From there, it will leak upwards to combine with the nitrogen rich excrement and carbon dioxide from the occupants above. Noah can also breed a few live cattle for sustenance and adding some methane. There's also a filtering process to regulate the required combination of air, recycling the rest.'

Uriel marvelled, 'A perfect ecological loop! But how will you get that sophisticated equipment to Noah without exposing yourself?'

'Oh, I already told him he will receive help. I have hired some mercenary human ship technicians from Lagash to deliver and install it as a mysterious gift from God,' He thrilled at his ingenuity—and he wasn't even done!

'A happy by-product for the inhabitants of that submarine Ark will be a natural air-conditioning system from that as well as exterior cold of the surrounding depths. That biological loop should sustain itself for about forty days, by which time, with the slow conversion and release of the liquid gas, I expect they can surface and thereafter rely on the resultant stabilised climate until Earth re-stabilises.' He finished with a flourish, as if expecting applause.

He left his meeting with Shalimar and her diary till later.

Giving excuse of a special gathering of Marduks, many now self-appointed kings of Gondwana had made their way to Eridu. To the few human astronomers remarking in consternation at the erratic behaviour of the second moon—forming a tail in its wake as it loomed larger on each successive orbit—they repeated Raphael's suggested mantra:

That is the purpose of the meeting – for the gods to rectify the aberration caused by that demon moon.

Nin maintained her distance from both her brothers, preferring to stand beside Uriel during the slow embarkation of the *Transporter*.

'You have been as much a father to me as Jova.' She said, taking his hand in endearment learned from her human servant, Delima.

'Unfortunately, that is both the necessary character and burden of a king, so don't judge him too harshly.'

'Oh, I don't judge him at all. And I miss him, more so as I am about to lose my mother as well. But also distressing is the loss of all that we have created and added to this planet, most especially humankind.'

Uriel hesitated, pondering whether to divulge what he knew. He decided against it. It was Ea's prerogative.

'There's always hope. But what if some of the hybrids or humans did survive?'

'That would be wonderful, and I don't believe our interaction on this planet was ideal. With his rigid conservatism, all Enlil did was to duplicate even lesser versions of us— creatively sterile. Cain's unpredictability in the freedom that Ea espouses is what makes mankind special - even if its solely in pursuit of pleasure. Neither of my brothers is interested in developing human higher faculties, only the development of technology – just by different means.'

Uriel inwardly remarked at Nin's growing acumen, *the student is becoming master!* He gave his full attention to her as she continued,

'But there's something in the hominid nature, which our language only hints at. I call it *Phileo*. But it can't be explained, it must be felt. I sensed it first in the hominid that saved me from the wolves, and have experienced it among them since—an altruistic sense of unity that we are all related parts. In that, I see potential for both our species.

'I'm not sure if we Marduks ever had it. Perhaps, as your astrology suggests, there weren't enough planets in our system to evoke that trait in our hormones. The huge evolutionary leap to humans has not yet enabled it to fully manifest in them - being too abrupt and deficient in the nobility to control that elevated consciousness. Yet that leap has initiated an eccentric spark, with the potential for brilliance that surpasses even ours. What took us millions of years of plodding progress, they could achieve in perhaps a few millennia.

'But now annihilation – what a waste! We could have guided them to merge that gracious altruism with their quirky creativity. And then we too could have evolved - using technology to serve as a means for overall growth instead of a narrow end in itself.'

'Spoken like your mother—but with more conviction!' Uriel enthused. He wanted to explain that such sentiment, or Phileo, was also found on Marduk, only absent in the *Nibiru* refugees, but he thought better of it.

'My brothers' objectives are already entrenched - petrified by our Marduk disposition for extremes. But both their objectives have value. What they need is mediation to balance them. As in a great building, one is drawn to marvel at the overt form and congratulate the use of materials, but it is as much the subtle joints and the cement that establishes its integrity and endurance,' she preached, before coming back to realities,

'But it's all for nothing now,' she added dejectedly as she took her turn to embark.

Scholar has turned to Priest and King. What a formidable combination! Uriel paused to revel at her retreating back, before following her to board.

Spiralling ever more erratically over the course of the following days giving off an entertaining display of fireworks to the enthralled global masses, the *Nibiru* dropped and pierced the marshmallow cloud cover. The meaning of that fiery streak was well understood by the inhabitants of distant Lemuria, who had watched in consternation that hitherto constant moon drift away from its position. To ancient Shtar, her partner Shalimar, and the elders of that great eastern civilisation, the outcome was patent and inevitable.

Around the inhabited world, other Marduks looked to the sky and prepared for their doom. The servants in Eridu were given extended leave to return to their folk with the excuse that the Marduk gods' convocation required privacy. The few remaining joined the forsaken Marduks and mutants there in an orgy of final revelry.

To mankind, the gods were simply putting on a show.

Upon the final *Nibiru* spiral, a *Transporter* had detached from the remaining reconstructed space station, marked as 'Phoenix'- which Gabriel stationed north of Mount Dilmun. Now engaging both Vril and combustion fuel, it carried the assembled gods, shooting up into a now seemingly incomplete sky. The stationary moon was missing, while Luna, its larger natural cousin now in waning phase, appeared like it wore a grimace.

The craft levitated into the heavens towards the *Nibiru* offspring, conceived from its mother's belly—a trivial runt compared to its former parent. Finally, the *Transporter* docked and was incorporated into the larger *Phoenix* from where its occupants observed events unfold as if in slow motion.

In the viewing dome, the escapees observed the last arc of the *Nibiru* planetoid, the womb that carried them from distant Marduk. Gabriel had steered the 'meteorite' on as oblique an entry as possible to incinerate as much of its material before eventually crashing into the distant ocean. But no amount of friction could burn off that immensity, and now the blazing fireball pierced the blue in surreptitious innocence, consuming itself and tearing off shreds that streaked independently behind in the process. As it hit the surface, it still contained more than half its original ten-mile diameter mass. Seen from space, the surreal streak slid surface-ward in sublime insouciance and style.

The projectile speared into the shallow ocean, east of Nanmadol. It tore through the few hundred feet of water, blasting deep into the planet's hitherto stable crust.

The released Vril energy was comparatively benign. And Gabriel had removed whatever radioactive material he could, relocating it on the *Phoenix* or jettisoning it in space. But remnants of that deadly substance and other explosives, now detonated, amplifying the cataclysmic impact.

'It's as if this *Phoenix* arose out of that fire and brimstone!' A poetic observer on the deck commented

Effects on the geology became visible. The shell of the planet fractured at first concussion. That initial crack, fed by shock waves silently reverberating within the orb, tore ever-wider fissures over the shell. As those grew - first around the epicentre - massive chasms yawned - vomiting jets of magma from the belly of the sphere in torrid shades of the colour spectrum.

'Ghost of Jova! Look!' An observer gasped as the bloated Antarctic continent imploded and like a frothy meringue, crumbled and collapsed into the tranquil blue. Massive icebergs folded domino-like in seemingly slow succession, pushing formidable swells that began their assault on the Antipodean coasts. The maelstrom was augmented by continental fragments, tearing off from Gondwana and separating on their crustal plates.

'Imagine the size of those behemoths!' Another yawped at the monstrous waves emanating from that collapse—visible even from their distant orbit.

And as its former inhabitants observed the *Nibiru* consume itself, burrowing into the planet, they were uniformly dumbstruck in introspection.

The ever-present disc - reassuring in the night sky – provided a link, a psychological and emotional tie to their erstwhile origins. It was an umbilical cord that kept their identity attached to their alien-ness. And as they watched the billowing smoke—evidence of that severed tendril—in unison, they experienced an awakening.

The cord now detached, they saw themselves in a new light, no longer tributary to mother Marduk, but adjuncts of this mother Earth, which had apparently aborted them.

Irania summed up the general sentiment, 'I feel even more trauma of separation than I did leaving Marduk!' Her words cast a bereaving silence and sadness upon the gathering.

On the southern shore of the river Pichon, Noah simultaneously felt the quake and spotted the upward streak of light behind Mount Dilmun, followed by the delayed thunderous roar, unaware of the *Transporter* or its rockets.

God had outlaid the detailed blueprint for a huge aquatic craft, and as promised he had sent the strange looking workers who said not a word while installing their devices.

He now recalled the instructions that came with those plans,

'At the appointed time, you will see a single long streak of lightning behind the mountain, followed by a loud thunder. That will be your omen to make final preparation. You will seal off the craft and descend to the depths as I have shown you, and remain within until it is time to disembark.'

And the zohar installed by those artisans will also indicate the appropriate time for disembarkation,'

The surrounding climate was arid, giving no hint of trouble. The sun blazed through a blue featureless sky. His neighbours, who also helped him build, relegated his warnings to raving or gross exaggeration, the recent quake just a storm gathering behind Dilmun.

And so, it was with some light-hearted ridicule from the townsfolk that the family entered the craft in apparent blind faith on such an unremarkable day. Relying on the belief that such an elaborate construction could surely not be for naught, the patriarch set about sealing the last aperture of his submersible vault, as instructed.

And soon it was to that cloudless sky that his kin looked up at in consternation as they felt the first trembles. They were closely followed by distant murmurs, harbingers of those soggy behemoths generated in the lower hemisphere and growing to many hundreds of feet as they approached land, was tearing into the southern coast. Shudders from the cracking crust were now unequivocal and growing in magnitude, causing wildlife to emerge from shelter and cast about in wonder and awe. What began as a bass rumble now grew to cacophony, augmented by the frenzy of prescient beasts that sensed before they saw, the vibrations of that approaching destruction. Throughout the planet, fauna took to panic and stampede, predator and prey alike, cowering into any accessible recess.

For Noah, it began with a comparatively innocuous up swell of tide that raised the Pichon, alongside his Ark. Bursting its banks, the river lifted the vessel from its earthen bed and set it afloat. It was followed within moments by a much larger tidal swell that swept swallowed his community, leaving visible only hilltops and impelling his Ark easterly, towards a gap that opened in Gondwana and what would become Europe.

As instructed, Noah now released some of the ballast air and allowed the craft to sink to the bottom. The action was fortuitous and timely. The surrounding depths sheathed the vessel from the next projectile sent forth from the southern abyss, sweeping everything in its path and blanketing all of Atlantis save Dilmun. And throughout the planet, the scene was replicated.

The watchers in space unified in silent awe, continued their fixation on the drama below, as collapsing ice caps doubled the volume of the ocean. Whole sections of fragmented continents were swept under—increasing separation between some, while others caromed into each other, redefining the geology and the very geography of the entire planet.

Relentless scouring of the crust exposed sections of liquid mantle below that disgorged in volcanic upheavals. As it did so, fragmented landmasses floated in jigsaw pieces on the now viscous surface. What would have taken geology millions of years, occurred in minutes. Rock deposited over aeons and in chronological order, were thrust up and now sat alongside recent deposits, rendering unintelligible the geological and the archaeological record.

Doctor Raphael bewailed, 'We witnessed Marduk's explosion from deeper space - this feels so close and *personal!*' His shaking went beyond his habitual hawkish facial twitch, as if sobbing. But that was too much empathy to expect from the crass arch-guardian, who added, 'what a fantastic spectacle!'

Gondwana split, crumbling at its separate coasts. This caused the immense upward extrusion of a mountain range that now blocked the previously westward flowing Amazonian River—reversing its flow eastward into the fast-expanding ocean of Atlantis.

In the East, Lemuria was swamped, leaving only ruins on remnant islands in that expanded ocean basin scoured out by the *Nibiru's* oblique entry. Nin sought out Uriel for mutual solace in their loss, but the sage was otherwise engaged with a tablet that Ea had apparently found and handed over.

And now the leading buttresses reached the temperate regions of Atlantis and other stains of intelligent endeavour that had gradually marked the landscape over recent millennia. Those miniscule etchings were erased from the topography, or shoved to the oceanic depths.

Aigar had long ago observed the unstable aberration of the *Nibiru*, nowadays visible even in his Central Earth, alarming him.

Having exterminated all the ogres within the Asian section save one abominable creature that had managed to hide himself in the snow-capped peaks to the South, he was now quite ancient and decrepit.

Zhulan, his hybrid companion and mother of his two children, was long gone. But their progeny – the khans as they were known - had multiplied, and he worried for their fate if the giant space station turned meteorite. Preparing for the unthinkable, in final effort he gathered his immediate tribe and marched them — to the very highlands where that last ogre had retreated.

And it was there, with mixed emotions he met Crius, the erstwhile toddy-finder of Tartarus. That last remaining Titan was in the process of erecting the corpse of recently deceased Atlas, positioning the body upright carrying a gigantic boulder - like he once found in the Tartarus goldfields. He had also carved out a niche for himself - to be encased in ice alongside their ten relatives that had died and were similarly mummified.

Following Aigar's point heavenward, Crius understood, and with a gentle wave and Titan moan of goodbye, he stepped into his self-made tomb.

His age and that journey into the barren mountains had taken their toll, but Aigar lived to observe the *Nibiru*'s final spiral. As it plummeted and then disappeared over the eastern horizon followed by a flash like an instant rising sun, his survivors heard his voice for the first - and last - time.

It was a cry of pure will, of scorn and derision, of hate and uncertainty, and love and all the emotions he could muster—a demand to the skies in sheer defiance,

'They say the universe is made up of protons, neutrons and electrons. They forgot morons! Send in the clowns you frauds - and let the show begin!'

CHAPTER TWENTY-EIGHT

As the fireworks and destruction subsided into a sloshing maelstrom, a shroud of ash, smoke, and steam soon obscured the atmosphere - as if shielding those watchers from any further trauma, and they broke away from their gruesome trance.

In the hushed lull that accompanied the hiatus, Irania returned to the topic of the future,

'So now what?' She asked her son again, who remained silent, still perhaps shaken by the sight.

A rarely heard Councillor Jeremiel commented, 'immortality is not all it was made out to be, but terrestrial life made it tolerable. We'll now have to put up with the desiccated store aboard for at least . . . a year you say, Gabriel?' His question ignored by the Captain, he turned to Nazarel for response.

But the farmer too was not in the mood for such inanity.

Jeremiel chose self-response, 'and then I suppose we would need to produce it ourselves from the sweat of our own brows when we return.'

Uriel had withdrawn, benumbed at the spectacle below. He was more absorbed in the electronic tablet Ea had passed to him from his daughter.

Shalimar's replica skull was unmentioned for the time being, Ea glancing back occasionally to observe the bittersweet sadness on the old sage's face. He had also felt inopportune to pass Shtar's sentiments to Nin at this time.

Receiving no valid response to her earlier innuendo, Irania added wistfully, 'We should have saved some of humankind, at least as slaves for the future.'

Not even that prospect roused any from their silent introspection. As a result, despite the silent tumult below, everyone managed to hear the soft response, which nevertheless appeared to reverberate around the chamber.

'Well... actually, I did.'

Ea had as much uncanny knack for stopping a discussion... as starting one! Nin observed. But her heart had skipped a beat nevertheless.

Upon hearing his nonchalant but cautious statement, delivered as it was with a recently emerging leer, the air grew thick. All eyes had turned to the geneticist, their faces betraying myriad expressions.

'Who-what-when-where-how-and-why? Irania's elision signalled her open fascination and spoke for the rest who were equally rapt in attention – except for Enlil who seemed murderous.

Ea initially appeared reticent, with even a slight wince. But with the barrage of erupting stares, he began to describe the choice of his refugees and the process of their salvation. Enjoying the gathering's endorsement and wonderment, he proceeded to explain the collection of specimens and the method of constructing his Ark, highlighting his foresight.

Nin by now knew him well and obviously he realised Noah's survival hung in balance. He thus turned to acknowledging the benefit to his brother,

'...Of course, I chose Noah - being a direct descendant of Adam and hence our king, Enlil.'

Nin's heart was bursting with elation. *My prayer has been answered!* But observing Enlil's mood, she contained herself.

Emperor Enlil, now devoid of empire, remained silent, as if expectant that Council would come to his same conclusion as his - outraged and condemned the recalcitrant's flagrant violation of their oath. But everyone's fawning enthusiasm indicated no such rebuke was forthcoming.

'You broke the oath, sworn upon the sacred Marduk Skull!' Enlil finally roared, 'Once again, you throw our laws into the dung-heap! Yes, we will rebuild on earth,' he stated emphatically in a voice laden with potency, 'and we will retain your fauna and flora, but our first act will be to exterminate all hybrids and any possibly surviving human stain!'

'No, Enlil! That's not necessary.' Nin's statement contained both plea and demand.

She was a little surprised at the nods of support from young stepmother, Irania, indeed on almost all the faces. But even if her tone was ingratiating, it was bad timing, coming as a challenge to Enlil.

About to flare out at his sister, he was held back by a modulated voice from his mother, preventing him in mid-act with her placating tone,

'Yes, son. It is true the oath was broken, and normally, such treason should never go unpunished, but this is a good thing. How else could we go back and live there again or rebuild with such a paltry number?'

Irania it seemed, had not wasted *all* her time illicitly. Her ethereal tonal quality showed she had been practicing some form of voice control that seemed to retard Enlil's rage. In any case it was supported and reinforced by the entire gathering, bombarding him with a hubbub of similar arguments.

'Noah is *your* protégé, directly from your line of Seth.' Ea also restated.

'But he went and married into *your* bastard line!' Enlil was calmer but still resolute.

So, he already knew. Ignoring that uncomfortable aspect, Ea argued, 'As you admit, the preservation of fauna and flora was fortunate. Well, who was to ensure their preservation? A Marduk volunteer? As it is, the Ark's survival is not yet guaranteed.'

'Well, if they survive, their purpose would have been served and thus will no longer be unnecessary. Your disregard of your oath is treason! Don't try to justify it. And don't try to patronise me! You don't have a monopoly on intelligence. Time and experience play as large a part in developing wisdom, perhaps more than self-deluded arrogance.'

'Agreed, and perhaps more than sudden elevation in status.' Raising both eyebrows, Ea seemingly couldn't resist the invitation to sarcasm and antagonism, 'while you dreamed of developing this planet with a single strain of Marduks with our sister, did you consider how any future invention and technology would come about? Where before you had the resources and expertise from so many on the *Nibiru*, you are now left with a bunch of "aristocrats" with little expertise or tools. And you obviously missed my failure to take the oath.'

In spite of the ship's fluorescent illumination casting everything as bland, Enlil's face was visibly turning colour as he prepared to explode.

Nin looked pointedly at Uriel who had had hitherto stayed silent, probably not wishing to further antagonise his king. But now the matter was critical,

'What says our Royal Sage?' She quickly prompted before Enlil could erupt.

Uriel stepped into the fray, in appeasing tone, 'Sire, with the limited remaining resources here in this *Phoenix,* I fear our kind would revert to primitives. After what has happened, the godlings are our only hope. As Enoch seems to prove, they are fast absorbing the sudden jolt of metamorphosis we introduced into their evolution. They could soon learn to cope with immortality and stand aside us, together propelling both species into a more productive future.'

Ea added supportively, 'For what it's worth, did not expose myself to your Noah, maintaining your image as their sole divinity and supreme God.'

It was as close to pleading as Nin had ever seen from the elder brother. Nin's sympathy was not for his argument, but for that noble species.

If my prayer was answered by Shalimar's 'underlying hand', then I shall be its instrument. Otherwise, I shall act in its stead for this planet's future while I discover that elusive missing piece! Nin resolved.

The congenital ache that had dogged her throughout life, now replaced by purpose, was liberating in its relief. It was up to her to provide the final thrust.

She took Enlil gently by the arm and led him aside, away from the melee.

'Are you siding with *him!'* He accused, while she weighed her words.

'Actually, I couldn't care less for either of your puerile and insipid motives. My interest is for mankind, who represent our best hope. Remember I was once saved by one of their primitive predecessors, and in the aftermath of that act, I glimpsed a quality we Marduks can only aspire towards.' Her confidence set him back a little, enough to gain his ear,

'You wish to return and repopulate with strictly our kind? But where would be the genetic diversity? Endless virtual clones of Jova provided by the two of us? And what of some dormant congenital defects?'

She let him mull questions, and her specific qualifications to ask them, before she continued,

'Well, I'll let you have your narrow wish of perpetuating your line and maintaining our bloodline's supremacy, not in isolation as Marduks, but as citizens of Earth. If, and only if, you agree to spare Noah and his family, I will agree to be your wife. And forget that silly Law of Inheritance, which no longer applies . . . your *only* wife! But for now, even though I admit you are an exciting bedfellow, I will remain childless.' Nin demanded, again giving him pause. 'And when you agree to that, I have one more condition.'

'What! There's more?' Enlil was nonplussed likely as much by her self-assurance as by the proposal, 'Go on,' he conceded warily.

She signalled to Uriel and beckoned Ea to join them,

'I wish to address this to both my brothers and call on our sage Uriel to act as witness,' she began, as others too gathered around her address,

'It's clear that both of your methods have failed, yet it is also clear that both branches of mankind have achieved great things – materially *and* spiritually - despite *both* your meddling!'

'Having experienced as much as our capacity allows, immortality has robbed us of enthusiasm and zest, and hence our creativity. The aspiration of *all* of us aspirations is to gain some purpose and evolve our kind. But this planet is for humankind, not ours. We can be no more than observers, watching over them and perhaps occasionally guiding them to eventually absorb us. The question is only one of approach—unfettered freedom versus dogmatic religion. I am at a loss as to which is correct.'

Uriel chimed in, 'I suspect it is a balance of both, but I don't believe anyone can determine the exact proportion.'

Gaining the ear of all, he continued, 'It is obvious the instantaneous evolutionary leap left their hominid based consciousness and morality still immature. They are unable to determine good or evil, or accept full responsibility for their actions – individually or collectively – thus reliant on the supernatural and appealing to an external God.'

Nin turned to Uriel with an imperceptible nod of mutual understanding, prompting him to go on,

'The matter cannot be resolved here. Lord Ea has amply exhibited he does not recognise, or at least refuses to follow any authority. From Eve's unique experience, even mankind seems aware of this "divine" conflict. So, why not let the humans, by their actions, determine the benefits or demerits of both their 'gods'. It will be *their* politics and religion, not *ours*.'

Nin was quick to add, 'but believing in the infallibility of gods, any opinion given by either Enlil or Ea will sway them - not daring to defy such divinity. Anyway, visible gods lose reverence with familiarity and by exposing their inevitable shortcomings. We must, thus, remain hidden.

'So, Enlil my final demand is that we all stay out of sight or contact, no longer actors in their drama, lest we influence them in any way,' she insisted. 'Most Marduks cannot reproduce, so let us adopt the entire human race as our children. And as voyeurs on this *Phoenix*, we can perhaps live vicariously through them.'

A masterstroke to exhort and encourage the survivors, reminiscent of Jova himself, Uriel mused. But Nin's sermon was not finished,

'And once they have reached our level, I will bear your child - he or she can then be true King of the World to lead us all rapturously into a Golden Age.

Uriel threw her a wink of acclaim and loyal support.

Within the submarine Ark, Noah was having his own epiphany.

I pleaded with god to choose another or at least to also perish, but that seemed to him an alien sentiment. My father's suspicion of those gods may be well founded and our salvation seems somewhat self-serving.

He, or they – in their earthly paradise of Eden and Eridu, appear omnipotent. But what have they really achieved save to wield those rumoured magical devices that they possess. From Eridu's servants I heard even those were inherited, or perhaps brought down from their heavenly home.

Flying machines; killing light-rods; viewing devices; measuring cord; and tablets of numbers and symbols—none were seen to be created here. And all the new inventions I witnessed in Cush were from human minds and hands.

Yet here is this wondrous contraption designed by God himself sitting under the sea. The design is extraordinary, keeping us alive and in comfort - and with live cattle for food! I'm torn between grandfather Methuselah's complete trust and father Lamech's suspicion.

I have yet to understand how those little capsules in the vaults below contain male and female animals, or how they can survive such icy cold. But the god assured it would be so and thus far - relating to this episode at least - I have no reason to doubt him.

Aboard the *Phoenix*, Nin's onslaught of conditions gained huge support with pleas for the Ark refugees bombarding Enlil into silent attentiveness.

And even Irania threw in her lot, 'It seems obvious that our salvation from Marduk was not to perpetuate our own species, but to propagate a new one, ending also this counterproductive patriarchy!' It seemed the mother was untying her leash, and in fact, creating some distance.

Raphael the Hawk, however, jumped on Irania's secondary suggestion,

'Yet an empty, primitive and savage world will once again require taming and rapid repopulation. It will take the positive dynamism and physical strength of male leadership to achieve that.'

Nin had gained full confidence in her pragmatic statesmanship, and she once again stepped in to mediate,

'Let the survivors determine their future! Under the conditions, it's likely patriarchy will continue. However, female equality in their future will be good indication of higher consciousness – proving their worthiness to integrate with us.'

Enlil had heard enough. 'By Jova, what optimism! But I share your aspirations for *our* heirs. Yet how do you propose we stay hidden and still observe them?' In his mind, the question was merely rhetorical.

But Gabriel came to the rescue. 'Well, the *Phoenix* could be taken around to dark side of their moon, maintaining identical lunar orbit and thus remaining perpetually blind-sided,' he suggested. 'It will also still allow us to visit and provision from time to time . . .' He caught Nin's disapproving glare. '...Surreptitiously of course.'

'Not bad!' Enlil admitted, turning an appraising eye at his captain, while more enthusiastic support followed.

'And how do you propose we determine their success?' Enlil sneered at those cheerleaders, nevertheless seemingly hooked.

That encouraged Uriel to make his suggestion, 'since proposing the sentencing of Cain, I have been devising an empirical method to measure levels of consciousness, and indeed the truth of any opposing condition. Perhaps I should explain?'

'Perhaps you should. Isn't that your role?' Enlil's sarcasm was growing, not happy about being side-stepped.

'Yes well, using a process I call kinesiology I have devised a scale from zero - inklings of awareness, up to one thousand—absolute enlightenment. Before we left, Marduks as a whole calibrated at 480, the realm of reason.' He avoided mention of the much lower level of the *Nibiru* contingent - due to the nature of their selection.

'Above 500 an individual can aspire to become a magus - the spiritual path to enlightenment and true divinity. The ogres, for example, scored only 25 - the realm of misery, shame and humiliation. The humans as a species, calibrated at around 80 – with punishment, tragedy, fear and regret being the prevalent attitude. Our elect hybrid Noah, at 245, has transcended to the level of courage and integrity, a critical step. For below 200, all actions and beliefs are negative and downward pulling.'

'Piffling pygargs!' Enlil trivialised the theory.

Nin, puzzled again by his reference to her cattle, nevertheless ignored Enlil's cynicism and pursued Uriel's premise 'So our goal is for all humans to evolve or mutate to at least our level of around 480.'

Uriel continued, 'Yes, and unlike us - driven only by law and logic, the humans have a greater capacity for relationship and selfless love. They may thus one day ameliorate our capacity and help us also cross the threshold into enlightenment.'

'And how long must we wait for this great illumination to come about? We're not about to wait till infinity!' Enlil's petulance continued.

I have considered that too. Please look at this chart.' Uriel projected a holographic star map.

'This sun circumnavigates an orbit around a galactic cluster, in a cycle of 25,920 years. I have split that into a zodiac or clock of 12 segments, wherein this sun's position points to those various star constellations as it orbits that centre – much like the hand of a clock. As this planet courses the sun, it too faces one or the other of those constellations. But each year, there is a fractional backward shift . . .'

'Yes, yes, enough with astronomy and astrology! So what?' Enlil interjected impatiently.

'Well, we arrived here around 65,000 earth years ago when this sun was in the constellation I call Aquarius – symbolised by a Marduk bringing intelligence to this planet. The other symbols are of earthly animals or concepts. As you can see, the sun is now leaving Leo, that king of animals representing the ascension of King Enlil,' Uriel managed to fudge with his explanation,

'I suggest we give Noah's heirs one astrological cycle or era. Uriel concluded, when the sign of the king will be prominent.

Enlil interjected, but surprised all by implying agreement with the concept, 'No, a full cycle is too long! Five thousand years should be plenty.'

But Uriel was keen on giving success every chance, 'From such low base, they cannot procreate or evolve so fast. Let's at least take them to the anniversary of our arrival, to Aquarius again – five ages and a full cycle from the creation of Adam - also in Aquarius.'

Gabriel was enthusiastic, 'By that time, and with our sowing information, they may achieve the technology to expand and restore this *Phoenix* to its *Nibiru* dimensions or more.'

Phanuel, the psychologist Councillor added,

'And we only need to kidnap random individuals to determine whether they have developed sufficiently—in all aspects including that scale of consciousness.'

'*Very* selectively and absolutely *covertly!*' Nin conceded.

'Six cycles until your Aquarius then,' Enlil accepted. 'And at that time, any that have sufficiently evolved consciousness – and by that, I mean technologically – will be integrated with us. The rest can perish.'

Irania seemed unable to contain herself, 'But we are *alive* and had a sense of at least some purpose on earth where before on the *Nibiru*, we simply *existed*! She railed, giving vent to the frustration that seemed to beset her since boarding the *Phoenix*.

'What are you getting at?' Enlil asked, clearly annoyed at his mother's increasing antipathy.

'I don't share all your noble but sterile aspirations! I personally still have an appetite for life and make no apologies. Much as I believe in guiding mankind, I will not sit around for another 10,000 years – living a flickering candle of existence - till they may or may not evolve sufficiently to fulfil our *lofty standards!* Once we return to Earth, I'm staying!'

Her outburst created a hubbub amongst the gathering and Nin herself wished she could have had such an option. That was now inconceivable. However, Irania threatened to subvert all their plans.

Enlil's face showed his bewilderment,

'Mother! All my life, you have been grooming me for this. Now that I have kingship, you want to abandon it, and me?'

'That time and reason is no longer valid. What's left of your kingdom?'

And Nin realised the nature of such expedient relationships – when the use was gone, attachment went with it.

Enlil too seemed to come to the same conclusion. While others also indicated agreement with his mother, he shared Nin and Uriel's looks of consternation. While those also offered their opinions, he again sat back as if evaluating.

Finally, he became emphatic,

'I thought and expected unanimous agreement. Nevertheless, the *Phoenix will* depart and with it goes any access to rejuvenation. As manna too has been removed from Earth, if anyone who choose to return to Earth, they will revert to mortality.'

But Irania was undaunted, responding to her son's earlier discouragement, 'Yes, I have changed, and wilfully because I *lived* and did not just *exist!* Your regimented manikins choose austerity and sterility instead of the valiant journey and jeopardy in living. I prefer the flaming bonfire of life and mortality, not as voyeur but as a participant!' Her lyricism emphasised her point, 'Who is with me?'

Twenty-six others expressed their wish to join her on earth, including Nazarel and, since her father's decapitation, orphaned nurse Dawn from Tartarus – endorsed for salvation by the three senior geneticists.

'My skills and interest serve no purpose here but will be invaluable to re-cultivate the devastated earth,' the agronomist Nazarel explained to any who cared to listen.

Enlil tried one last shot, raising his voice to ensure it fell within the earshot of everyone,

'I can't force anyone to stay against your will, and stripped of Marduk support you will be reduced to survival, in an even more savage environment than before. However, you must not jeopardise our recent agreement as outlaid by my sister and future Queen. Hence, you will take *nothing* artificial of Marduk origin from the *Phoenix* while also being isolated from any human habitation. And you will swear by the Skull that you will maintain the mystery of our origin, our existence, and the cause of that deluge! Failure will mean forced relocation to an uninhabited island!'

Despite that cold reality, only five defectors changed their mind to remain on the *Phoenix*.

Enlil continued, 'And there is another egregious crime—my brother's treason and history of disregard for any of our laws. Therefore, he will also be banished and live with you as outcast.'

Ea was quick to respond, 'I did not vote with the others, and I will not join them on the surface...'

'...More treason!' Enlil bellowed. 'You will *not* stay with us - even if Michael here has to hold you in shackles for eternity! Or do you prefer suicide?' Enlil indicted.

'Let me finish! I will not remain in this suspended tomb, preferring to have my nose to the ground, in earth's womb as it were.' Ea stated, as usual contriving suspense, and accompanied by that single arched eyebrow.

'In fact, I will go further than you dictate – into the catacombs I spotted while foraging for Ark specimens, in the highlands of Central Earth. I will make my home there, joined by my good assistant Galael here, and any others who wish to join me. Of course, I will recreate my radiation bath there, ensuring my immortality to witness which of our outlooks gains precedence.'

'No you w…!' Enlil began to countermand, but Ea held up his hand and cut him off,

…Restricted only to those who remain with me permanently hidden underground.'

Enlil deferred to his wife-to-be Nin, who gave a reluctant nod.

'Alright! We will reunite when it is time for what our sister expects as our "rapture" with the humans in the not-so-distant future.

Nin's voice showed her exasperation, 'So many deviations! I don't trust either the mutineers - who will at least die off – or my ever-recalcitrant brother!' She cast her displeasure over all of them,

'I demand a referee to watch over and report contravention to *any* of these contracts. The humans will need some help anyway. I propose that Uriel, if he consents, be secreted away on earth and with executive power to mediate on any vagaries caused by your conflicting philosophies. And to report on *any* deviant for banishment to Enlil's remote island!'

Enlil caught the approving nods from Michael and the other arch-guardians who chose to remain aboard,

'You have already understood that my sister Nin has consented to be my future queen, and she has made an astute suggestion. Do you, Uriel, accept the post?'

'And naturally he will have access to all *Nibiru*'s facilities, including rejuvenation,' Nin added.

While the argument raged, Uriel had withdrawn, introspective.

I have nothing more to offer King or race, and I feel so close to the mastery I have long sought. And our one-sided materialism ignores the other facet of cosmic duality required to expand consciousness. Humanity is still too primitive to understand that, believing anything inexplicable as an act of the gods. Yet, at least they have a future. But I'm too old to survive in that devastation. But what is this that Nin is suggesting? He stopped the internal chatter to listen to her proposal,

'What say you Uriel?' Nin was asking

So now Nin and fate are giving me another, final opportunity to gain mastery! I shall form a school of selected adepts – prospective magi following the Way to illumination—a religion aimed at eliminating the need for religion!

Reflecting again on Shalimar's underlying hand, he offered a blithe smile and consenting nod, 'Yes, I too was thinking in that direction.'

'Very well, so be it!' Enlil decreed.

Below, the planet seethed and writhed in the throes of its metamorphosis and rebirth. Above, the *Phoenix* emitted a different frequency, a lighter tune than its forebear. The *Nibiru*'s moaning hum of malaise was finally erased, replaced by a melody of fulfilment and purpose. Beyond *Phileo*—an inclination encompassing everything—*Agape*.

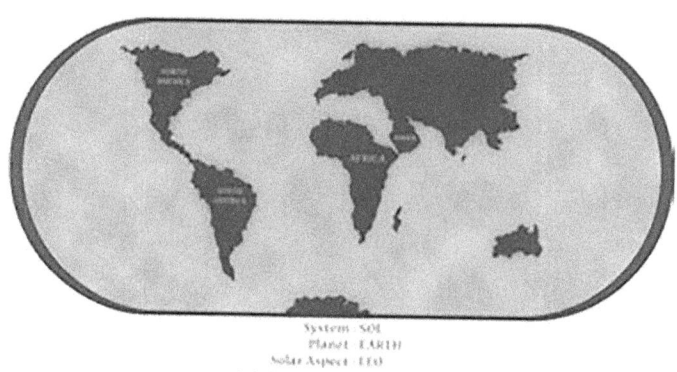

System SOL
Planet EARTH
Solar Aspect LEO
Arch Consul Gabri EL M.S.S. Nibiru

To Be Continued—

BOOK TWO

The Gilgamesh Legacy

Excerpt

"Dawn, bring me more of that slop we are forced to put up! I wish I could just go and mingle at will in the human beer houses." Irania ranted in habitual frustration at the cloistered existence imposed by her son King Enlil.

Dawn made no move, ever regretting her agreement to play chaperone and aide to the still stunning former queen. She had wished to accompany her foster father, but even he felt at the time that would have been far too risky. The few guardian deserters who abandoned the Phoenix and accompanied Irania had departed after securing this cave fortress for her. And now, Dawn was left alone with the shrew.

Anger mounted with gloom and she argued internally,

At least Irania occasionally goes off on her romantic forays with the lumbermen in our cedar forest - the only humans we encounter. I'm sure there's more to men than those boorish, brutish lumberjacks but I could not possibly stoop so low as to entertain one. Anyway, I have had enough of this place!

"Sorry m'lady, you'll have to learn to look after yourself!" She began practicing human talk, eliding words. And began to question why she felt the need to apologize.

"Whaaat?" Irania shrieked in melodrama.

Dawn was taken aback, briefly intimidated. But she quickly regained her wits,

"I abandoned the *Phoenix* to escape our stiflingly rigid Marduks. But these catacombs are hardly a party! Even my long-ago nursing days in the jungles of Tartarus, were more exciting."

"What can I do? I am equally constrained by that stupid edict to refrain from interaction with the surviving humans!" Irania whined like a spoiled child. No doubt that pout was successful with males, but Dawn found it condescending, adding to her claustrophobia in their dank grotto.

The fluorescent vril lamps borrowed from the space staion lacked the solar spectrum of colour. The mountain cave was cladded with the best cedar, but that constant pervasive aroma and the resonating acoustics felt like a mausoleum, deepening her oppression.

"As if they don't know all about us already. Regardless I'm leaving to join them." Suddenly Dawn's spontaneous plan sounded like a very good one. "I'll simply pass as a freak, one of the many mutants and half-breeds, just as my father Nazarel did."

"Go ahead! Alike all your parents you are no more than a peasant! What sort of name is 'Dawn' anyway? So un-Marduk!" Irania reverted to her natural haughtiness.

Dawn remembered nothing of her botanist mother. And little of her natural father, gruesomely decapitated by ogres when she was a child. Yet Irania's derision of her subsequent adoptive godfather, the former Head Agriculturist Nazarel, actually added the greatest sting to those cuts. But the intended mockery, described in human terms, evolved into a badge of honour.

"'Peasant' - sounds like a respectable calling! Anyway, your 'virgins' are more suitable companions." Dawn alluded to the daughters of influential humans conscripted at puberty as priestesses and schooled by Irania in erotica and the worship of their 'god' Enlil. The girls' selection was seen as a privilege. Upon returning to their communities, their 'madam' would provide obscure bulletins of far off events or imminent weather beamed to the ex-queen from the cameras aboard the Phoenix. And she redirected that information to her vestals via their secretive network. It gave them honourable professions as temple 'comforters' and oracles.

She left that day with only her clothes, some provisions, and the bow and silver tipped arrows gifted by Nazarel at their parting.

Descending from the mountain hideaway, she made her way across the fertile flood plains towards the mighty Tigris River, a remnant of the Deluge. Vegetation had re-appeared - the pristine landscape reminiscent of Eden's fringes - and provided her with fruit, berries and birds' eggs. But mankind was still sparse. She thus crossed huge distance without encounter as she made her way towards the city of Kish.

She was wary of the 'sons of man', aboriginal humans that had also survived the Great Deluge by taking refuge in mountain caves. Devoid of any civilising influence some had even turned cannibal in the subsequent absence of cattle. They roved the plains in bands, ransacking farms and towns that Nazarel had helped establish with the Ark survivors – Adam's and subsequently Noah's 'sons of god' as Enlil called those godlings.

Over the five days since leaving she regularly checked Nazarel's bow, which he had crafted from the hickory timbers of Noah's submarine Ark and reinforced with alloys from the Phoenix.

"Earth is nowadays more primitive than when we arrived and has become more dangerous since we evolved the humans, now stripped by the Flood." Her adoptive father had warned, giving her an emphatic stare with his single operative eye. A leather patch disguised his electronic other eye, adding some dash to his otherwise sombre rugged features

After her mother perished in the meteor strike on the Nibiru Space Station - that also gouged his right eye during their journey to Earth – Nazarel had drawn closer to Dawn.

The memory of that ship prompted her to look up, half expecting to catch sight of its daughter craft, the orbiting Phoenix, but it was invisible in the daylight.

The subsequent murder of her soldier father again happened in Nazarel's domain of Eden - the coincidences as if fated to bring about their relationship. And he had since adopted her, even as adult, after learning she too was deserting the *Phoenix*.

Marduk pragmatism prioritized safety and comfort above rapport. Hence, she was assigned to Irania in those early primitive and savage days

Restless in Irania's cave, she had practiced her natural proficiency in archery. And Earth was since recovering.

That brief reminiscence had distracted her vigilance, neglecting the pair of human marauders who had tracked her amongst the trees, and who now dropped ahead of her and blocked her path.

They baulked at Dawn's statuesque frame, giving time to draw her bow for a single shot, which felled the leader. But the other had charged too near for a second volley. Instead she wrapped the string over his head and dragged him by the bow, hitching it over an upward poking branch stump - temporarily entangling the man - and she fled with an involuntary shriek.

He soon unravelled himself and as she darted amongst the trees, began losing ground to her pursuer's familiarity with the woods. And unbeknown to her, his other tribesmen had circled the forest, following her yelps and anticipating her point of exit.

She emerged into a clearing, only to be confronted by a gang of naked savages of both sexes leering lasciviously at her finery and weapons.

Stalling while she considered her options, her pursuer caught up and pounced from behind. He was attempting to strip her artificial and valued 'god-skins' that protected the aliens from extremes of weather. The bonds that moulded those vestments to the body - as if an additional layer of skin - gave her some time while the brute, now joined by others in erotically excited frenzy, had difficulty removing the protective attire to rape her.

A glancing blow from an unseen female's club dazed her and she stumbled in collapse, briefly separating from the bunch.

The woman now lunged and hefted the club for a fatal strike on the kneeling Marduk.

Time expanded as Dawn surrendered to her fate, eyes closing in anticipation while a flood of flashing memories flittered across her mental screen.

Her eyes flickered in a daze. The flashbacks turned surreal as if the mind shutting down in its death throes.

She wondered at the glint of silver suddenly jutting from the woman's breast... white and red tendrils of tissue dripping off that tip...Welling blood from a torn chest...

Awakening, she looked up at the gentle gaze of aquamarine eyes in a deep-set brow surrounded by copper-red beard and shoulder length locks haloed by glints of light. The musky human smell was curiously pleasant.

Milton Keynes UK
Ingram Content Group UK Ltd.
UKHW030033180324
439604UK00002B/331